LOCKED & FOUND

MEREDITH REECE

To find out more about this author's
upcoming releases and free giveaways
visit the website & join the community at:
www.meredithreece.com

Or, come chat with me on Facebook at:
Meredith Reece - Author

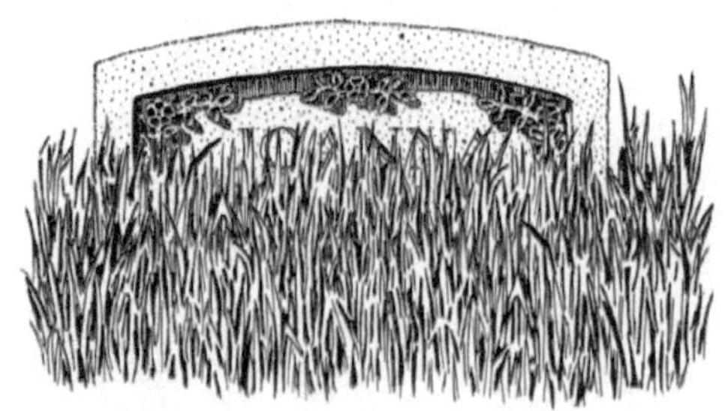

LOCKHEART MYSTERIES
LOCKED & FOUND
DISCOVERING YOUR FAMILY HERITAGE, MAY HAUNT YOU FOREVER
MEREDITH REECE

This is a work of fiction.
Names, Characters, places and incidents either are the
product of the author's imagination or are used fictitiously.
Any resemblance to actual persons, living or dead, business
establishments, events, or locales is entirely coincidental.

For my Daughter Hailey

Scottish Word Glossary

Aye - Yes (pronounced - I)

Ye - You (pronounced - yi)

Me - My

Dinnae - Don't (pronounced - 'di-nee')

Wee - Little

Och! - Oh! (pronounced Okh)

Greet'n - Crying

Skelp - Slap

A Skelping - A Thrashing

Tattie - Potato

Scunner - Nuisance

Bonnie - Beautiful

Bairn - Baby or Young Child

Auld - Old

Crabbit - Grumpy/Bad tempered

Battered - Open wound/bleeding

Baw heid - Ball head

Daft - Stupid

Contents

CHAPTER ONE

Sunday 20th March 2016

Jess

THEY WERE LATE - Embarrassingly late.

Tyres screeched, and the car pulled to a stop.

Jess slammed into the seatbelt across her chest, then reeled back against the front passenger seat.

"What? What's the matter?" Jess asked; a herd of cows trampling through her chest. "Where are we? Do you know where we are? Are we lost?" She moaned, already expecting her mother's denial.

Jess searched the sky. Blackness swallowed everything - even the car's headlights were dim. Not a single house light could be seen and worry gathered in the pit of her stomach. So this was it - the middle of nowhere - this was where teenage dreams come to die: At an intersection of country lanes somewhere in Scotland.

"Of course we're not lost. I know exactly where we are..." Mum paused and looked from left to right. The road to the right blinked orange from the indicator, but Mum pulled to the left. "It just looks a little different than I remember, that's all."

Mum's white knuckled grip on the steering wheel didn't relax until a battered metal letterbox came into view ten minutes later.

"This is it - we're here! Oh my stars - it hasn't changed a bit."

Navigating the ruts and rises of the pot-holed driveway, they made their way towards a frosted light struggling to illuminate a blue painted door. The odd puddle swallowed their car tyres more than once and threatened to strand them before they reached the house.

Dark shadows of trees and outbuildings stood sentry around a large stone farmhouse and the front door seemed too small for such a grand home. At each end of the three-story dwelling, two smoking chimney stacks puffed away like chain smokers competing for a nicotine award. A warm welcome and a hot meal was all Jess hoped for, but neither were likely given how late they were.

A light flicked on from an upstairs room and the curtain was pushed aside. Jess couldn't make out who it was, but knowing they were being watched put her centre stage in their production of: 'Strangers arrive from London.' The front seat of the car, screening their reality T.V show, bore little resemblance to a stage on Broadway. Jess turned to her brother, Brody, in the backseat and prayed the curtain would fall. If it were up to her the show would have been cancelled long before it ever hit the road.

Brody frowned then used his 'nature documentary - David Attenborough' voice to make light of their situation.

"Tullynessle. A place no one has heard of and is often forgotten on maps. Three Londoners - tired, disoriented, and desperately hungry, have wandered from the flock into the heart of the Scottish countryside, seeking refuge from the cold winter night. Will the native species accept them into the herd or will they freeze them out and leave them to die in the habitat of their Honda?" Brody laughed and Jess did as well.

"I have so much to tell you all, especially you, Jess. You're going to sleep in the loft with me... and Brody you're in with Steve and Jack. Aunty Vera, I've put you in my room. I think you'll be comfortable there and it's right across from the bathroom. I hope that's okay. I've cleaned it up really nice for you, and..."

Mum jumped in, eager to reassure her. "Thank you, Ella. I'm sure we'll be comfortable wherever we sleep, right kids?"

Brody grunted and Jess nodded.

Uncle Max greeted them before they made it to the front door and proceeded to take Mum's two suitcases inside. Placing them at the base of the stairs, he did the same with Brody's and her own. Uncle Max's face and moustache had only mildly weathered since she last saw him. His rosy cheeks and stiff body movements were evidence he'd been sitting by the fire waiting for them to arrive. On further inspection he did look rather rumpled - maybe he'd just woken up.

"Well, I don't know about you but I'm famished." He joked clasping his hands together.

Ella nudged her father in the ribs with an elbow. "Och, Pa! I've already told them we've eaten." She smiled and rolled her eyes. "I'll go get your supper ready, Aunty Vera." She disappeared behind a door.

Uncle Max gestured them towards the sitting room. "You folk look exhausted. What happened? Did you get lost?"

Mum's expression lacked any appreciation for the glint in his eye, and rather than give him cause to go on about their tardy arrival, she ran a hand and eye over the entrance of her old family home.

"Not much has changed, Max," She said. It wasn't a compliment, but it was true enough from what Jess could tell.

Cream textured wallpaper, browning at the joins, wore grazes and scabs like the children it had borne. The flattened pile and grey tassel edges of the Persian rug were still expected to receive grubby feet and visiting shoes. As were the coat and shoe racks. A wardrobe of jackets, scarves, and boots by the door, had only changed in length and colour - except for one. Jess wasn't the only one who noticed it. Aunt Gabby's caramel cashmere coat still hung on the rack like she'd worn it yesterday. Mum ran her hand down its sleeve and closed her eyes. On opening, she looked at Uncle Max for an explanation but a blank stare was all she got.

Jess hadn't given her Scottish relatives much thought since her aunt's passing, and it appeared nobody here had given much thought to clearing out her things. It was a little weird and uncomfortable. What was the protocol? Did they speak openly about her? Or was the house a living shrine that couldn't be altered? It hadn't occurred to Jess how their presence might affect them. The family re-union felt awkward - like strangers arriving for Christmas dinner. But dinner was over, so was Christmas, and sadly, Aunt Gabby wouldn't walk into the room with a gleaming smile to welcome them.

Uncle Max shifted their attention, "Come sit by the fire. Ella won't be long."

He gestured towards the door and Jess opened it. A waft of warm air engulfed them and smelt of smoked meat and stale fabric. Mum lingered in the foyer before hooking her jacket next to Gabby's and following them into the room.

"Thanks, for putting us up, Max, we won't stay too long, I promise. Just till I get a job and a place sorted."

Jess scanned the sitting room for Ella's younger brothers, Steve and Jack. She'd forgotten it was almost nine and they were likely already in bed.

The room was darker than the inside of a house ought to be. A solitary wood turned lamp stand in the corner of the room was the only other light source, besides the fire. The brass chandelier in the ceiling had a few bulbs missing, but it would have done a better job of keeping everyone awake than the muted glow from the lampshade.

Jess made herself at home in the corner of a green plaid sofa, removing a lumpy cushion to make room. Mum didn't seem interested in sitting, but her ten-year-old brother did. Taking the cushion as if it were a floating life-saver, he seated himself much closer than she expected. Normally she would have pushed him away, arguing he was in her space. But, given the circumstances, she made an exception.

Uncle Max stoked the fire with another log, sending a flurry of sparks and smoke up the chimney. Dusting the debris from his hands he sunk into a studded leather arm chair and lifted his legs atop a thread-bare ottoman. Beside him, a pile of old newspapers reached almost to the chair's armrests, making an unconventional side table of sorts. The paper on top was stained with rings of tea and Jess wondered how far back the papers dated. Had the collection been a result of her aunt's death too?

Jess lifted her eyes towards the ceiling imagining how tall seven years of newspapers might get. Her thoughts stopped as soon as she spotted several cobwebs clinging to the corners of the room.

A crack and fizzle from the fireplace distracted her search for spiders, and Mum's inspection of the walls continued in the sitting room. Jess wasn't sure what Mum was looking for, but when she stopped at the photographs on the fireplace mantel, Jess assumed she'd found it.

Ella returned with a smile.

"Supper's ready," she announced.

Uncle Max stood. "Aye, Well, Vera - mind I'll put you to work on the farm if you don't find employment. There's plenty work round here to keep you busy." He chuckled.

Mum's back shuddered with short inhalations.

Her face was hidden from the room so Jess couldn't tell if she was laughing or upset. Clearly it was the latter when Uncle Max's smile diminished. He wrapped an arm around her shoulders.

"Oh, Lass. Grant is a fool. It'll all work out for the best, you'll see." He kissed her on the head.

Jess fidgeted with the rough edge of a fingernail. Mum wasn't normally a crier. Years as an E.R nurse had taken care of that. There was simply no time to wallow.

But things were different now. A back-log of ignored tears slipped out almost daily - leaving puffy eyes and tissues everywhere.

The week before they left, Mum's stoic face was back. Farewells were given with practical sentiment and warm smiles. Jess thought her mother was over it and keen to move forward.

Now it seemed the haven of her old home had opened the flood gates. It was nice having Uncle Max there. Jess hadn't realised how long it had been since she'd seen a man cradle Mum like that. Dad's presence was sporadic at best. They really had drifted apart, like Mum said. Jess hadn't fully understood until now.

Ella's chipper voice broke the awkward tension.

"Well I say you're more than welcome to stay as long as you like, Aunty Vera. Isn't that right, Pa?"

Uncle Max nodded.

"Aye. It is. Now how about we go to the kitchen so you guys can eat?"

Mum turned and wiped the moisture from her eyes with a swipe of her hand. Ella pulled a tissue from nowhere and passed it to her.

Mum smiled, and Jess could breathe again. Tension exhaled from her chest and a warmth flooded her whole body.

Maybe moving to Scotland might not be so bad after all.

Good grief - Who was she trying to kid?

The fact was, that tomorrow she would enter a new life in a rural village high school. There'd be no drama department worth bragging about, and possibly no theatre to perform in either. How her life could get much worse she hated to think. All she could imagine was a class full of strangers who laughed at her accent and thought her acting was average.

Jess's stomach flipped and her head felt light. Had she been holding her breath again?

The room began to warp and hover and her stomach demanded she make an exit. She bolted for the front door and bent towards the garden - letting her body do the rest.

The cool air chilled her burning esophagus. Wiping her hands on the dewy grass she attempted to clean the surrounds of her mouth. Mum was quick to find her and pass her tissues.

"You alright, Luv?"

Mum's concern was a welcome relief - her touch soothing. Rhythmic circles on Jess's back distracted her thoughts and her breathing finally steadied.

"That was sudden. Perhaps the long drive all in one day wasn't such a good idea after all." Mum's body radiated heat, making Jess aware of how damp her skin was. She felt much better now her stomach was empty. The mix of junk food, motion, stuffy heat and anxiety had really done a number on her.

Eventually she felt able to stand and drew in a long cool breath. It was like drinking pure oxygen - no it was better than that. It was spectacular. Her mind emptied and she gazed at the few stars in the sky until the air made her shiver.

"Do you still want to eat something?" Mum asked.

"Maybe. What is it?"

"I don't know. How about we go see, and if you're not hungry you can head to bed. I think we all need a good night's sleep after such a roller-coaster day."

"Don't say roller-coaster."

"No. Sorry. Come on - let's go get you some water and a cool cloth."

Having a nurse as your mother had its benefits. Having a mother - full stop - was even better. Just being here made Jess grateful of that.

Back in the kitchen, Brody paused from gobbling a plate of stew.

"It's really yum, Mum. Ella's a good cook." He grinned and licked his fork.

Uncle Max smiled. "Brody and I have just been getting re-acquainted. It seems he's an *Arsenal* man. Not too sure how Steve's gonna feel about that. We support *Liverpool* here so you could be in for some stick. We've got a good team this season and I reckon they're gonna give your gunners a run for their money this year."

"Yeah right." Brody scoffed with food still in his mouth. "We whipped your arses last year. There's no way Liverpool even stands a chance."

"Brody! Language." Mum frowned.

"It's alright, Vera. Wait till you hear Steve. I've been a bit slack with him. But if you think Arsenal is gonna win, Brody - well - we'll just have to wait and see won't we." Uncle Max grinned.

Brody seemed relaxed now that football was being discussed, which made it easier for Jess to forget all about her sudden vomit dash.

Jess stirred the plate of stew in front of her with a fork. It smelt good and her tummy gurgled but she couldn't bring herself to eat it. Maybe no one would notice if she just kept moving it around.

Uncle Max took a big slurp of tea from his mug. "Steve plays in the school's junior football team - the Anglers. I'm sure you two will get along just fine once you sort out your team differences. If I were you, Brody it wouldn't be the first thing I'd mention though." Uncle Max winked at him then looked at Mum. "I've already spoken to Steve's coach..."

A loud crash, somewhere in the house, made everyone's eyes shoot to the roof.

Brody froze - his eyes wide. "What was that?"

CHAPTER TWO

Jess

A S SOON AS Jess ditched her fork in the unfinished plate of stew,
Ella twitched her head and glanced sideways, hinting they should
head up to bed.

Pulling her gently towards the doorway Ella whispered with a
mischievous grin, "I've got something to show you. Just keep quiet else
me brothers'll catch on you've arrived. Pa's sent them to bed already, but
they'll be listening at the door for sure."

Ella grabbed one of Jess's bags and gestured a 'Shhh' to her lips. It
must have been one of the boys Jess had seen pull the curtain when they
first arrived. Presumably they were responsible for the crash they'd
heard too.

Jess followed Ella up the stairs. The first tread creaked. Ella whipped
around before Jess could move another muscle. She indicated the next

safe positions on the worn carpeted steps so she could avoid making any more noise. Jess clamped her lips tighter and paid more attention to Ella's feet.

Reaching the first floor landing, Ella released a latch on the ceiling with a pole. A mass of timber and metal hinges squeaked - stretching like a gymnast to the floor. Jess tried hard not to giggle. With so much noise from the descending ladder, what was the point of avoiding creaks in the stairs?

The little staircase leading up into the loft rested to one side of the hallway leaving just enough room for the passage to remain clear. Her breaths shortened and her heart skipped a few beats. The confined entry looked like a black mouth and Ella had already been half swallowed.

Not keen to draw unwanted attention, Jess wiped the sweat from her palm, held her breath, and ventured up.

A warm flow of air followed her through the hole and dissipated quickly once she'd arrived. Ella pulled a chain - flicking to life a single bulb in the loft. The yellow glow illuminated the pitch of the roof and its dark wooden rafters. Childhood treasures, dusty boxes and antique furniture parts lay strewn and stacked without any order. It was like being inside a plundered pyramid.

A giant wardrobe caught her eye. Skinny and tall, it stood against the chimney stack. Jess imagined it to be a mummy's tomb of sorts and decided that if the light weren't on - a zombie might burst out at any moment and make her scream. She tried to bury the idea by searching for where they were to sleep.

Washing lines of cobwebs swooped between rafters, tensioning themselves in the draught. There would be no sleep tonight. Nor any night.

Ella flicked a set of switches on a partially-lined wall behind them and lights in a room at the opposite end of the loft blazed to life. Through the doorway Jess glimpsed a bedroom aglow with fairy lights. Two soft quilted bed tops with matching red and green pillow cases looked like Christmas came early. Jess longed to stretch out her legs on one of them and completely forgot about the spider webs in the storage end. A softly lit bed lamp and small vase of flowers rested on a chest of draws between the beds. It was cosy and warm, and her eyes weighed heavy. An unstoppable yawn stretched her jaw till it ached. If she could just lie down for a moment...

A loud clacking sound swung her attention back to Ella pulling on a rope to raise the stairs off the floor below. The light from the loft floor turned to darkness and her heart began to thump.

"What are you doing?" Jess's palms moistened again and her head dizzied - the room didn't warp like before - it spun. Her stomach wasn't to blame - this was different - yet familiar. She had to hold onto something or she'd pass out if she couldn't regain control. Her escape was now blocked and the symptoms that accompanied her Cleithrophobia were triggered. Dad suffered too - but his was the fear of small spaces. She wished he were here so he could remind her what to do. What was it?

Jess reached into thin air, trying to grasp hold of anything. The muscles in her hands cramped and panic choked her airways as if she were drowning under waves. Jess sucked at the air in controlled breaths, wildly searching for - Five things she could see. That's it!

Like photograph negatives, shapes blurred and changed colour, gradually becoming solid objects again. Her vision was clearing but her heart still raced. She grabbed at the folded staircase to steady herself. Bent in half paralyzed, Jess focused on four things she could touch. Her shoes, the wooden steps, her jeans, and Ella's hand - now being offered to her. She resisted the urge to take it and focused on what she could hear. Ella's voice was the only sound she could detect given how loud and concerned it was, but it was comforting never-the-less. Jess finally looked at her and swallowed hard.

"Are you alright? What's the matter, are you allergic to something? Can I help?"

"Uh… yeah…"Jess's breathing eased, "No. I'll be okay. I just like to have my exits clear at all times. Do you mind if we leave the stairs down?"

"I guess not, but then we'll be able to be heard and spied on, two things I was hoping to avoid by being up here. Don't worry, you'll get used to it." Ella replied, as if the mere statement would make it true. "We'll leave the stairs down, at least until you feel more comfortable. You scared me half to death. I thought the spirits were coming for you or something. Maybe you're allergic to the dust? It wouldn't surprise me after what happened this morning."

"It's not the dust, Ella." Jess pondered whether it was worth explaining. She decided not to, and instead unfolded herself to focus on Ella's face.

Ella chattered while Jess studied her features. She'd grown out of nearly all her freckles, and her teeth fit inside her wide mouth perfectly. Her coiling tresses of brown hair were striking - like her mother's. It wasn't the only comparable feature Jess recognised. Ella's fine cheekbones and sparkling eyes were familiar too. Looking at her was like seeing a young Aunt Gabby.

A lump caught in Jess's throat and she struggled to clear it. She was staring but she couldn't help it. Ella's almond brown eyes held the innocence of an eight-year-old and she found it difficult to believe her cousin was the same age as her. Due to Ella's accent, her words were easy to ignore. Her melodic undertones often confused Jess and had her doubting what she had said or meant. Ella was an enigma and Jess was captivated. Was she really as naïve as she appeared?

"Now, I've been dying for you to get here because something really strange happened this morning and I really need your help." Ella paused, her eyes unyielding.

"What happened? Help with what?"

The lights, now warm, had brightened and dust particles danced in its warm currents. Jess finally felt normal again. Hints of mystery beckoned from the boxes stacked two or more high all around her and all Jess wanted to do was to hunt for treasures.

Ella pointed to the top of the towering wardrobe. "See that box up there...that colourful one that looks kind of floral?"

Jess nodded.

"Well, this morning when I was up here looking for the bedside lamps, a really weird thing happened. See that window over there, in the middle." Ella pointed to a window sitting in its own little boxed out nook. Jess remembered seeing three dormer windows, evenly spaced along the length of the house, when they'd driven up the driveway. They looked much bigger from the inside. Jess went to inspect the cottage style window.

"Well, I opened the window to let in some fresh air. Steve and Jack were being a nuisance outside so I yelled at them and then went to look for the lamps. I found them over there. Then, just as I was about to leave, I had a weird feeling when I went to close the window. The hairs on the back of my neck stood on end and my arms felt like a plucked goose. It was surely a spirit, because it blew the window shut." Ella's eyes widened and she froze as if the spirit might reappear.

Jess cocked an eyebrow and restrained a laugh. Although her cousin's skill at story-telling was endearing, her elocution could use some work.

"A spirit-like spiral of dust moved from the floor - right where you're standing - to the top of that wardrobe." Ella said, in a semi-trance-like state. She motioned her hand along the course the dust had spiralled and issued an eerie whistle.

The air shifted, and a shiver fingered its way down Jess's arms.

Her breathing stopped.

She folded her arms across her chest and stepped away from the spot Ella had pointed to.

"That's when I saw it." Ella pointed at the box on the wardrobe. "I hadn't noticed it up there before. It must be important if the spirits have revealed it." She dropped her arm and then her head. "I tried to get it down but I fell off the chair. Will you help me get it? Please, Jess?"

Was she serious?

Jess was wary of being pranked. If her friends, June or Libby, had tried this story, she would have known if they were lying. Ella was not so easy to read.

Jess wasn't sure what to make of Ella's paranormal suggestion. Did she really believe in ghosts? If she did, then refusing to help her might make things worse. Either way, Jess's impression of Ella changed, and not for the better.

Regardless of how the box was found, Jess couldn't deny her curiosity and she wove a path towards the wardrobe. Taking care, and dodging anything that dangled, Jess arrived at the dark timber doors. Up on tip toes, she thrust her hands to the top and searched with her fingers for the box. She was taller than Ella, but annoyingly she still couldn't quite reach it.

She glanced around for something to stand on. The dining chair that was tipped on its side would have been perfect - if it weren't for a missing leg.

"Hmm, maybe a sturdy box might work?" Jess scanned around them. Nothing looked up to the task.

"I've got a better idea." She got down on one knee; like a man about to propose, and motioned Ella to climb her.

"Are you serious? You want me to climb you?"

Jess's curious mind went into over-drive.

"Dead serious, Ella. That box could have anything in it - expensive jewellery, mementoes, or maybe it was your mother's."

"Really - you think so? I hadn't thought of that." Ella chewed her bottom lip.

"It could be -who knows. But I do know this, I won't be able to sleep tonight until we know what's in that box."

CHAPTER THREE

Jess

ELLA HESITATED, WORRYING her eyes at Jess's raised knee. "Uh, maybe I should let you climb on me. I twisted my ankle this morning - stupid chair." She shunted the three-legged chair with a limp foot and winced. "It still hurts a bit but Pa mustn't know I've injured it again. It'll be fine in the morning."

Jess jumped up and let Ella take the proposal stance.

"So that's why you're limping." She gave a sympathetic look.

Ella frowned then offered her hand to aid Jess up.

Was Ella mad at her for noticing, or at herself for not hiding it very well?

After a wobbly start and a few giggles, Jess clambered onto Ella's good leg like a circus elephant balancing on a ball. Grabbing at Ella's head, to prevent falling herself, Jess tugged at her hair without thinking.

"Ooouwwch!" Ella cried.

Jess felt terrible. "Sorry." She grasped hold of the box with two hands. "Got it." She jumped down with a thud. Ella winced like she'd made the jump herself but then clenched a broad smile between her cheeks - her hands splayed expecting the reward.

Jess looked at the dusty box before handing it over. She concealed her disappointment by brushing thick bales of dust from her sweaty palms.

"Thanks, Jess... I mean it. I've been dying to get my hands on this box. It hope it's not just some old photographs. I reckon, if the spirits revealed it, it's got to be worth all this effort, don't you think? Shall we open it?" Ella eyed her for confirmation.

Against Jess's better judgment, she smiled politely and nodded.

A mystery box, found under mind bending circumstances?

Whatever.

Jess wouldn't believe it - but spirit-dust be damned, if this box contained anything remotely interesting, she'd consider it a win. If it turned out to be something valuable, then perhaps their move to the farm might not be as dull as expected after all.

Ella puffed away the top layer of dust then wiped it with her sleeve.

Jess traced a finger over the design on the lid. "It's really pretty. They're not flowers - they're letters. Let's open it. I wonder who put it there?"

"It's strange I never noticed it before. Who knows how long it's been sitting there. Our family has lived here a few generations and judging by all this dust I don't think it could be Ma or Pa's." Ella brushed her sleeve to remove the dust.

"Yeah, but it doesn't look that old. The white areas would be more yellowed if it were. It reminds me of a cardboard gift box - but I've never seen one decorated like this before. I love all the colours. What does that say there?" Jess pointed to a string of mis-matched fonts. Some of them were purple, her favourite colour.

"Free to choose, Free to heal, Free to Love, Free to feel." Ella drew out each word as she pieced it together; the various fonts making it difficult to decipher.

"It can't be more than fifty years old I reckon, Ella. It wouldn't have belonged to anyone really ancient." Her conclusion was based on little other than her own gut feeling.

Jess shoved aside a wicker picnic basket with its corner chewed off, followed by a cricket set that was short a few wickets. She then moved two small boxes, the top one contained a hard plastic doll with a missing eye and matted hair. It brought a flash of buried images into her mind like a bout of bad reflux and she cursed the day she ever let June convince her to watch, *Child's Play*.

Ella sat at the base of the wardrobe and placed the box between her outstretched legs. With little room left, Jess sat kindergarten style opposite her. Ella lifted a corner of the lid. She hesitated and closed it again. Jess wasn't sure why and frowned at her. Ella held her breath and in one swift motion, yanked the lid off the box and discarded it to one side. A sigh of relief left her mouth.

"What's the matter?" Jess asked with a chuckle. "Was a ghost meant to have escaped or something?"

Ella cut a stare of contempt in her direction.

Jess's cheeks glowed hot and her eyes dove inside the box for cover. She dare not look her cousin in the eye until she spoke again.

Ella explored the contents of the box. It wasn't full of photographs, in fact it was quite empty. There were a couple of official looking letters; one with a registries office letterhead and another with a typed address on its header. Ella obviously couldn't be bothered reading them and handed them over. Jess gave them a momentary glance, placed them on the floor and inched herself closer to see what else was in the box.

Under the letters sat a blue journal that was scuffed around its edges. Ella picked it up and opened it. Jess lent forward on her knees, cocking her head hard to the left to get a better look at it the right way up, but

Ella pulled away as if spooked. When she registered it was just Jess, she patted her chest and giggled.

Ella shoved against a brown cardboard box sitting next to her, sending fishing rods crashing against the roof. Now that there was room for two, Jess shuffled beside her and rested her back against the wardrobe door.

All was forgiven.

Ella opened the journal. The writing was quite swishy and difficult to read so she casually flicked through a few pages to see if anything stood out.

Some old newspaper clippings inside the box caught Jess's eye. She went to grab them, but as she did two old photographs fell out of the journal and landed in Ella's lap. Ella picked them up and Jess reverted her attention back to the journal with the newly found photographs.

The first picture was of a baby with dark hair wearing a white and pink outfit. The other was an old retro-toned photo. A woman, about twenty, stood coyly, wearing a short A-line summer dress made of yellow gingham. Crisp white straps and a wide collar trimmed the bust and matched a thin white belt snug about her waist. She was very attractive with big almond shaped eyes and full pouty lips, and a top her blonde bouffant do-up, perched a pair of the largest white rimmed sunglasses Jess had ever seen. She looked very glamorous, like an old movie star.

On the reverse were the initials C.S. 1972 and a lipstick mark of a kiss.

It reminded Jess of the time she and Libby plastered themselves with lipstick and made kiss marks in her friend's diary as practice. Worried they'd get caught, Libby had insisted they do it in the dark in her wardrobe, adding a sense of excitement.

"C.S," Ella pondered out loud, staring into space. "Hmmm, interesting, I wonder who it could be?" She turned the photograph back to study the girl further.

Jess rummaged through the rest of the items. Some newspaper clippings and a magazine advertisement for pantyhose. A blue piece of paper with a handwritten address had been torn off the back of an envelope. It was for somewhere in Denmark. No name was given at the top of the address though. On the reverse side, another address in Paris, had been written in the same handwriting as in the journal and this time the name 'Charlotte' was written at its top.

"That's strange." Ella took the blue piece of paper from Jess.

"What is?"

"Well, all of it. I don't know anyone named Charlotte and we still haven't a clue who these things belong to. So whose are they? And how did they get up here in our loft?"

Once all the bits of paper were removed and set aside, Jess noticed something else in the box. It was some sort of fine knit cloth. Its off white colour distinguished it as something older than present day fabric and she was desperate to see exactly what it was.

"What do you think that is?" She pointed to it.

Ella picked it up, bobbing it in the air, surprised by its weight. In haste she opened up the fabric.

'CLUNK-CHINK!'

A set of old keys dropped from inside the cloth and landed back in the box.

Jess and Ella jumped in fright and Jess screamed - wrenching herself as far away from the box as she could manage. Her hand clapped across her mouth, then dropped so she could speak.

"Sorry, I thought it was a spider. I hate bugs."

"Ew! Me too." Ella said, quivering with the fabric between her hands.

Jess couldn't believe it. Ella was a country girl - surely she wasn't as scared of insects as she was? With the mantra: 'You're safe' - repeating in her head, her pulse slowed.

Ella inspected the knit cloth. It appeared to be a baby's night dress and had a tiny pink bow embroidered on the front below the neck. After studying the gown for a moment Ella turned their attention to the set of keys. There were eight of them in total and all were different colours and sizes.

One was large and black and made from wrought iron. Ella said it looked like an old barn door key.

There were a couple of tarnished silver ones almost the same in size, one was much thicker and heavier looking than the other - which had a more circular head.

A small ornate brass key about the length of Jess's little finger had a pretty looped top and was instantly her favourite.

Next to it, sat a black key of similar size but it was very plain by comparison.

A tiny silver key dangled to one side. It was the smallest of them all and had just one nick in its teeth. It reminded Jess of a key she once had for a jewellery box with a twirling ballerina. She'd lost the key and never found it.

Another key; flat and brass coloured, looked like a padlock key and seemed very boring when compared to the rest.

The final key was the strangest of them all. Its very short cylindrical shaft was hollow like a whistle and had tiny rectangular cut outs all around it. The top had a chunky plastic, milk-white turn grip in the shape of a guitar pick. The hole it hung from was so tight that all the other keys clustered around it.

"What do you think that one unlocks?" Jess asked pointing to it.

"I dunno. I've never seen a key like that before," Ella said. "I bet it's for something custom made."

Jess couldn't fault her cousin's logic and she had no other suggestion.

All the keys hung from a single large ring - the kind you see a prison warden carrying. Jess remembered how much keys like that would jingle when they knocked together so she reached to pick them up.

Before she could, Ella beat her to it. She only held them for a second but dropped them almost instantly, looking at her hand as if stung by a bee.

Jess stood up. She wasn't sure why, but she felt safer on her feet.

"Whoa. That was weird," Ella said, clutching her hand and wiggling her fingers.

"What? What just happened?"

"When I picked them up my hand went all ting-gil-ly!" Ella dragged the word like nails on a chalk board sending a shiver down Jess's spine. Impressed by Ella's dramatic tone, Jess assumed she was trying to have her on.

"Sure Ella, your hands ting-gled," She replied in similar spooky jest, dancing her fingers above her head.

"I'm serious, Jess. I've seen things like this in the movies and it almost always has something to do with spirits or something like it. I don't wanna go upsetting no spirits. If you don't believe me - you touch them!"

"Oh hogwash, Ella, they're just movies. No spirits are gonna be bothered if we touch those keys. Get a grip."

From the look on Ella's face, Jess's abrupt dismissal must have come across as heartless. But before Ella could argue further, Jess picked up the keys...

CHAPTER FOUR

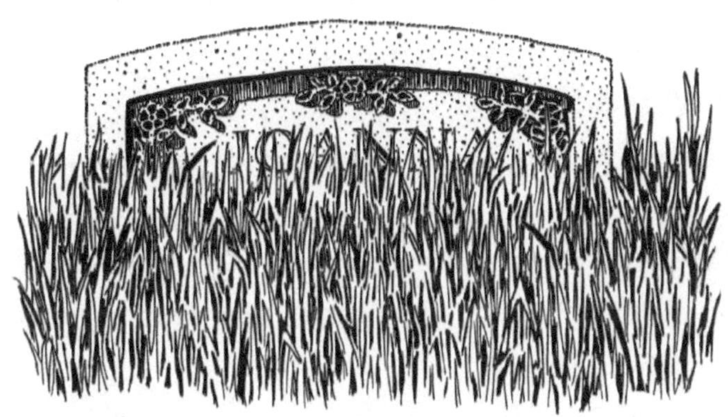

Jess

JESS HAD SEEN some creepy movies lately, which had heightened her interest of the un-natural and unknown. But she always reassured herself they were only make-believe. What happened next was way beyond mere tingling hands or movie tricks, and no one, not even her drama teacher - Mrs Buchannan, could have prepared her for it.

Holding the keys firmly in her grasp, a vision flashed before her eyes...

A woman was crying in front of a lone gravestone and in her arms, she held a baby. Leaning down she placed some flowers on the grave.

Jess squinted her eyes to read the inscription on the plaque but the grass was too tall and she couldn't make out the words.

"JESS!" Ella screamed.

Jess awoke from the vision and dropped the keys.

"What just happened?" Jess asked, suddenly afraid of what she'd seen.

Ella was standing now too and her face looked pale.

"I don't know, you tell me. One minute you're here and then you just froze holding the keys. For a few seconds, you said nothing and didn't respond when I tried to get you to drop them. I thought the spirits had taken you. Are you alright?"

"Yeah, I think so. That was weird - and creepy. When I picked up the keys, I had a vision."

"Really? What did you see?"

"A woman was holding a baby. She was crying in front of a gravestone." Jess paused to shake her hands - they were still trembling. "Jings, Ella! What's going on? Who do these belong to? I've never experienced anything like it. I don't wanna help with this anymore, I'm gonna have nightmares."

"So your hands didn't tingle at all when you touched the keys?"

Ella's question seemed irrelevant so she rebutted her again.

"I'm not interested in having anything to do with that box, or those keys. You got it." Jess poked her in the chest. Ella didn't flinch and wasn't the least bit deterred.

"You mean, your hands did tingle?"

"Ugh. No, they didn't tingle! But I saw something strange alright and I'm not keen to see anything like it again. So can you please just drop it!" Jess hadn't realised she was yelling until Ella shushed a finger on her lips. Jess wished she'd never helped retrieve the stupid box now. Keys lay splayed at her feet and she took a step back to avoid risking contact with them again.

Ella took the baby's nightdress and wrapped the keys inside it taking care not to touch them.

"What's going on up there?" called Mum from the floor below. "You alright, Jess?"

"Yeah I'm fine. Every thing's fine." Her voice jittered.

"I heard a scream and it didn't sound fine."

Her mother's concern, though over-bearing at times, was a great comfort and Jess wished she could flee downstairs into her arms. Pride prevented such an act and kept her feet glued to the floor.

"Sorry, Mum, we just got carried away with something that's all."

"Alright, well perhaps you two should get ready for bed. It's really late and Ella has school tomorrow."

Ella's face soured with a pout that beckoned a change of weather.

"Okay, we'll get ready for bed now," Jess answered, happy to comply.

Ella's eyes never left her and she could tell she wouldn't let the incident go without further interrogation.

Jess needed time - time to sleep. Maybe then her head would be able to figure it all out.

"Tomorrow, Ella. We'll figure it out tomorrow."

Monday 21st March 2016

Jess awoke the next morning to Ella moving about as she got ready for school. Her head felt groggy from the drive and arriving so late. Then she recalled what happened with the keys. She couldn't remember having any nightmares about it though.

"Good Morning, Sleepy," Ella said with the innocent glee of a five year old. "Do you know you talk in your sleep?"

"Oh no. What did I say?" Jess wanted to bury her head under the pillow and die of shame. But if Mrs Buchannan had taught her nothing else, Jess remembered that the best defence is always diversion. She'd become quite good at it during role play in drama class and it had saved her numerous times from one of Dad's lectures.

Jess sat up, cleared her eyes and waited for the interrogation to begin. To her surprise, Ella had no intention of discussing her sleep mumblings further and moved on. "Don't worry I won't say anything," She said, stuffing textbooks in her bag and glancing around the room.

Ella's cunning smile said otherwise and Jess felt cheated - then concerned. What had she said in her sleep? Would Ella use it against her? With her cousin unwilling to play, Jess had little choice but to forget about it too.

"Do you wanna meet up for lunch at school? Your mum said she's bringing you in later this morning to meet Mr Lees, our Dean. Something to do with your paperwork?" Ella glanced momentarily at the box sitting on the end of her bed.

"Sure I guess. If it's okay with Mum." Jess secretly hoped it wouldn't be and she'd have an excuse not to stick around. She hadn't figured out yet how to persuade Ella to forget about the box. It contained nothing valuable and she couldn't see any reason they should spend more time on it.

"Well, if you can't don't worry, I'll be home around four and we can catch up then." Ella disappeared down the hole in the loft floor without waiting for a reply.

Jess submerged her head back under the covers and hoped she'd never have to leave. How did Ella do that? In less than a minute she had made Jess forget about her sleep talking and somehow made her think about the box, all without saying much about either. Jess didn't know what to make her cousin. Was Ella even aware of her powers of persuasion?

Jess's thoughts were cut short when a different voice called up the stairs.

"Hey, Jess, you up there?" said Brody. At least it wasn't Mum telling her to get up.

"Yeah, Brody, what do you want?"

"Can I come up?" His tone was polite, which was unusual given the time of day.

"Sure…what's up?"

Brody's head appeared from the floor boards. He bounced his gaze about the loft, edged across the room, and took a seat near the foot of her bed.

"I was just wondering how you were. Did you sleep well?" His warm demeanour surprised her.

Jess nodded, "Alright I guess." She followed her brother's hand as he pointed to the sky out the window on the other side of Ella's bed

"Wow you can see for miles up here. It's really dark at night aye? I miss the street lights."

He's homesick - be nice.

"It's okay, Brody, you'll get used to it."

"And it's really cold, aye."

Jess hugged the cover to her chest and wriggled back down under them.

"Just stay under the cov…errrs!" Wet slime touched her feet. Jess screamed and leapt out of bed; flailing her arms and leaping from one foot to the other. Brody grinned like a frog. Throwing back the covers revealed a large number of worms writhing on her sheets. Brody's laughter disappeared down the stairs at great speed.

"You little twerp. Gross! Ew!" Her body convulsed. "I'm gonna get you, Brody Warren!" Her voice - a siren of impending doom.

Pulling on her dressing gown she ran downstairs to find her brother and bring him to justice. On the first floor landing, standing at their bedroom door, her two other cousins, Jack and Steve, stared and chuckled as she went past.

"You little brats, I'm gonna tell on you - then you'll be in trouble. You put him up to this. He wouldn't have been able to get those worms by himself." Both boys looked at each other and slammed the bedroom door.

Jess continued her rampage down stairs in search of Brody. She found him in the kitchen, innocently eating toast like he'd been there for ages.

"Mum. Brody put…"

A blast of cold air from the back door made her stop mid-sentence. Mum looked up from her steaming cup of coffee. Uncle Max entered, took a mug from a cupboard and filled it from the kettle on the stove.

"Morning," He said, unaware of what he'd walked into.

"Good Morning, Max." Mum's chipper tone annoyed Jess more than Brody's cheeky grin. She wasn't sure what to say next with Uncle Max there, but she had to tell Mum what happened. It wouldn't be fair if Brody got away with it.

"Mum, Brody put worms in my bed." Again, her body shook in disgust. Uncle Max stopped mid-slurp and gazed across the top of his cup. She crossed her arms and tried to pretend he wasn't there. "They were so gross. You have to punish him, or something. He can't get away with it. It's not fair."

Mum was a picture of calm and took another sip of coffee. She shook her head.

"Not today kids, not today. Today you will be on your best behaviour or I'm going to make sure that Max sticks you with the worst chores he's got. Doesn't that pig pen need cleaning out, Max?"

"Uh, sure, I guess so." He looked like a rabbit caught in the scope of a rifle and Jess tried not to smile.

"And how about collecting some firewood. What was it we used to have to get each night, Max? Five loads from the wood shed? I used to hate getting the firewood because there were always spiders and all sorts of insects in it. Now, what was the problem, Jess? Brody?"

Neither of them uttered a word. What planet had they moved to? If her brother could get away with this sort of thing, how would she ever survive out here?

Steve and Jack entered the kitchen, grabbed their lunches from the table and stuffed them in their bags. Ella came in a few minutes later, grinned at Jess and winked. Jess thought it was strange and worried it had something to do with her sleep-talking again. She couldn't tell if she should be embarrassed or mad. Not knowing was starting to irritate her and Ella's stupid grin wasn't helping.

"Now, you two had better hurry up and get dressed. We've got an appointment at the school this morning at ten and I'm not going to be late," said Mum.

Uncle Max raised his eyebrows and looked at his kids. "Right, you lot. You'd better head for the gate before the bus gets here. Steve, Jack, if I find out you've played any part in this prank, you'll both have extra chores this afternoon and the football game will have to wait."

Finally - at least one adult in the house was prepared to enforce punishment. So long as it wasn't Jess on the receiving end - she'd be happy.

The boys moaned and headed for the door, grabbing their backpacks and coats as they went.

Ella smiled "See you at school for lunch, Jess."

How would she get out of it now? Thankfully, Mum came to the rescue.

"Oh I'm sorry, Ella, but Jess won't be able to stay for lunch today. I'm taking them to Aberdeen after our meeting at the school. We need to get uniforms and school supplies, and I also have to drop off my CV at a few hospitals. We should be home before you finish school though."

"Okay. If I don't see you at school - I'll see you later!" Ella's voice disappeared out the door.

Jess re-wrapped her dressing gown about her chest in defiance and muttered all the way back upstairs. Flopping onto her bed she stared at the box at the foot of Ella's bed for a long time. Who did it belong to? Probably the woman she'd seen in her vision, she decided. She'd looked so sad and it reminded Jess of the last time she was here.

Aunt Gabby's funeral was the first wake she had ever been to. She'd never seen so many red noses and watery eyes in one place before. The memory was so well etched in her mind that she could even remember the dress she wore - her little grey one with the red shirt under it. She also recalled the pretty purple flowers everywhere and the smell of food in the oven. Thinking back, she'd probably caused her mother quite a lot of embarrassment during the service. At a quiet moment, between eulogies, she had asked, rather loudly, 'When do we get to eat?'

Aunt Gabby was a wonderful cook - according to everyone who spoke at her funeral. Jess had only tasted her aunt's baking once when she was about five years old. Aunt Gabby made pink frosted cupcakes for her and Ella to eat in the garden. She liked her aunt very much because her hair was so curly and her eyes sparkled whenever she talked.

No, the woman in her vision wasn't Aunt Gabby. Her eyes looked similar but her hair, although brown, wasn't curly at all.

"You done up there, Missy?" Mum called from the bottom of the loft stairs.

"Coming!" Jess scampered about, dragging on the first pair of jeans she found in her bag and her cute fox cartoon t-shirt. She'd almost forgotten about their meeting with the Dean and the reminder sent a stab to her gut. Ignoring her nerves didn't always mask the symptoms.

"Don't forget your jacket, Jess. And brush your hair! Brody, have you brushed your teeth?" The orders were coming thick and fast and Mum's voice tightened beneath each word. Jess could tell she was stressed and presumed she was just as nervous about their meeting at the school as she was.

Alford Academy had a newly built campus which only opened last year. Ella relayed that the teachers were very strict and that the work had been a lot harder.

No teenager ever wanted to face the gauntlet of changing schools - let alone part-way through the year. She'd have to work double-time to make sure she didn't fall in with the wrong crowd by accident. According to Mum her biggest asset in this scenario was meant to be Ella.

Jess grabbed her hairbrush, tugged it through the mess a couple of times to little effect.

But what if Ella's social ranking was lower than she hoped? Would it have a bearing on who she could hang out with? Or worse - who would *want* to hang out with her? Would she have to choose family obligation over potential friends?

Her stomach churned. She wished Libby were here - she'd say something smart to boost her confidence.

Jess ran the brush through her hair a few more times and checked herself briefly in the round mirror. She shrugged her shoulders and descended the loft stairs.

Approaching the bathroom, Jess waited at the door. Brody froze, bent over the sink during a final rinse and spit. He was cornered.

Jess scowled. "You little toad, I'm going to get you later on. You'll not get away with it!"

Brody walked towards her and on his way past, shouldered her into the door-frame.

Jess responded likewise, by placing her foot in his path.

He tripped. "Urgh, Jess!"

"What?"

"Nothing." His shoulders slumped and he went downstairs to get his shoes on.

Just as Jess started brushing her teeth she heard Brody scream. Next came a very angry cry.

"Jessie! How could you? Mum!"

Jess exited the bathroom with her toothbrush still in her mouth and peered down the stairs.

"What is it? What... what's the matter?" Mum asked in a panic. Jess made her way to the bottom of the stairs and saw her brother sulking with one of his shoes half on. Mum was by his side.

"My shoes! There's something squishy in my shoes. Jess put worms in them."

"No I didn't." Jess battled with her tongue to retain a mouthful of toothpaste. "Ow could I 'ave, I'v 'een up 'ere all morning." The foaming liquid was about to escape and she bolted back up to the bathroom to spit it out. It was then that she remembered Ella's wink in the kitchen. She must have done it as payback for Brody's prank.

Jess smiled to herself in the mirror. Now she couldn't wait to see Ella at school and thank her.

Brody moaned as he removed his socks and Mum sounded cross.

"Go and clean that off, Brody, and get your other shoes. Hurry up, or we're going to be late."

Mum's anger was on the cusp of a boil and Jess wasn't about to make herself part of the mix. Popping on her jacket and shoes Jess exited the farmhouse and waited by the car. A few minutes later Brody and Mum joined her and they all sat in silence on the drive to school.

Jess

"**G**OOD," SAID MUM. "We made it on time." She ushered Jess and Brody into the revolving front door and towards the school's main office. The lady at reception was busy typing on her computer and Jess couldn't tell if she'd even noticed them enter. Reluctantly the woman peered over her glasses and computer screen to acknowledge them.

"Hello, can I help you?"

"Hi, I'm Vera Warren and these are my two children, Jessie, and Brody. We have an appointment with Mr Lees at ten." Mum said offering the lady a polite smile.

"You're late," She replied with the snap of a Scottish spinster.

They all glanced at the large ticking clock above her head to read the time - 10:04 am.

"Well not by much," Mum said, joking off the receptionist's petty discrimination. Jess rolled her eyes. Why did Mum always insist on arguing with school staff? - It never helped. Couldn't she just restrain herself and remain civil, if not for her own sake then for theirs.

"Fill these out and take a seat. Mr Lees will be with you shortly." A clipboard of forms landed in Mum's hands and the lady went back to her duties behind the desk. Jess could tell it took a great deal of will power for Mum not to rebut the woman further and do as she'd been asked.

Looking for a place to sit, Mum and Brody took the two hard reception chairs, and Jess stood.

Fifteen minutes passed. Mum had filled in the forms and checked them twice. She tapped the pen against the clipboard, winning a stare of judgment from the woman behind the desk. Avoiding further eye contact with the receptionist, Mum pretended to look for something in her handbag. The only thing it yielded was her phone and pointless games of solitaire. Mum stretched her back and sighed heavily. Jess prayed Mum would hold it together long enough to avoid embarrassing them.

Mum's past bouts of impatience played like a video clip on loop in her head.

'If I'd had to wait this long to see a Doctor in the ER in Holloway, a gross negligence suit would have already been filed with the health board and the staff given a warning. This isn't just rude it's un-professional.'

'Do they think, they're the only people on this planet with things to do? If I ran my department like they seem to here, I'd have been fired ages ago.'

'You'd think that if they made the effort to send a reminder text about an appointment - that they'd make a similar effort to be on time themselves. It leads me to believe that they think their time is more valuable than mine.'

On and on, regrettably, Jess had too many memorable and embarrassing moments to count on just her fingers.

Mum stood to approach the lady behind the desk. Jess knew a demand to know Mr Lees' whereabouts would come next and likely an embarrassing scene she'd have to live with for the rest of her days at school.

Just then, a tall well-groomed man in a dark grey suit and blue tie entered the room. Jess released her held breath and watched her mother's cheeks flush with colour. A smile that would melt an ice cube radiated from Mum's lips and was one Jess had only recently noticed when her mother spoke to men that were marginally attractive. He was kind of nice looking - for an old guy anyway.

"Welcome. I'm Mr Lees, deputy head here at Alford Academy. Sorry to have kept you waiting. You must be Vera Lockheart." He held out his hand for her to shake with a smile that creased his cheeks with perfect symmetry.

"Well actually, I'm Vera Warren, I was a Lockheart before I married. I used to live here before I moved to London. My brother, Max Lockheart, made the appointment for us. My niece and two nephews go to this school..."

Mum was babbling again. She paused, caught her breath, and shook his hand.

"Well, follow me and let's see if we can sort out your enrolments, shall we?" He spoke with as much enthusiasm as her mother did. The whole process was awkward and embarrassing. In a room that smelt of clinical carpet and woody cologne, all three of them sat before his desk; uncommonly sparse for a school teacher.

To spice thing up a bit, and just for her own amusement, Jess decided to pretend she'd been abducted by aliens and was about to be studied by them.

Jess rubbed at the rough edge of her fingernail, which was now just a slither a top her finger. She sighed.

"Miss Warren, are you looking forward to attending a new school?" Mr Lees bore a hole in her temple with his stare and Jess gave one back just as good. Picturing him as a Cyclops - with just a single eye above his nose, she could almost achieve it by crossing her eyes.

"Ah, sure. I guess… Well no, not really." Her answer was confusing.

Mum micro-frowned, smiled at Mr Lees, and tapped Jess's ankle with her foot. She'd have to say something else.

"Well, I'm looking forward to going to this school if that's what you mean, but if you mean because it's a new school, it doesn't really bother me."

Mr Lees raised his eyebrows and cocked his head to one side as if trying to decipher her explanation.

"Oh, I see. Well, we have state of the art facilities here now; you won't be lacking anything in terms of what you might be used to from your previous high school. We aim to provide our students with as much of the latest technology as we possibly can. You won't be disappointed." Mr Lees smiled at Mum and turned to Brody. "And what about you Brody. I hear you're pretty good with a football. We'll be glad to have you on our team, Lad." Mr Less continued explaining the various facilities like a car salesman, while they all smiled and nodded.

Jess's mind wandered and she couldn't wait to get out of there. Each minute passed like an hour of homework and her opportunity to bump into Ella was fading away. A digital bell blared, followed by an encore of students migrating towards their next classes. Fingers on the clock above Mr Lees' shiny head of black hair, moved closer to eleven making it appear as though he sported some kind of Martian antenna. Jess fixed a stare on her alien creature, so much so that Mr Lees must have thought she was actually listening.

When the hour hand sprouted from Mr Lees' head like a lightning rod, he stood and asked them to join him on a tour of the school.

Jess was confused - she must have zoned out completely without even realising. *Blast - they'd got to her.*

Mr Lees' tight lipped chuckle confirmed that her little trip to la-la-land hadn't gone unnoticed.

Jess stared at her shoes and folded her arms across her waist.

Mum put a hand on her shoulder and spoke with the composure of a well-trained nurse, "They're still a little tired from the drive yesterday. How long do you think it might take? It's just that I have some other errands to attend to in Aberdeen, and we'll also need to get their uniforms sorted out."

He nodded in agreement. "I understand, it won't take long. I'll just get Jessie set up with a locker, and then take both of them to their home classes so they'll know where to come tomorrow morning."

Jess's shoulders tensed. She hated being called Jessie. Hearing Mr Lees say it, was even worse than when her father used it during one of his lectures. Jess glared at her mother. She understood.

"Ah, if you wouldn't mind, Mr Lees. It's best if you just call her Jess."

"Of course. And you can call Greg, Vera." Mr Lees said her mother's name with a little more breath than Jess felt was appropriate. Mum must have thought so too, else she wouldn't have turned so red.

"Thank you, Greg." She smiled. "I'm sure their cousins will show them around the rest of the school tomorrow."

As they walked across the large courtyard towards the junior area, Jess noticed a shadow of a person behind the corner of one of the buildings.

"Pssst, Jess," She heard Ella whisper. Her mother, Mr Lees, and Brody hadn't heard her and continued on walking while Jess hung back.

"Are you nuts? Won't you get in trouble?" Jess asked. Ella was brave. Jess tried skipping class once and got five days detention for it.

"It's fine. I asked to go to the bathroom when I saw you all start to walk across the courtyard."

"Hey, thanks for sticking those worms in Brody's shoes. He stuck his foot right in and mushed them all over his socks. It was gross." Jess giggled under her breath. "Well, I better go catch up with the others, else I'll get in trouble and I haven't even started school yet."

"Okay I'll see you after school."

Jess teased Ella with a smile. "I might be keen to help you with that mystery box after all. I've been thinking about it and..."

"Jess! Where are you?" She heard her mother call.

"Oops...gotta go. See ya."

Having endured the shortened school tour, all three settled in for a forty-five minute drive to Aberdeen. Seeing the countryside in the daylight made Jess appreciate they really weren't in London anymore. Long stretches of endless fields lay open to the skies above, and little villages would crop up from out of nowhere along the road side.

Arriving in the small village of Elrik, just on twelve, had Brody complaining of hunger again.

"There. The Braodstraik Inn." Jess pointed to an available car park on the side street. "That looks good. Please, Mum. Don't let him whine about food all the way to Aberdeen."

Mum pulled over and checked the GPS. They were still twenty-five minutes from downtown.

"You're right. Lunch and a coffee would certainly help my nerves. It's been a while since I've done any cold-calling for a job and I need to check the locations on the map - think you could help me, Jess?"

"Sure. Just don't call me SIRI." Jess gathered her phone and jacket.

Brody had practically placed his order before they'd even exited the car and asked if he could go check out the playground next door.

Mum nodded. "Not too long. I'll call you when your food arrives."

"Okay." Brody sprinted off.

"Can you keep an eye on him Jess? I'll go order our meals. What would you like?"

"Whatever you're having is fine." Jess sat at one of the picnic tables in front of the large white rendered building. Wandering her eyes over the black trim, and triangle topped turret bay windows. It reminded her of the backdrops they'd painted for their Shakespeare plays at her old school. They were doing Macbeth this term. She pulled her phone from her pocket to check her messages. Still nothing from Libby or June. She dropped the phone on the table and ignored it.

Eventually Mum called them inside to eat. Brody munched down a bowl of hot chips and a chocolate milkshake, while she and Mum mapped out the best route around the city between mouthfuls. Although the air was still cool, a smattering of sunshine peaked through the clouds keeping any threat of rain at bay.

When they finally reached Aberdeen, Brody was the happiest Jess had seen him since leaving London. Back amongst the hustle and bustle of cars and people, Brody all but leapt out the car window, panting like an excited puppy when he spotted the football stadium. Mum promised she would take him to the next match, but only because she feared being pulled over by the police if Brody didn't pull his head back inside the car.

Several stores and navigations later, Jess's patience grew thin. Despite her earlier reservations about the keys, she was surprisingly eager to return to the farm and resume the investigation of the box. In fact - it was all she'd been able to think about all day.

"One last stop," Mum announced. "Then we'll head back, okay. Woodend Hospital, Jess."

Jess tapped the next destination on her phone and huffed.

"I won't be too long this time, I promise. You guys can wait in the car if you like." Mum's attempt to appease them didn't work. She ignored their growing impatience and looked at Jess with a smile. "I have a surprise to show you on our way home too."

Jess attempted a smile and Brody's curiosity was peaked.

"What kind of a surprise. Ice-cream?" He asked.

"No, something way cooler than ice-cream." Mum winked in the rear-vision mirror.

Brody kept attempting to guess, while Mum went inside the Hospital. Jess was relieved when she returned sooner than expected and seemed excited about something. Was it because her cold-call went well, or did it have something to do with this surprise? Jess wasn't sure, but she also didn't care. If they were headed back to Ella's, Jess was happy to go along with whatever had improved Mum's mood.

They were making good time until Mum diverted off the main route. Jess grunted her annoyance as another tour of the back country lanes commenced.

"Mum, where are we going? You promised Ella we'd be back before they finished school." Jess frowned, wiping the joy from her mother's eyes.

Crossing the river Don, Mum took an abrupt turn onto a small winding track passing through mature woodlands.

"Cool," Brody sighed - gluing his forehead to the widow. "Where are we, Mum?"

Jess couldn't fathom a reason for the alternate route until they arrived at a magnificent stone building. It looked much like the castles of her childhood fairy-tale books, and the outlook, even from the car, was spectacular.

"This is Castle Ferlie, kids," Mum said proudly. "My grandmother was a Ferlie and grew up here.

I'd love to show it to you properly, but all we have time for is a quick drive-by today."

"Wow!" Brody was awestruck. "Really Mum? You never told us you had relatives that lived in a castle."

"Yes, we used to visit here occasionally as kids with our grandparents. It's a very special place, I'll see if Uncle Max can bring you fishing here one day during summer. Well, we better get going, it's almost 4 o'clock and I did promise we'd be back before the others." She eyed Jess for confirmation.

"Ah…Shouldn't we at least go and say hello to the owners, Mum? They'll think it's weird if we pull up and then just drive off so soon."

Jess knew she'd regret the suggestion, but her curiosity of meeting the people who lived in such grand building trumped any embarrassment she'd likely endure.

Taking her advice, Mum exited the car and went to ring the doorbell. Before she could even reach for the chain, the front door swung open.

"Hello, can I help you?" A small lady asked.

The woman was a picture of class, with a well-set ash-blonde bob that rested just above the collar of her crisp white shirt. Her beige coloured trousers were neatly creased down the front and her mustard yellow sweater was the colour of autumn leaves. She didn't look upset, so Jess got out of the car and went and stood by her mother's side.

"Oh, hello. Sorry to just drive up unannounced. I was just passing the area and telling my kids about how I came and visited here with my grandparents. You see, my grandmother was Rosalie Ferlie, she married Joseph Lockheart." Mum stopped and held out her hand. "Sorry, I'm Vera Warren, I was a Lockheart, before I married."

The petite woman accepted Mum's hand and shook it briefly, her fingers thinner than her smile. "Lovely to meet you, Vera… Lockheart was it?" She paused in thought, "hmm, yes I think I know that name from around here. I would invite you in, but Lord Ferlie prefers guests to make an appointment for visiting. I'm sure you can appreciate our need to verify your lineage - for security reasons, you see. My husband is very conscious of keeping our protocols."

"Oh yes, of course, I am very sorry for the intrusion. I wasn't going to bother you, but my daughter thought it might be rude not to at least say hello. We've just moved from London and I wanted to show the kids some of the great things up here. Since we were just passing through on our way home I thought I would just - drop by. So sorry. I'll be sure to call you next time."

By now Brody had also exited the car and come to stand with them. "The kids would love to see more of the castle, wouldn't you kids?" Mum looked at them, hoping childhood innocence would help dig her out of the hole she'd leapt into.

"Oh yes please," Jess said, picking up on her mother's desperate plea. "We'd love to come back, Lady Ferlie. Your home looks so beautiful and I'd love to learn more about the family's history."

"Well certainly, that would be wonderful. What did you say your name was again?"

"Oh, I'm Jess Warren. My mother's maiden name was Vera Lockheart."

"Well, Miss Warren, I shall look forward to meeting you again soon."

Mum ushered Jess and Brody towards the car.

"Thank you so much, Lady Ferlie, and again, I'm so sorry for the intrusion. Thank you for your time."

Turning the key, the car gave a hesitant rumble and Mum rolled down the driveway with a bit more etiquette than she'd arrived with.

CHAPTER SIX

Ella

T HE SCHOOL BUS pulled away with great plumes of exhaust and a rumble so loud, it rattled Ella's bones.

"When does Brody get home, Ella?" asked Steve

"Aunty Vera said they'd be home by four, so they should be here," She said.

Just then a horn tooted from behind and Aunty Vera's car pulled up alongside them.

"Hello! We made it, and this time - we're on time." Aunty Vera said with a chuffed smile.

Ella looked at her watch. "Well it is four-o-five, Aunty Vera," She said with a little cheek.

"What is it with you lot! Five minutes, five minutes! You'd think I'd arrived five hours late!"

Ella hadn't understood just how sensitive the topic of time was to her aunt. In future she would keep such comments to herself.

"Don't worry, Ella. It's not your fault. It's been a long day," Jess said.

"Hey, Brody. Wanna come check out the farm?" asked Steve, stuffing his head through the car window. "We're gonna go looking for rabbit holes."

"Ahh sure. That okay, Mum?"

"Alright, but try not to get your shoes too muddy. They're the only clean pair you have, and you'll need to wear them for school tomorrow."

"Okay." Brody jumped out of the car and the boys ran off.

Aunty Vera looked at her and spoke without any hint of humour, "You wouldn't happen to know how worms got into Brody's shoes would you, Ella?"

"Uh, well..." She squirmed.

"Mum, it's not Ella's fault. She did it for me. She'd never dream of doing such a thing. Besides, Brody deserved it, you know he did."

Aunty Vera seemed to accept Jess's reasoning and said nothing more. She could only hope her aunt would be as silent about it around Pa too.

Ever since her run in with Jess that morning, Ella's stock-pile of questions had grown and she was desperate for answers. After a brief download of her day at school for Aunty Vera's sake, she was bursting to talk to Jess in private. As soon as they were tucked away upstairs Ella fired off as many of her questions as she could.

"How was your day? Did you get your uniform? I hate wearing it, but it is high school I guess. What was your last uniform like? Do you have a boyfriend at your old school? I don't have a boyfriend, but I do like someone. My friend Holly has a boyfriend... Lucas Smart. Holly says that Lucas isn't really all that smart, but she doesn't mind a bit because he's braw! He does have quite nice hair I suppose. He's on the football team. They hang out at lunchtime with us, you'll get to meet them tomorrow. What was it you wanted to tell me earlier today?"

Jess stared at her with her mouth hung open and judging by her confused look, she wasn't quite sure how to respond to her Scottish word vomit. She sat on her bed, tucked her hands under her legs, and decided an inquisitive stare might help Jess engage in conversation.

Jess sighed, looked away, and tipped a bag of clothes and stationary over her bed. "Well firstly we got our uniforms, it's wasn't too bad. At my old school we had to wear a skirt. At least you guys have a choice of trousers or a skirt. Which do most girls wear by the way?" Jess waited for a reply. Ella was so keen to hear anything Jess had to say that she almost missed her cue to answer.

"Oh... Um... most wear the skirt I guess... particularly if you have a boyfriend or are trying to get one. When it's pure Baltic, I wear me trousers. They are more comfortable anyway. It just depends." She shrugged, not committing either way.

A couple more questions popped into her head and she was about to ask them, but Jess had more to say. "No, I don't have a boyfriend... anymore." She blushed. "But, I don't want to talk about that. What does *braw* mean?"

"Smoke'n hot!" Ella grinned like she was smelling cooked bacon. "Was your boyfriend hot? What was his name?"

Jess looked sideways and then changed the subject. "I was thinking about that box all day. Shall we take another look?"

Unwilling to jeopardise Jess's interest in the box, Ella shelved the topic of boyfriends for another time. It must be tough to break up with someone simply because you're moving. *Or maybe he dumped her - poor thing.*

Ella grabbed the box from the end of her bed and motioned Jess to join her. "Let's read the journal. Maybe there's a clue about who this stuff belongs to in there."

Jess seemed reluctant to get too close to the box so Ella placed it on the far side of the drawers, then patted the spot beside her so Jess would be able to sit closer and see better. "There's no name written inside the front cover like you'd normally expect. I always put my name in my diaries. How about you?"

"I've never kept a diary," Jess said, like it was normal not to. Ella struggled to hide her shock.

"Really? You mean you never… I don't believe it. Don't you have any secret thoughts you want to record?"

"Well…No, it's not really safe. I'm pretty sure Mum snoops sometimes and Brody probably does too. It's best if there's nothing to be found. I like drawing though. Eyes mostly. They're not very good, but it passes the time - when I'm bored."

"Cool, I'd love to see some."

"Uh…maybe, I don't really show them to anyone. Maybe that's why the writer didn't put their name in this journal; they wanted to remain anonymous."

"You're probably right. But at least the first entry does give someone's name."

Ella read from the journal.

"<u>November 12th, 1974</u>

Another blue letter arrived for Gerrard today. It had the same return address on the back."

Monday 2nd December 1974

Elaine

Elaine picked up baby Joseph from the cot. He hadn't napped for very long and she was weary from waking every couple of hours to feed him. The midwife was due to visit this afternoon and Elaine knew she should at least attempt to clean things up a little, including herself.

Glancing in the mirror, Elaine plucked her sunken cheeks trying to redden them to life. Nineteen? She looked much older. Her figure was returning to her usual shape, but her face had lost its supple exuberance since marrying Gerrard a little over a year ago.

Their over-sized house matched the excessive amount of cleaning it required, encouraging endless washing that kept her busy every day. Add baby Joseph to that equation and there was never a second to relax.

A momentary thought struck her, *what if I'd had two babies to care for? I'm barely coping with one.*

A tear rolled down her cheek and she felt guilty for even thinking she was better off with just one child.

Her son would have to grow up without his twin sister. Joanna had died in her father's arms on the way to Aberdeen to see a doctor. Her daughter was never far from her thoughts.

With baby Joseph's nappy changed he settled into a more cheerful demeanour and even offered up a smile for his doting mother.

Placing him on the sheepskin rug on the floor she sat in her chair to recount her findings from the previous day. Taking out her blue journal she jotted down the following:

<u>December 2nd, 1974</u>

Gerrard became quite upset with me when I asked what the blue letters were about. I told him I noticed he'd been getting them regularly and I wondered who was writing to him from Denmark. He said it was a business acquaintance he'd made during the time we'd lived there. I hope he's telling me the truth, but my intuition tells me he's not. I will find out what is going on and hopefully, my fears for my marriage will be put at ease. Baby Joseph is growing so fast. It makes me wonder what his twin sister Joanna would have been like. I visit her grave often with flowers, but the pain of losing her is still fresh in my heart. I miss you, Joanna.

Monday 21st March 2016

Ella

Ella closed the journal. "Well there's a few clues. We have a woman who has a baby. Had twin babies. But one has died, a girl called Joanna, right?"

"Yes I think so, that's what it sounded like to me. It's exactly as I saw it in my vision, Ella. A woman was holding a baby and crying at a gravestone. I didn't see the name on it - but it must have been for Joanna. I was wondering about this earlier. I tried to picture the woman again because I thought it might have been your mother. The woman and the gravestone reminded me of your mum's funeral. The woman in the vision seemed familiar somehow, but I'm pretty sure it wasn't Aunt Gabby. Besides, your mum never had twins, did she?" Jess's cheeks reddened and regret flashed in her eyes.

It had been a while since anyone had mentioned Ma's funeral and Ella wasn't sure what to say. Silence at seven was understandable, but at fourteen? Shouldn't she be able to respond by now?

Snapshots of Ma's funeral flashed through her mind: A thick mist blanketed the farm that morning and dark heavy clouds remained after it cleared. Blue & purple flowers covered Ma's coffin; her favourite colours; Ella's too. With a brave face, Pa had given her Ma's favourite scarf to wear to the funeral; a long length of silk dyed in vivid purple and pale blue; a gift he'd given Ma one Christmas. Ella's memory of it around her mother's neck was as strong to this day as it was when Ma had worn it last - just a week before she died.

Ella felt the pull of the treasured scarf and looked at the set of drawers where she kept it tucked in the back corner. She needed to touch it; to wind it through her fingers, wrap it about her neck and absorb the ever so faint scent of her mother from it. Somehow it always gave her strength.

"I'm so sorry, Ella. I didn't mean to..." Jess's apology was heart-felt and Ella could hold no grudge over it.

Instead she stared at the journal for a long moment and considered the words carefully. A moment of clarity struck.

"Of course it's not me mother's silly, look at the date." She pointed to it. "Ma probably wasn't even born, so she couldn't be the author of this journal. It's also not Ma's handwriting. This is very fancy and Ma's was not so swishy looking. But what do you make of this?"

Ella jammed her finger on an entry in the journal that was not like the previous handwriting at all. It was nearer the end of the book and the page before it had been torn out. The writing was so neatly printed, it couldn't have been authored by the same person.

Friday 5th October, 2007

I'm getting much weaker now and need to document what I have found or else it will be lost to my dear husband Joseph.

The owner of this journal was my husband's mother, Elaine Naudman. I have sent a request to the Registries Office asking them to send me a certified copy of the marriage certificate of Gerrard and Elaine Naudman. Joseph seemed to think that they were married in 1972 or 73. Gabby took me to the library today to look for any possible wedding announcements in the newspaper archives. I hope I hear back from the registries office soon as my health is deteriorating and I really must solve this mystery for Joe.

Wednesday 17th October 2007

Elaine writes that she turns 32 on the 18th January 1987, so she would have been born in 1955 - but I cannot find any birth recorded for her. The copy of the marriage certificate came today. I am in shock as Elaine has written that her maiden name was Lockheart. I can't believe it. Finally a breakthrough. Even though there is no birth recorded for Elaine Lockheart it makes my heart glad to hear that name. Gabby is going to be so shocked. Maybe Max is related to Joseph? That would be so nice if he was. I'd be surprised though as Elaine has written 'unknown' under her parent's section. So she could have been adopted?

Ella slammed the journal shut.

"What is it, Ella? Your mum's name is there. Do you know who wrote it? Do you know who this *Elaine Naudman* is? If she is a Lockheart she could be related to you... to us."

Ella appeared deep in thought.

"Well, I do recognise one other name that's written in here, Joseph Naudman. He's the person we need to talk to about all this."

"Great. Who is he? Can we go see him? Or perhaps we can call him."

A thought jolted Ella. "No way - I can't believe it! Ohhhh.... I'm betting that this other writing belonged to his wife, Flo. You see, Joe is an old family friend of ours. He and Pa have been friends for a very long time and I think he even went to university with Ma. Occasionally we went to visit him up at Rattray Heads on the coast.

"Anyway, Florence was his wife, we used to call her Aunty Flo because she was just like an aunty to us. She was really pretty even though she wore thick glasses. They bought the old lighthouse keepers cottages and ran a Bed and Breakfast. Ma used to take us on little 'Holidays', she'd call them, but it was usually just for a night. We'd play on the beach and toast marshmallows on the fire. It was so cool. I haven't been to the beach in ages." Ella paused, sadness consuming her thoughts once more. "Why does everyone I love die?" She whispered.

She hadn't meant to leap into the lake of depression but it was like quicksand. Once a thought had taken her mind she struggled to escape.

It often started as a puddle, then grew into the lake, which eventually became a swamp of sludge if she let it. Sometimes she would tread the memories for days, yet other times she could simply climb out if she just decided to.

Not having a mother anymore had affected her in more ways than she liked to admit. Overnight it felt like she had aged ten years, become more responsible than she really was, and transformed into a mother figure for her youngest brother, Jack. Her childhood was lost and her source of motherly advice was gone. Even though Aunt Flo died before Ma did, Ella had been completely unprepared for the loss of either. The void they left behind had chipped away at her hopes and dreams for a future without pain. All she could do was carry on, wearing a mask of bravery made of very little truth and a whole lot of pretence.

"Aunty Flo died of cancer about nine years ago. I was five and Steve was just a toddler. She and Joe had only been married for a year and they never had any children of their own. So we are kind of like Joe's only family. It's strange to think we might actually be related by blood though."

A glimmer of hope returned and she smiled. "I hope we are."

CHAPTER SEVEN

Jess

J ESS'S THOUGHTS RETURNED to family relatives and the embarrassing detour they'd taken to Castle Ferlie on their way home.

"Did you know that our great-grandmother grew up at Castle Ferlie?" She asked.

"Aye," said Ella. "Rosalie Lockheart was Rosalie Ferlie before she married our great-grandfather. Makes you wonder what it would have been like to live there when they were all alive, aye? Pa takes us fishing there every summer. The castle is so beautiful. I got to go inside it once. There are some really cool paintings and antiques in there too. Would you like to go see it?"

"Mum took us on a detour on our way home so I've seen it already. But I was thinking… I know it's a long-shot, but if Elaine Naudman is Joseph's mother and she was a Lockheart, then maybe there could be some clues at Castle Ferlie about her? She would have been a similar age as our Grandpa Erik, maybe they were cousins or something?"

Jess pulled out her phone and swiped the screen. "I don't have any data left and the battery's almost dead again. Do you have a computer we can use to search up a genealogy website or something?"

"You have a phone? Lucky. Pa won't let me have one yet. He thinks they're a waste of time." She frowned with annoyance. "Sorry, our computer's busted at the moment. Jack got on it and every time he does he seems to muck it all up. Pa's taken it to get fixed in town but he said it won't be back till the end of the week. Pa was real mad, he hates it when there's something he can't fix himself."

"Maybe we could use one at school tomorrow. Do they have some in the library?"

"Aye, they do, and I know Mrs Jenkins will be keen to help us. She's always doing ancestry research for the local folks. She's hilarious; looks just like what you'd picture a librarian to look like: glasses, hair in a bun, and dresses like an old lady… you know. But she is super smart and likes to joke around with us when it comes to checking out the books. She's really quirky… I imagine she probably has cats at home too." Ella giggled. "Hey, can we keep this just between you and me though? I don't want to tell Pa about it yet. I don't want to get his hopes up without any proof. I want to see if we can uncover the truth without him knowing if possible."

"Yeah sure, I get it. Sometimes they like to take over, aye? Mum can get like that. Once I had to do this project for science at school, and since she's a nurse she wanted to help me with it, but she totally took over the whole thing. I didn't mind too much though. I got an 'A' at least." Jess grinned with a glint in her eye and Ella laughed.

"I'm hungry. Is there anything to eat?" asked Jess.

Ella nodded, "Let's go get a snack and see if we can figure this family tree thing out."

Jess followed Ella as she stealthily tip-toed her way in silence down stairs. Jess thought it was weird since it was only four-thirty and the boys weren't in bed yet.

"What are you doing?" She whispered.

"I'm trying to avoid me brothers," Ella whispered.

"But they're out on the farm." Jess's full volume announcement earned a frown from Ella.

"Shhh. They've done it before. They sneak back in and hide around the house hoping to give me a fright."

"Booo!" shouted Jack, leaping from behind the bathroom door.

Ella screamed.

"Jack - you wee scunner! See I told you."

"Oh, I get it. Do they do this often?" asked Jess.

"Every day" - Ella face-palmed - "I fall for it every time. I'm sick to my eyeballs. I really wish they'd give it up."

"Well, we'll just have to see what we can do about that then as well - won't we?"

Optimism was a trait that came easy to Jess. The look of hope she inspired in Ella sent a spark of pride straight to her head. Jess had pulled off theatrical scenes more challenging than home alone pranks before. All they needed was some trickery of their own to get Ella's brothers off her back, and Jess knew just how to do it.

On the way to the kitchen Steve leapt from the stairwell cupboard and Brody from behind a curtain. Their tactics had little effect on Jess now that she'd been made aware of their agenda. Poor Ella, on the other hand, jumped a little every time.

Ella's hands shook as she poured two glasses of milk. Grabbing a handful of cookies from the jar, Ella stuffed one in her mouth before passing two to Jess. "Wwat bid ye 'ave in mind?" Cookie crumbs spilled with Ella words and she couldn't help but giggle.

"Well I figure it's only a matter of time before the boys try to set us up again. So *I'm* thinking we need to beat them to it. And this time - for good. Then they'll leave us alone."

Jess cleared her throat and prepared to raise her voice. "Ella, I heard something moving around the loft last night. Do you believe in ghosts? I reckon the loft might be *HAUNTED*." She winked as she spoke.

The boys were playing in the living room next to the kitchen and Ella heard one of them try and shush the others so they could eavesdrop better.

Catching on to her cousin's plan, Ella wanted to be sure her brothers had heard Jess, and added even louder, "Really? You think the loft is *HAUNTED!*"

Jess's eyeballs bulged in their sockets when Mum walked in through the back door. With one hand Jess swiped a double cut to her neck warning Ella to hit the pause button on their ruse.

"Gotta love the fresh farm air out here, aye Jess? It does wonders for your soul to breathe air that's uncontaminated by cars and smog." Mum sighed, smitten with farm life. "I just collected the eggs; there were eight, so I was thinking - maybe I could make a quiche for supper. That okay with you, Ella?"

"Yum. Sounds good to me." Ella beamed.

"I know Max said you liked to do the cooking but I'd like to do something to help out around here."

"Thank you, Aunty Vera!" Ella gushed, wrapping her arms around Mum. "You have no idea how nice it is having you here. I miss having another woman around to help with the house chores. Pa's been great and all, but he's been so busy with the farm lately that it's all left up to me." Happy tears rolled down her cheeks.

Mum hugged Ella tight and stroked her hair. It was a gesture Jess knew well and she could sense the relief Ella felt from her mother's touch.

"I understand, Ella. I left home at sixteen so I know how difficult it can be without your mother around anymore. Your Uncle Grant suffered through all my mistakes when we first got married; my domestic skills were non-existent, but we managed it together in the end. The least I can do is offer you some reprieve for a while."

Mum held Ella's shoulders and looked into her eyes. "Gabby was such a great cook. I'm not sure I could I ever live up to her talent. But, how about I take over the cooking for the next wee while and if there's ever a time when you want to make supper, you just let me know, okay?"

Jess sniggered. "That may be sooner than you hoped, Ella."

Mum scoffed feigning outrage from her smart remark.

They all giggled.

Jess decided now would be a good time to ask Mum if they could visit Castle Ferlie again.

"Mum...?"

But just as she was about to start, Ella butted in.

"Thank you so much, Aunty Vera. I'm so glad you came to stay. Thanks for making supper, Jess and I will just be upstairs." Ella grabbed Jess's hand and started to lead her out the door. Jess hesitated, but decided reluctance wouldn't remedy her frustration of being cut off. Ella might be emotional, but she sure had a way of getting what she wanted from someone without them realising what they'd given.

"Okay, supper will be at six thirty. Should I get one of the boys to tell Max, Ella?" Mum called after them.

"It won't matter either way if you do, Aunty Vera. He'll be here when he's done!" Ella called down the stairs.

"Wait up," said Jess. "What was all that about?"

"Oh nothing. I really am grateful that your mum's here, that's all. For once I'd like to be a kid again and not my mother's fill in for my Pa and brothers."

"It must be hard doing it all by yourself. Mum's always worked a lot, but she's pretty good at making sure Brody and I are taken care of.

"Anyway, about my plan. If we can trick the boys into thinking there's a ghost in the loft, they'll never want to come up here and if we play it right they'll also leave us alone too."

"Sounds good, but how are we going to get ghosts in our loft?" Ella asked." I know the spirits are there, but how can we get them to scare the boys?"

"Easy. All we need is some fishing rods and some carefully placed items around the room that can be tripped. Spirits or not, nothing makes a ghost move like nylon thread. The boys will wet themselves in terror before they ever catch on."

Since the boys had moved on to playing with the Lego and wouldn't be bothering them any further. Jess and Ella spent the rest of the afternoon setting up their trap in the loft; stringing and balancing objects about the room. Ella recommended they set a couple of trips in the boy's bedroom as well; ones they could set off remotely.

Jess insisted on a practice run; to be sure everything would go as planned. It took three goes and an argument over who would pull the strings, from inside the wardrobe before they knew if it would work.

Neither of them wanted to close themselves inside the ominous cupboard but if they wanted their plan to succeed then someone had to do it.

In the end it was Jess who faced her biggest fear and decided to tackle the challenge head on. Her first run was a disaster and resulted in another anxiety attack. But with Ella standing just outside the wardrobe door, she had been able to calm herself enough to complete the task.

The final run went perfectly. Jess managed to close the wardrobe door completely, while Ella stood much further away than she had before. It wasn't until Jess felt comfortable in her own role that she worried if Ella could play her part in their performance. Her cousin's excited nerves gave Jess plenty of cause for doubt.

The last half hour, before supper was ready, was spent coaching Ella to keep a straight face. Jess's stomach ached from all the laughing by the time they headed downstairs. All that was left was to lure the boys up to the loft after supper; setting them up for the scare of their life.

Ella came up with the perfect bait. At dinner she told the boys she'd found one of Grandpa's old fishing hats up in the loft. She thought Steve might like it. They all agreed, once the boys finished doing the washing up, they would come take a look at it.

The girls took off upstairs as soon as the plates were cleared away. Jess kept an ear on how close the boys were to being done and once she heard the sink start to drain, she turned on the shower and set the old tape recorder playing in the bathroom. The sound of her singing in the shower to Taylor Swifts, 'Shake it off,' would have her brother convinced that Jess was in the bathroom. Unbeknown to the boys she would instead be hiding under a blanket in the wardrobe, pulling the strings.

The boys went up to the base of the loft stairs and Steve yelled, "You up there Ella? Can we come up?"

"Come on up, boys." Ella peered from the top and gestured for them to enter. Steve came up first followed by Jack with Brody last to get to the top.

"Well where is it?" asked Steve.

"Here it is." Ella said handing him the khaki weathered hat, with its fly lures still attached. Jack and Brody peered over his shoulder trying to get a good look at it.

Just then a book fell off the shelf.

"What was that?" asked Brody. "Who's there?"

Ella began their carefully crafted story.

"Oh, that's weird. I've been wondering what's been going on myself. Ever since I came up here to find the lamps, I've been hearing strange sounds and sometimes things just move without me touching them. Jess thinks the loft could be haunted or something."

"Haunted!" said Brody. "Really? You think so? That's creepy."

Just as he spoke Jess made the lamp in the corner of the room flicker. Then she pulled a set of clothes tied together across the floor.

"Arrrrh!" screamed Jack.

"Whoa. What was that?" asked Steve.

Ella put on her scared voice. "I don't know, but it's never done that before. Maybe you boys have made it angry."

Jess kicked one of the wardrobe doors open. She could see through a small hole in the blanket but the rest of her remained hidden. Steve panicked and turned to run down the loft stairs, but Jack was clinging to him and Brody had blocked the exit.

Jess lowered the feather duster from a fishing line strung over the rafter beam. Steve felt a tickle behind his ear and cursed.

"What was that? - Let's get out of here."

Jack let go of his brother's legs and darted towards the stairs. He was much smaller and faster than Brody or Steve. He scooted past them; knocking them over as he took off.

Steve lay on the floor disorientated. The feather duster lowered further towards his face and a broom in the corner fell over. Books and boxes fell off shelves.

Steve clambered up and yelled. "Ella, what's going on?"

Jess couldn't see Ella but she must have kept a straight face as the boys sounded convinced. For the finale, Jess hit a button on her phone that played a sound bite she'd recorded back in London with June and Libby. A crazy high pitched voice like a witch cried out, "What are you doing here? Get out!"

Both remaining boys took off down the stairs and slammed their bedroom door behind them.

Ella and Jess waited a few minutes until the coast was clear for Jess to creep down in her dressing gown with a towel on her head. Once she was tucked inside the bathroom, Jess turned off the shower and music and prepared her own performance.

Jess exited the bathroom and Ella took over pulling the strings.

"What's going on? Brody?" Jess knocked and tried opening the door.

Brody stood just inside - his hands were still shaking.

"Jess, there's ghosts up in that loft. Don't go up there, Jess!"

"Oh hogwash, Brody, there's no ghosts in the loft."

Just then, Ella tripped a line through the floor boards in the loft to her brother's bedroom below. A toy plane began to swing around the roof until it finally fell off the line.

"Arhhhhh!" The boys cowered and darted for cover.

Distracted by the plane falling, the boys never noticed it was Jess who set the football rolling across the floor while simultaneously removing a wedge holding a series of items ready to fall. A book fell, then a plastic toy monkey flipped into the air, which set a car racing across the floor.

"It's followed us," said Jack. "Let's get out of here." The boys went running off down the stairs in a panic.

Jess muffled a laugh in her sleeve.

Returning to the loft she found Ella rolling in stitches on the floor.

"I've never seen Steve or Jack look so scared in all my life. I've never had this much success with a prank before. Did you see the look on Steve's face? Brody was convinced right from the start. Oh, this will last for ages, Jess. They'll never want to come up here ever again."

"Exactly. And that's just what we wanted. We better get into our pyjamas and into bed quick. I'm sure one of our parents will be up here expecting an explanation soon. I don't know about you, but I sure don't want to give one right now."

"Good idea. Lights out A-SAP."

Lying in her bed, Jess couldn't shake the feeling of sorrow in the loft. "Ella, do you think Elaine's spirit might really be haunting this loft?" She whispered, staring up at a shadow on the roof. She wasn't sure what it was but tried to cast all thoughts of bugs from her mind.

"I thought you didn't believe in ghosts."

"Well no I don't. Or at least I didn't, but now I'm not so sure. I mean… I saw that vision and perhaps Elaine wants us to help uncover something - a secret maybe? We've got to find out, Ella."

"I agree. She sure went to a lot of effort to keep a journal of what her husband got up to. There's something not quite right about it. It's pretty sad really. Joe's never had a nice word to say about his father, not that he talks about him much. But I do remember him saying that his Pa was not a very nice father to him. He said, if *he* ever became a father he'd never treat his children the way his father treated him and his mother."

Jess rolled to her side and raised up on one elbow. "I wonder what he meant by that?" Jess searched the darkness and eventually found Ella's eyes.

"I'm not sure but he really disliked him. I've never seen any picture of him at his house."

"Ooo…does he have a picture of his mother…of Elaine?"

"Sure. He loved his mother very much and took good care of her. She even came to stay with him after Aunty Flo died."

"Was she still alive then?"

"Yes - but I never met her. She died just a few months after Aunty Flo did. He didn't like to talk about it much. Poor Joe. Makes me wonder how he is doing now that we've been looking into all of this. We've got to find a way to convince Pa to take us all up to the coast to visit, and soon."

"I agree. I want to meet this Joe person, and visit the coast. I haven't been to a beach in ages…"

"…. Shhhh someone's coming," Ella whispered.

The girls paused and held their breath while whoever was at the bottom of the stairs decided that they were fast asleep and wouldn't bother venturing up to check on them.

After a long minute they left.

"Hey Ella, What shall we do about the keys?" Jess whispered.

"I dunno. I'm guessing they were wrapped in that baby gown for a reason. I think we should take them with us when we go to the castle. You never know, there might just be some key holes we could try them in. And if we don't have any luck unlocking anything, maybe we could touch them again and see if anything else happens. Let's just be careful to keep them wrapped up for now."

"Agreed. I don't want to touch them again, not unless I really have to."

CHAPTER EIGHT

Tuesday 22nd March 2016

Jess

AN UNWELCOME HAND rattled her shoulder.

"Wakey wakey," Ella cooed, holding a finger to her lips.

Jess's muffled objection was instantly rejected.

"Come on, Jess, get up," Ella whispered more forcefully.

Jess rubbed the sleep from her eyes. "What? What time is it?"

"It's six-thirty. If we hurry we can catch a ride with Pa to school early… *without* the boys."

Registering Ella's urgent suggestion, Jess raised herself on one elbow and assembled a reason to stay in bed.

"I'm not sure Mum will go for that. It's Brody's first day at a new school and she'll want me to take care of him."

"Oh, don't worry about Brody - Steve will look after him. Besides, the junior and secondary schools don't mix during the day unless there's a special event on or something. He'll be fine. Come on." She gestured.

Jess reluctantly folded back her bed covers and started to dress in her new uniform. Never had she ever wanted to get to school early but Ella made a good point. Avoiding the boys for as long as possible would delay an explanation about the alleged ghost in the loft.

To remove any scepticism the boys might still have, Ella set a small trip-wire by the loft entry, just in case they attempted to prove the ghost in the loft wasn't real.

The sound of Mum humming in the kitchen was as strange as the named lunch bags sitting in a row on the kitchen table. Tullynessle was clearly having an effect on Mum but Jess wasn't sure if it was for the better or not. In London, Mum was never awake when they left for school, usually having come off a night shift at 4am. Just to see her in the morning, let alone humming and preparing food was weird to say the least. Mum seemed more relaxed at the farm, yet somehow a part of her was on edge too. Jess couldn't quite pinpoint why and attributed it to missing her old job. She wondered if Mum was missing Dad too. She hoped so.

"Mum. What are you doing up this early?"

"I could ask you the same question, Missy. I've never seen you this ready for school before breakfast. Ella is already having a good influence on you."

"You've never seen me get ready for school - ever. You're not usually awake."

"True enough, but today is the first day at a new school for my kids and I wanted to make sure you guys have everything... I even made a special lunch for you all." She nodded at her morning's work.

"Wow! Thanks Mum. You've outdone yourself. Your hair looks nice too, are you using something new on it?" Jess cocked her head and looked her over. "Oh, me and Ella are gonna go to school early with Uncle Max. Okay?" Mum fell for the flattery but not the intent to leave early.

"Pa's got some supplies to pick up in town," Ella said, seeing Mum's wary look.

"Oh, I see. But don't you want to ride the bus with your brother, Jess? He'll be nervous and I'm sure he'd like it if you were there." Mum's glare trumped her comments, sending Jess's gaze to the floor. Avoiding contact with those eyes was like ignoring toothache. Jess crossed her fingers and hoped Mum would buckle. It hardly ever worked though. Mum was a master of persuasion, and more frequently than not, compelled compliance.

But on this occasion, what neither Jess nor her mother foresaw during their battle of wills, was Ella.

"Oh, don't worry about him, Aunty Vera, Steve and Jack will look after Brody. Besides, I have a big assignment I need to work on. Jess will need to get started on it too if she's gonna catch up."

Jess grinned. Mum couldn't argue with that. She'd won.

Jess - 1, Mum - 0. She could get used to this. Ella's powers of persuasion were much stronger than she realised.

Just then Mum's cell phone rang.

"Hello, Vera Warren speaking."

Uncle Max walked in and Jess feared Mum wouldn't give her final consent to leave early.

"You girls ready to go?" Max asked in a loud voice. He was either unaware Mum was on the phone or just as irritated as Jess was by her use of it - probably the latter, given Ella's comments about his feelings towards technology - *I mean what fourteen year old doesn't have a phone these days? That's practically Amish.*

Mum held a finger up, requesting they wait. "Oh, that's fine, I was up already. Uh huh... ...mmmm...sure I can do that."

Mum's sudden professionalism irritated Jess. Only seconds ago, her motherly concern about them starting a new school ranked top of her list. Now it seemed getting a job did. Fidgeting her annoyance by repeatedly tapping her mother's shoulder, Jess hoped the irritation would grant them permission to leave.

"Mum!? We really gotta go. Uncle Max is waiting,"

"Okay, hang on," She whispered, covering the receiver on the phone. She returned to her conversation. "I can come whenever you like..."

Jess rolled her eyes and grumbled a deep snort like a bull readying itself for a charge in the arena.

"...Tomorrow afternoon, at three thirty? Sounds fine. Okay, thank you very much, Good-bye."

Mum's gleeful satisfaction over-ruled Jess's frustration and no amount of arguing would get Jess out the door sooner.

"Well, that was Woodend Hospital and it sounds like they might have a job for me. I have an interview tomorrow at three thirty..." Mum paused worry creasing her forehead.

"Mum!" Jess huffed.

"...Oh, that means I won't be back before you finish school tomorrow. Is that going to be a problem?" Mum's brow twisted begging reassurance. Jess's own request seemed forgotten.

Lucky for Jess, Ella butted in, "No. It'll be fine, Aunty Vera. Thanks for the lunch...Pa's waiting in the van, so we'll see you later."

"Oh okay. Well, have a good day, Jess. I look forward to hearing all about it this afternoon. Okay?"

Jess was stunned. *How did Ella do that?* Unwilling to question her now and delay them further, Jess grabbed the bag on the table with her name on it, gave Mum a quick hug, and darted after Ella.

"Bye Mum!"

Ella

Skipping between drops of rain, the girls ran towards the school's main entrance. The large glass revolving door etched with the Alford Academy crest reluctantly turned and ushered them inside. Heading straight for the Library, Ella leaned herself into the heavy swing door and pushed it clear. A warm gush of stuffy air engulfed them as they entered the cavernous glass-walled room in silence.

Mrs Jenkins was already seated at her desk wearing the same clothes she had on yesterday. Ella wondered if she had ever left.

"Mrs Jenkins, I'm so glad you're here. This is my cousin Jessie Warren. She just moved from London."

Jess glared at her.

What was Jess's problem?

"Hello, Jessie, lovely to meet you." Mrs Jenkins smiled, peering over the rim of her glasses.

"It's just Jess. Everyone just calls me Jess. Only mum calls me Jessie, and that's usually only if I'm in trouble."

"Well alright then, Jess it is…as long as you do stay out of trouble" - Mrs Jenkins winked with a sly smile - "Now. What brings you two in so early this morning?"

Mrs Jenkins had spent countless hours researching Alford's inhabitants and its history over the years and Ella was certain she would be eager to help them once she'd heard their story too.

"Well, Mrs Jenkins, we were wondering if you could help us. We found an old journal up in our loft and we're trying to find out if the person it belonged to is related to us."

"How fascinating, girls. Do you have it with you? Have you read much of it?"

"A little bit. But most of it is just about a man named Gerrard and what he's been doing. We think it was written by his wife; Mrs Elaine Naudman," Ella said.

"That name rings a bell. Now let me think - Naudman. Oh yes, that was the name of a big shipping company in Aberdeen back in the 1950's and '60s. Did you know that we used to send shiploads of goods to Amsterdam and Denmark from Aberdeen?"

"No, but funny you should mention Denmark. You see Elaine talks about her husband taking business trips there," said Ella.

Jess tapped her fingers on the counter. "Can we use a computer, Mrs Jenkins, we'd like to look up an ancestry website to see if we can find a link?"

Ella was impressed; her cousin was learning fast. Ella learnt, at quite a young age, that the only way to get what you need is to be as direct as possible or simply take it outright and apologise later. It was the only thing she felt confident about when communicating with adults; likely a result of growing up with just her father's influence.

"I know just the one" - Mrs Jenkins typed in a web address - "It's very thorough for this particular area of Scotland. Come around this side of the desk girls and pull up a chair. Let's see..."

She entered Elaine's name into the blank box. "Do you know her birth date or even around the time she was born?"

"Well, my Aunty Flo tried to research this a few years ago but got stuck when she couldn't find an Elaine Lockheart born in 1955. See..." Ella opened the journal to where Flo had made her entry and read...

"October 22nd, 2007 - Elaine writes that she turns 33 on the 18th January 1988, so she would have been born in 1955 - but I cannot find any birth recorded for her..."

"Oh I see. Well let's try searching in the marriages shall we? ... Here you go, Elaine Naudman - Married Gerrard Naudman September 1st

1973. It says her maiden name was Lockheart. But no known parents? Mmmm, that's a bit strange." Mrs Jenkins frowned.

"Aunt Flo thought she could have been adopted," said Ella.

"Well I guess that's one possibility, but let's see. I'll just check out Gerrard Naudman. Here's his page. He is deceased and was the only son of Margaret and Frederick Naudman. He married Elaine Lockheart in 1973. They have a son named Joseph Naudman. That name rings a bell." Mrs Jenkins looked far off in the distance like she were trying to recall something important.

"Yes, he came to visit us lots of times." Ella informed her, "He's a friend of our family."

"No, that's not it" - Mrs Jenkins shook her head and re-joined reality - "Oh well, why don't we try looking up your family, Ella? If we scour all the different branches, perhaps Elaine's name will surface somewhere in your family tree."

"Well, my grandfather's name was Erik Lockheart. He married my grandmother, Marta."

"Are either of them still alive, Ella?" asked Mrs Jenkins.

"Grandpa died before I was born, but our grandmother is still alive. She lives in a rest home here in Alford, but she has dementia. We could try talking to her I guess, but it might be difficult. She has good days and bad days and I haven't seen her on a good day for some time now."

"Really?" Jess looked dumbstruck and Ella realised her cousin had no knowledge of their grandmother's condition. Ella wanted to discuss it further but Jess cut her off.

"What about Great-Grandmother Rosalie? She used to be a Ferlie. Is she in there?"

"Well there are a lot of Ferlie relations around here," responded Mrs Jenkins. "Here you go...Erik married Marta; she was an Ingles. There..."- Mrs Jenkins pointed to the computer screen - "See, Erik's parents were Joseph and Rosalie Lockheart - yes, she *was* a Ferlie. Well I never. I didn't know you were that closely tied, Ella," said Mrs Jenkins.

"Pa never talks much about our family background... What does it say there?" Ella pointed to the children listed for Joseph and Rosalie.

"Mmmm. It says here that your grandfather Erik had a sister, Eleanor. Looks as though she was ten years younger than him too." Mrs Jenkins mentioned.

Ella thought out loud, "I've never heard of a sister. Pa said he didn't have any aunties, uncles or cousins on his Pa's side" - She looked at Jess and smiled - "He said we were lucky to have you."

"Maybe your Pa didn't know," said Mrs Jenkins.

"What do you mean?" asked Jess, "Why would Grandpa Erik keep the existence of his sister, Eleanor, secret from Uncle Max and my mum?"

"I'm not sure. But there were lots of reasons back in those days. Maybe Eleanor wasn't Joseph's child and Rosalie had to give her away." Mrs Jenkins devious smile quickly vanished when Ella scowled in horror at her suggestion.

Mrs Jenkins searched the cavernous roof as if God would tell her what to say next. "Or, perhaps Eleanor disgraced the family; she might have gotten pregnant or run away. It did happen. Did you know you can marry without your parent's consent in Scotland, and you only have to be sixteen for it to be legal too."

Both girls stared at her, stunned by the proclamation.

Mrs Jenkins realised her mistake and tried to re-focus herself back to the task at hand. "Sorry, forget what I just said. Now, where were we...Oh yes, from the looks of this, Joseph Lockheart was the only child of his parents, Hamish and Heather Lockheart so there wouldn't be any other link from your family to this Elaine Lockheart, I'm sorry... ...Hang on a minute, wait...where was that entry about Elaine's Birthday?"

Ella opened the journal to the correct page and showed it to Mrs Jenkins so she could read again herself.

Mrs Jenkins muttered as she read, "33…1988…born in 1955. Well I never. I see now. Look girls…" - She pointed to the computer screen - "…Eleanor Lockheart was born on January 18th, 1955. It's the same date as this Elaine Lockheart-Naudman. You know what I think this means?"

The girls looked at her puzzled.

"I think that Elaine Lockheart **was** Eleanor Lockheart. She married this man, Gerrard - see he was born in 1935" - Mrs Jenkins skipped back to her search on Gerrard - "He was much, much older than Elaine. Maybe she ran away with him and her parents, Joseph and Rosalie, disowned her or they just might not have been able to find her. It wouldn't have been easy to find her if she'd changed her name."

"Oh, I get it," said Ella, "Well if that's true then that means that Elaine Naudman was our parents Aunty - and her son, Joe, is their cousin! Pa will be so pleased to know that they're related."

Jess didn't appear to be excited by the news at all. "Ella, don't you think it's strange that they've known each other all this time and not known that they were related though? Do you think it might be worth talking to our grandmother about it first? What if there's a really good reason they didn't tell Mum and Uncle Max. We don't want to cause any family rifts or anything."

"You have a point there, Jess." Mrs Jenkins said, "It's probably best you don't go talking about it to your parents just yet. What's the old saying? - Don't open the can unless you're sure there are no worms inside."

Ella and Jess both looked at each other at the mention of worms and giggled loudly.

Mrs Jenkins hushed them with a finger to her lips, pointing out they were still in the Library.

Ella stopped giggling abruptly and asked in a husky whisper, "Mrs Jenkins, do you think you could write us a pass to go visit my grandmother in the village during lunchtime? I know Mr Lees wouldn't refuse if it were you who wrote the note. You know he has a soft spot for you. Say it's for a family history lesson or something, Pleeease." Ella sang a one note chorus and Jess joined her.

"Pleeease, Mrs Jenkins. Ella was telling me yesterday how cool you were and that you of anyone in the whole village would be able to help us solve this mystery."

Mrs Jenkins blushed. "Well alright, I'll try. Now, you girls had better get off to your homerooms, the bell's about to go. Come see me during morning break and I'll give you the note. I'll even put in a good word to Mr Lees before lunch."

"Oh, thank you, Mrs Jenkins. Thank you so much." Ella gushed, wrapping an arm about the librarian's shoulder.

Mrs Jenkins smiled. "Well, we'll have to see if it works first. Normally we'd need your parents consent. But seeing it's a family issue, I'll do my best to help Mr Lees understand why they mustn't know about it just yet."

"Perfect. You really are very smart, Mrs Jenkins," said Jess.

Mrs Jenkins cheeks flushed an even deeper shade of red, and Ella learnt there may be some merit to flattery after all.

CHAPTER NINE

Jess

THE REST OF the morning passed by quickly and Jess struggled to stay focused on all the new assignments she was given. Feeling overwhelmed, she wondered if she'd be better off spending lunch time in the Library rather than visiting Grandma. Truthfully, the only reason she wanted to go today was to confirm that her grandmother actually existed. If this woman could tell them anything more about Elaine - well that would be a bonus.

Why had it not occurred to her to ask Mum about Grandma before? Mum was usually pretty open with her about almost everything else, so why hadn't she told them that Grandma was still alive? If Ella hadn't brought it up, it was possible she might never have known about their grandmother at all. The whole thing was unsettling and she wasn't sure why. What other past secrets was Mum hiding?

Her other Grandparents, Nana and Granddad Warren, lived in London, and they occasionally saw them on holidays, but they weren't really close at all, not like Ella sounded like she was with Grandma.

With all the talk of family relatives and digging up the Lockheart Family past, Jess considered who else had come before her. What other secrets and stories lurked in her family's history? For the first time in her life, she felt like she might actually belong somewhere; that she had ties to a place well beyond her own small world back in Holloway. It was a new beginning, and Scotland had opened its arms and welcomed her home like a long lost prodigal daughter. Jess hoped like crazy that whatever was to come - her family would survive. The life they'd left behind must never be repeated. As much as Jess missed her father, she would do whatever she could to keep the rest of her family from ever breaking apart.

"Hello is there anybody home in there?" Ella called as she approached, determined to resurrect her from no-mans-land.

"Sorry. I was a million miles away. What's up?"

"You coming? We need to go get that note and give it to Mr Lees."

"Yes, let's go." Jess discarded her worries and books inside her locker and closed the door, deciding instead to focus on what was really important - *her family*.

Lunchtime arrived and the girls went straight to the front office to check if their request had been granted.

With a pass to freedom in hand, they walked down the street towards the village centre, skipping puddles and munching sandwiches. It wouldn't take long to get there, so on the way they made a plan of what they would ask their grandmother. Ella said she just hoped she was having a good day and would actually remember who she was.

Entering the Angusfield rest home seemed completely normal for Ella, but for Jess, it was as foreign as another planet.

The smell got to her first. She tried to hide her discomfort from Ella who seemed completely unaware of the offensive aroma. Perhaps she was just more used to it, having probably visited hundreds of times. Maybe the rest home was the reason Mum hadn't taken them to visit their grandmother before. But what about before Grandma lived here? Why not then? She couldn't recollect ever having met her grandmother before, not even at Aunt Gabby's funeral.

Ella went to speak to a nurse with a bob of cherry red hair, and short legs.

"Hello, Luv, you here to visit your grandma? She's doing well today." She beamed a dimpled smile. "I put her out in the garden since the rain stopped and the sun's out. Would you do me a favour, Ella, and check that she's warm enough? I'll bring another blanket if she feels cold."

"Okay. Thanks, Freda." Ella led Jess outside.

Yes, Ella had definitely been here many times before.

Out in the sunshine, they quietly walked up to a woman in a wheelchair. Her head was bent to one side and she appeared to be sleeping. Champagne blonde hair spilled around her shoulders and was neatly pinned off her face; which still looked quite young for a woman in a rest home.

"Hello, Grandma. It's Ella, remember me? How are you today?" She crouched beside the wheelchair and touched Grandma's arm. The old lady lifted her head in response and stared intensely at each of them. "I've brought someone to see you; this is Jess, your other grand-daughter."

A smile of recognition wrinkled her eyes and cheeks. "Vera, is that you?" Grandma Marta asked in a soft broken voice, reaching for Jess's hand.

Jess obliged and clasped Grandma's hand in her own.

"No this is Jess, Grandma, she's Vera's daughter." Ella politely corrected.

"Oh, yes," She said. "You look like your mother." Grandma Marta patted the back of her hand softly.

"I get that a lot." Jess was surprised by Grandma's accent. It wasn't a thick Scottish tone like she was expecting but more English sounding. It puzzled her as she couldn't quite pick where it was from.

"How are you today?" Ella asked again.

"I'm good. And you?" Grandma returned the cordial greeting.

"I'm great thanks. Aunty Vera, Jess and Brody have come to stay with us at the farm. It's been so much fun. The boys have been very annoying though." Ella giggled.

"And how are Steve and Jack?" Grandma asked.

Ella's face brightened and she shot Jess a look of excitement. "They're fine. You are well today aren't you. Well, that's good because Jess and I would love to ask you some questions. Do you think you'd like to see if you know the answers?"

"Well, I'll try my dear," She exhaled her reply like she'd exhausted herself.

"Did Grandpa Erik ever have a sister called Eleanor?" Ella looked hopefully at Grandma.

Jess prayed the elderly woman's memory hadn't wandered off already.

"Well, let me think… Erik? Hmmm. His mother was very serious. She didn't like any joking around. She was straight to the point. She was a Ferlie you know."

"Yes, we know. But did she have a daughter?" Jess asked - her impatience hard to mask.

"Vera, stop being so insistent. And for heaven's sake, quit fidgeting and sit down!"

Grandma Marta voice was stern and Jess felt like a five-year-old. She did as she was told even though the ground was still wet from this morning's rain. Being mistaken for her mother was bad enough but she couldn't risk upsetting Grandma further or they might never learn the truth. Jess decided to leave the talking up to Ella, she seemed to have a way with her.

Grandma Marta shook her head. "Vera was quite disobedient sometimes and always seemed to do whatever I told her not to. She had a way with the boys too - got into so much trouble. It's why we had to send her to boarding school you know. It's my fault really. I worried because Vera was so much like her.

"Eleanor had these radical ideas and thought she should be allowed to do what the married ladies were allowed to. But she didn't have a husband; she was too young really. So you know what she did?"

The girls looked at her, their faces blank.

"Well, she just went off and married the first man that took an interest in her." Grandma shook her head and tears formed in her eyes. "She was only eighteen and he was twenty years older than her. He was smitten with her alright though. They ran away and eloped we presume. Rosalie was so distraught over what to do. I understand exactly how she feels. My daughter abandoned me too."

Jess was shocked. Was it true? Did Mum really abandon Grandma?

She'd obviously moved to London at some point. And boarding school? Mum never said anything about attending a boarding school. But then Mum had never told them about their Grandmother in Scotland either, why? It couldn't just have been because she had dementia, could it?

She really only knew about her parents lives once she had joined the picture. It had never occurred to her to ask Mum what she was like as a teenager. The line of questions grew like queues at amusement park rides. She could only conclude that if she wanted to make any sense of what Grandma was on about she might have to find the answers to some of her own questions too.

Since Jess's train of thought had changed tracks, Ella tried to keep Grandma from a derailment of her own.

"Do you know what happened to her? To Eleanor? Did she change her name, or have any children?" Ella asked.

"Well I don't know about any children, but Erik did go looking for her. He thought he spotted her once on a street in Aberdeen. But when he called out she never turned around. It took a few years, but eventually he gave up on finding his sister."

"Who did she run away with, Grandma?" Ella persisted.

"He was one of those devilishly charming types, a playboy you might call him - you know. You got a boyfriend yet?"

"No, not yet." Ella chewed her bottom lip.

"Good. There's no rush, you're too young anyway. Though I don't doubt someone's got their eye on you already to be sure." Grandma Marta squeezed Ella's hand and smiled.

Ella blushed and shrugged, she didn't seem to be getting any further. Jess sympathized. She was just as frustrated as Ella and decided to risk Grandma's scorn, once more.

"Was the man's name Gerrard? Did Eleanor marry Gerrard Naudman?" Jess squinted half-fearing the response.

Grandma's face hardened and her fists curled tight; baring blue veins and white knuckles. A feeble attempt to subdue her resentment slipped through tightened lips like a fish from the net.

"That good for nothing piece of dirt Gerrard!" she growled. "He ruined her. She told me he hit her, but she wouldn't leave him. He had his hook in her real good."

Grandma's bitterness turned to dismay when she saw Ella's horrified look. Her remarks had been quite nasty, and she smacked a hand to her lips to prevent further words escaping.

Jess hadn't a clue what to say. Grandma's sudden change in mood and body language was completely unexpected. She could see Grandma physically wrestling for control of her tongue and emotions. Eventually she won and a warm smile plumped her lips.

"Joseph is a lovely lad. They came to visit me yesterday." Grandma spoke the words so pleasantly and quickly that Jess wondered if she'd just witnessed the actions of a schizophrenic - not a dementia sufferer.

Ella seemed lost in thought for a minute. Jess hoped she knew what Grandma was talking about.

"She can't have come yesterday, Grandma, Eleanor is dead," said Ella.

"Oh no. I'm so sorry to hear that. I must write her mother a letter of condolence, she'll be so upset. When is the funeral?"

"No Grandma, she died years ago. But her son Joe is still alive."

"Well, give him my best regards, He's a fine young lad and I'm sure he'll find his sister one day. Eleanor was close to finding her too. She was more upset about Joanna than she was about Gerrard. I'm tired. Can you take me inside dear?" She tapped Ella on her arm.

"Sure, Grandma. We've got to get back to school anyhow. I'll get you in and ask Freda to take you to your room."

"Oh, thank you my dear. You're such a lovely girl. How is your mother? I haven't seen her in a while."

Ella rolled her eyes and seemed resigned to play along rather than explain another family member's death. "Oh, she's fine. She's been making a new quilt for when the baby comes."

"Oh, that's nice dear. Well say hello to my son for me and tell him to come and see me soon. Max was such a good boy…but that Vera." She sighed.

"I will, Grandma, I will." Ella kissed Grandma on the cheek. "Bye."

"Bye, Luv. Goodbye, Vera. Nice to see you." Grandma smiled, politely nodding at Jess.

"You too, Grandma," was all Jess could say.

Waving goodbye from the footpath Jess walked backwards beside Ella as they returned to school. It was the only way she could look Ella in the eyes to be sure she was telling the truth.

"Well that was weird…and she's not Scottish. I wasn't expecting that."

"I know, and that was her on a good day. Maybe that's why your mum never brought you to see her - she didn't want you to see her like that or something. Grandma is from New Zealand."

Jess turned to face forwards, satisfied with Ella's answer.

"Really? I never knew that. I never even knew she was still alive. It would have been nice if Mum had at least told us about her. It's like she never existed before today. Don't you think it's weird she never told us?" Jess's voice trailed off. She slung her backpack to her front and rummaged for the apple still in her lunch bag.

"Well maybe that's how Rosalie dealt with her daughter Eleanor too - just blocked her out. Perhaps it was too painful for her. I dunno… but what I do know is…we're going to be late to class if we don't start running. Race ya!" Ella took off, skipping lightly on her injured foot to maintain momentum.

"Oh, Jings." Jess chased after her, gripping the remainder of her apple between her teeth and wrangling her arms into the straps of her backpack.

CHAPTER TEN

Ella

ELLA'S JOY WAS about to explode as she twisted the latch on her locker and swung it open.

"I can't wait to tell Pa the good news about Joe. He's gonna be so pleased."

"I'm still not convinced it's a good idea, Ella. You saw how Grandma was when we mentioned Gerrard. There's a lot more to the story than I think we both realise."

"But what about Joe, doesn't he deserve to know?"

"Yes, eventually. But what if the reason they don't know they're related is because their parents kept it hidden from them for a very good reason. You wouldn't want to drive a wedge between your Pa and his friend, would you?"

"No of course not."

"Well, neither do I. I think we need to see what else we can uncover before we tell anyone about what we're doing."

Jess had a point but Ella was still vexed; Pa and Joe deserved to know the truth, didn't they?

"Besides," Jess said, "There's still the matter of those keys - don't you wanna find out where they belong? Mum and Uncle Max might never believe us if we tell them they're magical. Why don't we visit the castle first? If the keys lead us nowhere, then we'll tell your Pa and Mum and leave it at that."

"I suppose." Ella pouted and stared into her locker.

Jess struggled to get her locker open, and by the time she finally did, Ella had formulated a new plan.

"Well then, let's call Lady Ferlie today and ask if we can visit the castle tomorrow after school. Holly won't mind if we use her as our cover. She lives really close to the castle. We could catch her bus and then get your mum to pick us up on the way home from her interview tomorrow. What do you think?"

"Oh, Ella...that's a great idea. Mum's interview is at three-thirty. We won't have much time but it's better than nothing I suppose." Jess pulled out her phone and as soon as she swiped the screen a low battery warning flashed - then it died. "Oh, Jings!" She threw it in her bag, and grumbled, "We'll have to use a land-line." Jess searched the surrounding hallway of blue lockers for a phone. "Is there one in the library?"

"Not one we're allowed to use. There's a phone in the office but they won't let students use it until after three-forty, and, only if your parent hasn't arrived to pick you up. There is a pay phone in the cafeteria, got any money?"

"No, I left my wallet in the car yesterday. You?"

"Why would I ask if you had any money if I had some myself?" She hadn't meant to sound spiteful, but attempts to be witty often back-fired. With Jess in a sour mood already - it wasn't unexpected she'd take it the wrong way.

"Never mind." Jess moaned. "Let's just call the castle from the office at the end of the day. What do we have next?"

"Science with Mr Stevens." Ella grabbed an armload of books from her locker and slammed the door shut.

"Cool, I actually like science." Jess's mood seemed to lighten but she also looked lost.

Feeling sorry for her snide remark, Ella gestured the direction with her head. "Come on, it's this way."

The period passed quickly and when the last bell sounded, the girls made their way to the school office. Just as they were about to enter Ella caught sight of Brody coming towards them. She whispered to Jess, "I'll distract him, keep him busy. You go and make the call to Lady Ferlie. Tell Mrs H you're not sure if we're meant to catch the bus or if your mum's picking us up. They're more likely to let the new girl use the phone than me."

Ella dodged her way past the other students to cross Brody's path and walked with him to the schools front entrance.

"Hey Brody, how was your day?"

"Okay, I guess. I got to play football at lunchtime. Mum said she'd pick us all up this afternoon. I suppose she'll be waiting outside. You coming...where's Jess?"

"Uh... She'll be here soon. She's just got to make a quick phone call before we go. I'll go find her. Can you tell Aunty Vera to wait for us?"

"Why can't she just use her own phone?"

"It's dead."

Just then Steve and Jack came down the hall towards them.

"Let's go, Brody. Your mum said she was gonna pick us up, remember?" said Jack.

"Uh...yeah, but I wanna wait for Jess."

"Wait for your sister? You baw heid! You daft or something? Come on, let's go." Steve shoved Brody towards the revolving door, tipping him just enough to make him stagger.

"Steve, ye wee scunner. Leave him be. Jess won't be long. I'll go find her. You boys go and tell Aunty Vera to wait for us." She pointed a stern finger into Steve's chest with an eye of warning. Steve recoiled and stepped backwards into the revolving door; his mischievous grin and glinting eyes gave a warning of their own. Ella sensed something was up. She had better find Jess, and fast.

Jess handed the phone to Mrs Hodges over the counter. "Thank you so much, Mrs H. Mum's on her way now. She had forgotten we finish earlier than our last school."

"Jess, come on, we gotta go - Now!" As surprised as Ella was to see a smile on the usually stern-faced, Mrs H, she was more concerned about missing their ride home.

"Sorry. It took a bit longer than I expected, but Mrs H is really funny when you get to know her. Did you know she's a big Michael McIntyre fan?"

"No. But if we don't move it, we're gonna be stuck here." Ella swept a hand in the direction of the door.

"Lady Ferlie has agreed to us coming after school tomorrow. I mentioned that Mum couldn't come with us due to her interview, which she seemed okay with. I hope I don't do or say anything to embarrass myself. She seemed very refined, Ella. We'd better use our best manners tomorrow. Okay?"

"Sure. I have met her before you know. Lady Ferlie is really nice. She and Lord Ferlie are very generous contributors to the community and the school. Now, come on!"

"Wait." Jess stopped in her tracks. "I forgot my geography book. I gotta go get it from my locker."

"No time. You can borrow mine."

"Why the rush?" Jess followed a few steps behind.

Ella felt the rumble of buses as they filed out the driveway. Even though she knew she wasn't meant to be on board, she couldn't help the sinking feeling in her gut.

"Come on, hurry up. Aunty Vera is waiting and I'm worried Steve's up to something." Ella pushed her back into the revolving door and faced Jess

"Like what?"

Internal dread etched itself on Ella's face. Jess nodded, and they ran for the car park.

Their car was nowhere to be seen.

Ella face-palmed and slumped to the pavement.

"Noooo!"

"Where's Mum, Ella? Was she in our car or yours? Probably yours aye, I don't think we'd all fit in ours."

Jess was clueless to their current dilemma and Ella hadn't the heart to tell her straight.

"This is all Steve's fault. Sorry Jess. He once told Pa I was catching the bus home when I wasn't. I had to walk all the way home and it took me almost an hour. I was so mad at him that I burnt supper that night. I didn't want to, for Pa's sake, but Steve deserved to go hungry for that."

"What are you saying, Ella. Are we stuck here? Did they leave without us? But Brody would've said somethi... Oh crap! Well what are we gonna do now? I could call Mum I suppose..."

"No you can't - your phone's flat, remember?" - Ella rolled her eyes exasperated - "And we can't use the phone in the office again either - we've already used the missing parent excuse. We'll get caught if we try it again."

"Darn it. Well, maybe we could ask one of the teachers to call Mum for us? She might be mad that she has to come back to get us but what other choice do we have?"

Ella gazed up at the sky and the direction of home. Sunshine attempted landfall between puffs of cloud in a hurry to cross the great expanse. The horizon's flat hills were bordered with dirty cream streaks heralding rain by the time supper ended. "Let's just walk. It's nice enough and I'm sure we can make it home before twilight."

"Alright. I guess it's our only option. I'm gonna tell Mum though. We can't have this happen every day or I'll never catch up on all my homework."

"I can help you if you like."

"Thanks. Think I'm gonna need it." Jess sighed and followed her out the school gate. It appeared as though all hope of a remedy to their predicament was gone and so was the sunlight now hidden by a cloud.

The girls started on their long walk home. The sun intermittently rippling over the freshly sown fields of oats and barley. Before too long they would start to green and the shoots of young ears would soon grace the tops of the plants. Ella gazed out across the rolling landscape.

"Isn't it beautiful, Jess?"

"What?" Her city cousin asked naïvely.

"The land, silly. The hills and the fields. Listen… hear that? The soft breeze passing through the trees, it's such a lovely sound, don't you think?"

"I guess so. But all I can hear is the sound of a car coming."

"Look Jess! That's our van. Maybe Pa's come looking for us." Ella yelled, pointing across the field. The van pulled to a stop, took a right turn onto the road they were walking and headed towards them.

The girls jumped up and down waving their arms to flag the vehicle down. As the van slowed to a stop, both girls were surprised to see Vera and not Max in the driver's seat.

"What are you doing out here, then?" asked Aunty Vera.

"We're walking. What does it look like?" Jess's smart talk at her mother startled Ella and she felt embarrassed for her aunt.

"But Steve said you girls had caught the bus though." Aunty Vera's excuse was exactly what Ella expected and her sympathy deepened for her.

"Well. There's your problem, Aunty Vera. Never listen to a word Steve tells you. He's always lying." Ella sent a scathing look towards her brother seated in the back.

"Well aren't you going to punish him, Mum? We've been walking for ages."

"Just get in and we'll sort it out when we get home."

Both girls hopped into the front seat of the van.

"I like your haircut, Aunty Vera. Did you have that done today?" Ella grew anxious that they might have been spotted during their lunchtime walk to the rest home.

Aunty Vera combed her fingers through the freshly styled hair. "Yes. I just had it cut after school. The boys had ice-cream while they waited for me."

Aunty Vera turned red with guilt. Steve had played her real good. What would her aunt do? Ella would back her so long as she didn't make excuses for the boys' nasty trick. Justice must prevail and if Aunty Vera didn't have the back bone for it, she'd make sure Steve paid - one way or another.

"Brody, Steve. I want you both to go to your room and get started on your homework when we get home. We'll talk about this later when Max is home." Aunty Vera spoke through gritted teeth and made the next turn more sharply than anyone expected. She was mad alright, but would it help or hinder the outcome they wanted?

That night around the dining table a feisty course of accusations were exchanged across the table. 'She said this' - 'He said that.' It was enough to drive both parents mad.

Ella jumped when Pa slammed a fist on the table and stood.

"Right you lot. Listen here. There'll be no more trickery. We've all got to learn to get along together, you hear?!"

Pa paused to regain his composure and looked at Aunty Vera who nodded, happy to agree with whatever he decided.

"Steve, Brody, you boys will have to come straight to the shed after school and help me with sorting the seed. You've obviously got too much time on your hands if you've time to annoy your sisters." - He looked at Steve -"It's time you grew up lad. What kind of an example are you setting for your wee brother when you go telling lies? What would your mother think if she saw you behaving like this? I won't stand for it, and Ma wouldn't 'ave either. Now off to your room with you!" Pa placed a hand over his face and sighed.

The pain in his voice at the mention of Ma garnered faces of remorse from Steve and Ella. There were no more protests, no more excuses.

"Sorry, Pa." Steve choked the words out before quietly removing himself from the table and disappearing upstairs. His apology, though genuine, would never remove Pa's heartache of bringing up their mother in that way.

Ella hadn't seen her father this mad since Steve made her twist her ankle on the loft stairs nearly a year ago. She worried for him. He dearly missed Ma when it came to disciplining them and avoided it unless completely necessary.

Although saddened by Pa's outburst and on the verge of tears herself, she felt oddly relieved that consequences had been dealt. She'd tried many times to set Steve straight but Pa never backed her up when really needed. Ella realised then that the presence of another adult in the house had more benefit than just an extra pair of hands. She'd forgotten what it was like to have the influence of a mother and couldn't help a subtle smile at her aunt.

Aunty Vera looked around at them all, settled on Brody, and broke the awkward silence.

"That goes for you too, Brody. Just because Steve says you should do something, doesn't mean you should. Use your conscience, I know you know better. Now off you go please."

Brody sulked out of the room tailed by Jack, leaving the girls sitting with their parents.

"Now, don't think you're not to blame in any of this, Jess," Aunty Vera said. "I know you had something to do with scaring the boys last night and I haven't forgotten about it. Don't go pushing your luck girls." Aunty Vera eyed her and Ella's cheeks burned.

"No Mum, sorry," Jess said quietly.

"We won't, Aunty Vera," Ella said admiring her aunt, "But how can we make sure this doesn't happen again - the school pick-up-mix-up I mean."

"Well it shouldn't now that this has happened," Aunty Vera looked at Pa and nodded, "But we'll inform you of any plans for pick up and drop offs in future and changes won't be permitted. Okay?"

"Okay. Thanks, Aunty Vera. Oh, that reminds me. Tomorrow we were hoping to go to my friend Holly's place after school. We thought since you'd be coming back from your interview you could pick us up on your way home. Would that be alright?" It was a brave thing to ask, given the evening so far, but she had to try.

"Sounds like you've already made plans without asking first," Aunty Vera said. She was wiser than she looked and it threw Ella off her game. She was used to getting her own way with Pa over things like this. He could never read her like Aunty Vera seemed to. Ella cowered her eyes, unsure what tactic to try next. If Aunty Vera denied their request, they'd also have to cancel with Lady Ferlie and that was a call neither she, nor Jess, wanted to make.

Fortunately Jess saw her mother's hesitation and pushed for an agreement.

"Please Mum? Holly's in my Drama class and I'd really like to get to know her...get on her good side - you know - before she decides I'm competition. We don't want another Mary Mossop incident - do we? I just want Holly to like me."

Aunty Vera considered it a moment.

"Sounds fine to me, Max? You okay to watch the boys tomorrow afternoon?"

"Yeah, that'll be fine. Looks like I'll have them in the sheds with me anyhow. I'll sort something out for Jack in the morning." Pa nodded thoughtfully and left the room.

"What time do you want to be picked up girls? It's just... I thought I might check out some properties after the interview."

"You're moving already?" Ella couldn't help but pout.

"Well no, not yet, but we can't live on the farm off Max forever. Besides you kids already need some space by the sounds of it." Aunty Vera looked worried.

"Awwwe, but I love having you all here."

"Don't you worry about that for now. Write down your friend's address and I'll try and be there by six. That okay? How about we pick up some fish suppers on our way home?" Aunty Vera rubbed Ella's shoulder.

"Alright. Thank you."

Her Aunt's offer was feeble. Ella would have agreed to make dinner herself if it would keep her aunt and cousins from leaving. For now the takeaway peace offering was a nice gesture - but it would take a lot more than battered fish and greasy chips to buy her satisfaction.

CHAPTER ELEVEN

Wednesday 23rd March 2016

Jess

HOPPING ONTO THE bus with Holly the next afternoon, Jess's stomach swirled with butterflies.

Ella turned in the seat to face her. "It'll be fine Jess, your mum's not gonna find out we went to the castle, and even if she does, we'll tell her we went there on a walk with Holly. She does it all the time - it's mostly true."

"I know, but we just can't afford to lose track of time, okay?"

The bus finally pulled up outside Holly's house and they confirmed their plan to meet back in her driveway at five minutes to six, just before Mum was expected to pick them up.

Holly waved briefly after they'd crossed the road, then disappeared. The girls made their way up the long bending driveway towards the castle.

"Holly's really nice, not a bit like Mary Mossop. But don't tell Mum I said that." Jess wanted to believe it, but she couldn't let her guard down around Holly - not yet anyway. She hoped to someday, she needed some new friends - not just Ella. Having her cousin at school had been helpful, but not when it came to establishing her own personal friendships. Every girl Jess thought about be-friending, Ella seemed to dismiss - citing multiple reasons why she shouldn't. Jess was beginning to wonder if Ella wanted her to have her own friends at all. She should feel flattered, but she saw the negative side too. Living with her cousin and attending the same school would eventually become tiresome and possibly even difficult. To her surprise she was actually hopeful Mum would find a suitable property, sooner rather than later.

Early spring shoots of daffodil bulbs were starting to crop up and the trees would soon begin to bud also. It was an impressive sight as they emerged from the giant beech trees flanking the entrance. The whole castle stood in its wooded surroundings, wearing neatly cut stones like a coat, and fairy-tale crenellations as a crown on its head. The dominating four-storey circular battlement tower stood like a staff to the south-west. The view from which, Jess imagined, would be spectacular and fitting for such a historic clan as the Ferlies'. Ella had given her a crash course on the Ferlie clan and Jess became enthralled by the long list of Lords, Ladies, and all the fascinating twists the Ferlie heritage had taken.

Entering the enclosed ivy draped portico through blue arched doors, Jess grasped the chain of the doorbell and donged it twice. The daunting sense of intimidation returned along with the spiders inside her stomach.

Waiting in front of the white trimmed glass doors the girls admired the pretty flower shaped top light. So engrossed by it, they both startled when Lady Ferlie swung the door open.

"Hello, girls. Come on in." Lady Ferlie's warm smile and casual attire soon relieved Jess's insecurities and she was glad to relax - at least a little.

Gesturing the girls inside Lady Ferlie led them to the sitting room. Jess gazed around; stunned into silence by its cavernous grandeur.

Pale mint walls stretched high above to a picture rail bordered by the most intricate crown moulding Jess had ever seen. Giant gold gilded portraits of past family members commanded attention whether you wished to look at them or not, and elaborate tapestry rugs divided the parquet floors into sections. Jess couldn't bring herself to sit on any of the dusky pink seats until Lady Ferlie asked them to.

Eager to maintain the formalities such a setting deserved, Jess decided the politest thing would be to introduce her cousin. "Lady Ferlie, this is my cousin, Ella Lockheart."

"Hello m' Lady. Ella held out her hand.

"Come now, we don't need such formalities girls. Please just call me Janice." She smiled at them. "I think we've met before, haven't we?" Lady Ferlie looked at Ella.

"Yes, m' La..." she paused, "I mean Janice...Oh, that's just too weird. Can I stick with Lady Ferlie?"

"If you like." She smiled.

"We met at the Country Fair you held at the castle last year," said Ella.

"That's right. You won a prize for your baking if I'm not mistaken." Ella blushed. Jess was impressed by Lady Ferlie's memory.

"Now, Jess, I think you mentioned you'd like to look at the Library. Is that correct?"

"Yes please, if you don't mind."

"Are you looking for something specific, your family ties perhaps? Or are you just generally interested in the clan?"

"Well if I'm honest, we're really just interested in Rosalie Ferlie. You see we found out yesterday that she had two children, not just our grandfather. We visited our grandmother in Angusfield rest home yesterday and she mentioned that Rosalie had a daughter called Eleanor. We'd love to see if there are any photographs or records of Rosalie's family."

"I see, well - follow me. We'd best start in the Library." Lady Ferlie led them down the main passageway and off into a side room just past the grand main staircase. The Library; just as tall and awe-inspiring as the sitting room, was thick with woody brown shelves housing hundreds of books from floor to ceiling in all manner of muted reds, browns, blues and greens. A cologne of knowledge filled the ancient bindings and their equally aged pages. Jess felt sick with envy at the ability to have such a collection of books at ones fingertips. The fifty seven books she stored on her kindle seemed feeble in comparison to the overwhelming amount of books in this room.

"Well, I'm not sure if you'll have much luck." Lady Ferlie gestured to the huge expanse. "The trick is knowing where to look. But let's try, shall we? Now let's see. Here is the section of the family albums. Photography was a pastime of my husband's father so there are lots of photos, but not all of them are labelled with the names of who's in them you see. There are some really old ones too - which I find fascinating. The clothes, the hairstyles, and even some of the castle's alterations it's had over the years. I have spent many hours looking through all of them but I'm not sure exactly which of ones may have pictures of Rosalie in them."

"Oh, that's okay. It's worth a try." Ella stared in awe at the surrounding walls of books.

"Lady Ferlie, I almost forgot," said Jess, "Do you know if you have any furniture in the house that's missing a key? Or perhaps something that's never been able to be unlocked?"

"Mmmm... let me think... There was a writing desk that we couldn't seem to open. My husband, William, didn't seem to mind. It just sits in a room as decoration more than anything. Why do you ask?"

"Could we take a look at it?" blurted Ella.

Jess bugged her eyes at her cousin and shook her head.

"Well, you see, Lady Ferlie, we've sort of been on a journey of discovery. We found a box with some items in it and amongst them were some keys. So naturally, we're curious to find out what they might unlock. We think they might have belonged to Rosalie's daughter, Eleanor, or maybe even Rosalie herself. Would you mind if we took a look?"

"Ooo you've got me curious now too, follow me." Lady Ferlie seemed quite excited. "It's upstairs in the, *Girls Room*. You'll see why we call it that."

Jess and Ella followed Lady Ferlie back out to the entrance hall and up the grand main staircase, pausing on the mid-way landing. A gallery of proud ancestors hung solemnly on the stark white walls. "This is Alistair Ferlie." Lady Ferlie gestured, mentioning it like he were actually alive and standing there in person.

A magnificent painting of a man standing proudly in his Scottish kilt with a loyal black and white border collie by his side was framed in gold; commanding the entire left wall and all who passed him. Ella admired the portrait courteously while Jess was hypnotised by the real tiger skin draped length-ways like a trophy over the handrail. Its head; still attached, lay flattened with glass eyes boring a hole into space and its once deathly sharp teeth consumed the handrail they rested upon. Jess's forearm hairs raised sending a chill up her spine.

"Marvellous isn't it?" said Lady Ferlie, running her hand down its pelt. "This way." Lady Ferlie motioned the girls to follow.

Ella eventually stopped glaring at the unnerving portrait of Alistair Ferlie only to unwittingly run her hand over the tiger skin. In a panic she quickly hurried to catch up with them waiting at the top of the stairs. The second floor was just as excessively decorated with narrow hall tables, random chairs, pictures of art and travel memorabilia, all placed at distracting intervals down the hallway.

Reaching the end of the castle where the battlement tower stood all three began climbing the dark stained spiralling staircase. Broomstick balustrades topped with a smooth curving handrail led them up an intriguing route of African tribal masks, each one scarier than the last. Jess's excitement grew with each step. Where on earth were they going?

Once she realised she'd lost track of their location in castle, Jess desperately tried to suppress her instinctual flight response. Her eyes swam and her head felt light. *It's just from the change in altitude - You're fine.*

She stopped on the stairs and took a few deep breaths. Without Lady Ferlie's help, they would struggle to find their way back through the labyrinth of corridors and doorways. She fought hard not to let her panic take over completely.

"You okay, Jess?" Ella's voice bounced around the walls, and her head.

"Yeah. I'll be fine." Jess looked at her feet and focused on the stairs beneath them. The staircase carpet was springier and less worn than other areas of the castle but the boards beneath it still creaked.

"Not far now. It's just at the top of these ones," Lady Ferlie called over her shoulder.

Upon reaching their final landing, a glow of pink emanated from the doorway of the *Girls Room*. Standing at the entrance, both Jess and Ella gasped at the luxury of it.

A beautiful crystal chandelier dripped from the decorative ceiling rose. The florals of spring colours graced not only the wallpaper but the draperies as well. All around the room were treasures that any young girl might find delightful.

Jess was particularly in awe of the giant dolls house beside the window. It was as detailed as the very castle they were standing in. Its miniature form was so intricate she believed that any doll that resided there would be as well catered for as the inhabitants of the real castle itself.

"Wow! It's *amazing*. Whose room was this?" Jess asked Lady Ferlie.

"Well it's housed numerous generations of Ferlie girls over the years and some boys too I'd imagine. This part of the house was last decorated by the 17th Lord Ferlie's wife, Anne-Marie. It's not particularly to my own tastes, but when you're around it long enough it kind of grows on you. Over here is the writing desk I was talking about. It doesn't appear to have a key broken in the lock."

Jess slipped her backpack off her shoulder, setting it down on the chair by the desk. Carefully she reached inside to retrieve the swaddled keys. Lady Ferlie looked on with great interest. Jess unfolded the baby's gown, taking extra care to avoid any contact with the keys.

Spreading the keys apart with her fingers beneath the fabric, she looked at each of them carefully.

"What about…that one?" Ella pointed to a small black key that looked about the right size.

"I'll give it a go." Jess carefully slipped her other hand under the garment and took hold of the chosen key.

"What's she doing that for?" Lady Ferlie asked in a hushed tone, noticing their changed demeanour.

"We think the keys are *enchanted*," Ella whispered.

"Really - Why?" Lady Ferlie whispered out of reverence.

"It's a long story, Lady Ferlie," said Ella.

Jess placed the key in the hole and tried to turn it.

Nothing. It wouldn't budge.

She removed it and looked at the keys again puzzled.

"Try that one, Jess." Lady Ferlie pointed to a brass one, "It looks like a key I have for another bit of furniture I have here."

Jess tried her favourite key, the one with the pretty looped top, and this time the lock released.

29th June 1973
Eleanor

Eleanor buried her face in the pillow. How could her mother do this to her? She felt tricked.

Not only would she not be returning home from Albyn boarding school, but she was to stay for the whole summer with her aunt and uncle at Castle Ferlie.

Locked up like a prisoner in a castle tower; she now understood just how Cinderella felt.

How would Gerrard know where to find her? If she could just get word to Lydia, she would give a message to him. Eleanor sighed as if the whole world was collapsing around her. Her hopes had been dashed and her plans ruined. Her only consolation and companion was her Harlequin romance novel she'd put in her coat pocket for the journey. Her mother berated her sternly for reading such 'rubbish' she called it. But to Eleanor, it was a world in which she could imagine herself with her beloved Gerrard as her hero.

Looking over at the open writing desk she noticed the Ferlie Crest printed at the top of the stationary. Uncle Arthur, the great Lord Ferlie, was a well-known Politician in Scotland. If she ever did anything to disgrace him she'd probably end up locked in her room in the battlement tower with the key thrown away. Eleanor had spent many summers holidaying with her aunt and uncle at the castle, especially during the harvest when the dust got particularly bad for her lungs. But each time it had been at her own request, not forced on her. All those days she'd spent role playing as *Rapunzel* locked in a tower had unwittingly come true.

Regaining her composure, she wiped the tears from her cheeks and took a seat at the desk to pen a letter.

Dearest Gerrard,
It is of the saddest news that I am loathe to share with you, but Mother has taken me away to my uncle's castle. I may never be able to see you again. I am distraught and I fear that you will not come looking for me. I miss you my darling with all my heart. My body aches for your touch and the memory of your kisses fades faster each day we are apart. If you ever loved me please, please come rescue me from Castle Ferlie. Let's run away together like we said we would. Just you and me.
Yours faithfully forever,
Eleanor XX

Eleanor took out an envelope and carefully wrote the address of her best friend Lydia Macrae on the front. Quickly she drafted another note to Lydia explaining the urgent request for her to pass on her letter to Gerrard. Wrapping her letter to him inside the note for Lydia, she slipped them inside an envelope and closed it with the Ferlie Crest wax seal. She placed a stamp on the front corner and slipped the letter inside her skirt pocket. Now all she needed was the right person to give it to; someone she could trust who would post it for her.

If she succeeded in getting word to Gerrard, she'd also need a plan for her escape.

What social events were on the calendar this month? Probably not much out here in the country. What about the Farmer's Ball?

She'd often heard her mother talk about how she had met her father at the Tullynessle Farmer's Ball. But that wouldn't be till the end of summer once the harvest was in, almost three months away.

Eleanor decided it was likely her best and only shot at escaping and would formulate a plan around it if she could. Gerrard loved taking her out dancing and she had always found a way to go. Even though Mrs Fox, the boarding house matron, expressly forbid them to leave their dorms after 7:00pm - Eleanor escaped frequently, whether she was allowed to or not.

CHAPTER TWELVE

23rd March 2016

Jess

J ESS HELD HER breath and lowered the writing desk lid. Ella and
Lady Ferlie peered in with child-like fascination. They fossicked
around the various compartments looking for anything out of the
ordinary. The Ferlie seal and melting wax still sat as if it had just been
used the day before. A neatly stacked pile of paper with the printed crest
awaited a pen to give it purpose and the embossed envelopes stood ready
for their orders. There was nothing really interesting at first glance. But
then Jess spied an orange book placed near the back; behind a small
dictionary and a book of quotations.

Jess picked it up and read aloud, "Summer Season - by Lucy
Gillen...My mum used to read these kinds of romance novels."

Its pages were only slightly yellowed on the edges but otherwise, it
was in pristine condition - compared to the tatty books her mother kept
on the shelves back in Holloway.

Jess flipped through the pages, stopping unexpectedly in the middle.
Wedged between two pages was a piece of stationary neatly folded in

half. Jess pulled it out. Ella and Lady Ferlie waited with barely contained glee.

"What does it say? Read it aloud," said Ella.

Jess opened the letter and a photograph fell to the ground. Picking it up, they studied it carefully together.

"Wow, she looks like you, Ella." Jess looked from the photo to her cousin.

"Yes, I can see a very close likeness there," said Lady Ferlie.

The photograph depicted a pretty young girl of about seventeen, with long brown wavy hair tied back off her face. She looked earnestly into the eyes of a much older man wearing a stiff looking suit and a well-groomed moustache. He, standing proudly beside the green Jaguar sports car, had his arm draped lazily over the bewitched girl's shoulder, with a nonchalant look of charm about him. Jess passed the photo to Ella and began to read:

"<u>31st August 1973</u>

Dearest Mother.

I wish I could be the daughter you hoped I would be. I love you dearly, but tonight I am to run away with Gerrard. He loves me and I know will take care of me. I had hoped you would come to know him as I do. But you never gave him the chance to prove himself. I know you think he's not right for me. But whatever your reasons, I am sure he will prove them to be untrue. I hope you know that I still love you and Pa very much and I pray you can forgive me one day. I plan to start a new life with Gerrard and I will close this chapter of my life, here at Castle Ferlie. No longer shall I be known as Eleanor Lockheart.

Your Loving Daughter, E"

"Oh my goodness. It looks like you've found a clue girls," said Lady Ferlie.

Jess closed the note and looked at Ella. "I believe what Mrs Jenkins said earlier today is true. Eleanor must have become Elaine."

"I wonder if what Grandma said is true too. What if Elaine did go to visit her with Joe? She seemed to think so," said Ella.

"She could have been confused. You saw how she was yesterday. She thought I was my mother." Jess smiled, trying not to let her manners slip in front of Lady Ferlie. "Do you think there could be anything else at the castle that might tell us what happened to Eleanor, Lady Ferlie?"

"Well now, let's go back to the Library and see what we can find in the albums, shall we? It should be easier now we have a reference picture of Eleanor."

Jess tucked the keys and note into her backpack, and followed Lady Ferlie back down the stairs.

To their surprise, Lord Ferlie exited the library when they reached the bottom.

"Oh, there you are darling. You're home early today. How was your walk?" asked Lady Ferlie.

"Very fine thank you. Spring is on its way, the River is looking good and Murray thinks we'll have a fine season of fishing this year."

"Oh, that's wonderful news. William, may I introduce Miss Jess Warren and her cousin, Miss Ella Lockheart. They are doing some research about their family history and have found a link to the Ferlie clan."

"Well now, that's wonderful. And how are we related?" He asked, his formality akin to a Gentleman.

"Well, you see, our great-grandmother was Rosalie Ferlie." Ella took the printed piece of paper that Mrs Jenkins had given them yesterday from her pocket and handed it to Lord Ferlie. "She was Arthur Ferlie's youngest sister." She pointed out the name. "She married my great-grandfather, Joseph Lockheart and had Erik and Eleanor. Erik is my… *OUR* grandfather." She grinned looking at Jess.

"Oh, I see. Yes, I know that name, Lockheart. Did you know that Joseph Lockheart used to be the Estate Manager here? Come take a look at this girls."

He led them into the Library and took out a very large book. Opening it to the correct date he pointed to the name. The Estate ledger entry noted the following:

December 3rd, 1938.
Mr Joseph Lockheart hired as the Estate Manager.

"That's the year my grandfather inherited the castle. I dare say he wouldn't have chosen a new estate manager the same year if the old one had been doing well, so there must have been a good reason for him to like Joseph Lockheart. They might have been childhood friends or something. I suppose if he was engaged to marry a Ferlie girl that would be a pretty good reason to hire him too. Aye, what I wouldn't give to go back in time and ask them some of these questions. But 'tis something we'll just have to wonder and suppose at I guess…

"…Look, see here, my grandfather states that he paid Joseph Lockheart a bonus of 1400 pounds and two loads of lumber on the 6th of May 1940. That was a lot of money back in those days. I'd say Joseph could have purchased his own farm for that. Look here's another entry that mentions him. Joseph Lockheart was given another 150 pounds for a new tractor. It was paid to him on the 2nd of May 1946. It says here; A gift to Rosalie and Joseph Lockheart at the birth of their son Erik.

"That's odd you see, because there's never a mention of another family's birth in here unless it was a baby born in the Ferlie direct family line. I'd say Joseph was a very good friend indeed of Arthur Ferlie."

Lord Ferlie finished his chronicle, and the girls, astonished to learn such a lot of information about their family heritage, sat speechless.

Lady Ferlie was looking at another bookshelf and seemed intent on finding what she was looking for.

"So that's how we came to live at Lockheart Farm!" Ella's realisation came with a grin that pinned to her ears. "I guess that means that Great-Grandfather Joseph probably built the farmhouse we live in now. It's a lovely big house you see, Lord Ferlie, not a really small one like a lot of the other homesteads around here. I guess he had to buy the land and build a house for Rosalie, so they could marry. She would be used to living in a big castle. So he couldn't have built her a small house.

"But if that's true, that means that Rosalie would have lived in my house… and maybe some of her things are still there. Oh, Jess, we'll have to go look on the farm again. Maybe there's something else in the loft that can help us. I've a sneaky suspicion I know exactly which box to look in too."

"Oh look, girls, here is the photo album for the years 1938 to 1945. I knew it was this one. Not many photos were taken those years because of the war," said Lady Ferlie.

Flipping through the pages she stopped at one with a photograph of a man in uniform next to a bride adorned with a crisp white veil that reached to the floor. The dress was entirely modest with an upright collar at the neck, long sleeves, and a small amount of lace trimming the hem in front. Her flowers were possibly the nicest part of the whole picture. Beautiful roses dotted in amongst ferns and ivy, cascaded from her hands and the man at her side was smiling very contentedly.

"This is Rosalie Ferlie and Joseph Lockheart," said Lady Ferlie.

"She's not very pretty," said Ella.

"Well, no. She wasn't quite a picture of traditional beauty, was she? But what she lacked in looks, I'm sure she more than made up for in her character." Lady Ferlie chuckled.

"Her purse too no doubt," said Lord Ferlie with a glint in his eye.

"She looks so serious." Jess frowned.

"Your grandfather, on the other hand, is quite a looker. I can see why Rosalie liked him. He was a lucky man to be sure, and I think he knew it too." Lady Ferlie stroked a finger across Joseph Lockheart's image.

"Uh, Ella... look it's quarter to six." Jess pointed to the large grandfather clock swinging its pendulum from side to side at the end of the Library.

"Oh my goodness! I'm terribly sorry, Lady Ferlie, Lord Ferlie, but we really must be going. Jess's mother is picking us up at the gate at six."

"We're very sorry, Lady Ferlie, but you see my mother doesn't actually know we are here. She thinks we are at Holly Garret's place across the road. We wanted to do the research ourselves and then present the facts, but not until we have them all. So, for now, we hoped to keep them secret. Do you mind?" Jess crossed her fingers behind her back and cast a sideways glance at Ella.

"Well, it's not a position anyone likes to find themselves in, girls. I'm not of the mind to lie to your mother. If she should ask me, then I would most likely give you up. But if she never asks, then you can be assured I will conceal your quest as best I can. I myself would like to learn more of your story and of this Eleanor. I'm curious to know what became of her too. I won't hinder your progress. In fact, I feel inspired to continue the search at the castle for you."

Ella's face lit up. "Oh thank you, thank you, thank you! Lady Ferlie. We promise we'll keep you posted of any developments. And if we need to return here, or if you find something else, we'll be sure to make a plan that doesn't involve lying to our parents."

Jess nodded.

"We promise, Lady Ferlie. And next time we'll leave you with the key to that desk, once we find a way to get it off the ring."

"Oh, I certainly would like to have it. Well, you best get going or you won't make it to the road in time." Lady Ferlie led them to the front door.

"Bye girls!" She waved them off.

"Bye, Lady Ferlie. Bye, Lord Ferlie. Thank you!" the girls chorused and shot off down the driveway.

Jess and Ella made it to the road with less than a minute to spare. Cautiously they paced across the road and up Holly's driveway. Jess was instantly relieved when Mum's car was nowhere in sight.

Holly was outside waiting; kicking a football ball against the fence.

"Thank God you're here. I was getting worried. I could have stalled your Mum for a little while, Jess, but I'm glad I won't have to." Holly kicked the ball to Ella.

"Sorry Holly, we didn't mean to be so late. At least we made it before Aunty Vera - that's what matters." Ella kicked the football back to Holly but it veered off in the wrong direction.

"Remind me never to have you on my team." Jess laughed. Ella responded with the protrusion of her tongue that made both Holly and Jess giggle at her.

The familiar sound of Mum's car made Jess signal the others of her imminent arrival. She pulled into the driveway and Jess and Ella got in. "Thanks Holly, you're a life saver!" Ella waved goodbye before closing the door.

With their secret visit to the castle concealed, Jess and Ella kept discussions in the car on the topic of Mum's interview and their school work; insisting they still had math homework to complete.

Relieved there was no washing up required after supper, the girls sped straight upstairs to the loft eager to hunt for evidence of Rosalie's life in the farmhouse.

Jess sat on her bed and searched her bag for the note and photograph.

"I can't imagine being eighteen and running off to be married. And to a thirty-eight-year-old too. No wonder Rosalie and Joseph were mad about it. I'm sure Mum would be too if I did such a thing."

Ella didn't bite. She was too busy rummaging through boxes and shuffling things around the storage end of the loft.

"Jess, I know it might not seem very interesting to you, but somewhere in amongst all this stuff are some of Rosalie's things. Do you think you could quit your jabbering for a second and come help me look for it?"

Jess did her best not to take Ella's stab personally and went and busied herself with items close to the main light. Distracted by an old typewriter, Jess didn't notice Ella was waiting to hand her a box. Ella huffed, shoved a box beside her, and balanced the other one awkwardly on top.

"Jess, I could really use your help here." Ella's exasperation was evident but lacked any kind of humorous sarcasm that Mum usually injected.

"Alright. Don't get your knickers in a knot." Immediately Jess was distracted by an old hat box. She inspected it closely and became lost in her own thoughts. She wasn't the least bit aware Ella was again waiting for her help.

"Where should I put this?" Jess looked for a place to deposit the hat box.

Ella expelled a great huff and pointed to a stack of boxes. "Just put it down, and come and help me with this one. It's heavy but I'm sure this is the box we're looking for." Jess clambered over to Ella like a heron picking its way through a marsh-land. Something stuck to the bottom of her shoe but she dare not stop to see what it was or Ella might bite her head off entirely.

Together they awkwardly shuffled the large box all the way over to the mat in their room and dropped themselves on the floor beside it. The box was rigid and sturdy, not like the ones Jess had packed her things in for their move north. This box had a stamp on the side with a 'Fergusson' manufacturers label on it. Neither one of them had seen or heard of it before.

Ella lifted the flaps, pulled out a fur stole and placed it on the mat. Jess immediately picked it up and wrapped it around her shoulders.

"Oh, Ella it's lovely. I feel just like one of those old movie stars," she gushed, stroking the fur.

Jess glanced down to the left. Her eyes met with the cold black beaded eyes of a dead fox.

"Arhhhh!" Her high pitch scream wheeled about the loft and she flung the stole across the room with such velocity that it almost looked alive. Ella laughed so mercilessly that Jess became cross.

"It's not funny. You knew it had a head and didn't tell me."

"Oh come on, I didn't mean to trick you. But the look on your face was priceless." Ella giggled.

"Ha, ha." Jess attempted to humour herself. "Well, I suppose at least we know what a flying fox looks like now." She joined Ella giggling until they forced themselves to calm down.

"Look at this." Ella pulled out a flat white box. On it, the words, ABERDEEN TAILORS, were embossed in gold letters.

Lifting the box's lid, the girls found a white gown laid carefully folded to fit neatly inside.

"I think this might be Rosalie's wedding dress," said Ella.

"Oh yeah, it looks like the one we saw in the picture at the castle. I wonder if there are any more photos of Rosalie in this box?" Jess peered over the box flap, wary of what other creatures might lie within. Spying a pretty little jewellery box she picked it up and tried the lid.

"It's stuck." Looking more closely she noticed a keyhole. "Ella, look, another locked box." She held it up for her cousin to see.

"Where are the keys?" Ella held her palm open in front of Jess.

"Hang on, hold your horses." Jess grabbed her backpack and reached inside for the keys. Feeling the baby's gown, the cloth loosened and the keys slipped out brushing her hand.

Without thinking she grabbed them. Another vision flashed before her eyes...

...Eleanor sat on the edge of a bed with the jewellery box beside her - The same one which Jess currently held in her other hand - Eleanor opened the box and inside was a gold and ruby ring with little diamonds all around the centre stone. She picked it up and placed it on her ring finger.

"Mrs Naudman," She said to herself. "I'm going to become Mrs Eleanor Naudman and nobody, not even Mother, will stop me." Eleanor smiled and admired the ring. She removed it and placed it back inside the box alongside a silver locket. A lock of her own brown hair tied with a little pink ribbon sat in the bottom of the box also...

...Jess awoke from her vision by herself this time. Ella didn't appear to have noticed her absent look and was focused intently on the jewellery box in Jess's hand.

Jess grinned.

"I bet you ten pounds there's a lock of hair in this box."

Ella looked sceptical. "Well how would you know that? Where are the keys - Let's see if you're right."

Jess handed her the keys. Holding them carefully with the baby's gown beneath, Ella picked out the smallest one.

"This has to be it." Quickly she installed it in the lock and turned it. Opening the lid, there sat a silver locket and a lock of hair.

Jess was gob-smacked. Having seen them in her vision she knew they had been there once. But seeing them now was like she'd travelled in time.

"But - how did you know there would be a lock of hair in there? You can't have known. It was a guess, wasn't it?" Ella looked completely puzzled.

"I saw it. I touched the keys in my bag, and I just saw it. I saw the locket too, but I didn't think that would still be there." She picked it up and immediately went to try it on.

"Oh Jess. Are you sure you wanna do that?"

Too late. Jess had it on and didn't seem the least bit affected by it - at least not in the vision sort of way. Her vanity, however, was most definitely altered and she ogled it on her neck in the mirror. "It's got to be worth a pretty penny for sure."

Ella didn't look happy so Jess diverted her attention.

"Her engagement ring isn't here though. "She lifted the lock of hair to check underneath. "It was in here, I saw it. Eleanor said, 'I'm going to be Mrs Naudman and no one, not even Mother can stop me'." Jess mimicked Eleanor's Scottish voice as she had heard it in her vision. She laughed at her poor imitation. "Well I guess her mother couldn't stop her from marrying Gerrard - Joe's proof of that."

"Don't be so pretentious." Ella frowned. "It broke her mother's heart when she ran away to be with Gerrard. Would you want to break your mother's heart like that? I know I wouldn't. I'd just be pleased to have mine back."

Ella's eyes welled with tears. She bowed her head and wrapped her arms around it to hide her face.

"Oh come on, Ella, I was only playing around. I'm sorry. Of course, this is serious. I want to know what happened to Eleanor as much as you do. But what do all her mother's things have to do with finding out about her? I think we need to talk to Joe and get some real answers. That image of his mother standing at the gravestone still gives me chills. I'd like to know if there's anything he can tell us about that. What if he has something that's locked, don't you wanna find out?" Jess touched Ella's shoulder, trying to distract her from the heavy heart she now possessed.

Jess peered into the box again and pulled from it a large photo album. Imprinted on the front it had the words:

'*The Lockhearts.*'

Opening it to the first page, there were pictures of even older generations still than Joseph and Rosalie. In them, other siblings sat or stood beside very serious-looking adults. She concluded they must have been Joseph's or Rosalie's parents, grandparents or even great-grandparents.

After turning a few pages Jess saw a picture of Castle Ferlie. A very young Rosalie stood outside with her two sisters and older brother, Arthur.

On the next page was a picture of a horse in the field. Below it was written the name, '*Whinnie.*'

Then there was a picture of Rosalie in a very formal gown, looking about sixteen or so. Perhaps she had been a debutante. She did look quite serious, like Grandma had said she was, but her image didn't offer any clue as to her thoughts. Rosalie wasn't entirely pretty and her face certainly didn't match her name; in her opinion anyway. Not like her daughter, Eleanor, who had more defined cheek bones and round full lips like her father. Rosalie's oval face was very aristocratic and stubborn looking by comparison.

"Look, Ella. Here's the farmhouse, *this* farmhouse."

Ella looked up and cleared her eyes. She was very interested to see the photo and pulled herself up beside Jess to look at it.

"Woooow. Look, there's not one tree around the house, it looks so barren. I bet Rosalie planted all the trees that are here now. She would have missed them when she moved from the castle. I know I would have."

Ella seemed consoled by the old photograph and Jess was glad. Turning the pages, they enjoyed more of the family's holidays and notable achievements, finally resting on a page that held a family portrait.

There sat Joseph and his wife Rosalie, with Erik standing behind his father. Their grandfather, Erik, looked about fifteen years old. A chubby-cheeked five-year-old Eleanor, dressed in a pretty little smock, stood beside her mother. Behind them was the farmhouse with its steep-pitched roof and abundant flowering garden in front. They all looked very happy and healthy.

Next were some pictures of the children on their own as they grew up. Jess and Ella took special note of a photo of Eleanor at about sixteen or seventeen years of age. Had she met the charming Mr Naudman yet? Quite possibly, they decided. She did have a somewhat cheeky look about her. With her hair down and hands clasped behind her back, she appeared as if she might be concealing something. Her crooked smile and warm coy eyes made her very lovely to look at. She wore a beautiful short white 60's baby-doll style dress made of polyester with a sloping empire waistline. Even though the Victorian laced neckline plunged very low, the slightly puffed full length sleeves made up for modesty where the neckline lacked.

"Look she's wearing the locket" - pointed Ella - "I wonder if she had a picture in it?"

They hadn't looked before. Ella held out her hand and waited while Jess un-latched it from her neck and carefully handed it over. Ella opened the locket and inside was not a picture of her beloved Gerrard, but a picture of her mother.

"Oh, Ella," Jess's tone sombred. "She must have loved her mother very much."

"I bet Eleanor wished she'd worn it the day she left Castle Ferlie."

"She must have worn the engagement ring."

The girls resumed their study of the photo album.

"Oh my goodness, Jess, look." Ella repeatedly tapped a photo of a dance hall with lots of people formally dressed. "Look there are Rosalie and Joseph. She's wearing that fox stole. And I think that's Erik, he's so young, and really handsome. I bet Grandma Marta is in this picture somewhere." Ella pulled the photo closer.

"I can't believe it. That's Gerrard, isn't it?" Jess's excitement made her own ears ring.

He was dancing with a blonde haired girl and looking so jolly happy about it too. It was only his side profile, but Jess was sure it was him. "Look over the back there, Ella" - Jess pointed - "Isn't that Eleanor? She doesn't look too pleased about what Gerrard's up to."

CHAPTER THIRTEEN

31st August 1973

Eleanor

ELEANOR HAD WAITED three months for this night. It was the longest time she'd waited for anything.

Uncle Arthur and Aunt May had left almost an hour ago and she was expected out by the road in the next half hour - otherwise, she would miss her ride. Gerrard had arranged for his friend James to drop him at the hall and then take Lydia to pick up Eleanor from Castle Ferlie. Gerrard couldn't risk being spotted anywhere in the vicinity of the castle himself. If Eleanor was discovered in her plan to escape then Lydia would help extract her without additional trouble. But first, Eleanor had to get passed Great-Aunt Susan.

Aunt Susan was a good twenty years older than Aunt May and had silver grey hair which she wore coiled atop her head. She always wore a shawl around her regardless of the temperature and had the pointiest nose Eleanor had ever seen. Aunt Susan wasn't a family relative at all, but an old friend of the Ferlie family, who had no husband left alive to care for and not much means to support herself. She came from Dundee but prided herself on being just as refined in her mannerisms as the distinguished Ferlie family.

It wasn't just out of charity that Aunt May had asked Susan to stay with them for the summer. Her presence would offer another set of eyes over their mischievous niece. Susan was most grateful to Aunt May and Uncle Arthur for their generous offer and as recompense would do all she could to prevent Eleanor from getting into trouble.

It was nearing the end of the summer harvest and the sun sat lower in the sky heralding the onset of autumn. Great-Aunt Susan was reluctant to return home but would do so just as soon as Eleanor was back at school.

Susan had stayed up watching the hallway and clock from where she sat reading in the library. Eleanor knew that if the stairs creaked ever so slightly, her plan would unravel and she would end up locked in her room; just as she had been a week after her arrival at Castle Ferlie.

She had gone to the gate to watch for the postman who came around noon each day. Fortunately, her letter had made it into the postman's hand before Uncle Arthur caught sight of her returning from the driveway. Her punishment for such a reckless act was to spend the next week confined to her bedroom, with nothing but her book to amuse her. Meanwhile, Uncle Arthur had called Great-Aunt Susan and asked her to come stay as Eleanor's summer chaperone.

Tonight, all she had to do was make it past Great-Aunt Susan's all-seeing-eye. The thought of what might happen if she didn't, was far too unbearable to even consider.

Seated at the writing desk, Eleanor placed the ruby stone engagement ring on her finger. Retrieving the note she'd written for her mother earlier she slipped it inside her book along with a photograph. Placing it far in the back of the writing desk, she smiled mischievously.

Eleanor couldn't resist turning the key in the lock and did so without considering the consequences of such an action. Even as a little girl she had loved to lock things. Once, she had even locked her mother out of the house. Although she had loved the thrill and power she felt, she'd been severely punished for it. Eleanor rubbed the knuckles on her left hand as she recalled the pain her mother inflicted with the wooden spoon. The writing desk had such a dainty key and she wanted to keep it. Against her better sense, she removed it from the desk and placed it in her purse.

Grinning like a Cheshire cat, Eleanor quickly changed into her burgundy rose gown. The shiny taffeta skirt was terribly noisy and would be difficult to conceal, but it was Gerrard's favourite and she was determined to wear it at their wedding for him. A delicate sheer chiffon overlay; laden with crystals, covered her bodice to the neck and long sleeves, as sheer as the overlay, caressed her arms with each movement. Strands of gems burst forth from one shoulder and spread across her breasts like a star-burst, making her feel like a crown jewel. A pin-tuck sash outlined her waist and a generously full skirt fell like a bell to her ankles.

Eleanor admired herself in the mirror. Nervous flutters of excitement coursed through her body like sparks of electricity, heightening her sense of touch. Twisting a wine coloured lipstick she pouted and applied a round of the tint; pressing her lips together to permeate the stain. It was far too bold a shade to wear everyday but she was determined to captivate Gerrard with her lips as soon as he saw her.

Pinning soft waves of hair to each side behind her ears, Eleanor fixed a matching silk rose on one side like the Spanish heroine on a cover of one of her romance books.

Grabbing her black clutch and tucking it under her arm, she collected her co-ordinating strappy bow tie heels from the floor; she would have to put them on once she'd escaped the castle.

Edging herself down the top of the curved handrail she slid slowly backwards, so as to not creak any step. She had enjoyed sliding down the banister many times as a young girl, but never as a young lady dressed in a ball gown.

Dismounting at the other end proved more difficult than expected and in the process she banged her knee quite badly on the end pillar. As much as she wanted to groan in agony, it was vital she restrain herself and conceal any cause for suspicion if her plan was to succeed. Silently gasping she clutched her bruised kneecap and hobbled the rest of the way through the corridor.

One way or another she was determined to slip away unnoticed. The housekeeper and maid had finished for the night and the only other person who might interrupt her escape was the chauffeur. He'd taken Uncle Arthur and Aunt May to the Farmer's Ball already so he wouldn't return until they did.

Eleanor's last hurdle would be the grand staircase. It wasn't clear if Great-Aunt Susan had gone to bed or not until she reached the 2nd floor landing. Light emanated from the library and Eleanor knew that the next thirty seconds could determine her whole future.

She had spent the past week memorising the positions on each step, to avoid any indication that mischief was afoot.

With the final step cleared Eleanor tip-toed across the entrance hall and silently out the front door.

Outside and with freedom attained, Eleanor breathed deeply. Giddy with adrenalin and un-willing to tempt fate, she abandoned her plan to put her shoes on and instead ran like a school girl late for class. She was sure glad she did because just at the very moment she arrived at the road Gerrard's green sports-car pulled over.

"Miss Lockheart? Eleanor?" asked the gentleman inside.

"Yes, that's me."

"Good. I'm James. Gerrard sent us to pick you up."

"Oh, I'm so glad you're here, I only just made it out. If you'd come and gone any sooner I'd have missed you altogether!"

"Get in!" said James, urgently scanning the surrounding roadside and fields.

Eleanor got in the passenger seat and beamed a smile at Lydia seated in the back.

"Lydia! Thank you so much for coming, I've missed you so much. If it weren't for your letters and help with all this I'd still be stuck in that castle." The girls smiled and held each other's hands; grateful to be re-united after a long summer apart.

"It's been terrible at the castle. I have died of boredom more than once and I can't tell you how glad I am to finally be free of it. I've left with nothing but the clothes I'm wearing mind you, but I'm sure Gerrard won't mind fussing over me. I'll have a completely new wardrobe by the end of the week. Just you wait and see."

"I'm sure you will, Miss Lockheart," said James with a sly grin.

They all laughed.

Eleanor waited outside the dance hall while Lydia went inside to let Gerrard know they'd arrived. Eleanor took out her compact mirror to check her make-up and decided some lip gloss was needed. Music echoed from the hall and she was dying to see if her parents were inside. If she could just get herself up to one of the windows she could peek in and check. Eleanor scanned the area for something she could position below a window to stand on. Nothing availed, so she crossed her arms and huffed. A moment later Lydia burst out a rear side door used mainly by caterers and musicians.

"Eleanor, quick. Over here." Lydia whispered gruffly.

"Well, where is he? I should think he'd be eager to see me after all these months. What's taking so long?"

"He's ah...well, he's coming. He's a little busy at the moment. I tried to get his attention, but he, um..." Lydia was stalling and Eleanor sensed something was afoot.

"What? Who's he with, my parents? Are they in there?" Eleanor felt sick playing a guessing game. Why wouldn't Lydia just give her a straight answer?

"Your parents are here, but Gerrard...he's...um..."

"Spit it out - What's he doing?"

"Well he's dancing with someone. I tried - I really did - but I couldn't get his attention."

"What? Who's he dancing with?" Eleanor fumed.

"Just some blonde girl."

"Was she pretty?"

"Yeah, I guess so. But nowhere near as pretty as you, Eleanor," Lydia said. Eleanor wished she couldn't read her friend's face quite so easily. They'd been friends ever since they started school and Lydia had always struggled to lie when being questioned. Eleanor, however, could lie without batting an eyelid which made her seem endearing to others. It was a talent and skill she'd tried to impart to Lydia, but no matter how many attempts she'd made over the years, it was still a skill she had failed to master; evidenced now by the look of discomfort on her best friends face.

"Do you think he doesn't want me anymore, Lydia?" Eleanor's mood changed; her hot headed childish nature smothering all apprehension. "Well if he's not out to see me in the next ten minutes then I'm done waiting! I'll just march right up and give him a piece of my mind! I'll skelp him too if he dare gives me one of those grins." She looked at the ring on her finger, it would be terribly sad to have to return it. Eleanor's heart ached and her hands twisted in battle.

Lydia placed her hands on Eleanor's shoulders and looked her square in the eye. "Gerrard loves you. He wouldn't dream of upsetting you. I'll go get him and this time I won't fail. He'll be standing in front of you before you know it, okay?" Lydia wrapped her in her arms.

"I need to see him, Lydia - and who he's dancing with. I won't marry a man who thinks he can have his own bit of fun on the side. Can you sneak me in?"

"Alright, but keep your head down. We don't want your parents seeing you or the whole evening will be a bust. Stay behind me and when we get to the stage stay behind the curtain, okay?"

Eleanor nodded and the girls shuffled together into the hall from the rear. Lydia left her tucked out of sight and made a beeline straight for Gerrard, disregarding the fact he was still dancing and her actions might draw unwanted attention.

Eleanor caught her breath when she saw who he was dancing with. Elizabeth Stratford.

Elizabeth was a gorgeous girl from Alford. Long ago she had been a childhood friend of Eleanor's but the two had fallen out of kinship over Harrison Flanders. Elizabeth stole Harry from her during summer break, while Eleanor was away on a family holiday. She was heartbroken.

Eleanor clenched her jaw and narrowed her vision on her nemesis. It was no wonder Liz caught his attention, she was dressed in red -

Gerrard's favourite colour - and she had a mouth to match. She was laughing as they twirled around the floor, her pearly whites glossed with Vaseline no doubt. Liz was a terrible flirt and often cast a web of flattery much like her beloved Gerrard did. What irritated Eleanor most though wasn't anything to do with Elizabeth, it was how happy Gerrard looked in her arms. It made her nostrils flare and temples steam. *How dare he!*

Before she noticed that the curtains had pulled further aside leaving her exposed on the stage, a camera flashed - stealing her attention. Less than a minute later Gerrard was by her side.

"Good God, Eleanor, let's get out of here before anyone sees you!" Holding her arm he discretely guided her outside.

"Oh darling, I've missed you so much." He gushed embracing her, placing a fierce kiss on her lips. At once she forgave his transgressions, but resisted letting him know it.

"What were you doing with Elizabeth Stratford?" Eleanor pressed - her face cross. "I saw you dancing with her and you looked to be having a pretty good time of it too." Her cheeks burned and she parted from his embrace. Raising her finger to his face, with a scowl on her own, "I'm not happy Gerrard - we're engaged. How could you dance with another woman?" Her bad temper and infuriated demeanour only fuelled his charm and grins.

"Oh darling, I was just pretending, that's all. Your parents were there and I thought if I danced with another girl they'd think we were over and they'd never suspect us of our plans."

Accepting his desperate excuse she gave in fully to his charisma and believed every word, sad that she had ever doubted his promise to her.

"Come on, we'd better get out of here before anyone spots us and tells your Pa. I'm not fond of the thought I'd take a beating from him tonight. This is our night darling. It's all arranged, you'll see."

Lydia and James stood waiting by the car. Gerrard opened the passenger side for Eleanor and she promptly climbed in to the back seat followed by Lydia. But before Gerrard could get in the car, someone had spotted him.

"What are you doing here, Gerrard? You're not from these parts, so what's your business here?"

Eleanor ducked behind the front seat to hide. It was her brother, Erik.

"Elizabeth asked me to come, Erik. It's not so suspicious for me to be here any more than it is for your Marta."

"Eleanor is glad to be rid of you for sure. She's not for you Gerrard, don't go causing her any trouble now, you hear me!"

Eleanor was stirred by her older brother's care, but she also wanted to scream at him for delaying Gerrard from their plans.

Peaking from behind the car seat, Eleanor watched Gerrard casually walked towards Erik with confidence. "I'm leaving now. So your little Farmer's Ball may continue without the risk of your dear Marta falling in love with me too."

Erik struck him with a punch to the nose.

Eleanor gave a tiny squeal and clapped a hand over her mouth. She ducked out of sight until her brother spoke again.

"Get out, you dirty cheat!" Erik pointed his finger at Gerrard. "And if I **ever** see you around these parts again, I'll do a lot more than break your face."

Gerrard stumbled backwards with his hand wrapped over his nose. James jumped to help him and guided him back to the car.

Erik walked off shaking out his fist. The sound of the band echoed out as the door to the hall opened and closed behind him.

Tears rolled down Eleanor's cheeks. It would probably be the last time she'd ever see her brother. The reality of her decision fully sank in, and her heart twisted in pain.

Eleanor tended to Gerrard, who seemed slightly less than tender towards her now. He sat with his head back against her shoulder while his bloodied nose dripped into his moustache.

"Your brother's a mean brute. I bet he was a bully in school." His scathing words weren't meant to be answered. "Let's go, James." His voice was bitter and dark. It was a side Eleanor had not seen of him before and it frightened her.

James rumbled the engine to life.

Revenge glinted from Gerrard's eyes and a crooked smile thinned his lips. Eleanor wasn't sure whether to laugh or cry. Instead, she muffled the alarm bells ringing in her head and gave a twisted smile of her own. He turned to face her, his mood shifting to the charmer once more.

"Eleanor, from tonight and for the rest of my life, I shall call you Elaine. My dearest Elaine."

And they drove off to Aberdeen to get married.

CHAPTER FOURTEEN

Wednesday 23rd March 2016

Jess

J ESS CLOSED THE album when she heard footsteps coming up the loft stairs.

"And what are you two up to?" Mum asked.

"Um, we've been looking at some of the things in the boxes." Ella was eager to change the subject. "Aunty Vera. Jess and I are working on a history project for school and I was wondering if it would be possible for us to go and visit our friend Joe up at Rattray? His father used to own one of the shipping companies in Aberdeen you see, and his help would really make a difference. We could all go," She said hopefully. "The sand dunes up there are great fun to sled on. Ma and Pa used to take us all the time and I know the boys would love it. It's Easter this weekend and Joe will probably be busy, but maybe we could go next weekend. What do you think?"

"Is that Joseph Naudman?" Mum asked. Jess thought she detected a small glimmer of worry on her mother's face, but it disappeared as soon as she noticed Jess watching her.

"Aye," said Ella.

"Gosh, it's been ages since I last saw him. Do you really need to go and see him though, couldn't you just call him, Ella?"

"It won't work, Mum. We have to do a video report and we can't do that over the phone can we. Ella says Joe is the only person she can think of that we could ask. Besides wouldn't it be nice to go to the beach?" Jess knew her mother loved the seaside and would struggle to say no.

"It does sound like a lovely idea if the weather isn't too bad. It's been a long time since we've been to a beach, aye Jess? Brody was about two when we went to Camber Sands and he loved it. Jess, on the other hand, was very shy of the waves; it took ages for Grant to coax her into the water. Remember those wee red swimmers, Jess, with the black spots? Dad used to call you his little Lady Bug. Hmmm..." Mum sighed and snapped back from the happy memory. "What does Max think?"

"Oh, we haven't asked Pa yet. I thought maybe you could help us to persuade him."

"I guess it'll depend if he has anything important to tend to on the farm. If not then I suppose it's alright with me. Where would we stay?"

"Oh, that won't be a problem, Aunty Vera, Joe owns a bed and breakfast property with lots of rooms. There are three other buildings near his own cottage, they were once the old lighthouse keepers' cottages. Ma used to love going there; we'd spend hours sledding down the dunes and collecting shells." Ella closed her eyes as if to picture it. "Oh, it'll be so much fun, I hope we can go." Ella's eyes fluttered open again, and begged Mum without blinking.

"It does sound lovely, Ella. Let's ask Max at supper tomorrow night, shall we? I'll make his favourite meal, shepherd's pie. Just like our Ma used to make it."

"That reminds me - how come you didn't tell us about Grandma, Mum? Ella says she lives right here in Alford. You never told us she was still alive." Jess could tell from her mother's delayed response she was thinking on her feet for a plausible answer.

"Uh, well, she was just getting so forgetful, and she always got upset with me when I did go and visit her. I used to call her when we were in London, but she never knew who I was, so I just stopped bothering I guess. She moved into the rest home two years ago and I didn't want to take you kids there. I suppose I should go and see her." Mum stared into space as if mulling over her own suggestion.

Jess didn't want to give away their secret visit to Grandma, so she didn't ask her mother anything more. She wished she could have told her how pleased Grandma was to see her. Even though it was Jess who'd been mistaken for her mother. Jess worried. What if Grandma told Mum about the girls visit? Grandma did seem very confused about things, maybe she wouldn't remember. But then, she had remembered a visit from Elaine and Joe as if it were yesterday.

That will have to wait. We need to see what Joe can tell us first.

Saturday 2nd April 2016

Mum's shepherd's pie succeeded where two begging girls might have failed, and the whole family now sat in Uncle Max's van as it sped towards the coast. Joe was expecting them soon after lunch and the boys had been talking non-stop about all the things they wanted to show Brody when they arrived. Ella and Jess weren't quite as enthusiastic with their chatter, given that their late night excitement had drained their respective batteries.

Wild with delightful fantasies about the things they might find at Joe's to unlock, the girls flung questions and answers back and forth across the room, along with clothes they wanted to pack. Ella entertained Jess with a myriad of memories from her visits to Joe's; distracting them both from the task at hand.

"What shall we take?" Jess asked, sitting on the mat with piles of books in front of her.

Lady Ferlie had dropped a stack of albums and books off to the school for the girls. Thinking smartly they'd asked Mrs Jenkins to store them safely, bringing just one home each night, so as not to arouse any suspicion. Jess sat in a sea of books and photo albums. Each had its points of merit, but Jess thought just the ones that directly related to Elaine and Joe should be packed.

"But what if Joe tells us something and we need to check one of the others?" Ella asked. She seemed desperate to have everything with them for the sake of efficiency.

"That will look very obvious, Ella, Our bags will be too big and way too heavy for just one night."

"We're girls. We're supposed to have large bags. Besides, the boys won't bring much.".

"All right, but if Mum or Uncle Max questions us, you'll have to answer for it. And I'm not carrying all of them, let's split them."

"Sure, fine with me." Ella smiled and divided the pile in half. "Here're yours."

"Thanks." Jess took the pile and shoved them in her bag. "I've got the keys."

There were six remaining keys on the ring that they hadn't found a home for yet and Jess was determined to check every single lock they could find at the lighthouse cottages in Rattray. Ella assured her there would be plenty of places to hunt for them and Joe was pretty good about letting them explore anywhere they wished.

With the sun higher in the sky, playing peek-a-boo from behind the clouds, its faint warmth cloaked them in contentment, and the rhythmic motion of the car made them all feel sleepy. Field after field of barley and oats were starting to sprout and the early spring sunshine and rains would work their magic on them in no time.

"Ten more minutes and we'll be there," announced Uncle Max.

His steady driving had sent the inhabitants of the back seats into a wonderful dreamland and the sudden sound of his voice had stirred all but two of them from it - Ella and Brody.

"Wake up, Ella!" shouted Steve. He leaned back and shoved his sister in the leg - too excited to care if she got angry with him or not. "We're nearly there."

"Owwwh, Steve! I was having the most wonderful dream." Ella roused herself fully and looked over at Jess. They exchanged smiles and Jess lent forward to brush a finger over Brody's nose. He roused a little and rubbed his nose. Ella pressed a button which wound down his window and a blast of cold wind snapped him awake.

"Huh, What - where are we?" Brody pulled himself upright in the seat and looked around for someone to blame for his rude awakening. Jack was giggling and Brody gave him a slap on his leg.

"Owww! It wasn't me." Jack pointed to his sister. Brody rubbed his eyes and face, unwilling to confront Ella about the window.

Ella beamed a satisfied smile. "Smell that, Jess. We're nearly there."

Joe exited the little white monopoly house shaped cottage before they'd even pulled to a complete stop. The wind was gusty, but his footing was steady and sure.

"Hello!" He yelled his greeting through the closed windows of the van.

The sliding door burst open and both Jack and Steve jumped out. Running straight for the tall wiry man, they embraced him around the waist with grins as wide as their arms.

Joe's sandy brown hair thrashed about in the wind and looked quite unkempt due to its length and fullness. His blue eyes matched the plaid shirt he wore; unbuttoned at the neck and sleeves rolled to the elbow. A snug caramel knitted vest clung to his torso, and brown trousers flapped about his legs in the wind.

Uncle Max got out and went to greet his old friend with an extended hand and a grin. "Joe. It's been a while."

Returning the sentiment, Joe smiled, grasped Uncle Max's hand firmly and took him in for a hug; patting him soundly on the back.

"Aye, too long. It's good to see ye." Joe ruffled Jack's hair. "Look at ye Jack, ye've grown at least another three inches since I saw ye last. Aye, and where's ye'r sister?"

"Here I am, Joe!" Ella leapt towards him for a hug; barely touching the ground thanks to the wind. Joe caught hold of her before she could be blown over.

"Well, well, my you're a wee young lady now. Ye look more and more like your mother every time I see you. And your hair, it's so long. You'll have trouble keeping it from tangling if this wind keeps up. Come in, come in. Let's get you out of it shall we?" Joe ushered the party of seven into his little cottage and out of the weather.

"I've some bed and breakfast guests in the big house this weekend, so I hope you won't mind staying in the other wee cottage girls. It's the one with the red door over there, Vera." He pointed it out to her.

Jess was surprised by the familiarity between her mother and Joe as he spoke, and wondered how well they knew each other. Clearly, quite well, judging by her mother's smile when she looked at him. A nagging worry clawed her mind momentarily before she dismissed the thought as ridiculous.

"There's a kitchen and bathroom, and the living area should provide enough room for ye all, so not to worry there. And Max, if you and the boys are happy to, you can stay up in the hostel. The boys can sleep in one room, and Max, you can have a room to ye'self if ye prefer. There's an Australian couple staying in the south end tonight, but they leave tomorrow, and a pair of young ladies hiking the trail should arrive late tomorrow afternoon - so they told me," said Joe, pleased to inform everyone of their accommodations.

"Aaawe, can't we stay with you, Joe?" said Jack.

"Well, I'd have liked that very much, Jack, but I think we might be too crowded if all five of us lads tried to sleep in here, don't ye think? You'll like the hostel, it has bunk beds and ye can see for miles from the upstairs windows."

"I guess," said Jack disappointedly.

"Come on Jack, It'll be fun," said Brody. "We'll pretend we're Pirates. You can keep a look out from the crow's nest and alert us of any invaders. I'll be the captain, and Steve, you can be the first mate." The boys kept a look out towards the hostel, announcing whatever they could see from inside the small window of Joe's cottage.

"Sounds like you keep very busy here, Joe," said Mum. "It's good to see you again and very kind of you to put us up like this. Ella says you're more like family than just friends. I'm sure Max feels the same."

"Well we've certainly had some laughs over the year's aye, Joe?" Uncle Max patted Joe on the shoulder.

"To be sure, we have indeed. I'd say there are probably still some very upset Italian ladies who curse our very names for stealing their flowers that summer."

"Ooooh, I'd like to hear that story," Mum took a seat at Joe's table.

"Can I take Brody to the beach, Pa?" asked Steve. "I wanna show him the dunes and we're gonna go look for treasure."

"Sure, but take Jack with you and stay out of the water until we get there. Promise?" He gave Steve a stern look.

"Sure thing, Pa, we'll just stick to the dunes."

"Well, just stay on the paths, boys. You don't wanna go upsetting any nests" said Joe.

"Yup, we won't. I mean, we will - stick to the paths," said Steve.

"What kinds of birds are there, Joe?" asked Brody.

Steve butted in before Joe could answer.

"Who cares, come on." He flung open the cottage door and all three ran off towards the beach.

"You girls going to go too?" Mum asked.

"Maybe after we've unpacked. I wanna show Jess the old store room," said Ella.

"Alright, I might come take a look too if you don't mind. I'm curious to check this place out as much as everyone else." Mum opened the cottage door, "But let's unpack the van first, shall we?"

Mum marched towards the van planting her feet as solidly as she could amidst the blustery assault.

Uncle Max, Joe, and the girls followed trying to face themselves into the wind. Gusts whipped about hair and limbs making the whole process look quite comical. Mum grabbed hold of Jess's bag and soon realised it wasn't about to budge without considerable effort. Heaving it with all her might, she managed to grunt, "Here, Jess, cor…What have you got in there? Lead weights?"

"Um…"

"It's just books, Aunty Vera. We bought some school work with us to do, remember… for our project that we've got to talk to Joe about?" Ella interjected, half yelling as the wind stole her words.

"Well, don't work too hard girls. Make sure you have a little fun too."

"This *is* fun, Aunty Vera." Ella faked her ease at holding her bag. "We'll just need some quiet time, without the boys around to talk to Joe. Think you can help us?"

"Oh sure. I'll head over to the hostel after I've dumped this. Max and I'll take the boys for a good walk along the beach. That'll tire them out." She smiled to herself at the thought.

After a short tipsy trek, Ella opened the red cottage door and ushered Mum and Jess inside. Mum looked around with interest at the dark timber roof beams and quaint cottage décor. Duck egg blue cushions dotted two cream covered sofas, and the nautical touches of rope, sail boats, and oars created a cohesive maritime theme.

"Ooo, it's lovely. This reminds me of my honeymoon in Portugal with your father, Jess."

Jess wasn't sure she wanted to know anything more about that subject and beckoned Ella to say something, and quick.

"Why don't you take the master room, Aunty Vera?" Ella opened the door and let Mum take a look. A stark contrast to the living area, it contained one very pink floral queen size bed and two bedside tables.

"It's definitely not Portugal in here," Mum said, tossing her bag on the bed. She wasted no time unpacking and quickly pulled on her jacket and headed for the door. "We'll be a few hours, girls, so make the most of it." Mum marched off towards the hostel.

"Good she's gone," said Jess.

Ella smiled. "Let's go find Joe before he gets busy with anything else or decides to go with the others."

"Good thinking. We've got a lot to search by the looks of it and the sooner we start, the better chance we'll have of finding…well - something." Jess really wasn't sure what they'd find, but at the very least, was certain it would be something.

Joe was over at the hostel helping Uncle Max with the bags and it looked like they'd just finished. Uncle Max headed for the beach to join Mum and the boys and Joe looked like he was going too.

With desperate urgency the girls called out, "Joe! Joe!" gesturing him with a wave to come over to them.

Joe broke into a jog, looking back over his shoulder towards the beach. "Aye, what do ye need, Ella?"

"Could we talk to you for a bit, Joe? We have some questions about a project we're doing at school and we could really use your help." Ella batted her eyes innocently and Jess wondered if Joe would fall for it.

"Well, I'd be glad to, girls. I did tell Max I'd join them though." He looked hesitantly at them.

"Don't worry, Joe, my mum knows that we need to work on this, so she said she'd keep the boys entertained for a few hours so we could concentrate. She'll tell Uncle Max why you didn't come."

"Well alright, I guess that'll be fine then,"

"Can we go to your cottage, Joe? I've missed this place and I love your sitting room, it's so cosy."

"Are you sure? It's a bit messy in there."

Ella's look of insistence paid off.

"Alright, that'll be fine I guess. I'll make us a nice pot of tea."

Ella smiled and nodded. "We'll just get our books and be over in a minute."

Joe left for his cottage and Jess flashed a triumphant smile.

"I kinda feel guilty about lying to him, Jess. I hope he won't be mad at us."

"He doesn't strike me as the kind who'd get mad, Ella. You'll see, everything will work out fine."

Jess had reluctantly agreed to tell Joe the whole story once they were here in person. She just hoped he'd go along with keeping it secret. If he wouldn't keep quiet, they'd have to resort to plan B - emotional blackmail. Ella hated the thought of using her mother's memory in that way. Jess just prayed they wouldn't have to.

Comfortably seated on Joe's old brown leather sofa, Jess pulled out the Lockheart family album. The recollection of the moment they'd found it in the loft made Jess shudder when she pictured the fox staring up at her.

Ella took the album and chewed her bottom lip. "Joe, I'm sorry to have mis-led you, but we're not really here to talk about a school project."

"No? Well, what is it then?" He looked concerned.

"Oh, it's nothing to worry about. Jess and I have been sleeping up in the loft back on the farm and we came across this." Ella held the album out to him. Joe took it and opened it to the first page.

"Och, that's real fine isn't it." Joe said it like he were commenting on a piece of art Ella had drawn herself.

Jess giggled. Ella squinted at her then smiled at Joe.

"There's a lot more to it, Joe. In the loft we found a box too, and inside it, we found this."

Ella handed him Elaine's blue journal. Joe's eyes widened in recognition of it and he became quite reserved.

"It's me mother's journal." He stood and paced the room, turning the journal in his hands. "But how did it get in your loft?"

Jess rummaged inside her bag. "Well that's not all we found. We also found these magazine clippings and this baby's gown." She held it carefully in her hands with the keys wrapped inside. Joe didn't seem too interested in it and focused on the journal.

"I remember me mother writing in this journal. She hid it from me father because if he'd found it, he would have beaten her." Joe's eyes darkened and Jess was shocked by his abrupt honesty.

"We have a lot of questions, Joe, but we also have some answers too. Perhaps even ones you may not know yourself." Ella took the journal from Joe and motioned he take a seat.

Over the next hour, they told him everything; from their visit to see Grandma to the deceptive plot to get to Castle Ferlie without their parents finding out. Joe was very surprised to hear about the keys unlocking the writing desk at the castle and he asked to take a look at them.

Jess unwrapped them carefully to show him while they both told him about their surreal experiences when touching the keys. He thought it was very unusual.

"But where did the keys come from?" He asked.

"We don't know, we thought you might," said Ella. "See, the last person to have the journal was Aunt Flo. I'm guessing she gave it to Ma when she became too ill and that's how it ended up in our loft."

"Do you have the box?" Joe asked.

"Yes, it's in the cottage. Do you want to see it?" asked Ella.

"If it's really colourful with writings all over it, then no. I know where it came from; it was Flo's box. She used to keep her research in a box like that. She had it with her at the hospital near the end." Tears welled in the corners of his eyes and Jess could see Ella's empathy for him.

"I'm sorry, Joe, we didn't mean to make you feel badly. I've got some wonderful news for you though. I've been saving it till last. See when we told you about Eleanor being stuck at the castle and planning to run away with her boyfriend, what we didn't mention was that his name was Gerrard Naudman." Ella's excitement was about to burst. "You know what that means?" She expected he'd realise immediately, but when Joe didn't show any sign of comprehension, Ella explained further. "It means that Eleanor Lockheart was Elaine - **YOUR** mother, Joe."

Ella thrust the printed piece of paper from the ancestry website which proved Eleanor was Elaine.

"Your Ma was our grandpa's sister; you and Pa are cousins." Ella's eyes sparkled - just like Aunt Gabby's used to. "That makes you my second cousin. Isn't that wonderful Joe? I've been so excited to tell you about it ever since we found out, but Jess convinced me to wait till we could tell you in person. You see, we don't want Pa and Aunty Vera to know just yet. We've much more of the mystery to solve and the rest of these keys to find locks for."

Joe looked astonished and tried to take it all in. "I knew Flo was researching me family heritage, ancestry was always a fascination of hers; to think she came so close, but couldn't piece it together. Och, I am grateful girls and very pleased to find there's an actual link to Max. But it'll be hard not to tell him. Don't you think he ought to know?" He looked earnestly at Ella.

"Well yes, we do Joe," Jess interjected. "But please - can we just have a little bit more time on it? We had hoped to look around here and see if there are any locked doors or cabinets you might have. Did your mother leave you any boxes or furniture, Joe?"

"I see...well, let me think. I did put some of her things in the big house for decoration. And there was a wardrobe I put in the hostel, but that's not locked. I mean it has a key hole, but I don't recall it ever having a key. When she died I put some of her boxes and things in the storage shed, ye've been in there Ella. Ye know where it is. Mmmmm, keys?" He sat contemplating the question. "I do remember Flo and I found a key once. It looked similar to that padlock one there on your ring. I found it in the cottage you're staying in. I assumed it was left behind by some guest. I gave it to Flo to follow up.

"Ma had been staying with us that weekend. In fact, now that I think about it, she's the one who said she'd found it in the cottage if me memory serves correctly."

"Maybe it was her key all along," said Jess excitedly. "Maybe she locked something in the cottage and left it there for you or Flo to find?"

"Why would she do that? Why wouldn't she just give it to me?" asked Joe.

"I dunno, she must have had a good reason. Maybe it was too difficult for her to share with you," said Ella.

"Well, why didn't she tell Flo then? She loved Flo like she were her own daughter. I was so pleased that she did because I never would have married anyone that Ma didn't like." He smiled.

"That's it." said Jess, "You said it yourself. I think maybe she did tell Flo. And I think that Flo found where the key belonged. I wonder if it's still there in the cottage?"

Jess leapt up to go and start looking immediately but Ella stopped her.

"Wait. What if what Flo found, were the keys and this baby's gown? Maybe that's how they came to be in that box in the loft."

"You might be right, Ella. Come on - let's go see."

Joe stood. "Well don't let me stop you girls. Go take a look and keep me posted."

"Oh, we will, Joe. And before we leave tomorrow, if we haven't found anything more, then we'll tell Mum and Uncle Max the whole story, okay?" Jess crossed her fingers behind her back. She only wanted to tell *half* the story if she could get away with it.

"Good. I'll be mighty pleased not to have to keep that secret too long. It's such a warmth to me heart to know that I have a cousin. Me Pa was an only child see, and Ma never really talked about her family upbringing. I guess that means that your Grandma Marta is me Aunty, and Vera's me cousin too."

Joe's last comment disturbed Jess more than expected and she couldn't understand why. With no time to waste, the girls headed straight for the cottage and left Joe to piece all the family ties together.

CHAPTER FIFTEEN

16th September 2007

Elaine

ELAINE STOOD BY the open red door to the lighthouse keeper's cottage in Rattray Heads. Gusts of wind chased invisible wisps about the dunes and the last of the summer tourists were scarce about the property. Her son was busy fixing a door latch on the hostel and Flo was headed towards her with a tray full of breakfast.

Elaine was tired and although the fresh salty air had done her good, she still had an ache in her heart. Seeing Joseph and Flo so happy together had finally put her worries about her son to rest. But it also stirred up the memory of the lost girl she had never had the chance to know, Joanna. What would she have been like? Would she look like her? Elaine wished more than anything to find her, but time was no longer on her side. Her health was not as good as it should be, and she wasn't willing to let anyone know it, especially Joseph. She was dying and the doctors said she had six months maybe, if she was lucky. At least Flo would be here to take care of Joseph and that helped ease her mind a little.

"Hello Flo, Oh thank you dear. Are you feeling any better today? You looked a little pale yesterday and you're looking thinner than ever. Are you sure you've nothing to tell me?" She winked at her and smiled. She thought Flo might be pregnant and suffering from morning sickness.

Flo set the tray down on the dining table. "I'm alright. The summer's been really busy and I've been run off my feet that's all. I just need a nice long quiet winter to rest up. How about you? You took a long rest yourself yesterday afternoon."

"Well I've a bit of driving to do today and I'm not as well as I should be, but I'll be fine." She reassured Flo as best as she could. "I'm so glad to see you and Joseph so happy together. It sets a mother's mind at ease to know that her child will be loved by another as much as she has loved him in his youth. I dare say that you'll have made your mother a lot happier than I ever did mine. I made such trouble for her."

"I've never heard you mention your parents before, what were they like?" asked Flo.

"Oh, I never really knew them much myself." Elaine knew it was a half-truth, but it was all she could say. "Now…I have something special to tell you, Flo. Come sit with me." She motioned to the sofa. "I once had a little girl you know. I only ever saw her once. Oh, how I wish I could have met her now. She was born the same night as Joseph."

Flo looked at her astonished.

"Joe's a twin? - I never knew that. He never told me so himself that is."

"Well, he might not remember. He was very young when I took him to visit the grave, but after a while I stopped taking him there. I didn't want him growing up thinking that he was never enough for me. He was a good wee boy, he helped me immensely in those early years of marriage. I don't know where I'd be if it weren't for him. His father, as you know, was not a very nice man and I regretted marrying so young. I could have saved myself and my parents a lot of trouble if I'd just listened to them. But youth is fraught with foolish arrogance, one mistake can lead you down a path you'd not expected. I'm sure you can understand that yourself to a degree.

"Now…I want you to have my journal. I've kept it ever since Joseph was born. If there's anything of help to you in it, then you must use it. Joseph was a good baby, although he did have a short spell of colic, which I nursed him through. There are some other things I want you to have and I've left them in a box under the bed - It's locked."

Elaine smiled with a sneaky look on her face. "I love locked things, it makes you feel like you can keep a secret buried for all eternity and perhaps some are if ever the key is lost. But there's something quite mysterious about a locked box or cupboard or a shed. The anticipation of what you might find is all the more to relish, don't you think? I know it'll drive you mad to know, but I'll send you the key when I hear some good news from you both." Elaine winked at her. "Some things are best kept between us women" - Elaine paused and looked desperately into Flo's eyes - "Got it?" Flo nodded but Elaine wasn't convinced she had understood what she really meant. She'd have to find another way - somehow.

Elaine went to the dining table to eat her breakfast. "Well, I'm off home after this. And I shall miss you both dearly. I know you're coming for Christmas, so I shall look forward to seeing you then."

Flo got up and headed for the door, leaving Elaine to enjoy her breakfast in peace.

"Yes Christmas." Flo's tone was weak and conveyed not an ounce of excitement. "Well, I have a pile of sheets to wash and dry before the days end and then Joe and I are going to run some errands into town. Are you sure you'll be alright to drive home?"

"Yes, I'll be fine." Elaine livened up her eyes as best she could. Flo kissed her on the cheek and slipped out the door.

Elaine had hoped the thought of a locked box in the cottage would peak Flo's curiosity enough to go looking for it. But if her suspicions of Flo being pregnant were incorrect, would she even bother?

Elaine felt a weight in her heart. *Something's not right - What aren't they telling me?*

Elaine sat quietly and ate her breakfast. She looked at her bag.

What should I do? What if I die before I get the chance to give the key to Flo? I have to leave some clue for Joseph, some hope, or else it'll all have been for nothing. I suppose I could leave the key for the solicitor to pass on. The thought made her uncomfortable. It wasn't quite the personal touch she had hoped to give Flo.

Anxious that her time was shorter than expected she decided to leave one of the padlock keys here before she left, but where? How could she make sure it got into the right hands?

She slipped one of the keys off the ring and tucked it in her pocket. When Joseph came to load her bags into the car she slipped the spare key, still on the ring, into her handbag pocket.

Joseph opened his arms to hug her goodbye.

"Goodbye, my dear. I've had a lovely time visiting. You take good care of Flo and make sure she doesn't work too hard. She's a good girl and I'm so very proud of you both. I'll see you at Christmas... Oh, I almost forgot." Elaine retrieved the key from her pocket. "I found this key in the cottage. It's probably been left behind by another guest at some point. Give it to Flo, she'll know how to track down the owner."

"Okay, I will. Bye Ma. It's been good to see ye. Look after ye'self and take care on the drive back home. I'll give you a call this evening to make sure you got home alright. Okay?"

"Alright, thank you, dear. Don't forget about that key will you." Elaine hopped in the car and drove down the rutted dirt road, giving a short wave at the gate.

Flo

Joe came inside to wash his hands for lunch. "How are ye today, Sweetheart? Coping alright?" He asked, wrapping his hands about her waist and placing a kiss on her cheek.

"I'm fine I suppose. The medication isn't helping much with the pain anymore though." Flo shook the water from the lettuce leaves and sliced them into chunks.

"I'm not sure if I'll be up to a trip into town later. Do you mind?"

"Och, no that's fine, you rest. Perhaps we need to go and see Doctor Flynn again. He could increase the dose maybe? I don't want to think we've reached the end of our options, just yet."

Joe set about helping with the remaining lunch prep and then lay out two of the new plates they received as a wedding gift. Flo picked the cutlery from the drawer and delivered them to the table, along with the bowl of salad and a plate of cold meat.

Taking their seats, she clasped her hands and lowered her head.

"Dear Lord. Thank you for Elaine's visit. May you keep her safe as she journeys home today. Thank you for the food before us which thou hast provided and bless it to our bodies, Amen."

"Amen," agreed Joseph. "Oh, that reminds me. Ma found this in her cottage." Joe placed the key on the table. "She said to give it to you. A past guest must have dropped it; think you might be able to track down its owner? It should be in the ledger. Who was in there last, can you remember?"

Flo did her best not to show any kind of recognition or excitement about the key. "Leave it to me, Joe, I'll sort it out." Flo picked it up and put it in her pocket. A light flutter circled her stomach and she instinctively placed a hand there. If only the sensation wasn't simply nauseous excitement over a key.

She and Joe spent six months trying for a baby and were desperate to share some good news with everyone. But sadly, they received a devastating diagnosis instead. Flo had been racked with guilt over it all summer. But Joe had been so good about it and had kept any personal disappointment about their situation to himself. He was so strong. He deserved to be a father. He would have been so good at it too.

Tears welled in her eyes once again and Joe took her into his arms, like he always did, and hushed her painful thoughts away. He led her to their bed to rest, stroking her hair until she calmed.

"Here. Take these." He handed her two powerful pain relief tablets and a glass of water. She took them, swallowed hard and lay her head back on the pillow. "I won't be long, Sweetheart, just an hour or so. Okay? Back soon."

Joe bent to kiss her and she gave him a faint smile of hope to take with him. He touched her hand and then he left.

Although she was tired, Flo was determined to find the box Elaine had left in the cottage for her, even if it only contained items relating to babies. It was true, there was something about a locked box that lifted her spirits and now that the nausea had subsided she felt able to move around again. Grabbing her coat she pushed each arm into a sleeve and wrapped it closely about her shrinking frame. Dull clouds had blotted out any earlier impressions of sunshine and she was relieved to see that Joe had already brought the washing inside.

Flo marched with added concentration on her feet towards the red door of the cottage. She prayed Joe hadn't locked it before leaving, otherwise she'd have to return to the house for the spare key.

Flo exhaled, audibly relieved when she turned the door knob and it opened. Once inside she went and looked under the bed. Nothing.

What are you up to Elaine?

Then she remembered the other room. As quick as her head and stomach would allow, she made her way there and lowered herself to the floor with care. She felt a little dizzy, but she couldn't stop now. Lifting the bedspread, there, tucked in the darkest corner was a box with a medium size brass padlock on it. It was tricky to reach but with great exertion she eventually managed to retrieve it with the help of a broom from the kitchen. Exhausted she sunk into the sofa.

The key? Where did I put it? In my pocket - Yes that's right.

She felt for it in her pocket and pulled it out.

Like a school girl, ready to tuck into a birthday lunch, she placed the key in the padlock and turned until it swung open. She lifted the lid. A simple folded note sat on top of a number of other items. She picked it up and read it aloud to herself:

Dear Florence,

The items inside the box are just for you. I hope you will keep them safe and treasure them always, including the journal I gave you. Maybe you'll have more luck than I did piecing it all together. It would put my mind at ease to know you continued on searching. And maybe, Joe might one day know the truth about Joanna. Please don't ask me to explain any further. It's too painful. I have made my peace with it all. I can only hope that maybe this will help Joe in the future somehow.

All my love,

Elaine.

Flo picked up the other items in the box, a pile of magazine clippings of old advertisements were scattered in the bottom. Sitting on top of them was a baby's gown with a pink embroidered bow at the neck. Tears formed in the corners of her eyes. She unwrapped it carefully noticing there was something encased inside it.

"Keys?" She said aloud. "Oh Elaine, what sort of game are you playing at?" She removed the items and replaced the lock on the box. She wasn't sure why, but she shoved the box back under the bed. Telling herself, that if it remained in situ, it would be as if nothing had changed. And, if Elaine visited again, maybe she might add some more clues.

More suspense and questions would arise than answers from her find over the coming weeks. But nothing, not even a mystery to solve, would help her battle the aggressive ovarian cancer in the coming months.

Elaine's mystery box proved a wonderful distraction and Flo was grateful to have a reason to fight for another day, even if it was from the confines of a hospital bed. She knew it was important. And until the last breath left her body, she'd do whatever she could to find answers.

2nd April 2016
Ella

"Found it!" called Ella. She squirmed under the bed and retrieved the box. It was about the size of a large shoe box and a brass padlock sat holding the two halves of it secure. "Where are the keys? Did you bring them?"

Jess pulled them from her pocket. "Yes. Put it on the bed and let's take a look."

Ella picked herself up from the floor and placed the box in front of Jess. Looking at the keys, they both knew the flat brass key was the only one that would fit.

Inserting it, Jess turned the lock until the metal shackle popped up and she swung it free from the box loops. Opening it revealed two handwritten notes. Ella recognised the paper as being from the journal; it was folded into quarters. The other had the floaty style of writing on it and was folded in half neatly - just like the one they'd found in the desk at the castle.

"Read that one, Jess," She pointed at the one folded in half.

Jess picked up the note and read aloud.

"Joseph,

I don't know if you'll ever find this, but if you do, then perhaps you have found the original contents of this box. Inside it, I left a number of clues regarding your father and a set of keys wrapped in a baby's nightgown which I made for your sister. I left them here for Flo and I had hoped she would be able to help you find your missing sister, Joanna. When I'm gone, my belongings will no doubt end up in your care. I beseech you to not throw away the old Naudman shipping crate. I know your father has

hurt you immensely over the years, and I'm determined that someone should find out the truth about poor wee Joanna and what became of her. I love you my darling boy and I always will,
Ma.

It's dated November 20th, 2007," finished Jess.

"That's only a couple of days after Aunty Flo died. Read the other one. What does it say?" asked Ella.

<u>Sunday 16th September 2007</u>.

Elaine left yesterday and gave me this, her Journal. It is most interesting and has me very perplexed. She told me Joseph was a twin and had a sister. Elaine said she'd only seen her once when she was born. What happened to her I wonder? She mentioned taking Joseph to visit the grave but stopped doing so around the time he started school. Why? I need to find out who Elaine's and Gerrard's parents were. Maybe they knew something of the baby girl and where I could find her gravestone. Gerrard has long since passed away. According to Joseph he was a terrible man who hit his mother and whipped him whenever he got angry. Elaine said something that gives me the chills. She said that she - *'wished she could have met Joanna now'*. What an odd thing to say about a child that died long ago. I guess it's probably the wish of many parents who lose their children before they're grown. But what if Joanna didn't die? Elaine mentioned in her note that she wanted me to 'Piece it all together and find out the truth about Joanna'. I'm not sure how I'll manage to do it, but I'll try. Elaine. If you read this I'm sorry if I have failed you. I don't have long to live and I'm not sure who I could pass this onto to keep searching. I understand why you didn't give it to Joseph. He probably would say 'leave the skeletons in the closet.' But a mother would never give up hope I guess.

<u>Wednesday 19th September 2007</u>

I'm booked in for a Chemo treatment in the city next Tuesday. Gabby is going to come with me. Perhaps she can help me solve this mystery.

"That's it. That's all it says," said Jess.

"Wow, that's a lot to take in. Read that bit again where she says that Joanna might not be dead."

"She said that she 'wished she could have met Joanna now.' Flo also said that she guessed it's 'probably what many parents wish for when they lose a child. But what if Joanna didn't die?' It says, 'Elaine mentioned in her note that she wanted me to 'Piece it all together and find out the truth about Joanna'." Jess folded the note and looked at her. "So I guess it's up to us now. It's obvious Flo gave this to your mother to continue with, but I guess she never did."

Ella didn't like what Jess was implying. "Well, she might have tried. Steve was just a toddler when Aunty Flo died, and then Jack came along soon after. She wouldn't have had a lot of spare time you know."

"Oh yes, Ella, I didn't mean that she hadn't tried. Your Ma was there helping Flo with the research when she was sick and I'm sure she knew how important it was to her and Joe. She probably just got busy. Your family and farm wouldn't have run on its own without her."

"Well, we've been managing perfectly fine thank you." Now her feelings really were hurt. She'd looked after Pa and her brother's since she was eight, and she thought she'd done a pretty good job at it so far. Jess hadn't a clue what it was like to live in her shoes. Although Ella's pride was a little bruised, her feelings would have to wait. She was not about to let them stand in the way of a new lead.

"Anyway - how did these two letters come to be in this box do you suppose?"

"Well, look here at the Journal. See a page has been torn out. I think Flo wrote about what she found and then left the page in the box again for Elaine to find if she came back to the cottage after she had died. She did, didn't she? You told me Joe's mother came to stay with him after Flo passed away."

"Oh yeah, she did. I never met Joe's Ma because she was unwell and couldn't come to Flo's funeral."

"My guess is, that when Elaine came here she must have added her note to the box."

"But if Aunty Flo had the key to this box, and then gave it to Ma, how did Elaine unlock the box?"

"Perhaps she had another key for the padlock. You often get two when you buy them, in case you lose one."

"Oh yeah - you're right, Jess. Well if Elaine's belongings were left to Joe, we better go ask him if we can take a look around for them."

Jess nodded. "Particularly that Naudman shipping crate she mentions. It must be important and I bet one of these keys is going to open it."

Ella wished she could wipe her cousin's satisfied smile off her face, but for now she'd go along with the excitement.

"Well, we still don't know where these keys came from, but I'm betting Elaine had something to do with it"

Excited by the new information they had found, the girls ran with the letters back to Joe's cottage. He was busy in the kitchen chopping vegetables for what looked to become a very hearty stew.

"Joe we've found some notes. Here - this one's from your Ma. Read it." Ella thrust the piece of paper in front of his face. His startled look then eager response gave her a feeling of success.

Wiping his hands on the already dirty hand towel he went to the sofa to find his reading glasses on the side table. He scanned the note silently.

"Och my - Girls!"

He sat on the couch and stared at it for a long time reading it over slowly. Finally, he stirred and looked up at them with disbelief.

"I'm speechless. Eight years, and it's been there all this time."

"Do you still have the shipping crate, Joe?" asked Ella. "I mean, it must have been important if she wanted you to keep it. Perhaps one of the keys will open it."

"Have you thought of anything else your mother might have brought with a lock on it when she came to stay with you after Flo died?" asked Jess.

Ella flashed her a look of disgust at the blunt question about Joe's mother and wife.

"Sorry, I didn't mean to be rude, Joe," Jess rushed her apology.

"Och that's alright lass, Ma and Flo have been gone a wee while now, but this note just brings back a flood of memories is all. The crate is in the store room. Like I said, Ella, you know where it is. The shed's unlocked so you won't be needing your keys for that, but the crate I believe could be, so take 'em with you."

"Thanks, Joe. We also found this note too. Well, it's a journal entry really, but Aunty Flo wrote it."

Ella placed the unfolded piece of paper in his hands and motioned for Jess to follow her outside.

Out in the blustering wind Ella half-screamed at her cousin, "Come on let's go find that crate before the others return from the beach. We're running out of time!"

Jess's hair completely lost its way in the wind and slapped her about the face mercilessly. Ella loved watching her struggle to regain her control of it. Nature had a way of dealing its own form of justice.

CHAPTER SIXTEEN

Jess

OPENING THE DOOR to the shed, it was dark and dusty and they soon wished they'd brought a torch.

"I'll run back to the cottage and get one." Ella took off before Jess could argue with her.

Standing alone in the eerie shed with garden implements and years of stored junk all around her, Jess felt uneasy. She reached for the keys wrapped in her pocket and took them out. Unwrapping them, she made a guess which key might unlock the crate, and on a whim, she touched it…

… Jess looked into the distance. A woman kneeled next to a dug out hole in the ground with a shovel abandoned to one side. A small white wooden box smeared with dirt sat close by.

The sun had set a while ago and the clear sky radiated purple-pink hues all around. The long grassy fields had dulled to a sombre pale brown and branches of willow danced in the breeze behind her.

The woman's hands were muddied and her tear stained cheeks looked red against her pale complexion. She looked all around - as if scared she might be seen. Jess then realised what the little white box was.

A coffin.

It wasn't shiny and ornately carved like her Aunt Gabby's one, but on top of the lid was a small wooden cross. The woman seemed too distraught to move at all, but then she took from her pocket a key and started to unlock the box...

Frightened by what she was seeing Jess screamed.

"What is it?" Ella panted at the shed door trying to catch her breath. "Did you see a rat or something?"

"No" - Jess turned to look her cousin in the eyes - "Something much worse!"

7th October 1988
Elaine

Elaine was anxious for her husband to leave. Gerrard had been awfully preoccupied lately and as the summer days hurried towards autumn, he'd only gotten worse. His temper grew short, his dress became rumpled and he seemed to be spending more hours at the office than he ever spent at home.

'Business isn't good' he'd told her.

With another of his business trips to Denmark planned, he would miss Joseph's high school basketball game for the third time.

"Why do you need to take another trip so soon?" She had queried, trying to determine if the story he told bore any truth.

When they first returned to Aberdeen, after their year spent in Copenhagen, his business trips back to Denmark seemed perfectly normal. She would wish him well and eagerly await his return and the inevitable gift he would bring back for her. Their first year of marriage, was a roller coaster of lovesick emotions and major arguments. Each instance, resulting in passionate apologies, expensive jewellery and a plateful of flattery - Gerrard's star talent.

But over the last ten years Elaine's desire for such superficial expressions of his love had waned, and Gerrard's interest in keeping her happy with trinkets had been abandoned as well.

Elaine had done her duty, looking after Joseph and keeping things running smoothly while Gerrard was away. She would do everything he asked her to and keep up their social engagements during his absence - not the easiest task for a practically solo parent.

But in the last two years Gerrard's trips had become more frequent and his reasons less believable. She suspected her husband was keeping something from her and she couldn't wait for him to leave so she could find out what it was.

The blue letters had stopped coming from Denmark, but in their place white ones now came from Paris. Elaine could see they were from the same person because of the handwriting. She dare not ask him about it though. The last time she made an inquiry, he'd left her with black and blue marks up her arms and a swollen eye from the back of his hand. She told Joseph she'd fallen down the stairs. Even at seven, he didn't believe her, but he never said anything more.

Now in her thirties, she had grown more cunning than the innocent doe she once was as a teenager. Just as Gerrard had tried to keep his life more private from his wife, Elaine became just as crafty at finding the trail of breadcrumbs he left behind.

She would take note of the magazine and newspaper pages he'd leave open on his desk, cutting them out once he'd discarded them. She kept a written record of dates and times he had come and gone, even if it was just to get something from town for her. She had even tried to follow him one day after picking Joseph up from school, but her attempts to be stealthy failed when he called out to his father as they walked down the street. She gave an excuse of needing to get Joseph new socks for school, which seemed to satisfy him.

After that, she had attempted once more to follow him to town while Joseph was at school. But all he'd done, was go to work at his father's shipping company. She'd given up by 3 o'clock and went to collect Joseph from school.

It wasn't until she took Gerrard's smartest navy blue suit to the dry-cleaners, after he returned from his last trip, that she got a solid clue.

Mr Anderson, their usual dry-cleaner, was apparently ill and a new clerk, named John, stood in his place behind the counter.

Taking the suit from Elaine he inspected the marks on the collar and then asked if she had checked the pockets.

No, she hadn't.

He promptly emptied them onto the counter and she gathered the items. A couple bits of paper, some coins and a matchbook from the Normandy Hotel in Paris.

The coins were French and the folded piece of paper was his boarding pass - to Paris.

But Gerrard hadn't been to Paris on the 16th September. He only ever told her he went to Denmark.

Elaine tucked them into her writing desk when she returned home that afternoon and never broached the subject with Gerrard for her own safety. He was definitely up to something and now that he was leaving again she would have time to do some digging.

Dropping Gerrard at the airport was her usual practice, but today he'd decided to take the shuttle. She'd told him it was completely unnecessary, trying to play her best at pretending she didn't mind taking him. But this time he flat out refused and stubbornly stuck to his plan. She wasn't about to argue, and gave a practical farewell without any sentiments of love. "Travel safe, See you Sunday."

Waving from the front door Elaine exhaled deeply when the shuttle left at 8:00am. It was Friday and a whole weekend ahead without Gerrard cheered her spirits immensely. Elaine hurried to get Joseph off to school. Pulling out of the school's parking lot, a satisfied grin caught the corners of her lips; she was finally free to search their home at her leisure. But today, leisure was not something Elaine would allow herself to consider. She had one goal - find as many clues as possible about what Gerrard was hiding and preferably without any evidence of having done so.

Entering his office she went straight to his desk and tried all the drawers. Only the bottom two opened - the top one was stuck. She fingered through files and papers in the two bottom drawers and found nothing notable.

Turning her attention to the top drawer she noticed it had a hole for a key. She searched the desk surface and other various cabinets and shelves for it - but nothing.

Taking a pin from her hair she attempted to jimmy it open like she'd seen them do in movies, but she had no clue what she was doing. Elaine worried she might damage it and then Gerrard would know it had been tampered with.

She resumed her search for the key, checking every object in the room thoroughly. She was about to give up when she glanced over at the framed photograph of wee Joseph sitting on the desk. He was standing next to his go-cart he'd gotten for Christmas when he was nine. She picked it up to study it closely. As she did, she noticed that the stand would not sit flat on the back of it, something was stuck underneath it. She felt up under the stand and sure enough, it was the key.

Quickly she tried it in the lock and the drawer slid open. She lifted the items up carefully one by one and made a mental note of exactly how they were positioned. Tucked at the back were a pile of blue letters with a few of the white ones on top. All of the letters near the top had been placed back in their envelopes, but a number of letters near the bottom weren't. She pulled out the top white letter, it was postmark dated 2nd, June 1980. Opening it, she read

Dear Gerrard,

Thank you for the gift you sent for Elle, she just loves the purple dress and has worn it every day this week. I tell her I'll need to wash it sooner or later and she just says 'Later'. She is doing very well at school and has started to read on her own. Perhaps you could send her one of your favourite childhood books. I have been a little unwell of late, but I feel I am on the mend now. Elle is very much looking forward to your next visit. All our love,
Charlotte.

Elaine went to the first blue letter at the bottom of the pile. Inside was a picture of a pretty woman with blonde hair wearing a yellow gingham dress. Turning it over were the initials C.S 1972 with a lipstick kiss mark. *This must be Charlotte, his mistress maybe?* She read the letter:

Dearest Gerrard,

Oh how I miss you desperately. It feels like the world has dealt me a very cruel blow to take you away from me. How I miss your embrace and your tender kisses. Your father is very mean to forbid you from seeing me anymore. I shall love you always my dearest. If you should ever be able to steal yourself away from your world in Aberdeen, you must know you can escape it with me here in Copenhagen. I know I will never be able to

give you the child you wanted, but don't abandon me forever my love.
I will remain forever yours, and will love you till my last breath,
Charlotte.

Elaine was furious and grew even more so when she saw the date on the letter; 4th of March 1974. Not even a year after she had married Gerrard and just a few months before she had the twins. *So he did have another woman!* Her eyes hardened and her jaw locked tight.

She slipped the letter back and tried one more in the pile. This time the last blue one nearer the top. It had its return address top fold removed. This must have been the envelope she had found in the trash. Gerrard must have retrieved it after she had brought it up with him.

She touched her cheek, remembering the consequences of doing so. Lifting out the letter, she read:

Dear Gerrard.
Thank you for the money you sent. It is most generous of you. As I have not heard from you in a while and since you won't come to see me and the child, I have decided to come to you during the summer. I plan to bring her on the 22nd June. We will arrive on the noon flight. If you are not there to meet us, I will arrive by taxi to your offices in town. I don't want to cause you any trouble, but it's high time you meet Elle and explain yourself.
Regards,
Charlotte.

Elaine thought back. Where was she when Charlotte came to visit? June... She flipped the envelope in her hand and checked the date stamp - 1977. Was that the summer Gerrard suggested she visit her friend Lydia in Glasgow? He'd asked her to take Joseph at the last minute when some important business meeting came up. "So Charlotte must have come…Here?!" The thought of it shocked her and she gazed around the office wondering if this Charlotte woman had been in her house and maybe even her bed!

Although anger pooled in her veins, Elaine couldn't help but be intrigued by the double life her husband had been leading. Against her better judgment she decided to sit down with a cup of tea and read all of the letters in sequence. Even though, as she read each one, they made her cry till her heart ached, she just had to know the truth.

A whirlwind of emotions thoroughly wrecked her body. She struggled to keep them all in check as they poked their ugly heads from beneath her calm exterior. Elaine battled her temper all evening; through Joseph's game, his excitement of their win and through supper as well. Poor Joseph copped more than a few short words from her and she spent most the evening apologising to him. Elaine collapsed on the sofa after he'd finally settled in bed.

Not only had she found the letters in Gerrard's desk, but also a number of drawings, obviously done by the child Charlotte called, Elle.

Although it had never been stated in the letters, Elaine could easily read between the lines that the child was Gerrard's. But she couldn't figure out why or how Charlotte came to be raising the girl. Charlotte, in her own words, had written that she couldn't have children. But then Elaine had heard of other women, diagnosed as barren, who had gone on to have a herd of children to their name. Perhaps Gerrard had yet another mistress who didn't want the child or perhaps even died giving birth! She wouldn't doubt any possibility now that she had read the letters and the depth of his deception was clear.

The whole scenario puzzled her greatly. But with all that she'd learnt, Gerrard's mistress and illegitimate child were not the most puzzling thing she'd found in that drawer. Gerrard had a key in his desk, for what purpose, she did not know. But it was stuffed inside a long envelope with the words Joanna written on the top.

What did it unlock?

All night she battled with the demons in her mind. Joanna lay crying in a cradle somewhere and Elaine, try as she might, just couldn't seem to find her. The echoes of Joanna's cry swam inside the corners of her mind haunting her until daylight finally relieved her of the torment.

Her little girl was buried in a hollow of the field beside their house. Next to it, along the fence line, willow trees swayed as a shield from the wind and wildflowers were left to grow where they wished. She hadn't been to it in years, although it was rare that a day passed that Joanna didn't enter her thoughts.

Joseph will be away for the day, I'll go and visit the grave.

Joseph, in his excitement about the Scouts trip, hadn't noticed how tired and distracted she was and talked non-stop in the car on the way. "It's gonna be great Ma. I get to lead my own team. I think I have four with me: Jase, Mike, Tommy and Matthew. And, if we can reach the top first, Scoutmaster Ben said we'd get an extra ribbon at the finish line."

Joseph was so proud to be earning his leadership badge and had worked hard for it all year. The hike was a final test to see if he could demonstrate all that he'd learnt. In Elaine's eyes, Joseph, at fourteen, still seemed too young to be a leader but she'd encouraged him despite reservations. He was honest and sensible, and she knew he would act responsibly if the need arose.

Elaine parked a few metres away from the Bridge of Dee Scouts hall where everyone had gathered to catch the bus. The Aberdeen boys were joining up with the Kincardineshire troop for their adventure race up Bennachie ridge. The atmosphere, when the boys joined ranks, pinged with the static of fully charged atoms. The six or more Scoutmasters tested their own leadership skills, and battled bravely to keep them all in line.

A round of Scouts cheers filled the air as each team clustered and entered the bus in an orderly fashion.

Elaine stood waving at the bus full of boisterous young lads and out the corner of her eye she thought she spotted a familiar face. Amongst the other mothers fare-welling their children, was none other than, Marta, her brother's wife.

Guilt stabbed her conscience over her past actions and she was unable to forgive herself for not attending Erik's wedding. She'd seen the announcement in the newspaper and begged Gerrard to let her go. She promised to stay out of sight and not make a scene, but he'd forbidden it. If she'd disobeyed he would have eventually found out, and the extent of his anger could have frightful consequences. Fearing her husband more than the joy of seeing Erik married, she resigned to the fact that her family really was lost to her.

Elaine quickly shielded her face with the scarf around her neck and made her way behind the crowd. Tucking herself swiftly into the car she observed the crowd as it dispersed, noting which car Marta got into. Her eyes locked on the license plate and she watched Marta leave - oblivious to their close encounter.

Elaine left with a charge of conflicting emotions; tempting her mind to be consumed by them. She had to focus. Now was not the time for guilt and remorse. Knowing she had time to enjoy sunshine and solitude, Elaine was determined to carry out her plan.

Elaine opened the lichen cover wooden gate at the far corner of the grounds of the house and slammed it shut once through. Never had she visited her daughter's grave in anger before. Sadness? Yes, but not anger.

No, Gerrard had plenty of that for the both of them and she hated the thought of bitterness consuming her like it had him. She paused for a moment, closing her eyes and letting the cool air engulf her lungs. A sense of calm settled over her allowing a warmth in her spirit to return.

If only every day could be this peaceful.

At a much slower pace, she could enjoy the strands of long grass as she ran her fingers over their tops. A flurry of spice coloured leaves escaped tree fingers and floated on the wind. She lay in the grass and looked up at the wide expanse of blue; dotted with plumes of shadowy clouds. Echoes of wind whispered through applauding leaves as the grass bowed to its audience.

Elaine felt a stillness that had eluded her the night before. This was where she was meant to be - right here where Joanna lay. She looked over at the gravestone. It was somewhat buried in amongst the grass now and it pained her to see it looking so neglected.

"Joanna Naudman, Beloved Daughter of Elaine and Gerrard. Born 27th, September 1974."

'Funny…' she thought to herself, '…it doesn't say died 27th, September 1974. Normally they put the date the person died, don't they?' she pondered. 'Well I guess it was the same day, so probably wasn't necessary. But why not say born and died on that date?'

Elaine closed her eyes and relived the memory of that day. She had only seen her daughter just the once soon after she was born. Gerrard's face looked grim. The little blue baby girl didn't cry and lay very still in his arms. As Elaine cradled Joseph, Gerrard whisked the baby away, saying he was taking her to a doctor in the city.

Joanna was swaddled in the shawl she had knitted for when the baby came; she wasn't expecting two. It warmed her heart to know that at least Joanna had that comfort and gift from her mother. She would just have to knit another one for Joseph.

She had dozed on and off and eventually a midwife came to care for her later that morning. Gerrard didn't return home until four in the afternoon. His pale face looked sadder than when he'd left. He got out of the car and opened the back seat passenger's door. He pulled out a tiny white wooden box. Atop it sat a small wooden cross; the symbol of death. Its image was burned in her memory like an internal scar. Gerrard had brought their baby girl home to be buried on the property.

Elaine clutched her nightgown to her chest as if squeezing the fabric might reduce the pain beneath the cotton. Moaning in agony she hadn't realised she had torn it so badly until later when she went to feed Joseph. The sting in her breasts as the milk let down when he cried, made her own tears start every time and she wondered if her heart might stop beating from the pain of her loss. Gerrard tried to comfort her, reminding her she still had wee Joseph to care for and that grieving for their baby girl would not bring her back or benefit anyone. She had hated his words and seen just how heartless he could be. Her parents had warned her, but she didn't want to hear it.

She was sad that she never got a chance to hold Joanna and say a proper goodbye. Gerrard had given her some pitiful reason why it was best not see the dead baby lying in the box. He quoted the doctor's instructions about, infant death protocols and the rehabilitation of the mother, like it were some sort of instruction manual for dealing with grief.

What harm could there be to look at her dead child? To touch her tiny hands and give her a Mother's kiss goodbye?

Then a thought hit Elaine quite out of the blue…

What if he never put Joanna in that coffin?

She'd never know if he hadn't.

"The key!"

CHAPTER SEVENTEEN

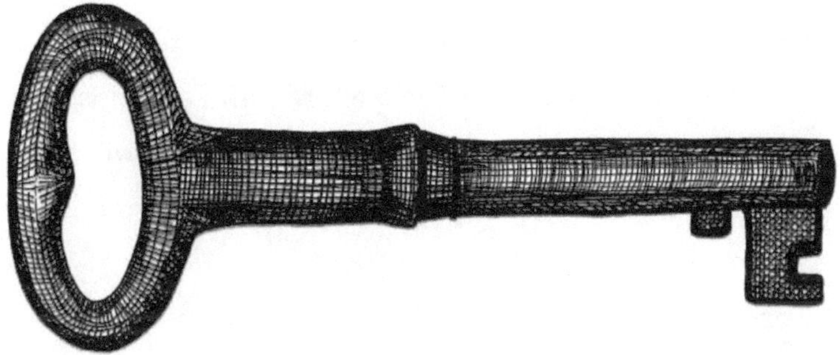

2nd April 2016

Jess

“THERE IT IS - I see it!” Ella squealed like a mouse who'd found a piece of cheese.

Jess scrambled over the lawn mower and garden tools, carefully squishing herself around the boxes to reach her cousin.

“Where?”

“There at the bottom,” Ella pointed at a large grey timber box.

“Oh, Jings. It would have to be on the bottom.” Jess frowned.

“Help me with these, will you,” demanded Ella.

Jess took the boxes sitting on top of the crate from Ella and did her best to re-home them out of the way. Finally, they had cleared enough space to free it.

The weathered wood bore the Naudman Shipping Company badge on its top and both sides. Its stencilled letters now faded into the silvering timber like a memory of a bygone era. It was quite large and could probably have fit both of them inside it. The old black padlock was large and chunky and Jess knew exactly which of the keys would unlock it.

Taking the black iron key between her finger and thumb beneath the cloth, she slipped it into the padlock keyhole. It felt rather clunky compared to the other locks she'd turned, but sure enough, the barrel released and the padlock could be unhinged from the crate. Lifting the lid the girls gasped when they saw the little white coffin sitting on the top. The cross still sat as an emblem of hope for the body that would lie therein. Jess went to lift it but Ella caught her arm, "Do you think we should?"

"Don't worry, I'm betting it's empty. Usually, the ones with bodies in them are in the ground." She laughed, but she couldn't completely hide how unsettled she was.

"Oh, I guess that's true enough." Ella relaxed her grip on Jess's arm and together they lifted the little coffin out of the crate and sat it on top of another box resting beside them.

"It's got a keyhole, Jess."

"I… I knew it. It's like I saw it."

"You saw it? You mean you had another vision?"

"Yes and it was the same lady at the gravestone, but she was much older. She dug it up. Elaine dug up the coffin!" Jess was thrilled she understood what she'd seen, but it still didn't remove the feeling of dread in her gut.

"But why?" asked Ella.

"She must have had a good reason to I suppose. Let's open it."

"I'm not sure I want to - at least not until Joe's here to see it."

"Well, go get him then." Jess demanded, her impatience half excitement - half dread.

Ella disappeared out the door again and Jess was very tempted to take a quick peek before they returned. She tried to lift the lid, but it was stuck.

"Oh yeah, the key. Who locks a coffin anyway? Unless you're trying to bury someone alive." Jess shuddered at her own conclusion.

Picking up the keys again, she looked them over and decided one of the little tarnished silver ones would probably fit the keyhole. Without a second thought, she placed the heavier looking silver key into the slot as Ella and Joe returned.

"What are you doing? - I told you to wait!" said Ella.

"Well I… I was just checking to see which key would fit, that's all. No need to get your nickers in a knot, I haven't opened it." Joe looked on in disbelief, while Ella got closer to inspect if she was telling the truth.

"You sure you girls wanna open that?" Joe looked a little worried. "It ain't good to be opening auld wounds of the past."

"We won't if you don't want us to, Joe," said Ella.

It was admirable her cousin wanted to respect Joe's wishes, but Jess was gripped with panic. What if she never got to find out what was inside the coffin? "But don't you want to know what happened to Joanna, Joe? What if she never died?!"

"Well alright, but mind that I warned ye."

Jess turned the key and the lock released. Lifting the lid Ella made a squirming squealing sound, anticipating the horror of its contents.

"Boo!" said Jess.

Ella screamed properly and she jumped in fright. Jess laughed, but then stopped as soon as she saw the contents of the coffin.

A neatly folded note sat just like the others on top of a loosely knitted baby's shawl. Jess knew the note would be in Elaine's handwriting. Picking it up, she immediately began to read.

<u>26th, October 1988</u>

My dearest Joanna/Elle,

I don't know where you are, or even if you are still alive, but please know that I love you. You would have been very much loved if I had ever had the chance to know you. My only hope is that your brother might find you someday. Your father has taken you and hidden you from me, but I will not rest until you've been found. My darling girl. I wish I could have known you.

All my love,

Elaine Naudman (Eleanor Lockheart)

P.S – Joseph, I have left this coffin in the condition in which I found it, except for the shawl. I placed your baby blanket on top of the rocks as a clue for you. Joanna was wrapped in a shawl I knitted exactly the same way. If you can find it you will know that you have found Joanna. It breaks my heart to know that I buried and mourned a pile of rocks!

"Wow, look at that. She signed it - Eleanor," said Ella. "I guess she really wanted Joanna to find her. What do you think, Joe?"
Joe looked as if years of troubles were lifting from him and new thoughts were entering his mind for the first time.

"I don't really remember much about my sister. I knew that I had one, of course, Ma took me to visit her grave. But whatever possessed her to dig up the coffin?"

"Look Joe." Jess had pulled back the shawl revealing the pile of rocks sitting on the bottom of the satin lined casket. "What a mean thing to do."

"Well, he was mean." Joe fumed. "How could he do this to her. Oh, Ma. You must have been so mad and worried and all types of confused when you found this. I'll never forgive him for this. I'm well to be rid of ye." He moaned as if starting a new grieving process all over again.

Joe picked up the shawl and clung to it.

"We've got to find her, Joe - We've got to find Joanna." Jess felt sorry for him. What must it be like to learn your sibling is still alive? She was desperate to find the truth for him.

"We'll help you too, Joe, won't we Jess?" Ella's eyes fixed on Joe.

"I think we need to tell your parents. Max needs to know, Ella."

"I agree." Ella looked at Jess with a fragment of contempt. "Tracking down your missing sister might be harder than we think and we could sure use your help."

What was Ella's problem? They'd discussed the reasons why they couldn't tell their parents. Jess worried that if Mum or Uncle Max found out, they might halt any further investigations.

"Let's just tell them the facts though, okay? They don't need to know how we came to find them just yet, do they?" Jess looked between the two of them. "Let's just say that you found some information that Flo had written in a journal... that's true enough. And we'll tell Mum and Uncle Max that you are cousins. They'll be happy just to know that, Joe."

"I suppose that'll be alright." His mournful tone didn't inspire much confidence.

"Cheer up, Joe. We'll find your sister," said Ella.

Joe gave her half a smile and then left.

"She's alive, Ella. Joanna is alive - I can't believe it." Jess grinned.

Joe

Retreating to his cottage to finish the stew, Joe stared out the window and spotted Vera and the boys returning from the dunes. He wished he'd gone with them now; it would have been better than reviving old memories he'd long suppressed and rather forget. But what of this unknown sister? Surely she had died soon after she was born, just as his mother had told him numerous times. What if the girls were raising his hopes for nothing? It would be crushing to know that he was still all alone in this world. For now, at least, the thought of new cousins had greatly cheered his spirit and he couldn't wait to share the news with his good friend Max.

Joe went outside to meet them all.

"Joe! Joe! Look what I found." Jack raced over towards him as fast as his legs could go, and with an outstretched arm offered the treasure up to Joe as a prize.

"Well, that's a mighty fine looking piece of emerald you've got there." Joe patted Jack on the back and held it up to the sky.

"I know." - He panted trying to catch his breath - "We found it on the beach. I reckon those Pirates buried their treasure somewhere nearby too. We're gonna go looking for it again tomorrow. Wanna come with us next time, Joe? What have you been doing anyway?" Jack questioned him with intensely curious eyes.

Joe turned the sand smoothed bottle green piece of glass in his hand and handed it back to Jack.

"Well, I've been making your supper. We're having Black Beard's Jack stew. Argh! 'me hearties," He said in his best pirate voice and lunged to grab him. Jack laughed, trying to escape and successfully dodged Joe's tackles. "I'll make a stew out of ye yet, Jack!"

Jack screamed and ran back to Max who was lagging behind the others on his way back from the beach.

"Where are the girls?" Vera asked when she was closer.

"Oh they're in the storage shed still I think," He said.

"Did they get their homework done?"

"Uh, yeah I think so. After we got talking, Ella said she wanted to show Jess the old pinball machine out there and no doubt all the rest of the junk." Joe stared blankly past her to the sand dunes beyond.

"Are you alright, Joe? Is something wrong?"

"No. I'm fine. Just memories that's all. Sometimes they're better forgotten. You can understand that, can't you, Vera?" Joe looked straight into her eyes. She searched his momentarily and then looked away biting her bottom lip. Her concern was barely visible but Joe knew it still existed - how could it not?

"Okay. Well, do you mind if I go take a look in the shed?" She asked, seeming to have swept her own thoughts under the carpet once again. Joe knew exactly how she felt and he wouldn't dare broach the subject unless she did first.

"No that's fine. Supper won't be for another hour or so; about six-thirty. I have some other jobs to tend to but I'm looking forward to catching up with you all later. We'll eat in your cottage; it has a bigger dining table. Perhaps once the boys are occupied with a game or something, we can have a chat," He said, trying to hint that he had something to tell her and Max. He saw the same concerned glint in her eye and needed to reassure her. "Don't worry it's not about that. It's something good - you'll like it."

Vera nodded she understood, then headed for the shed.

Jess

"Girls? Jess! Ella? Where are you?!"

Jess heard her mother first and froze in panic.

"Ella - that's Mum," she whispered loudly. "We better get that coffin covered up or she'll be asking all sorts of questions we don't wanna be answering."

"You're right. This tarpaulin should do it." Ella covered the white box with the green plastic sheet just as Mum opened the shed door.

"You in here girls? Ah, there you are. Why didn't you answer me, Jess?"

"Ah, we were just busy. I didn't even hear you," She lied. "How was the beach?" Jess asked trying to distract her mother from firing any more questions at her.

"Oh, it was lovely. The sand was wonderful under my toes, so soft and fine. And the lighthouse is quite a pretty picture too now the sun's a little lower. You should have come, girls. How was your chat with Joe, did you get the information you needed? What was it about again?"

"Aye, we did, Aunty Vera. Joe was very helpful. Thanks so much for keeping the boys busy for us." Ella said. Thankfully, Mum seemed distracted by all the clutter around them and didn't seem to notice they hadn't answered her last question.

"Ooo. Look at that. I've never seen an old wringer washer like that before," Mum went to crank the handle. The shaft didn't budge even though the effort she exerted should have moved the rollers easily. "It must be rusted." she clapped the dust from her hands. "Joe has quite a collection of stuff in here, doesn't he? Ooo, I'd love to rummage around, see if he has any old bookshelves or cabinets I could refurbish. It might be fun to have a wee project." Mum eyed around the rest of the shed scanning for anything else interesting.

Jess was getting anxious, and Ella, sensing her urgency, re-directed her mother's attention to a cabinet close to the shed door.

"What about those shelves over there, Aunty Vera. There's a cabinet at the bottom too I think." She ushered Mum towards the unit. Boxes were stacked against the front of it and Ella eagerly shifted them away so Mum could get a better look.

"Ooo it's lovely - look at the carved detail. It's an old cottage style buffet. Look at the knobs, aren't they just the cutest?" Mum started opening its cupboards and drawers and checking it over thoroughly. "Mmm, this drawer seems to be stuck. Oh look, it has a keyhole. It could be locked. I wonder if Joe has the key somewhere. Keys for old furniture like this are usually long gone. Chances are this one's key is missing too. I could jimmy it open I guess. A missing key won't matter once it's opened. It's still a really nice piece of furniture."

"Why don't you ask Joe if he'd sell it to you? He obviously has no use for it if it's just sitting out here," said Ella.

While Mum was preoccupied with the cabinet, Jess stared at Ella like a bomb was about to explode, franticly mouthing an urgent evacuation. Her silent pleas were met with subtle gestures to calm down and be patient. Ella did seem to have a way with her mother but Jess still had difficulty trusting her.

"Joe's not especially attached to anything in here, Aunty Vera. I think the only reason he keeps it, is for us to play with when we come to visit. The boys love the old tools and Joe's old go-kart's here somewhere too. I'm sure he'll pull it out for them to play with tomorrow. You should definitely ask him about the cabinet, he won't mind." Ella motioned for Mum to leave the shed and seize the moment now.

Jess wondered if it was wise to encourage Mum to spend time with Joe, but with her so reluctant to leave, Jess made a concession.

"Joe's working on supper, maybe you could go help him and bring up the cabinet then."

Mum gave her a look; Jess knew it well. "What are you girls up to? You seem awfully keen for me to leave?"

Mum could be very intuitive when it came to situations of secrecy. On many previous occasions, Jess had failed to conceal her true agenda, so she did the only thing she could think of - she lied.

"You're right Mum. Uh, we're planning a surprise for tonight after supper and we'd like to work on it privately or it won't be a surprise, will it?"

"Oh." Mum smiled, "What sort of surprise? I love surprises."

"I know. But...but we don't want to spoil it for the others now, do we?"

Although Mum was still dubious, she gave a sigh and relented.

"Oh, All right, I'm going. But you don't have too long to get whatever you've got planned ready. Supper's at six-thirty, okay?"

"Sure, Mum, we'll be ready."

Mum left and a stunned Ella stood at the doorway looking more worried than ever.

"What did you do that for? I had it under control. Now we've got to come up with a surprise for everyone. What on earth are we going to do, Jess?"

"Never mind that, we'll think of something. What about that cabinet drawer - it's locked. Let's see if we have the key."

Jess walked over to join Ella by the door. Her mother had disappeared into Joe's cottage and they were safe to continue their investigation of the cabinet and its keyhole.

"We don't even know if this was Elaine's," Ella said. "If we get caught out by your promise of a surprise, I'd like it noted that I warned you.

You're very impulsive and thoughtless sometimes, Jess. Now, a surprise, hmmm, what would make a good surprise for everyone?"

CLICK.

Jess had unlocked the drawer with the other daintier tarnished silver key.

Sliding open the drawer, Ella stopped dead in her thoughts, "I don't believe it. What's inside?"

Jess bent to peer into the corners of the drawer and reached in to collect up its contents.

"It's a pile of letters."

CHAPTER EIGHTEEN

26th October 1988

Elaine

ELAINE SAT IN her car a short distance from the St. Andrews church parish. A navy and red silk scarf covered her hair tightly and a large pair of tortoise shell shades concealed her eyes.

Watching intently as the ladies arrived for their weekly meeting, she peered over her sunglasses and surveyed them all carefully.

For what purpose they had gathered she could not determine and she cared not for its attendees except one.

Marta Lockheart stood in a pale blue winter dress and jacket. Her smart attire might suggest that she and Erik were doing well, but then, Marta always looked smart and proper. She had always been terribly concerned about being a topic for gossip and she couldn't bare anyone who might speak a harsh word about her appearance or character.

With a plate of baking in one hand and her Bible in the other, Marta patiently waited for a woman, dressed just as formally, to enter the building. Hugs of etiquette and smiles abounded and Elaine suddenly felt very alone.

She'd never intended to become so recluse, but Gerrard had become unbearably judgmental if she dared to acquaint herself with anyone new. She'd unconsciously given up all attempts of friendship after returning from Denmark and denied that she was unhappier for it.

But seeing Marta and her friends so gloriously thrilled by each other's company gave her a most uncomfortable ache in her heart. She had acquaintances herself, of course, but none that she could ever dare to tell all her secrets to, not even Lydia anymore.

Elaine picked up the magazine on the passenger seat and flicked through the pages without looking at them. Marta would be inside for the next hour plus and she was determined to catch her this time. She had to talk to someone about the coffin. But who would ever believe her? Even Marta probably would laugh at her, but she would have to risk a little embarrassment for the sake of her own sanity.

Soon after the clock ticked past noon, a sudden flurry of chattering got her attention and signalled the end of the meeting. Elaine had watched this group of modestly dressed woman exit the parish over the last two weeks and had come to name some of them by their traits.

"Oh my, Miss *Luscious Locks* is looking very colourful today. And Mrs *Know-it-all* is singing her own praises again." She chuckled to herself.

The ladies all dispersed and then Marta finally emerged, closing the parish door behind her as she went.

In haste Elaine exited her car and walked towards her, scanning the surrounds to check no one was watching.

"Mrs Lockheart?... Marta!" She interrupted the down headed woman trying to place her Bible into her handbag. "Could I have a word with you?"

Marta looked up as if awoken from a troubling dream and a puzzled look crossed her face.

"Yes... Do I know you?...Eleanor is that you? My goodness girl, where have you been? Oh, Erik will be thrilled to know I've found you. He was mighty troubled when you disappeared. You know he looked everywhere for you for at least three years after you vanished. You did a terrible thing running off like that. Your mother was sick with worry and became very ill you know. You've been gone for, let's see...almost fifteen years. Where have you been my dear?" She finally paused for an explanation.

"I'll tell you everything you want to know, but can we go somewhere? I can't be seen here in Alford. I can't risk it." Elaine glanced around, anxious she'd be recognised.

"Alright, follow me." Marta walked back towards the parish. Elaine hesitated.

"Are you sure, we won't be seen or interrupted?"

"I'm sure dear. The hall is booked for our ladies prayer meeting for the whole morning. No one would dare interrupt our vigil," She said with satisfaction. "Besides if you can't confess in a church, where on earth would any of us be? Lost I tell you, that's what." Marta opened the door and ushered Elaine inside.

After a lengthy explanation about the night she ran away, Elaine revealed that she and Gerrard had gone to live in Denmark so the family couldn't find her. She confessed her regret over the betrayal of her family. She had been so happy that Gerrard had decided to return to Aberdeen when she announced she was pregnant. But her hopes of a family reunion were dashed when he forbid her to have any contact with her parents and brother on their return. She had cried over it until her eyes were so red and puffy that he had slapped her across the face to snap her out of it. He'd apologised and promised never to lift his hand to her again while she was pregnant. A promise he had kept and a change which Elaine thought might remain in permanent effect. But sadly this was not to be the case and once the babies were born he resumed his physical abuse; taking better care to avoid her face.

"You see, Marta, Gerrard has a lot of faults, and I see them now. He can be a very cruel man and his temper can be erratic. I know I provoke him sometimes, but his outbursts often leave me with more permanent reminders, if you catch my drift." She lifted up her sleeve revealing bruises on her arms.

"Oh my dear, All these years what you've had to endure, I'm terribly sorry for you. You don't deserve that even if you were naïve to run away with him. Well, you're here now and the Lord knows of your repentant heart."

Elaine worried that Marta hadn't quite grasped the reason for her sudden re-appearance.

"Well, that's not really why I'm here. I've come to ask your advice and also to warn you. You see, if Gerrard learns about what I've done I'm worried he'll do something that could land him in prison." Tears welled in the corners of her eyes and she did nothing to prevent them from trickling down her cheeks.

"Sounds like that's where he belongs anyway," muttered Marta. "What is it you think you've done?" She finally asked.

"Well, I've suspected him of cheating for a while now; he gets these letters you see. They came from Denmark first, and then they stopped. But then they started coming again…but this time from France."

Marta listened like she were hearing something too scandalous for her own ears.

"Anyway, while he was away on his last business trip I had a wee snoop around his office. I found a pile of letters locked in his desk drawer - so I read them.

"The letters are from his mistress, Charlotte, and she has a child called Elle. I believe they live in Paris. I'm fairly certain the child is his."

Marta looked at her in astonishment.

"I was very jealous you must realise and overcome with anger when I read them. It stirred me deeply and the night after I read the letters I had such a tormented dream; Joanna was crying out to me from the grave."

"Bless my soul." Marta bowed her head and kissed a crucifix around her neck as if paying her respects to the dead.

"You see, when I went into labour, it was too late to go to the hospital. The babies came very quickly. Joseph came first. He was big and cried loudly. Then Joanna came, but she was limp and blue. Gerrard raced her to Aberdeen hospital to try and save her, but it was too late. He brought her back in a white coffin which was locked. I never got to see my little girl again."

"The Lord will have her in his hands, my dear, rest assured you'll see her again in heaven one day." Marta patted her leg as a gesture of comfort.

"You don't understand!" cried Elaine. "We buried the coffin on our property, she was never christened you see, so we couldn't bury her in the church cemetery.

"In amongst Charlotte's letters was an envelope with Joanna's name on it. In the envelope was a key. Oh Marta, I'm terribly worried about what Gerrard will do if he ever finds out what I've done. I was so tormented by the dream that I dug it up!" Elaine blurted.

"Dug what up?" Marta paused, trying to understand what she had said. "Oh my Lord. What have you done, Eleanor?"

"That's not the worst of it. I dug up the coffin, and the key; the one from his desk, it unlocked it... and... There was nothing but rocks inside, Marta. Gerrard made me bury a pile of rocks." Elaine sobbed. "Oh how I've mourned for my little girl, yet she were never there. What shall I do?"

Marta cradled Elaine in her arms and rocked her gently.

"Oh my dear, what a cruel, cruel thing to do. I've never heard of such a thing. I don't know what I'd have done in your shoes. Lord knows I've had to keep some secrets in my time, but nothing good ever comes of it. Perhaps if we asked Erik, maybe he could talk to Gerrard?"

"Oh no, he mustn't ever know, Marta. Erik would be so ashamed of me, my parents too. If Gerrard ever found out that I came to see you he'd probably kill me, or heaven forbid, do something to hurt Joseph." Elaine's bottom lip trembled.

"Oh come now… He won't kill you, Eleanor, you're the mother of his child. It'll be fine. And what of Joseph? How old is he now?" Marta asked, distracting her from her thoughts.

"He's just turned fourteen. He really is good, Marta. He's the best part of me and I wouldn't take any of it back now that he's here. But that's also why I've come. You see I saw you a couple of weeks ago at the Scout's hall when the boys went up Bennachie. Do you have a son?"

"Yes, my eldest is Max; He's thirteen. He's a strong young lad – looks just like Erik. He'll do well when it's his turn to run the farm. Boys can be terrible trouble sometimes, but we love them no matter what mischief they get up too. I'd love for you to meet him."

"Maybe I shall. You see I think perhaps Joseph and Max might have already met on that hike and I'm fearful that your son might say something about Joseph Naudman and it'll only be a matter of time before Erik figures it out. Erik clocked Gerrard in the nose quite badly the night we ran away. He warned him to leave me alone or he would do much worse than hit him in the face. If Erik finds out that Gerrard's been beating me, he might take things further."

"Erik wouldn't risk it, Eleanor, and Gerrard won't hurt you *or* his son, he's his heir remember."

"I'm sure you're right…but can we at least try to keep the Lockhearts and the Naudmans from ever finding out about each other, Marta?" Elaine hoped Marta's wisdom was greater than her own.

"Well now. What if I ask Max if he met Joseph on the hike and find out if he knows his surname yet? If not then I'll tell him that I met Joseph's mother, Eleanor… Newman after they left for the hike. That way he'll only know him as Joseph Newman. And you do likewise. Ask Joseph if he met Max and tell him you met his mother, Mrs… Lawson, will that do?"

Elaine turned red with embarrassment.

"Oh that's perfect except for one thing, I go by the name Elaine now - not Eleanor. So if you are going to tell him my name, say Elaine Newman." She smiled, happy for an outcome that would preserve her family.

"Alright then, Elaine Newman it is. Now, what about the coffin? What did you do with it?"

"I put the coffin in an old shipping crate in the barn, it's locked and Gerrard doesn't go out there so he won't find it. I filled in the hole in the field…as best as I could anyway. I put some rocks from the fence in it to fill it up a bit first. But if Gerrard goes to the grave he'll notice something is not right."

"So he hasn't gone to it yet. Does he go there often?"

"No. In fact I can't remember the last time he visited it. He's so busy with work that he's hardly ever home."

"Well I wouldn't worry then. Chances are he'll only go there if he follows you or you ask him to go. Remember he knows that Joanna is not in the coffin, so he only has to keep up his pretence for your sake. But if you're still worried, you could have the field ploughed for planting to be certain there's no risk of him finding out.

As for the letters, I'd take them and lock them away with the coffin. He can hardly question you about the whereabouts of them without giving himself away in the process. Maybe then you can look into finding his mistress, and the child. Do you think the child - what was her name?"

"Elle."

"Yes, Elle. Do you think it might actually be Joanna?"

"I hadn't thought of that. I guess it could be, Oh Marta. I thought Joanna might still be alive, but to think that Gerrard has known all along and kept her from me is…is… unbearable. I must find her."

"Well now, see you be careful, Eleanor, I mean, Elaine." Marta tried out her new name to get into the practice of it. "It's not worth your life now, is it? If you can give me an address for his mistress in Paris, I'll see what I can find out for you. I have a friend who works in Paris, she's there with the missions."

"Oh, would you Marta? But Erik mustn't know. Could you keep it a secret?"

"A secret it shall remain for now, but there will come a day when not even my best efforts to prevent your brother from finding out the truth will stop him. Be sure of that."

"How shall I contact you?"

"Leave me a note at the post office, box 22. I always collect the mail, so you've no concern of Erik ever picking it up. Perhaps don't sign it though… just in case." Marta smiled, and wiped a tear from Elaine's face. "You'll be alright. But whatever you do, make sure you're not the victim of Gerrard's next outburst. Well, I'd best be off. I've got some errands to run before the children finish school."

Elaine put her scarf and glasses back on, and she and Marta moved towards the parish's front door.

"Thank you so much, Marta. I really am so grateful to have it all off my chest. You've been a wonderful listener and I'll be in touch soon.

Gerrard heads away again mid-November, so I'll get you that address. Give my brother a kiss for me. I do miss him so. I can't believe he's a father. It feels so strange to think of him that way."

"He's a good man, Elaine. He'd do anything to be re-united with you again. It can't stay a secret forever. Okay?"

"Okay, I'll find a way."

The two women hugged each other tight and then exited the church. Elaine looked around, checking if anyone might see the two of them together. The pavement was empty given that a light rain had begun and she hurried towards the car. Once she was safely inside she looked to see if Marta was still there - but she had vanished and Elaine felt relieved.

As soon as she returned home after her visit with Marta, she wrote a note to Joanna; or Elle if that could be her name now. Taking the note and Joseph's baby blanket, she went to the barn and locked them both inside the coffin. Then she went to her room and wrote in her journal.

26th October 1988

Today I went to see Marta. I think Joanna could still be alive and go by the name, Elle. Gerrard leaves for his next 'business trip' on the 16th of November. What shall I do? Should I take the letters from his desk? I could ask to go to Denmark with him and try to find the address on the envelope. Virginia might help me. But what if he's not going to Denmark, what if he's planning to go to Paris? He might get angry if he thinks I'm getting too close to discovering his secrets.

She stopped in her train of thought as paranoia took hold, 'What if Gerrard found her journal? He might find it if she took his letters and then went looking for them.'

Elaine tore out the page she had just written and tossed it into the fire then lit a match to burn it. It didn't take long for it to melt away to ashes. 'I must find another place to hide the journal.'

She looked around the house and spotted the buffet drawer with its little silver key inserted. Immediately she placed the journal inside and then retrieved the suit pocket items from her writing desk and placed them in the buffet drawer, along with the key to the shipping crate in the barn.

She locked it and slipped the buffet cabinet key onto a piece of narrow cream ribbon. Stuffing it inside one of her handbag pockets, she zipped it closed. Holding her bag to her chest she said a prayer. "Lord if you're there. Please help me find her, and please don't let Gerrard find out."

CHAPTER NINETEEN

2nd April 2016

Jess

"WHAT ARE WE going to do Jess?"

"Well, first we need to get these letters back to our room without Mum or Uncle Max noticing. Do you think you can distract them while I sneak past?"

"For heaven's sake, Jess. Would you just quit it with the mystery letters. We've got other things to worry about, like what this surprise is going to be?"

"Oh never mind that. If we don't bring it up, maybe Mum will forget about it."

"I doubt it. You heard her, she said she loves surprises. She won't forget about it and neither will I. My stomachs in knots just thinking about it."

"Well, why don't we just… sing them a song or something. You know any? My old drama teacher said my voice isn't too bad. I can hold a tune at least."

"Um, well, what about the old Scottish folk song '*Wild Mountain Thyme*'. You know it?"

"Uh, how does it go? Hum it for me."

Ella tried her best to hum the tune and then gave up and just sang the words. "...*and the wild mountain thyme grows around the blooming heather. Will ye go, lassie go?*"

"... Oh, I know that. My mum used to sing it to us when we were little. Great, we'll just sing that if they ask us what the surprise is. Okay? Now, how are we going to get these letters back to our room?"

"Ooo, I know. I'll go inside and open the bedroom window and you sneak over and pass them through. Got it?"

"Good idea. But what if the boys see me?"

"Improvise. Com'on, it's almost six-thirty, let's go!"

Jess tucked the other items they'd found in the drawer inside her pocket; some French coins, a matchbook and an old airline boarding pass. They'd make an excellent decoy if Mum made a fuss about anything. Tucking the pile of letters underneath her jumper, Jess hung back in the shed while Ella made her way towards the cottage.

Ella jogged, glancing back over her shoulder. A rise in the ground tripped her up, but she caught herself from falling over just in time. She slowed her pace to a walk.

Jess giggled a little too loudly, but thankfully Ella kept going. The boys were just crossing the lawn between the Hostel and the cottage and would be there in less than a minute.

Hurry up Ella!

Just as the boys reached the cottage door Jess heard the bedroom window creak open.

She waited till the boys had all entered the cottage and then crept up from behind, keeping out of sight till she was sitting beneath the window.

"Here, Ella," she whispered. There was no reply.

Fearing she'd get caught, Jess dropped the letters through the window opening and they clunked to the floor.

"What was that?" She heard her mother ask from inside.

"Uh, nothing. It's probably just Jess," said Ella.

"Well, how did she get inside? I never saw her come in?"

"Um…"

"Here I am!" Jess announced, walking through the front door. "I was playing a trick on you all, did I scare you?"

"Nothing scares me, Jess," said Steve.

"Really? But you never come up to the loft anymore, why's that?" She smiled audaciously.

"Uh, well, you girls are up there that's why. And it stinks of perfume up there, what do you do anyway, soak in it or something? I can't even breathe."

Jess lodged the suggestion of overpowering scents to her list of brother deterrents.

Giving Ella the eyes, she cocked her head back to the right, towards their bedroom. Quickly they scampered off and closed the door behind them.

"Dinner's almost ready girls. Don't go getting started on anything. We'll be serving in a minute."

"Okay," they chorused behind the wooden door.

Just as Ella picked the letters up from the floor they heard Joe's voice enter the cottage. Although the voices were muffled the girls paused to listen.

"Here we are. I'll just pop this on the stove. It's all ready to go, Vera."

"Thanks, Joe. I've made us a rhubarb crumble for dessert, I hope you don't mind."

"Yum, I haven't had that in years. Ma used to make it a lot when I was younger."

The girls were eager to hear more of Joe's stories so quickly tucked the letters out of sight and re-joined the others in the living room.

"What was she like, Joe, your Ma?" Jess asked, taking a seat at the dinner table opposite him.

Ella tried to do the same, but she couldn't get her chair out from under the table. It was stuck by the leg. Yanking on it, she managed to free it but also went tumbling back against the wall, banging her elbows in the process.

"Ouch!" She dropped the chair and rubbed vigorously.

"Ooo, are you alright, Luv?" Joe winced sympathetically.

"I'm alright. Thanks Joe." She attempted to smile. Ella sat on her chair, looked at Joe and repeated Jess's question. "What was your mother like? I bet she was caring like you are. Did she punish you when you were naughty?"

The others joined them at the dining table and Mum served up the stew.

"Well she was caring and she always had plenty of sticking plasters, which I often needed. I liked to climb things and be high up, you see. I know I frequently made her worry that I'd fall out of a tree; injuring myself beyond the remedy of a simple plaster. So I guess in that respect she might have thought me naughty for it...Thank you, Vera." Joe paused as Mum set a plate of food in front of him. "Other than that, I was very good. I had to be, else Pa would beat me. He often skelped me when I was young for telling lies. But I was just telling stories that he thought were lies. Maybe some were exaggerated but I liked to make my tales more interesting."

"Me too," said Jack. "I know this isn't a real emerald." Jack twisted a piece of glass in his hands and placed it on the table. "But it looks like one to me and it's nice to pretend it's an emerald while I'm playing with it."

Mum set the last of the plates on the table and took her seat. Joe reached for Mum's and Jack's hands and bowed his head. Without registering what was happening, Jess followed the others example and joined hands also.

"Dear Lord. Thank you for family and for friends and for the food which you have provided for us. Bless it for us this day. Amen." Joe looked up and everyone said, "Amen."

His eyes were filled with joy and Jess thought she even caught a glimpse of a tear.

"Were your parents religious, Joe?" Mum stabbed a gravy covered carrot. "Our mother was aye, Max, not that she'd know it now. She once told me she was having tea with the angels when I called her from London. I played along and asked if Jesus would be coming too. To which, she said, 'Of course - He comes daily!' I left it at that." Mum ate the carrot and a chorus of laughter circled the table.

"Well maybe He does visit her daily, Aunty Vera." Ella said in all seriousness. "She has her good days and she still attends church on Sundays if she's well enough. She hasn't left us completely."

Mum stabbed a few more vegetables without so much as glancing at Ella.

"Well, I've never really believed in the Bible myself, but perhaps there's some merit to it," Mum looked at her niece and smiled with squinted eyes.

"I should say so." Joe's voice was a welcome change. "Lord knows we all need saving from ourselves. Me-self especially. I read the Bible daily, and it served my Flo well in her last days - Ma too. She was very peaceful when she died, so I've stuck with it. It's very reassuring to know where you'll be going when your time comes to an end. Me Pa never went to church mind."

"What was your Pa like?" asked Brody. Jess was pleased not to have to ask the question herself. Even though she probably wanted to know Joe's answer more than her brother did, she was glad to be relieved of that inquiry.

"Me Pa was a troubled man. I remember the first skelping I ever got from him and I'll never forget it as long as I live. I was about five or six and I'd left some mess on the living room floor. He'd come home from work early and was really upset when he saw the mess I'd made with me cars. He was terribly wild with me; skelped me across the cheek before Ma had the chance to get between us. She was furious and told him never to lay a hand on me again. Which he didn't, if Ma was around. But after that he turned his anger into words too. From then on I could never do anything right by him. He'd fuss and criticize my every move. I tried real hard to please him, but he was a troubled man.

"I once saw him in his office at home, after he returned from one of his business trips; he was unshaven and seemed quite out of sorts - possibly drunk. He took out a picture and kissed it. I was so shocked because I'd never seen him kiss anything!

"He never kissed me goodnight, not like your Ma and Pa would have" - Joe looked at Ella and winked - "But I never even saw him kiss me mother. I'm sure he did, but he wasn't the sort of person who would show his affections readily. I think maybe he resented me and Ma because we got along so well together, while he had to travel a lot working for his Pa.

"Grandpa Fredrick Naudman owned the Naudman Shipping Company and he was a really mean man. He worked the men hard and docked their pay for the slightest of mistakes. Once he had the whole mechanical team pull apart an engine because one of the new boys couldn't tell him where a specific nut went. They had to stay late every day for a week and finish it, with no extra pay. Needless to say, that boy was fired once the job was done too.

"Grandpa was a very busy man and Pa wouldn't let me come to work with him at the shipping company. He said it was too dangerous and no place for a little boy. He was probably right, but occasionally he'd take me to see a new ship that had just been completed, or if a big new boat had come to port from somewhere overseas.

"I loved watching them load and unload the ships and on those days Pa would be in a most generous and happy mood. The shipments of grain and beef often went to Denmark or Oslo.

"Did I mention that Ma and Pa used to live in Denmark before I was born?" Joe paused and looked at the others who were contently listening and feasting on their stew.

Jess looked at him and shook her head, then asked, "Did you ever go to Denmark, Joe?"

"Aye lass, I visited once or twice after me Pa died, but it wasn't my cup of tea - too cold and the Dane's are hard to understand. Grandpa Naudman sent Pa to work in the port offices in Denmark to 'learn the ropes'. Pa said he liked living in Denmark and didn't mind being away from home.

"When Grandpa Naudman became too unwell to run the company, Ma and Pa decided to return to Aberdeen. Pa took over as chairman of the shipping company. I think it made him very stressed and it's probably why he was so grumpy all the time. He must have liked living in Denmark very much though because he always seemed happier after his trips back there. I was born soon after they returned to Scotland."

Joe finished telling his history and scoffed down the last of his stew. He realised he must have been talking a lot since all the others were well finished.

Ella helped Mum clear the table and then got the bowls out so she could serve up the dessert.

"When I grow up," said Steve, "I'd like to be a sailor and visit all the ports especially the ones in Italy, they look the best from the photos I've seen. Have you ever been to Denmark, Pa?" Steve passed the bowls of rhubarb crumble down the table and settled one in front of himself.

"Well, no I haven't been to Denmark. But I have been to Italy. You know that of course. It's where I first met your mother," Uncle Max said and shovelled crumble onto his spoon.

"Oh please tell us the story of how you and Ma met, Pa. I want to hear it. I miss you telling us your stories," said Ella.

"Ooo Aye, Pa, tell me the story. I don't remember Ma much and I'd like to hear it too," said Jack, licking his spoon of crumble and cream.

"Alright. Alright," said Uncle Max.

"And don't leave out any of the details, Pa," Ella said with a stern look and an upright spoon in his direction.

"Well now, Joe, you start us off, it's because of you that I even went to Italy..."

"Well sure if ye like. I was nineteen I think, and I'd just finished my first year of university at Oxford. I was taking business studies so that one day I might be able to work for Pa's company. Max was eighteen and had just finished high school." Joe looked at Uncle Max and he nodded in confirmation. "We first met at Scouts when we were younger and although we knew each other, we never got to spend any time together outside of that.

"The summer had only just begun and I was keen to catch up with me auld troop who'd planned a rafting trip down the River Tay. A few of the older Aberdeen boys decided to tag along with us and we all had such a great time. The river was ice cold mind you and it's a wonder none of us ended up with hypothermia."

"Aye, it was cold alright. I couldn't feel me fingers or toes till the next day." Uncle Max chuckled.

"Anyway, when I got back, Pa was home - which was unusual. He was very excited to tell us something. Ma was in town doing the messages and Pa was getting impatient. He was eager not to spoil his surprise, so he didn't get cross like he normally would."

"Excuse me Joe. But what are messages... was your Ma getting the mail, or something?" asked Jess.

"No lass. Doing messages is ah...getting the groceries. Anyway, when Ma finally got back, Pa told us that he was taking us on a two week holiday to Italy. Ma was excited but not nearly as much as I was.

"Ma had never gone anywhere. Well, that's not entirely true, she did go to Denmark a couple of times. Once to spend Christmas with Pa when he was working and another time for one of his business trips. Ma went to catch up with some of her auld friends from when they lived there... I, on the other hand, had to stay with Grandma Naudman." The gloomy tone of Joe's voice and forlorn look on his face made the children giggle. "But that's nothing to do with Italy," He flicked his hand to dismiss his theatrical detour.

"Pa had arranged for us to stay in a villa in Tuscany. Ma was kind of wary of the whole plan but didn't want to deny me the experience, so she asked Pa if I could bring a friend along with us; that way if I wanted to go exploring, I wouldn't be alone.

"Pa thought it was an excellent idea and asked me who I'd like to join us. I wasn't sure as most of my friends from University had summer jobs and wouldn't be able to come. Then Ma suggested I ask you, Max."

"Well, I'm sure glad she did because if she hadn't I might not have met the most beautiful girl in all of Italy." Uncle Max beamed. "So, of course I said yes. The next hurdle was getting Ma and Pa to agree. At first, Ma didn't approve and when I asked her 'why' she said we needed a serious talk. Ma wouldn't give me permission unless I made her a solemn

promise to never mention my real surname to anyone while I was away —
not unless there was an emergency.

"I thought it was a strange request so I asked her why. Ma explained
that Joe's surname was not, Newman, but was actually, Naudman. For
reasons she couldn't tell me, she said it was crucial that Pa never know
Joe's real surname - and that I be known as Max Lawson. No questions
were to be asked - or she would not help me get Pa's permission. I was so
desperate to go to Italy, so I agreed."

Ella frowned - puzzled by her father's story.

Didn't she already know this story? Perhaps not all of it.

Uncle Max opened his palms wide. "Well, Ma had to use all her
charms on Pa to convince him to let me go. He was annoyed because I'd
miss a good portion of the harvest and my help would certainly be
missed. I was very grateful to have Ma on my side otherwise there's no
way I would have been able to go.

"Your Ma kept hold of my passport and tickets for the whole trip, Joe,
and told me to never mention my real surname to you or your Pa. She
said that your Pa had some grievance against the Lockhearts; I can't
imagine what it might have been, but your Ma said that you and I had
the chance to mend it for the future. We were just never to bring it up."

"Aye, you were always Max Lawson to me. You only told me your real
surname after Pa died. That was a really strange day. Wonder what past
grievance caused the rift between our fathers?"

Ella looked at Jess and a heat rose in her cheeks.

"Who cares anyhow?!" Uncle Max shrugged his shoulders and reached
to slap on Joe the back.

Joe gave half a smile land looked at the girls. Jess could almost see the
penny drop in his eyes. He finally understood, and all Jess could do was
mouth a silent *please* at him to keep quiet. Joe rubbed a palm over his
forehead and held it there until Mum spoke.

"I remember that summer. It was a bumper crop too and Pa was always muttering to himself in the evenings about how you should've been there working."

"Never mind now, Tell 'em how you stole the roses, Max." Joe said, clearly wanting to divert the attention back to how Uncle Max and Aunt Gabby met.

"We had such a great time visiting villages, the beach, not to mention all the wineries too, aye Joe?" Uncle Max winked at his friend and tried to jab him in the ribs. "It was all so glorious - nothing like our summer's here. Anyway it was close to the end of the trip and Joe's Pa had gone into Florence to meet someone. I was upstairs gazing out the window, and then, there she was. The prettiest, most beautiful girl I ever saw. She was talking with her mother as they walked down the street."

"What did she look like?" asked Ella.

"Your mother had the loveliest smile with dimples on each side. Her dark hair was half pulled back with a ribbon; just like you do yours, Ella."

Ella blushed and twirled a finger through her hair.

"Your Ma saw me looking down at her from the villa window and she smiled back." Uncle Max looked pleased with himself.

"What was she wearing? Did you follow her?" Jess asked.

"Well, I'm not sure I remember." Uncle Max paused to think it over for a minute. Mum topped up the men's ales and Jess hoped it might aid his memory - though it was doubtful.

"She was wearing a dress, it was pink - no yellow I think. They must have been out walking because Gabby had a string of white and yellow daisies in her hair. I was smitten and ran to tell Joe all about the beautiful young lass I'd seen. I made him promise to help me find her.

"That night, Joe's Pa returned in an awful mood. He was meant to meet an associate or something in Florence but they didn't show up.

Anyway, he said he would stay on in Tuscany for a few more days to wait for them and insisted we return home as planned. My hopes were dashed. We were leaving the next day but I couldn't leave without trying to find your Ma." Uncle Max looked seriously at all three of his children.

"So, Joe and I convinced his mother to let us eat out by ourselves for our last night in Italy. We wandered the cobbled streets for a long time, and I decided to pinch some roses growing over a fence to give Gabby in the hope I would find her again. A couple of auld Italian women saw us and were most intent on making sure we were held accountable for the offense. Yelling at us, we ran as fast as we could up the darkening alley. Out of breath, I looked at the roses in my hand and they were mostly ruined - so was my hand. I bled from the thorns which pierced me when I'd grabbed them; serves me right really.

"But then I saw her again; my bleeding hands didn't seem to matter. She was sitting at a restaurant across the street with her mother and I was so full of adrenaline from the chase that I just went straight up to her and handed her the ruined flowers saying, 'These are for you. I shall never forget your beautiful face.' She smiled very shyly and our eyes met." Uncle Max paused, lost in the memory for a few seconds before snapping himself back to the table. "Her mother seemed very pleased by my brazen declaration and introduced us to her daughter, Gabriella. She allowed her to come sit with us and chat till the waiter arrived with their meals. They were the most wonderful minutes of the whole trip.

"I introduced myself as Max Lawson. But I was desperate to tell her my real name. When the time came to say goodbye I was nervous and couldn't decide if I should kiss her or not. I gave her a peck on the cheek, which made her smile and blush.

"Joe alerted me to the sounds of the old ladies still looking for us, so we had to run again. I thought, 'That's it, I'll never see her again.' Well, I was so wrong, and here you all are to prove it." Uncle Max finished, grinning with a raise of his glass and took a long swig of ale.

"But how did you meet again, Pa?" asked Ella.

"Oh, you know, Ella, you've heard me tell the story hundreds of times."

"I know, but Jess and Brody haven't. Does Aunty Vera know?"

Mum shook her head. "Well, I knew he met a girl in Italy, but I had no idea it was Gabby. I thought Joe introduced you to Gabby at Oxford, what are the odds of that, aye?"

"Aye, It wasn't luck, Vera, it was providence," said Uncle Max.

"I'll say," said Jess. She was so enthralled by her uncle's story that she'd forgotten where she was.

CHAPTER TWENTY

17th November 1988

Elaine

ELAINE DECIDED NOT to take the letters in Gerrard's desk drawer, she didn't have the courage to follow through with it. Instead, she would try and win back her husband's affections, even if it were only in pretence. Should she fail in her act, at the very least she might catch him out in his lie.

Gerrard would be away on business in Denmark for the next week. It would be his last trip away before Christmas and he'd promised Elaine he would take some time off over the holiday period so they could enjoy some family time together.

Elaine had heard nothing from Marta about the address she'd given her in Paris, but it was probably not high on the priority list of someone working in the French missions. Why she had bothered to ask for Marta's help in the first place seemed reckless now and it was probably for the best that she hadn't heard anything.

Picking up the phone Elaine circled each number on the rotary dialler and waited for someone to answer.

"Good morning, Naudman Shipping Company, this is Ailsa speaking. How may I help you?"

"Ah, hello, this is Elaine Naudman. I would like to be put through to Gerrard's secretary please."

"One moment please, Mrs Naudman," came the reply.

"Mrs Naudman, how can I help you?" came Shona's cheerful voice on the other end of the line.

Gerrard's secretary was young and bubbly and Elaine might have been jealous of her if Shona had been single, but since she was married, Elaine knew Gerrard wouldn't bother her.

Besides, Gerrard was over fifty now and his often unshaven appearance gave him a hardened look. His hair and moustache were well silvered and the creases on his face grew deeper each year. Elaine was ashamed to say that she found him very attractive. His charming ways, although less often expressed, sometimes made her feel like she was still under his spell. She still loved him despite how he treated her. Even after reading the letters, she still had hope she could regain the distance that echoed between them.

"Well, I would like to surprise Gerrard and accompany him on his next business trip. He said I could come the next time he went to Denmark. So I was hoping you would book an extra ticket for me. When is his next trip?"

Shona was very good at her job and Elaine made a point of saying so every time she visited Gerrard at the offices, insisting he give her a generous Christmas bonus every year. As such, Elaine was confident Shona would help her.

"Well he's not scheduled to visit Denmark for another two months, Mrs Naudman, on the 13th January," was the prompt reply on the other end of the line.

"Well, that will be fine. Can you please book flights for the two of us for that date?"

There was a long pause at the other end.

"Yes, of course, Mrs Naudman I will see you are booked on the same flight. Would you like me to inform Mr Naudman?"

"No, I'll let Gerrard know myself that it's all been arranged. Thank you for your assistance, Shona. Goodbye."

Elaine would start her investigation in Denmark and see if the address on the blue letters bore any result in finding, 'Charlotte. S.'

While Gerrard was away, she would take the photo of the woman and get it copied. Unlocking Gerrard's desk drawer for the second time, she rummaged through to find the photograph in the correct envelope. As she did, she noticed a thin book underneath the pile. She hadn't noticed it there before and tried to recollect if it had been there all along or if it was a new addition.

Regardless of its origin, she took the book out and flicked through the pages. It was a book of Italian poetry and right near the back, she found a photo of a baby in a pink and white smock. The child had soft curls of brown hair. Pain tugged her heart. Could this be Elle - the child referred to in the letters? Surely it must be.

She studied every detail intently. The eyes were like Gerrard's, fierce and determined. But her hair and round face were like her own. Elaine didn't have any photos of herself as a baby so she couldn't compare the two images side by side to make any true comparison, but she felt certain it must be Joanna.

Taking both photos in her purse she went to the printers in Stonehaven to have them photocopied. The gentleman at the counter was very prompt and gave no judgment of the photos, except to say that she had a very 'Bonnie wee bairn.'

Fighting back the tears in her eyes, she held her composure till she was safely inside the car. She cried a lot over the next few days and then just an hour before Gerrard was due home from the airport, she turned her tears off and put all her energy into playing the good wife.

"Darling. You're home. We missed you. How was your flight? Have you eaten?" All the usual routines just slipped back into place keeping Gerrard fooled that she was ignorant of his misbehaving ways.

"I miss you when you're away, Gerrard. Next time I'm coming with you to Denmark. Joseph can stay with your mother and we can spend some time together. Besides, I want to catch up with Virginia while I'm there too, so I won't be any bother while you're working. It's all arranged darling. I had your secretary book our tickets."

Gerrard had tried to protest, but he could see there was no way to put her off without giving her a valid excuse, but he could think of none. Resigned to the fact that his wife would accompany him on his business trip, he sulkily accepted.

"We could pretend we're newly-weds again, Gerrard, just like old times."

Gerrard seemed excited by the proposition and tried to make it seem like it was his idea for her to come all along. He promised he'd make an effort and Elaine felt a charge of hope zap at the heartbeat of their marriage. But would it be enough to bring it back to life? Elaine remained unconvinced he would make any such romantic gestures. "Well if you think you can sweep me off my feet, Gerrard, you're going to have to do better than strawberries and a bottle of Champagne."

At least she could be assured of a decent meal at Ravage's, and, with any luck, she would see a change in his demeanour towards her too.

13th January 1989

Upon landing in Copenhagen, Elaine managed to leave Gerrard to his work and made her way around her old familiar haunts of the city. It was freezing and dirtied snow still sat on the ground all about the city. Icy draughts crept about the streets along with the cars and bicycles. However, no amount of cold would hinder her from a stroll along the water's edge to see the new fountain in the Amalie gardens, or to the Marble Church beyond it.

She had arranged to meet Virginia at the Nyhavn 17 restaurant for lunch. Once the formalities of greeting were seen to and her hands started to thaw, Elaine vigorously questioned her friend's life over the last fifteen years. Of utmost importance to her was whether or not Virginia had seen or heard anything from Gerrard since they'd left Denmark. Certain and relieved that no contact had been made, Elaine openly divulged her suspicions about her husband, to which Virginia's horrified response was properly justified.

"Oh my Elaine, I had no idea. Yes, of course I'll help you try and find this Charlotte. But without a surname, it could be impossible. Are you sure you want to do this?"

"No I'm not sure, but I must know the truth and I think my own daughter deserves to know the truth too."

"Yes, of course. Where do you want to start?"

"Well, I have this address for her." Elaine handed her friend a note with the hand written address on it. "I'm sure she doesn't live there anymore because the letters come from Paris now. But I have this photo of her and one of the baby. Surely someone in the neighbourhood might remember her."

"Well we can only try I guess," said Virginia with a sigh.

They spent the next few hours knocking on doors all down the frosty tree lined street. One person said they thought she looked familiar but didn't know where she had gone. Another elderly lady across the street said she would often see the woman taking the baby for a walk in the pushchair but she didn't know her name. "She kept to herself and had a gentleman visit her once. I only remember the man's visit because they had a very heated argument on the street one evening and he grabbed her arm. I didn't call the police because the woman was begging him not to leave, but he did anyway," said the old woman.

Elaine pulled out a photo of Gerrard for her to confirm if he was the gentleman she'd seen. The old woman took the photo and held it up close to her glasses.

"Well it could be him I suppose, but it was nearly thirteen years ago and my memory is not as good as it once was. Sorry dear," She said.

Elaine felt discouraged by the end of the afternoon and returned to their hotel to take a long bath. She wondered if Gerrard might make any attempt of intimacy towards her. But he was tired when he returned late and promised to take her out for dinner the next day.

The rest of the trip was a daze. Her hopes of finding any further information about Charlotte and the child faded along with her promise of a romantic dinner.

Gerrard had worked till 10 o'clock the next night. Elaine, having given up, ate alone at Ravage's and took a cab back to the hotel. Climbing into bed she knew she would probably never win the affections of her husband back from his foreign mistress and likely never find her missing daughter either. She fell asleep before Gerrard returned and in the morning, made her own way to the airport early, so she wouldn't have to hear his pitiful excuses. She left him a note on the pillow stating as much.

An electric fence of silence hung between them during their flight home. He apologised, reasoning with her that it *was* a business trip. But she ignored him mercilessly. It wasn't until Elaine was home and had Joseph in her arms that she uttered a word.

"My dear boy, I've missed you so much!"

Gerrard knew he'd blown it and seemed determined to show his remorse for neglecting her in Denmark. The next day he'd returned home from work with a stunning emerald necklace for her. She thanked him formally and promptly put it in her dresser drawer instead of trying it on. His temper gave way and he gripped her arm tightly.

"For God's sake, Elaine, put the damn necklace on! I got it especially for you." And he threw her arm away forcefully. She heard it crack; as did he. Agonising pain splintered through her shoulder like shock waves of an earthquake. She let out a short cry of pain and fell on the bed, clutching it tightly and holding her breath until she could control the surges in her mind.

"Oh no! I'm sorry darling, I didn't mean to." Gerrard motioned to offer his aid but she pulled away from him and cowered against the wall. "Oh darling is it broken, can I fix it?" He looked around as if trying to remember what just happened.

He'd never broken her bones before, but Elaine felt certain it could be this time.

Sniffing back her tears, she lied, "I'm fine. It's probably just sprained. I'll bandage it in a sling and it will be okay," She reassured him. From then on he was much more careful with her and kept his distance.

The years seemed to blur into one another after that and Elaine was happy to keep house and tend to Joseph's needs as long as Gerrard restrained himself around her. She hadn't intended to cause the gap between them to widen, but after the trip to Denmark, the few strands that still held them together seemed to have broken completely. Nothing, it seemed, could repair their damaged marriage and like the tendon in her arm; was unlikely to heal completely.

Elaine felt more alone than ever. Gerrard had taken to sleeping in the spare bedroom after he returned home late from work for a number of weeks and the habit stuck.

As the years pulled Elaine and Gerrard apart, her independence and confidence grew, leaving Gerrard with less control over her than he once had. Joseph, now a young man, attended his first year of university which succeeded in broadening his ambitions and horizon's, where his own father had failed him.

Then out of the blue Gerrard suggested they take a family holiday to Italy at the end of the summer of 1994.

Elaine thought it was a lovely idea, but worried Joseph would become more fully aware of the distance between his parents. It wasn't easy for Gerrard to hold his tongue, nor his hand when stressful situations arose. Joseph wasn't stupid and Elaine feared more than anything that he would find out how bad things had become.

Under the guise of Joseph's loneliness, Elaine suggested to Gerrard that their son might be able to explore more of the area if he had a friend along. To her surprise Gerrard agreed and she encouraged Joseph to ask Max to join their odd little family holiday. Max, none the wiser, was more than happy to come, but it did put her in somewhat of a conundrum.

How would she ever keep the boys from realising they were operating under false names?

CHAPTER TWENTY-ONE

2nd April 2016

Ella

"**W**EREN'T YOU GIRLS going to give us a surprise tonight?" asked Aunty Vera.

Ella stood and moved over to the living area beckoning her family to come and sit on the sofas.

"Um, yeah, come on Jess. Uh, we would like to sing you all a song," Ella said with slight trepidation.

Jess stood beside her and whispered into her ear, "I'm sure glad you know what you're doing. You start us off, okay?"

"Okay." Ella, giggled nervously.

> *"Oh the summertime is come'n,*
>
> *And the leaves are sweetly bloom'n,*
>
> *And the wild mountain thyme,*
>
> *Grows around the bloom'n heather..."*

Jess joined Ella at the chorus.

> *"Will ye go, lassie go?*
>
> *And we'll all go together,*

To pluck wild mountain thyme,

All around the bloom'n heather,

Will ye go, lassie go?"

Ella and Jess smiled at each other. Steve, Jack and Brody covered their ears, unimpressed by the girls singing.

"Make it stop!" said Steve. Pa looked sternly at him, and Joe carried on with the next verse.

"I will build my love a bower,

Near yon clear crystal fountains,

And on it I will pile all the flowers of the mountain,

Will ye go, lassie go?"

Aunty Vera, and Joe joined them with the chorus while Pa sat listening with the boys.

Joe started a final verse of his own with slightly glassed eyes.

"If my true love she were gone,

I will never find another,

In the starlight you will shine,

Even through the greet'n weather,

Will ye go, lassie go..."

Everyone joined in the final chorus of the song and the final effort was enjoyed by everyone. With smiles and cheers from all, Aunty Vera said, "Thank you, girls. I doubted you had any such surprise actually planned but you have done us proud and warmed our hearts." She hugged each of them and then went to the kitchen to put the kettle on.

Joe wiped a tear from his eye and Ella's heart ached for him.

"Oh Joe, are you alright? I bet you must miss Aunty Flo a lot, aye?" asked Ella.

"Aye lass – very much. She was the sweetest girl I ever knew."

"Well how did you meet Flo? We know about Uncle Max and Aunt Gabby, but what about you, Joe? What was Flo like?" asked Jess.

"Well, I will tell ye, but first ye've got to keep ye'r promise to me."

Joe stared at Jess as if looking through glass. Ella shared her cousin's discomfort but was also relieved. It was time to come clean to Pa and Aunty Vera.

Joe stood and went to pour himself and Pa a glass of whisky. He motioned to Aunty Vera to see if she would like some too. She declined.

"Here, you'll want one of these," Joe said, passing Pa a glass filled with the rusty brown spirit.

"Uh, Max, Vera. The girls and I have something to share with ye. And it's about that rift we spoke of between the Naudmans and the Lockhearts."

They both turned to listen to Joe, but before he could utter a word, Jess butted in. "Well you see, we've sort of been looking at our family history. Joe told us that Flo had been researching his family tree before she died. She made some discoveries and found that Joe's mother, Elaine, used to go by another name."

Ella wanted to be the one to tell Pa the good news so she jumped in before Jess could continue.

"Aunt Flo couldn't find the names of Elaine's parents but she did manage to get hold of her marriage certificate. At school, Mrs Jenkins helped us look up Joe's parents on a genealogy website and it showed Elaine's maiden name was *Lockheart*."

Pa shifted forward in his seat and Ella was pleased to have caught his interest. "So we wondered if there might be a link to our family. Unfortunately we couldn't find any record of an Elaine Lockheart ever being born. But we knew Elaine's birth-date, so we typed that in with the name Lockheart and we found that an Eleanor Lockheart was born on that same date.

"So you see Elaine used to be called Eleanor. Then we looked at our family tree. Pa, you said you didn't have any aunties or uncles on the

Lockheart side, but that's not exactly true. Great-Grandpa Joseph and Great-Grandma Rosalie had a baby girl ten years after our Grandpa Erik. Her name was Eleanor. So you see, that makes Joe your cousin." Ella's joy exploded on her face.

Pa looked at her in disbelief and for an agonising thirty seconds or so Ella feared he was getting angry.

"Wait a minute, go back, said Pa. "So Great-Grandpa Joseph, had my Pa, Erik, *and* a daughter. Her name was Eleanor. And you're saying that Eleanor was actually Elaine, Joe's mother? Well what do you make of that, Joe? All this time, and I never knew you were my cousin." Pa smiled at Joe, who looked far more pleased than he did when they first told him.

"So Joe is my cousin too - we're related?" asked Aunty Vera. She looked puzzled and a little sad. Ella hadn't a clue why.

Jess stared at her mother intently. Something was bothering Aunty Vera - but what?

Jess fidgeted with a fingernail and spoke without looking at anyone. "What we think happened is…Eleanor was sort of cast out of the family because she ran away and eloped with Gerrard - Joe's Pa." She eyed him. "You see she was only eighteen when she married Gerrard and he was thirty-eight. He took her to live in Denmark so her family couldn't find her."

Pa looked confused. "Well why didn't Elaine tell Pa when they moved back to Aberdeen?"

"Who knows really?" said Joe. "My father might have forbidden her. He was abusive towards her and perhaps she was too scared. Ma obviously made contact with Marta at some point, because we met at about fourteen, if I remember correctly. Maybe your mother kept it secret from Erik for a reason."

Joe's assumptions prompted Pa to suggest his own thoughts.

"Aye, Pa might have gone and bashed Gerrard senseless for stealing away his sister so young." Pa's voice was tight between his jaws, but he stifled his emotion when he saw the pain on Joe's face. "Sorry Joe, I didn't mean to upset you. It's not your fault. Pa never told us he had a sister. I can barely believe it. So your Ma, Elaine, was my aunty. Oh, I wished I'd known this a lot sooner." Pa took a swig of whisky and sunk his head to his chest. "Hmmm… I'm glad she came to me and Gabby's wedding. I think Ma probably had a hand in that if she knew all along. I wonder what else Ma knows?" said Pa.

"Obviously a lot more than we do!" Aunty Vera was mad, and she picked up Pa's whisky and downed the last of it. "But it's unlikely she'll ever be able to remember now." The chill in her aunt's voice was undeniable and Ella sensed there was much more to it.

"But what about after your Pa died, why didn't Elaine, or Ma, or even Pa tell us about being related then?" Pa asked Joe, who was pouring himself another drink. Joe offered Pa another round, but he shook his head.

Joe downed his drink in one swig. "Dunno. Maybe too much time passed and she didn't wanna stir up the past. Sometimes it's just best to leave things be for everyone's sake."

Ella knew there was more of the story to tell, but since they didn't have all the answers, they kept quiet about their visits to Castle Ferlie, Grandma Marta, and about Joe's missing sister. Ella could only hope there would be more answers to their questions in the letters.

Jess was either completely unaware of the tension in the room or she just didn't care.

"Well now that everyone knows, Joe, will you tell us some more about Flo and how you met?"

"Och lass, I would be glad to, but it's awfully late and I aft' to be up early in the morn'n. How 'bout we have some more stories t'morrow even'n, Aye?" Joe said slurring his words, demonstrating his inability to hold his liquor.

"Oh okay, I guess so," said Jess.

"Night Joe." Ella stood to give him a hug.

"Max, 'ow 'bout we go fishing t'morrow? Bring the boys and well make a day of it, aw'right?" Joe swayed towards the door.

"Aye, that sounds great, Joe. We'll see you tomorrow then," said Pa.

Joe left the family in the cottage and made his way back to his own quarters, where he would no doubt continue to drown his sorrows in private.

The boys who had lost interest in the adult discussions were happily playing a game of Bluff on the dining table and protested as soon as Pa told them they were headed for bed.

"Would you like me to help with the washing up, Aunty Vera?" Ella wanted to talk to her aunt about what was bothering her and she wasn't sure how to do it without tempting Jess's curiosity.

"Oh no, Luv, that's alright, I'd like some time to think about everything. You two can head off to bed now too if you like."

Ella opened her arms to give her aunt a hug.

"Alright. How about we go for a walk on the beach tomorrow? I'd love to spend some time with you, Aunty Vera."

"Awe, that would be lovely, I'd like that very much."

"Oh I almost forgot. How did it go with Joe - with the cabinet? Did he let you make an offer for it?" Ella asked.

"Yup, it's mine if I want it for twenty pounds. I said I'd take it. Not sure how I'm going to get it home though. But seeing as we're now cousins - I'm sure he won't mind storing it till I'm ready for it."

Jess jumped up from her seat, pulling the items they'd found in the drawer from her pocket.

"That reminds me, Mum. After you'd gone we tried that drawer and it wasn't locked - it was just stuck. We found these inside."

Aunty Vera paused from her washing up to take a look at the items closely. "Hmm, a boarding pass for Paris. What's the date on it, Jess?"

Jess pulled the paper closer to read the fine print. "It says, the sixteenth of September 1988."

"Hmmm," Aunty Vera furrowed her brows. "What's it say on the matchbook?"

"Normandy Hotel - Paris," Jess said.

"You don't see those around much anymore, but I guess it was still popular to *fumer une cigarette* in *Ol' Paree* back then." Aunty Vera's French accent was severely exaggerated and Ella couldn't help but giggle.

"The coins are French too, see." Jess held them out for her mother to inspect. Aunty Vera glanced at them before resuming her dish washing.

"Well, I guess the last person to use that cabinet took a trip to Paris."

"You don't say." Jess rolled her eyes full circle.

"Well now, let's have a think. Those items are from 1988, so let's see...I would have been about seven, so I'm guessing it must have been one of Joe's parents. Aunty Elaine? Aunt Eleanor? Hmmm it's weird. I never knew I had an aunt all this time. And now that I know I had one - she's gone. I have so many questions." Aunty Vera swirled the dishwater in the sink and stared at the window. The glass reflected her odd expression and Ella wished she could read her aunt's thoughts.

"Come on, Jess. Let's go get into our pyjamas." Ella tapped Jess's shoulder and she followed.

Jess kept her voice low once they were tucked inside the bedroom. "That boarding pass wasn't Elaine's, Ella. Joe said she never went anywhere except Denmark. And I guess she also went to Italy. I bet those things were Gerrard's. Let's take a look at those letters, shall we?"

"Careful though, we don't want to get busted with them by your mum."

"Okay, let's just take one out at a time and keep the rest in the drawer. I'll read the first one and you can read the next. Shall we start at the bottom of the pile or the top?"

"I dunno, I guess the oldest one first. Then maybe we'll have a better picture of what happened and when."

Ella lay her head back on the pillow and listened to Jess as she began to read.

They spent most of the night reading through the pages of Charlotte's letters to her beloved Gerrard. It seemed she genuinely loved him and was devastated when he left her. Although it was clear that he returned her affections, Charlotte's words always seemed to be of the begging kind. That was until the last few letters when she seemed to be more confident of Gerrard's love towards her.

In a letter dated 1975, Charlotte mentioned their quarrel in Denmark when Gerrard told her he would not come to visit her again. And then she had written telling him she was coming to visit him in Scotland with the child in 1977.

Ella wondered how he had managed to keep that a secret from Elaine. The next letter told of Charlotte expecting Gerrard to come any day, but she seemed concerned that she hadn't heard from him. Gerrard had obviously told her he was going to leave Elaine and come and be with her and Elle.

But her next irate letter in January 1988 was full of devastation that he wasn't coming and that Elle deserved better from him.

As they read on, late into the night, Ella almost felt sorry for this woman called Charlotte. She had lived her whole life in hope, waiting for a man who never came, or hardly ever anyway. And when Gerrard did come to visit, he never stayed long.

"Charlotte must have loved him very much to have waited for him for so long," said Ella

"And I think Gerrard must have loved her quite a lot too, seeing as he kept visiting them," Jess replied.

"Let's skip ahead, what does that last white letter say, Jess?"

<u>24th, June 1994</u>

My Dearest Gerrard

Elle is away at university and I am so lonely here all by myself with no one to talk to or spend my nights with.

She will return for the summer and I would very much like to spend one last holiday together as a family before she is too grown up and travelling with a companion of her own. She is doing very well and you would be so proud of her. She is exceedingly beautiful Gerrard and I see the young men staring at her when she does come home to visit during term breaks. I know it won't be long before she has a boyfriend, and I will be forgotten by her too.

Please, my love, say you will come and be with me forever. Surely your son is now just as grown and can manage the company. Come and spend your golden years with me in Paris, your wife has kept you long enough, while I have had to endure a life wasted in patience. If I don't hear from you or see you this summer, then I will leave you Gerrard and I will no longer be waiting for you in Paris.

I hope we will be together soon.

All my Love,

Charlotte.

"Wow, so she finally gave him an ultimatum. That must have taken a lot of guts after waiting all those years," said Jess.

"Yes, but what did that mean for Elaine? Did he leave her to be with Charlotte?" Ella asked.

"Well, how did Joe's dad die? Didn't I hear your Pa ask why they never told them they were related after Gerrard died?"

"Hmmm, you're right, Jess. He did say that. Joe doesn't like his Pa much, you saw how he got when we found those rocks in the coffin and tonight when he told us how mean he was. I'm not sure I want to ask him anything more about Gerrard."

"Well we've got to try, Ella. How else are we gonna find out what happened?"

"Let's ask him about Aunt Flo, he likes to talk about her and then perhaps we might get him to answer some questions about his Pa in the process. Slip them in, so he doesn't really notice. What do you think?" asked Ella.

"That's a brilliant idea, Ella. But you'll have to bring it up. I don't think he'd take too kindly to me asking him about Gerrard. And whatever you do, don't mention Charlotte. He might not know about her and I'd hate to be the one who told him his Pa was cheating on his mother her whole life."

"You're right there," said Ella.

"Girls it's so late," Aunty Vera spoke wearily.

Both Jess and Ella jumped in fright by the sudden interjection of her voice in their conversation.

"Do you think you can go to sleep now? I've been dozing on and off and I can't believe you two are still talking." Aunty Vera yawned more tired than angry at them.

"Sure Aunty Vera, sorry. We'll be quiet now. See you in the morning,"

"Sorry Mum. Night."

CHAPTER TWENTY-TWO

29th September 1994

Elaine

ELAINE SETTLED HERSELF in the aisle seat; with Joseph and Max sitting next to the window. The aircraft was due to take off from Paris to Aberdeen at 4:50pm and they had only just made the connecting flight with few seconds to spare. The boys were thrilled with the excitement of it all but Elaine was just grateful to be heading home.

Florence had been truly wonderful and Gerrard had been extra nice to everyone. It had been years since she had seen such a smile on his face; that was up until the last day. Why she had ever let Gerrard convince her to leave without him was beyond regrettable.

Gerrard's business associates had not arrived on the intended flight and it had put him in a most fidgety mood. All she could do was assure him they would arrive the next day. He was apologetic and promised he would be on the next flight home once his work was sorted. The only compensation was that she had two wonderful young men to help rush and direct through the busy Paris airport. Joseph had cheekily asked if she would like a ride in the baggage trolley to get there faster.

She'd refused, saying, "It simply isn't dignified, Joseph. You young lads might be able to get away with it, but I'm not so old yet as to require you to push me around on wheels. My two legs are perfectly fine."

The boys shrugged and laughed, and strode their much longer legs farther ahead of her. Elaine wished she could have stayed a couple of days in Paris. See the sights, and look up that address for Charlotte that she'd given to Marta. But time and her boisterous company certainly wouldn't permit any such delay this evening. *Pity*.

The sun was just starting to near the horizon and the orange glow, draped across the sky, was a backdrop anyone would desire when in the city of love.

Closing her eyes she took long slow breaths. The aircraft brakes released and the engines screamed to action; speeding them towards the end of the runway. Once lifted in the air, she relaxed and pulled a novel from her handbag. Its title - '*Whispers*,' had intrigued her when she perused the tiny bookshop in the village. She bought it on a whim thinking it might distract her from her thoughts. Now its task was to still her panic of being over the fields below, and the oceans which were to come. Elaine paused with a finger in the page to reminisce their holiday.

The Italian sun had certainly soothed her spirit and the creases on her face seemed to soften with each glass of wine she sipped. Elaine closed her eyes and pictured the four of them enjoying their lunch under the shade of the vined pergola above. The white-clothed table top hosted a feast of breads, cheeses, and fresh garden vegetables. The dry heat pressed on her face and the hum of insects sang in chorus with the birds.

Yes, it had been wonderful and filled with happy memories that would likely have to last her for years to come. But for just how many years, she never would have suspected.

Landing in Aberdeen, Marta was there to greet them, Elaine had telephoned ahead that Gerrard would not be returning with them from Florence, which meant their carefully planned rendezvous wasn't necessary.

Max threw his arms around his mother, surprising himself as much as her of his affection.

"I missed you, Ma." Max placed a kiss on her cheek. "We had a great time, aye Joe? How's Pa? Did the harvest go alright?"

"Yes, the harvest's in and he seems pleased enough. Where are your bags then? We best be getting you home for supper. I can't thank you enough for taking him, Elaine. Looks like it's been a good experience for him."

"It sure was, Ma, and I met someone too."

"Well did you now. Well, don't go mooning over some lass you'll likely never see again, you hear? Pa won't be too pleased if you're distracted. There's still plenty of work to do."

"Oh I wish you could have met her, Ma. She was the prettiest girl I ever saw." Max swooned.

Elaine chuckled. Marta would no doubt hear all about it on their ride home whether she wanted to or not.

A week passed and still no sign of Gerrard. Elaine wasn't too concerned, he'd been away often enough. She felt sure nothing ill had happened. Something ill-advised, however, was much more likely. She pondered whether he really was still in Florence - or perhaps he'd not been able to resist stopping in Paris. Elaine had called his office twice and they assured her that Gerrard was still away on business.

Joseph was due back at Oxford and even after two weeks with no word from Gerrard, Elaine insisted he return to his studies and not worry about his Pa's absence. With much protest, he obliged and returned to the city with a promise that as soon as she heard anything from Pa, she would let him know.

3rd April 2016
Ella

"Jess, wake up." whispered Ella. "Jess. It's nine o'clock."

"Huh mmugh," Jess mumbled, stretching and propping herself up on an elbow. She rubbed her eyes with her palm and stared blankly.

"What, what time is it?" She asked, now ready to process conversation.

"It's nine. I can't remember the last time I slept in till nine. Isn't it wonderful, I wish I could sleep till nine every day." Ella smiled, lying on her back, staring up at nothing in particular.

"Me too." Jess yawned.

"What shall we do today? I think we should go for a walk on the beach. I wanna show you the lighthouse. Pa took me out to it once in Joe's row boat. I was so scared to fall in. The water was choppy and it made the hairs on my arms stand up. It was thrill'n to be out there with the water all around us though and Ma waved to us from the shore holding Steve." Ella closed her eyes and was picturing the memory.

"I don't really like boats much. Dad took us on a punt in East London once. He used to be a tour chaperon at Cambridge University, and took hundreds of tourists up and down the River Cam. He must have been out of practice when he took us though, 'cause he nearly went in - us too. I'll stick to dry land thanks, the water's not for me." Jess swung her legs out from under the covers and sat upright. "I'm starving. I wonder where Mum is." She stood and opened the bedroom door.

Thin beams of sunlight lasered through gaps in the living room curtains, reaching almost to their bedroom doorstep. Ella hesitated, then threw back her covers and got up too.

"You're up. Finally. I was beginning to wonder if your dreams were detaining you from entering the land of the living. You girls were awfully chatty last night. Anything you want to share?" Aunty Vera asked.

"No, nothing important to report. It's a gorgeous day. I wonder if the boys are up yet?" asked Jess.

"Oh, they're long gone. They left about six this morning. Gone fishing. They'll be back later."

"Do we have to leave today, Aunty Vera? I feel like we only just got here."

"Awe, I know, Luv, me too. But Max has a farm to keep running, and you've school tomorrow too."

"Can we at least stay till dinner, Mum? I wanna hear the rest of Joe's story."

"Well, I think we should at least do that, especially if they catch anything. How about we take that walk on the beach after some breakfast?"

"Sounds good to me," said Ella.

"Me too," said Jess.

Mounting the top of the dunes, Ella flung open her arms and embraced the windy gusts with a smile. She loved the feeling of the air pressing hard against her whole body and the difficulty of breathing in just the right amount of air through her nose. With her 'Titanic moment' complete, she took off as quick as her legs could go, slowed only by their sinking in the sand. Her feet; caught momentarily too long beneath the surface, sent her tumbling face first down the dune; a mouth full of brown grit finding every crevasse in her teeth.

Ella picked herself up, terribly embarrassed by her clumsy fall. With airways clogged, she coughed and spat sand filled globs of saliva downwind. Seeing the waves she ran to the water's edge, shaking the remaining particles off as she went. Bending to catch a bowl full of surf in her palms, she swilled the icy water around her mouth - clearing the tiny stone particles from inside. She rinsed and repeated at least three times before any sense of normality returned around her tongue.

Finally, Jess caught up with her.

"You alright? All I could see was your red cardigan rolling. You wouldn't have heard me scream, but I did." Jess wrapped an arm around her shoulder.

"I'm alright, I just got stuck in the sand is all. I'm fine."

"Oh, Luv, that was quite a tumble. You okay?" Aunty Vera puffed when she finally caught up to them.

"I'm fine, Aunty Vera, but please don't tell anyone. I'm glad me brothers didn't see me. They'd tease me no end about it."

"Not a chance! My lips are sealed." Aunty Vera, twisted an imaginary zip across her lips.

Together they spent the next two hours playing up and down the beach, collecting shells and practicing their cartwheels on the firmer sand - Aunty Vera included.

Risking the chill of the water, Jess and Ella paddled their toes in the wash. Side by side they sank themselves in the sand, waiting to see who could remain standing as the swell wrapped around them.

Dizzied by the rushing water and the loss of feeling in their toes, they held onto each other to keep upright. The salty air was damp and slick on their skin making the girls hair twist into wild thick tassels.

Kicking the water up at each other, what little sun there was was no match at drying. Before long they were soaked and starting to chill from the mix of damp cloth and cool breeze.

"Time to head back girls!" Aunty Vera called with a cupped hand.

Giggling they all climbed the steep dune to the opposite side where it was more sheltered.

Tussock grasses wiped goose-bumped legs and unconscious feet as they trudged their way back to the red cottage door. Sitting outside in the faint sun for a moment longer to dry, they dusted off the sand while Aunty Vera went inside to make lunch.

"Here you go." Aunty Vera handed them each a hearty sandwich with cold beef and leafy fillings.

"Thanks, Aunty Vera… who's that coming over there?" Ella pointed towards the dunes.

"It might be those women Joe mentioned he was expecting. I'll go find out." Aunty Vera wrapped her coat about her and made her way towards the beach.

"What shall we do now?" Jess said through her last mouthful of sandwich.

"I dunno. Wanna take another look in the shed? There's heaps of stuff to look at, and play with. We could see if there's anything else in that crate too."

"Okay, sounds good. Shall I tell Mum?"

"No, she looks happy enough chatting to those ladies. Let's leave a note on the door though so she knows we've not gone missing, and come looking for us."

"Perfect. I'll go get the keys - just in case."

Flashlight beams bounced about the shed walls as they explored around boxes, under garden tools, bicycle parts and endless crates of empty glass bottles and jars. Pulling out an old rusty wheel and various different oil cans, their hands began to darken with the grime of days past.

Back at the shipping crate, Ella bent herself in half over its edge to reach the bottom and found an old trench coat. Patting it down, dust fled the dark cloth and made her sneeze.

"I wonder if this belonged to Gerrard?" She folded it over the edge of the crate, and beckoned Jess to come check out what else might be inside. The coffin still sat shrouded by the green tarpaulin. Neither one of them wanted to look at it again.

Jess tucked her hand inside her pocket with the keys. She didn't take them out. Ella looked warily at her - had she seen another vision? Something in the crate caught Jess's eye and she lunged inside to pull it out. It was a green round box about the size of a curled up cat. Opening it revealed a deep purple plush velvet hat with a round box top. Clustered to one side of it were several plumes of black iridescent feathers and carefully positioned loops of dark green ribbons. It was very elegant and Jess looked eager to try it on. She gave a few puffs to remove any invisible dust mites, then placed it on her head - tilting it to one side.

"How do I look?" She asked in an aristocratic voice.

"Why you look lovely my dear," Ella replied in a deep voice imitating Pa. They giggled.

"Put the coat on." Jess picked up the heavy coat and held it to her.

Ella frowned. "Uh, I'm not sure I want to, it's really dusty."

"Come on. Be a sport."

"Alright." Ella cautiously slipped each arm into the large heavy sleeves, and stood swamped by the coat. "There - you happy?"

Jess laughed.

"Is there anything in the pockets, Ella? Come on, let's see."

"I'm not sure I wanna put my hands in there. What if there's a cockroach or something? Steve did that to me once and I hardly ever use my pockets anymore."

"Nonsense, Steve hasn't been anywhere near this coat, Ella. The only thing you'll find in there is what the owner left behind - Now do it."

"I can't." Ella's lip quivered and she grimaced at the thought of doing so.

"Fine. I'll do it. Turn that way so I can reach."

Ella shuffled closer to Jess and turned. Reaching her hand into the left-hand pocket Ella felt Jess's hand search the cavern.

"Anything?"

"No, it's empty, what about the other one?" Again Jess's hand swam the deep recesses.

"Nothing." Jess frowned. "Hang on, is there a breast pocket inside - in the lining?" She asked excitedly.

Ella opened the coat to look. "Aye, there is." She leaned closer so Jess could check inside.

"There's something in it, Ella. It's a slip of paper, and there's a clip on it."

"Well open it. What's on it?"

Jess pulled the mirror-like money clip off the slip of paper. Inside was a hundred pound note, and printed on the paper was a five digit number.

"Cool. I wonder if this is an old account number or something?" Jess held the slip of paper towards the light as if looking for another clue within the parchment.

"I dunno, but it truly belongs to Joe, don't you think? We ought to give it back to him." Ella had always been taught to give things back to their rightful owners. She'd been rewarded for doing so once when a lady dropped two ten pound notes in the street and she had raced to pick it up and give it back. The lady was so taken by her honesty that she gave Ella two pounds as a reward. Steve thought it was very unfair since it took him nearly three weeks of collecting firewood to earn that amount.

"Yeah, I guess so." Jess put the money inside the paper and slid the clip back over them. She handed it to Ella and put her hands in her pockets.

"Hey I was thinking, you know how I have a vision every time I touch the keys?"

Ella wasn't sure she liked where this was headed by the tone of Jess's voice.

"Yeah."

"Well, there's only two keys left right? Why don't I touch them and see if I can get us any more clues about what they might unlock?" Jess's sly grin was loaded with mischief. "What do ya think - shall I try?"

"Umm, you sure you wanna do that, Jess? It's just, it's creepy when you just stand there staring into space and I can't get you to snap out of it." Ella fought to find a hand within the coat sleeve so she could tuck a loose strand of hair off her face.

"Oh, I'm getting used to it now. It doesn't scare me like it used to, but having you here makes me feel safer."

"Alright, I guess it's worth a try."

CHAPTER TWENTY-THREE

Jess

J ESS REACHED INTO her pocket and pulled out the wrapped keys.
The light in the shed had dimmed as the sun dropped lower in the
sky behind the clouds. Opening the cloth, she held her breath and looked
at the two remaining keys they hadn't found homes for.

"Touch the small black one there, Jess. That weird looking one we can
touch later." Ella shivered nervously.

Jess pointed out her finger and placed it on top of the little black
key…

…A flash of a woman standing in a bedroom appeared and she was
wearing a slim white gown. A crown of white and yellow daisies rested on
her loose auburn curls which framed her face. She bent to unlock a
wooden hope chest. Lifting the lid she pulled from inside the box a
framed photograph. There were two people in the picture, but Jess
couldn't make out their faces. The woman smiled and a single tear rolled
down her cheek. She kissed the picture once, then placed it back inside
the box and locked it again…

Jess awoke from her daze and her face lit up.

"Ella, I think I saw your mother. She was wearing a wedding dress and had a crown of daisies on her head, just like your Pa said she wore when he first saw her. She had curls just like your Ma's and a round face too."

"Really, Oh I wish I could have seen her." Ella frowned and cast her eyes to the ground. Tears dripped from her cheeks to her jumper, staining the fabric with wet circles.

"Well, why don't we try?" Jess locked eyes with Ella and battled her cousin's fear. She held out her palm. "Here, hold my hand and we'll touch the key together. But whatever you do, don't let go of the key - Okay? Even if it starts to tingle."

Ella nodded and lifted her chin. Jess prayed it would work. She hated the thought of crushing Ella's hopes.

Ella held the top of her hand and lay a finger directly next to her own. Cautiously, Jess guided them both towards the key...

... Jess's hand tingled - buzzing like her fingers were being pricked by a hundred pins. It had never stung this much before and she struggled to focus on the vision. It was like looking through a rain soaked windscreen. Finally the vision cleared and once again she saw the woman.

She didn't touch the hope chest this time, but instead just stared straight at them with light emanating from around her. Jess looked out the corner of her eye and saw Ella beaming with joy. Her eyes ran with tears but she was happy. Then the woman moved. Her eyes were desperate. Aunt Gabby reached out her arm towards them - her lips moving but without any sound. She was drawing closer and her hand was within inches of touching them...

Jess screamed. Never had a vision been that intense before.

"Are you alright, Jess?" Ella's face looked iridescent and appeared to be glowing, like Aunt Gabby's just had.

Jess was afraid. Had she woken from the vision or not?

"Did you see her? She looked straight at us." Jess said, still shaking from the trauma. Ella's face started to look normal again.

"I saw her! You were right, Jess, it was Ma. Wasn't she beautiful?"

Jess wasn't sure what to make of any of it. Never had one of the visions tried to interact with or touch her before. She couldn't tell what was real and what wasn't, and she still trembled from the whole experience.

"Jess. Was that you?!" Mum called.

"Umm yeah, I'm alright!"

The girls quickly abandoned their costumes and headed for the door.

"That was creepy, Ella. I'm not sure I wanna touch that last key after all… I'm alright Mum! It was just a rat I think - scared the living daylights outta me." They exited the shed. Jess attempted to laugh to help ground her back to reality.

"Oh, never mind we all catch a fright sometimes. Look, here come the lads. They're smiling so I guess we'll be eating fish for supper." Mum smiled and walked them back towards the cottage.

"Wow looks like you had a great day," Mum said, eying up the boys catch. "What have you got?"

"This here is Cod," said Joe.

"And I caught a Bass, Aunty Vera, but it wasn't big enough to keep so we had to throw him back," said Jack disheartened. "Steve caught that one there and Pa caught that really big Skate."

"How about you, Brody, how did you go?" Mum asked.

"I had some nibbles, but they all got away. I'm not very good at fishing."

Joe came and patted him on the back. "Well now, it was only your first time, ye've got to give it another chance, Brody. Don't give up so easily, those fish never do, it's what keeps them swimmin' in the ocean, lad. You'll have better luck next time; I guarantee it." Joe smiled. "Well now, are ye stay'n for supper?" He asked Mum.

"Well, I'd like to if Max doesn't mind driving home in the dark."

"That's fine, Vera, I don't mind. I'd sure like to cook up some of this fish while it's still fresh."

Mum clasped her hands together pleased. "Well, I peeled up some tatties in the hopes you'd be successful, so I'll go and put them on now. You two can see to the fish and show the boys what to do. I may be a nurse, but I'm no expert at gutting and cleaning fish."

"Aye, not to worry, Vera. I think we'll manage just fine thanks," said Joe.

Uncle Max worked at removing the fish scales, while Joe slid his knife from head to tail along the underbelly to remove the guts. The boys watched the gory massacre with mischievous intrigue.

"Don't go getting any ideas now," Jess said. "If you think a pile of fish guts is gonna scare me then you'd better keep a lookout for the ghost of the lighthouse. I hear it roams up and down these shores at night wailing for all those men who lay dead at the bottom of the sea."

"Oh Jess, come on, there's no ghost at the lighthouse," said Brody. "You're just making that up."

"Am I?" She asked without blinking.

"I don't believe in ghosts anyway," said Steve.

"Joe, can you tell us about you and Aunty Flo now? Pleeease." said Ella.

Jess was relieved when Ella changed the subject. It was probably for the best since her last lot of ghost stories had landed them in a bit of trouble. Besides, the fact that she thought she really had seen Aunt Gabby's ghost sent a full blown case of goose-bumps over her whole body and she needed something to take her mind off it.

"Alright lass, I'd be glad to," said Joe "Let's see now... It was my second year of University...

246

CHAPTER TWENTY-FOUR

October 1994

Joe

JOE NOTICED HER immediately; how could he not? Air caught in the back of his throat.

She moved to take a seat in the second row of the classroom. Her celestial cream hair shimmered in the light and her complexion was almost as pale. Had he died and not realised it? He stabbed a pen into his thigh just to be sure.

Who was she?

With a nervous smile, she glanced back at the other students gathering in the seats behind her. The fluorescent lights above reflected squares of light on her glasses. The frames were thick and black but they didn't detract from her best feature - her full crimson lips. Joe watched their every move as words shaped them into various positions while she chattered to a friend. He'd let her talk all day - just to watch them.

God I want to kiss her. How am I gonna stay focused with those lips in the room?

The lecturer, Professor Scott, arrived and Joe watched the girl smile like she knew him. Scott's appearance wasn't unattractive for someone of his era, but Joe had little regard for the man as an inspirational lecturer. History of Economics was not a subject he thought anyone enjoyed, himself included, but this girl seemed as eager to learn the material as Joe was to meet her. He could only hope that her expression indicated pure educational interest, and not some university crush on the professor. By the time five minutes had turned into forty, Joe hadn't heard a single word spoken by Scott. But of all the subjects this term, History of Economics was now his favourite.

Joe thought he'd nodded off when bells signalled the end of class. Lulled by Scott's voice and the angel in the second row he was certain he'd floated out of his body to some dream-world. The room promptly emptied and with it went any hope Joe had of running into the lass who had unwittingly consumed his thoughts. Joe tripped down the stairs, along the corridor and out the double doors of the lecture hall. Scanning the sea of bobbing heads ambling to their next lectures, Joe spotted his angel walking alone on a path towards the library. With strides that doubled his peers, he followed her from a safe distance and tried to think of a pick-up line that would make her laugh.

Nothing sprang to mind and he cursed his memory for failing him. All he could do was watch her and pray an opportunity might present itself.

Gazing skyward, the girl seemed more interested in the trees above than the uneven cobbled path under foot. He wasn't paying attention either and almost tripped on a raised cobble.

Saving himself from a fall and likely great embarrassment, his angel didn't succeed with the same dexterity he expected. She stumbled to her knees and then onto her palms, grazing both in the process.

Having seen the impending mishap about to occur, Joe ran to try and catch her; narrowly missing his opportunity to do so. Regrettably he was faced with aiding her messy recovery instead.

"Are you aw'right, lass?" His bleeding angel sat on the path clasping at her knees with whitened grit-moulded hands. Tears welled in her eyes and she blushed with embarrassment at her clumsiness.

"Oh, I think I'm fine." She pulled back her hands to check if it were true or not.

"Ouch, ye'r knees are battered, canna help ye?" Joe smiled and bent to help collect her things lying scattered over the path. Handing them to her, he took her other hand and eased her up off the path. She squinted at the pain but tried to put on a brave appearance.

Joe reached to correct the twisted frames over her eyes and inspected the blue irises through the glass barriers and beyond. The intensity of her stare had him lost. If she'd not looked down to check her hands again, his gaze would still be locked on hers. As it wasn't, he did the only thing he knew how to do well - introduce himself.

"My name is Joseph Naudman." He held out his hand formally. She looked at her dirty grazed hands and tentatively offered just her fingers for him to shake. He looked at her hand and turned it over. Gently, he brushed away the granules of dirt wedged in her palm, and resisted the urge to bring it to his lips and kiss it - like his mother used to when he fell over. He didn't want to scare her. So instead, he cupped her palm inside his own and reached for her other hand to give it the same care.

She watched him closely, catching her breath when he brushed her skin.

Eventually, she stammered, "I'm Flo. Well - Florence actually, Florence Rogers, But everyone just calls me Flo. What about you? Do you shorten yours?" She was flustered and a little nervous too if he wasn't mistaken.

"Aye. My friends call me Joe. But me mother calls me Joseph." It wasn't usual for him to mention his mother when meeting a girl he was actually interested in, but then there was nothing usual about this angel.

"Well, thank you, Joe, I really appreciate your help. Do you go here?" Flo asked to sway the attention from her embarrassment.

"Yes, I just had History of Economics with Professor Scott."

"Oh I was just there too, he's terribly hard to listen to, isn't he. That monotone voice makes me want to fall asleep. I didn't see you," She said as if apologising.

Joe couldn't help himself from grinning. *Scott's not competition then - that's a relief.*

"Oh, I was hiding up the back, it's a pretty full class," He said.

Flo winced when she changed the weight on her feet.

"Well, I'd better go and clean myself up if I'm gonna make it to my next class. Thanks again Joe. I hope we meet again - under nicer circumstances next time."

"Well, ye'r not gett'n away that easy, lass. Me mother would scalp me behind if I left a bonnie lass like you to make her own way. No, you'll be hard to rid me of ye till ye'r patched up,"

Flo beamed a smile and gave a short laugh. He couldn't tell if it was because of his chivalrous attention or because of his Scottish way of speaking. Either way he didn't mind. She appeared to like him and that was compensation enough for his ego.

Putting his arm around her small frame he bent to offer her his shoulder. When he realised their height was no great partnership, he simply picked her clear up off the ground and carried her, books and all, towards the library and the nearest first aid station.

Seated on the nurse's bed, Joe wrapped his arm of protection firmly around Flo's shoulders. His eyes fixed on her profile as often as he could without her noticing. As the nurse sat before them with a tray of cotton swabs and antiseptic cream. Flo turned to face him; unable to watch her wounds be cleaned. Pain swelled in her eyes as moist cotton balls dabbed at her broken skin.

Joe, keen to distract her, offered up random comments and odd questions causing her to think carefully about her replies.

"What sort of a name is Florence anyway? Are you from Italy? Did your parents meet there?"

Flo went to respond, but then inhaled shortly when the swab touched her skin. "W...Well, my parents aren't Italian. They haven't been there, at least I don't think they have, they never told me if they did. You know I'm not really sure why they called me Florence, perhaps it was after Florence Nightingale?"

"Well some nurse you'd make" - Joe paused to catch the eye of the nurse cleaning Flo's wounds - "I think she makes a much better patient. Would'nee ye say?" He said with another wink. The nurse smiled, rolled her eyes at his jest, and left the room giving an excuse of needing more bandages.

Was it just a reason to leave the two of them alone?

Joe didn't care. It was his opportunity to make a move and if he missed it he'd never forgive himself.

"You're from Scotland if I'm not mistaken and your accent, it's from the north isn't it?" She asked.

This was going to be harder than he thought.

"Aye, true enough. Though don't hold it against me. I'm here to study business and economics, as per my father's wishes. It's me second year. Honestly, I should've taken that history class last year, but I could'nee fit it in. I'm sure glad of it now though, for if I had I would'nee've been watching ye...I mean, I..." He paused. Now it was his turn to blush. "You know, I've been to Florence. I went there with me parents this summer. We explored the villages and vineyards... Aye, 'tis bonnie true. But not near as bonnie as you, Flo." He looked through her glass shields once more into a vortex of ice blue shards and took his chance on a kiss. She didn't refuse and in fact returned his gesture with equal interest.

A sting of desperation arced through his chest making his heart pound with rays of heat. He didn't notice he'd bumped Flo's glasses off her nose until the nurse cleared her throat and re-entered the room.

Joe felt cheated. If the nurse hadn't come back he might never have stopped. Flo seemed into it.

Her lips were red - like a drug, and he wanted more. Instantly addicted, He needed another fix. How long would he have to wait?

The nurse, although clearly entertained, had little time for their shenanigans and began wrapping Flo's knees and palms in white bandages. Unable to do anything else, Joe resorted back to formality.

"Can I take ye out for supper, Flo?"

"Yes, I'd like that very much, as long as you don't mind these." She held up her bandaged hands.

Joe smiled. "How about I cook us a meal at my place then, that way ye won't have to worry about trying to use a knife and fork in a restaurant. I'll take ye out somewhere fancy when ye're all better." Joe didn't want to put her off with his obvious enthusiasm, but she seemed delighted by his offer of not just one but two dates.

"That's very kind of you, Joe. I look forward to it...just as long as I'm not the only thing on the menu." Flo lifted her chin and blushed. Flo slunk her eyes beneath her lashes. He could tell she was waiting for another kiss. Desperate to please her, but equally keen to let the tension build, he looked away.

Joe's mind wrestled with his body in a tug of war of desire, his forced resistance to her tempting lips necessary if he wanted things to progress further than they had in any of his past relationships.

Joe stood and put his hands in his pockets. "I'll come pick ye up at seven. I assure you, Flo, I'm a perfect gentleman. You'll not regret it. My food, on the other hand - well, ye can decide on that for ye'self later."

Having professed himself to be a gentleman, Joe pulled one hand from his pocket and offered it to Flo to help her stand. Flo looked disappointed. He hated himself for it. But if he'd learnt nothing else over the last year, he knew that delaying fulfilment often enhanced the reward.

Helen Tisdale was to thank for that. Before her, Joe had hopped from one girl to the next - taking little care with their feelings, or his own. Helen was far more challenging. The chase was exciting and during the months he pursued her, he'd gotten to know her better than anyone else. That's what made breaking up with her so difficult. He could see they had no future together and ended it before leaving for the summer. He regretted breaking her heart and questioned whether he'd done the right thing. Max was good in that regard. He'd taken his mind off it and made him forget all about Helen. Joe was determined not to repeat the same mistake again.

Joe could tell from the moment he'd looked in her eyes that Florence Rogers was not going to be just another chase - she was his future - he just knew it in his bones. Even though he liked her more than any girl he'd ever met before, he worried that if he rushed their physical attraction, he might spoil his chance at a proper relationship. This time he would not allow himself to be so carnally swayed.

Flo

Flo enjoyed her dinner at Joe's so much that she wouldn't wait for her hands to heal for a second date. Their discussions had been a welcome change from the typical guys she'd dated. She knew she wasn't always the easiest girl to approach; too filled with day-dreams to notice when others took notice of her. Her suitors had been few since she often attracted the quiet and reserved men. More often than not she found them difficult to engage with in topics of political debate or historical points of interest. Joe was a welcome injection of colourful banter and often put a fresh spin on things. His unpredictable take on the world engaged them frequently in deep conversations that could last for hours. Flo liked it. In fact she found herself liking it so much she worried she'd be too caught up to notice any of Joe's possible flaws. He was attracted to her - she knew that much. But he'd been patient and respectful in that department - maybe even a little too patient for her liking.

Their chemistry was undeniable and she fought hard to hold herself back from letting go completely. He had her head which was no easy feat, and she wanted him to have her heart also. But there was something that kept her from giving it all. She wasn't sure what it was. She'd glimpsed moments in Joe's expressions that gave her pause to think them over. What did it mean when he rubbed his chin? Why did he always insist on leaving just when things started to heat up? She could only suppose someone hurt him once and he was just as afraid as she was to let go completely.

After a week of flirtatious lunches and dinners, they had taken a big step last night and he'd stayed over. Nothing happened - though she had to admit, she wished it had. He just wanted to hold her as they fell asleep and she was more than happy to let him.

Somehow, without realising it, their night together had deepened their bond, and solidified their feelings for one another. Kisses were all he'd permitted, but she could tell he wanted more. The longing in his eyes bore a stunning resemblance to her own and she was desperate to know what was holding him back. The only way she could think to pry it out of him was via her friends and family. She decided that morning that he needed to meet her parents. Joe could be the one for her and she'd be stupid not to seek their guidance before allowing herself to commit further.

She agreed to meet Joe for lunch the next day in the Cafeteria. She'd ask him then if he'd be willing to meet her parents. And - if Gabby were there - he'd struggle to say no to her.

Flo confidently strode across the cobbled pathway without a hint of stumbling. She spotted Joe waiting at a table. In front of him sat a single red rose - the fifth one this week.

Waltzing up behind him, she asked, "This seat taken?"

"Aye, Sorry, I'm waiting for me girlfriend," Joe spoke it with such a solemn face that he caught her off guard. What did that mean? Seeing her confused look, he promptly smiled and winked. "I hope that's you by the way."

Flo laughed once she caught his meaning and rather than sit across from him where the rose sat, she slid into the seat next to him and kissed him fervently to give him his answer. Joe was flustered by her sudden move on him in public and struggled to pull away. When he finally managed, he got up, pulling a large bouquet of at least a dozen red roses from beneath the table.

She was speechless.

"What would you like for lunch, m' Lady?" They were the same words he'd spoken every day. She always replied, 'the salad'. But today she was inspired by his spontaneity and said, "Surprise me."

She trusted Joe. They'd discussed food often enough on their dates and he would know what to get her.

Joe raised an eyebrow at her and grinned.

"Well I'm not sure that's such a good idea," He joked in seriousness. "I mean, I don't want you to end up in anaphylactic shock or anything. It's only our fifth…sixth, no, seventh date." He smiled. "Alright, one salad, come'n right up."

Joe sauntered off in confidence while she sat and sniffed the roses. Never had she felt such a rush of power and influence over a man before and rather than feel thrilled about it - she panicked.

She loved him, she couldn't deny it. But did he love her back?

Joe

Before Joe could make it back with their food, a girl with a familiar smile and set of curls had joined Flo at the table.

"Joe, I'd like to introduce you to my friend, Gabby."

Joe placed the tray on the table and offered out his hand.

"It's a pleasure to meet ye, Gabby." He held out his hand for her to shake

It was her alright, but he didn't want to ruin Flo's introduction by announcing they'd already met. He wasn't sure how his new girlfriend might react, so he kept quiet.

Gabby arched her brow and clasped his hand. "Joe, have we met before?"

Phew - she remembered. Now he wasn't the one to bring it up.

"Aye, we met in Italy. Me friend Max was so taken when he saw ye that he made me promise to help him find ye again. We ran all over that village looking for ye that night."

Flo jerked her head when she heard Joe's story.

"What night was this?" She asked.

Gabby blushed at the mention of Max's crush.

"He was so sweet," she conceded. "Mother liked him too. I was wary of encouraging him when he mentioned you were leaving the next day. I didn't want to break his heart." Her confidence conveyed she was the one used to breaking hearts, and not the other way around.

"Well, he'll be over the moon when I tell him I've seen ye again. If ye don't feel the same way, mind, then I'll no say a word." Joe took a bite of his burger and grinned. Gabby was cornered. She'd have to decide one way or the other if she wanted to see Max again. Joe liked watching her squirm.

"Well… I never said I wasn't interested. There's something awfully charming about you Scottish men that I can't seem to put my finger on. I guess it's because my father is Scottish."

"Oh, what area is he from?" He asked.

"I'm not really sure. He moved around a lot, but grew up mostly in around Copenhagen. I remember taking a holiday with him in Scotland once when I was little. I loved seeing all the castles. It was magical."

"What does he do?" Joe's interest wasn't for his own sake, but for Max…and for Flo, come to think of it.

"He's a salesman - travels a lot. I hardly see him. But it's been like that for most of my life, so I'm used to it. When he is home, he's the best father a girl could wish for though. Spoils me lots - but I let him." Gabby smiled.

"Yer lucky then, my father's fair crabbit. Works a lot too. Wants me to follow his footsteps. I'm not sure it's really what I want to do with my life, but I don't think I have a choice. If I did, Pa hasn't said so."

Joe hadn't really given his studies much consideration beyond what his father had enrolled him for. It hadn't occurred to him to suggest some other kind of career path. And, if he had - he couldn't think what it might be. Business studies was just something Pa said he would do. Go to University. Study Business. And take over the Naudman shipping company when Pa said he was ready. His whole future had been decided and he hadn't thought to question it. Until now that was.

What did he want to do with his life?

Would Flo be in the picture? He hoped so.

But what if Pa disapproved?

For a flitting moment he felt an odd sensation he'd not had before. *What if he refused his father's plans and instead, went off on his own with Flo?*

Ma. He could never do that to her. It was the only thing he was sure of.

"Well, my father is not Scottish, but I still love him all the same." Flo slammed her fork into her salad, making Joe acutely aware he'd been staring at Gabby and neglecting Flo from the conversation.

He blushed, then grinned at Flo. He'd never seen her like this before. Fumes of jealousy seemed to fog her glasses near the tops of her cheeks and he lifted them off her face for a moment. She blinked a few times but didn't break their stare. He wiped her lenses on his shirt without drifting his eyes for a second. "Och, really? Well - he's a lucky man to have you for a daughter. I only hope I'm as lucky when me own turn comes."

Joe turned red when he realised what he'd actually said. Flo lips twisted tight, she was trying not to laugh. But she burst into a fit of giggles. In truth he didn't really mind how she took it. There was certainly some truth to it. Everything was going great with Flo and he expected it to continue if he didn't put his foot in his mouth too often.

"You big Oaf." She pecked him on the lips. "You'll make a great dad one day."

"He's a good one, Flo." Gabby nodded, "You could do a lot worse. These Scots are terribly good at sweet talking though. If you've any sense you'll keep him waiting for you. Don't do what my mother did; wait your whole life for him to propose. My father has never proposed and probably never will. She doesn't mind though, they love each other anyway. Still, best to wait for the ring, Flo."

Joe couldn't believe Gabby's candour and noted it for future reference if he decided to tell Max. Perhaps he should get to know Gabby a little better before he informed his friend. It might save Max a whole lot of heartache.

Even though the revelation could be risky, he didn't care if Gabby and Max didn't work out - so long as it didn't affect his chances with Flo. By dinner time he'd resolved that the benefits outweighed the negatives and he would let Max know he'd found his 'true love' once more.

But how would he tell him? He didn't have a phone number for him. The only way he'd ever made contact with Max was through his mother.

Joe needn't have worried. It didn't take long for the grapevine to have its intended effect, and the very next weekend Max arrived to visit him in Oxford.

CHAPTER TWENTY-FIVE

3rd April 2016

Joe

"**Y**OUR PA WAS so love struck, I never saw any man act so pathetic in all my life." Joe chuckled.

"Oh come on, Joe, admit it. You were head over heels for Flo too. She had you wrapped around her little finger every bit as much as Gabby did me. We were helpless and at the mercy of whatever rules they had for us - and boy there were plenty. Gabby was very reluctant to get involved with me. She blamed her father - said she had abandonment issues, but she never really explained why. I never knew much about her parents. They died so suddenly and she didn't like to talk about it." Max scraped the back of his knife along the body of the fish, lifting and removing its scales with short swift movements.

"Aye, it was pretty tough for her. She must have felt so alone when she lost 'em. I'm sure it's the only reason she actually agreed to marry ye, Max." Joe laughed - Max didn't.

"Really? You think so, Joe?" Max handed him the last fish.

"No, I was only kidd'n. She loved ye, Max. She told Flo you were the only man who ever cared so much for her, even more than her own father. You were right for each other - right from the start."

Joe finished his filleting and filled a bucket with fresh water to wash up.

"So what happened when you went to Oxford to meet up with Aunt Gabby again?" Jess asked Max.

"Well, she was just as I remembered her, beautiful eyes, gorgeous smile. I was more nervous the second time because I had no Italian women chasing me to boost my adrenaline. But even so, my heart was thumping out my chest. I was certain she'd notice. It was awkward at first, I didn't know what to say, except to compliment her of course, which was easy. But then I wasn't sure if she actually liked me; she hardly knew me. We went on a double date with Joe and Flo; remember that Joe? We went to that Jazz club."

"Aye - that was Flo's idea." Joe hadn't enjoyed the music much. Some of it was okay but it got old pretty fast.

"Yeah, it was okay I guess - but some parts were terrible." Max smacked a palm to his forehead, then rubbed it briefly before wiping his expression away.

"What d'ya mean, terrible?" Joe asked like it was news to him.

"Well you and Flo were helpful in getting the conversation started, but then you were so wrapped up in each other that you completely forgot about us."

"No, we didn't," said Joe.

"Aye, you did," Max said flatly.

"Och maybe we did, I dinnae remember. Flo said we should give ye some time alone. I wasn't about to disagree cause it meant I got to be alone with her, if you catch my drift." Joe winked.

"Ugggh, this story is getting way too gross," said Jack.

Max tousled Jack's hair in jest. "Well long story short; it took me a while to win Gabby's trust, but after my third visit, she knew I wasn't going to stop. She finally gave up her resistance and we couldn't see enough of each other after that. It was tough through the winter and spring, mind. She at least had school to focus on whereas I just had the farm mostly. Pa said I didn't need to go to University since farming would be my lot. Which turned out to be a good thing, because it meant I was working and could afford to take trips to visit Gabby more often."

"Come on, we better stop jabbering and start cooking this fish." Joe gestured them all to head inside.

Butter sizzled in the cast iron pan and Joe sank the fillets into its browning bubbles. Immediately it popped and cracked; searing the skin and turning the flesh into creamy white flakes. Joe removed the last pieces from the pan and within minutes, Vera announced the potatoes were ready. Everyone gathered at the table to sample the various types of fish they had caught. It was the best meal Joe had had in a long time and he was sad the visit was coming to an end.

"Right boys, ye best go and get the rest of your bags packed," said Joe. "You too girls. You'll need to get going as soon as ye'r finished here."

"Aye. You've all got school tomorrow and we best be gett'n home before the rooster crows. Now go on," Max said.

His instructions weren't as well received as Joe's. But once the threat of pig pen chores was added, they all scurried off to pack.

Joe laughed. He would have loved being a dad if he'd had the opportunity.

Ella

Waving at Joe they pulled out of the driveway to begin their journey home.

"Well that was a wonderful weekend, wasn't it?" asked Ella to no one in particular. The sun had sunk well below the horizon and a lavender twilight replaced the melon glow in the sky. The boys settled into silence with full tummies after their long day of fishing; dozing on and off in the back seats. Jess and Ella, on the other hand, sat up front close to their parents, too alert and energised to sleep. The stories Joe and Pa had shared of their budding relationships had been a dessert of curiosity for them, and ones Ella wanted to savour for as long as possible.

Ella found it difficult to imagine her mother as a twenty-year-old. She was always so wise and motherly in her memory that to think of her in any other way seemed too weird.

"So how did you propose, Uncle Max? Was it a grand gesture or an understated request nowhere special?" asked Jess. "Dad told us he proposed to Mum on the *London Eye*. Planned the whole thing. Had a meal waiting with waiters and everything. Personally, I'd hate to be that high off the ground eating dinner and being proposed to as well. Seems a little cliché to me. And then what's a girl to do - say no? It's not like she can leave in a hurry. He must have been certain Mum would say yes."

"Well, I did say yes." Aunty Vera interrupted, "It was so romantic too." She smiled remembering.

"So, what was your deal, Uncle Max?" Jess prompted. Ella wasn't sure if Pa would want to explain the specific details and was surprised to hear him speak so readily.

"I'd been working to save some money for a ring. But when I told Ma I wanted to ask Gabby to marry me, she insisted that I give Gabby, Grandma Rosalie's ring.

"On my last trip to Oxford, before the summer break, I took her to this spot in the Botanic Gardens, we'd picnicked there many times before and it was her favourite spot. I had the ring in me back pocket. I couldn't decide if I should put it in her glass of Champagne or on top of the mini chocolate gateaux I'd bought her. Neither seemed right. I remember her lying there on the picnic rug with her ringlets about her face. She seemed so peaceful and happy. She looked over and saw me staring at her and started talking about how we had to make the most of the summer we would have together. She was heading home to Paris but would fly to Aberdeen first to spend a week with me at the farm before she left." Pa paused and looked at Aunty Vera. "Well actually, Ma would never have let her stay at the farm with us – it wouldn't be proper. No. She was going to stay in Aberdeen in a holiday let.

"When she did finally arrive, we saw each other most days." Pa smiled at Aunty Vera again, and she smirked back, obviously concealing a private joke.

Ella was not pleased to see Jess grinning ear to ear, having cottoned on to Pa and Aunty Vera's secret.

What's so funny?

She hated not knowing - but couldn't let on she didn't She smiled broadly.

"But how did you propose?" Jess asked again.

"Oh, aye. Well, Gabby was saying something about how much harder the next year would be, her study commitments and all. I said I didn't care how long I had to wait. I reached into my pocket and pulled out the ring. Then I asked her to marry me," Pa said, finishing his story and expecting that would be it.

But Jess was like a tabloid reporter and probed further, "And did she say yes?"

"Of course she said yes, Jess." Ella rolled her eyes. Had her cousin not understood the stupidity of her question?

"Well, not at first she didn't," said Pa.

Ella was shocked; she'd never heard him tell it that way before.

"She was happy that I asked her, but she didn't give an answer, I had to prompt her. 'Well?' I said. And in true Gabby fashion, she said, 'I have to think about it' and she frowned looking at the ring. I was confused and thought she was just joking or that she didn't like the ring. She told me she needed the summer to think it over. I was more than a little disheartened I can tell you. But I agreed to wait and wouldn't accept the ring back until she could give me a definitive answer."

Ella wasn't sure if she liked knowing more of the specific details about her parents engagement. It somehow seemed less romantic and more real life than it ever had before. Pushing it aside in her mind, she instead focused on the few stars she could see amongst the shards of grey clouds dimly lit by the moon and imagined her mother sleeping on one of them.

October - December 1994
Elaine

Three weeks passed and still no word from Gerrard. Elaine wondered if she should be worried. He'd never been away for so long and not contacted her. What if something bad had happened to him? She picked up the phone and decided to call his secretary again.

Satisfied, she hung up the phone. Shona had informed her that Gerrard had been out of contact for two weeks, which had them all in a bit of a spin at the office. Finally, they had received a call from him three days ago saying that he would be returning to Aberdeen in four more weeks. Apparently his business meetings in Italy had gone so well that he'd been invited to stay on longer. Also, he'd take a stop in Denmark on his journey home; he said he had some 'loose ends to tie up,' Shona relayed. He was expected back in the office the following Monday, the 28th of November.

She was afraid to ask why Gerrard hadn't informed her of his plans himself, but was reluctant to allow his business associates to know how distant they'd become. Their time in Italy had given her hints of hope again. She was foolish to allow it and now Gerrard's delayed return only proved it.

When the 28th of November came and went without so much as a word of from him, Elaine suspected there was more going on than she was being made aware of. If Gerrard thought he could hide away from his responsibilities then she would have to make certain that he knew he still had some. Deciding on the most direct approach she could think of she went straight to his offices at the port.

"Where is he?" Elaine demanded upon entering the reception. Shona stood from behind her desk and went to guide her to a more comfortable seating area away from the front desk.

"Mrs Naudman, Gerrard is still in Denmark. Did he not call you?"

Elaine shook her head.

"Oh, I'm so sorry Elaine. I just assumed he would let you know his change of plans himself. He stayed on to head up a new project over there and isn't expected back till the end of January. It really hasn't made too much difference here. He conference calls in for all the board meetings and the company seems to be in good order as far as I can tell."

Elaine let a tear roll down her cheek.

"I'm sorry, Shona, he's been distant lately and when I didn't hear from him, well I suspected the worst I guess. I'm glad you're all doing well without him - wish I could say the same. There hasn't been any money put into our joint account for some time and I was worried there never would be again. What should I do? Could you contact him and ask him to at least inform me when he intends to input the funds? I have some bills to pay and if I do, there'll be little left for my daily expenses. I don't want to worry Joseph about all this, he's busy with his studies at University."

"Yes of course, Elaine. Would you like me to set up a meeting with the company accountant so you can check everything over for yourself?" asked Shona.

"Can I do that?" Elaine asked, ashamed to admit she didn't know her own rights.

"Of course you can - you and Joseph are shareholders. You have the same rights as any of the others do to look at the financial records."

"Well, I don't want to make Gerrard upset with me for checking up on him. Perhaps I'll just wait till he's back and then he can go over it with Joseph." Elaine worried she wouldn't understand a word the accountant might say and she'd feel even more foolish than she did presently.

"Alright, if you wish. What about your bills, shall I make the payments for you?" asked Shona with a softening smile.

"Can you do that? Oh no, I wouldn't want to get you into trouble. I'll work something out. I'll be fine."

Elaine left the office a little embarrassed by how she had handled herself in front of the staff. She should have just telephoned instead of making a fool of herself. Shona had been very understanding, but she knew Gerrard would be cross with her once he found out Shona knew their private business. Elaine would just have to trust that Gerrard was where he said he was and that he would deposit the money in their account in the next couple of days.

After another week passed she'd not only run out of money but patience as well. Nothing had changed.

That's it, I've had enough. What are you up to Gerrard?

I'm not waiting here any longer for answers - I'll find them myself.

Picking up the phone she made arrangements to catch the next flight to Denmark. With little cash left in the account, she had no other option but to use her credit card, something she only ever reserved for emergencies.

Well if this doesn't qualify, what does?

As soon as she had her tickets booked she quickly packed her bags and arranged for a cab to pick her up the next morning. A quick call to Joseph proved pointless as she couldn't get a hold of him at his flat and had to leave a message on his answer phone.

"Joseph - it's Ma. I'm off to Denmark to spend Christmas with your Pa. I know you wanted to spend Christmas with Flo and her family, so you've no need to worry about me. I'll be fine. Have fun my love and I'll give you a call on Christmas Day. Bye."

None of her past travels had brought her much joy, and this trip was unlikely to change the tide. Facing a solo flight was one thing but facing Gerrard and how he might react at the other end was terrifying.

Nervous and alone, Elaine sat trying her best to wear a face of bravery, like a soldier ready for battle. Knowing her facade was so faintly painted on, she was certain she could break down into tears at any moment and wash it all away. Fortunately, no one seemed interested in her anxious state and didn't bother offering to assist her in any way. Thanks to an ever increasing feminist movement it was lucky if a girl even had a door opened for her these days, let alone help with her luggage. She hadn't booked a return flight and didn't know how long she'd be gone for. This made packing light more difficult. It wasn't a vacation but she wasn't used to the life of a corporate traveller, where clothes served multiple uses. An outfit, to Elaine, consisted of at least five pieces and each outfit never utilised the same garment or accessory twice. It was also winter and the snow would have already packed the streets in Copenhagen.

She had booked a suite at the same hotel she and Gerrard stayed at almost six years ago. Later she'd be gobsmacked when the hotel bill was cast in front of her with a pen to sign.

For now, her ignorance served well and her surname held the weight she hoped it would until she tracked down the whereabouts of her husband.

With key in hand, and bags and bellboys dealt with, she opted to walk the four blocks to the port. Even though the streets of Copenhagen were hedged with snow, it was clear enough for one to tolerate the cold. Red Nordic Christmas decorations perched happily on lamp posts and tree tops and Elaine stopped frequently to enjoy them all. Come nightfall the streets would glow in a wondrous constellation of fairy lights and Elaine was almost giddy with anticipation for it.

Just before she visited the Naudman Shipping offices on the port front of Toldbodgade, Elaine paused at the Amaliehaven fountain where the shipping company offices had once stood. The buildings had been in dire need of repair, but rather than refurbish them, like Elaine suggested, Gerard sold them. Choosing to relocate to a more modern set of offices instead. She'd been heartbroken. The new building held none of the charms the old one possessed. But Gerrard reassured her that the developer had plans to build a garden with a fountain on the levelled plot of land.

Elaine walked the gardens and circumnavigated the foaming spouts of water shooting skyward from the Amaliehaven fountain. She was thrilled that everyone could enjoy the space now that the old buildings had gone. The company offices were now set a street back from the water's edge, but still had a stunning view of the harbour and the Amaliehaven Gardens too. Elaine pushed open the heavy door of the building and climbed the stairs to the first floor. Opening another door to the office reception she entered and offered her name to an attractive young blonde girl seated at the front desk. She looked surprised when Elaine asked to see Mr Naudman.

"Sorry, he's not here," She said.

"Well, when do you expect him back?" Elaine asked, ignorant of the situation.

"Mrs Naudman, I'm sorry to tell you, but Mr Naudman hasn't been here for some time. He left for Paris two weeks ago."

"But, he's working from here. He told his secretary in Aberdeen that he was staying on in Denmark to finish up a project." Elaine was certain that she was correct and not the other way around.

"Yes. Mr Naudman finished that project two weeks ago. He said he would inform the Aberdeen office of his new addresses in Paris." The girl smiled, unaware of Elaine's mounting frustration.

Elaine's lips tightened and she squinted at the girl.

"Well he never did, Miss..." Elaine searched for the girl's name badge and found none. "... Miss?"

"Chambers," the receptionist filled in Elaine's blank.

"Yes, Miss Chambers. Can you explain why?"

"No I'm sorry, but he expressly told us to route all correspondence with him through his Paris location in future."

Elaine paused and took a deep breath, her temper was starting to escalate. She straightened her jacket. "Well, what might that address be then, hmmm?"

"Uh, just a moment." Miss Chambers promptly uttered something in Danish to another woman across the room with a look of uncertainty. The woman looked up but refused to engage with her, choosing to resume her duties instead. The girl was clearly more worried for her own welfare than that of Miss Chambers' situation. Miss Chambers slowly turned the pages of her diary eventually stopping at the location bookmarked with Gerrard's contact details. She looked up at Elaine hesitantly.

"Can I see some ID please?"

Elaine felt indignant. She had always been well known as Mrs Gerrard Naudman in her husband's business circles. To have the fact questioned was not something she had anticipated, nor expected. Outrage would have been her usual response, but memories of her trip to the Aberdeen office surfaced and she bit her tongue. Obtaining the whereabouts of Gerrard was far more important than giving Miss Chambers an earful.

Fishing for her driver's license in her purse she handed it to Miss Chambers and smiled through gritted teeth. The girl only glanced at it briefly and Elaine wondered if the request had been made merely to scare her away.

Miss Chambers took a pen and wrote on a small notepad.

"It's, 3 Rue d'Abbeville, 75010 Paris." She handed the slip of paper to Elaine.

"Thank you, Miss Chambers." Elaine smiled politely, satisfied she had got what she came for. Finally, some solid information.

It wasn't until she was out on the street that she wondered if she should have asked for his contact phone number as well.

I'll call and ask from the hotel, I'd rather not face the Danish inquisition again.

Her presence had obviously made them uneasy, a more passive approach might yield better results.

Taking her time, Elaine enjoyed a cold but leisurely stroll along the water's edge. Boats navigated in and out of the harbour along with drifting chunks of frozen ice, broken up by the passing ships. She decided a bite to eat might help unravel her mounting confusion and made her way towards the nearest restaurant. Upon reaching its main door, however, she had changed her mind and didn't much like the thought of eating alone. The promise of hot chocolate and refuge from the outside air was little comfort in her current state. She tried to suffocate her memories and thought about calling Virginia. But she really wasn't in the right sort of mood for company. Besides, it would likely result in yet another lengthy explanation of her husband's dubious actions and it made her sick just thinking about it.

No, she decided it would be better to head back to the hotel and perhaps enjoy the spa.

Back in her hotel room, Elaine dialled the port office phone number and waited for Miss Chambers to answer.

"Hello Naudman Shipping Company, Copenhagen, You're speaking with Alice Chambers, How may I help you?"

"Ah, Miss Chambers - it's Elaine Naudman, Would you be a dear and get Gerrard's phone number for me in Paris?" Elaine said in a tone of sympathy.

"One moment please." She could hear the worry in Alice's voice, but a moment later she came back on the line. "The number is 00+33+1+77 23 59 10. Please, Mrs Naudman, don't say where you found it, I beg you." Her voice sounded desperate and a little scared.

"I appreciate your assistance, Miss Chambers. I won't say a word." Elaine heard an audible sigh of relief before the receiver went dead.

What should she do now? If she phoned Gerrard straight away, they wouldn't have time to warn him. But if she did call, maybe he'd know how she had tracked him down anyway. This called for some serious thought.

What if I call posing as a local business or something? Then I can just say it's a wrong number if he answers.

Elaine concluded it was a good enough plan.

Elaine's heart thumped inside her chest as she tried to work out what she would say

Grabbing the hotel notepad & pen she began scribbling and after a few minutes had something plausible.

She dialled the hotel's front desk.

"Mrs Naudman, how may we help?" asked the front desk concierge.

"I'd like to make an international call please. Can you connect me through?"

"Why yes of course," he replied.

Elaine relayed the number. "One moment please." He placed her on hold.

The phone began ringing - so were her nerves. She looked at the paper. Her mouth was dry. Would any sound come out when someone answered? Her heart beat faster.

"Allo, Charlotte speaking." The voice was deliciously French.

CLICK - Elaine hung up immediately.

CHAPTER TWENTY-SIX

11ᵗʰ December 1994

Elaine

SAFELY BACK IN her homeland, Elaine whispered a prayer of thanks when the wheels touched down on the tarmac. Her trip had been fruitful even if it hadn't yielded the results she had hoped for. At least now she knew Gerrard had left her for his mistress and the likelihood of his return was doubtful. But where did that leave her? She had no means to support herself and had relied on Gerrard for everything since she was eighteen.

By the time January rolled around, she feared her only option was to tell Joseph. With trepidation, she decided to try Marta instead. Elaine was sure the resulting reunion with her brother wasn't going to be pleasant but she had to do something.

Sitting alone at the Broadstraik Inn in Elrik, a familiar car pulled in. Elaine recognised it from the many times she'd seen Marta driving it.

She held her breath watching intently when Marta and an older version of her brother exited the vehicle. Tears welled in her eyes at the sight of him and she held herself back from running straight outside and into his arms. Elaine stood when they entered through the main door. Her eyes met Erik's confused gaze and she sobbed a smile at him with half extended arms.

"Eleanor! I don't believe it." He embraced her. "I thought Marta was joking till I've seen you now in person. Oh, Eleanor where have you been lass? You know Ma's gone and Pa went soon after her, he died of a broken heart I reckon. He was devastated when you left too. He never said as much, but I heard him greet'n after, and you know how he never let himself cry. Ma got so ill... Oh lass, why'd you do it?" He grasped her shoulders tight, searching for answers in her eyes.

"I don't know, Erik, it seems like such a long time ago now. I was young and silly. I never thought it would cause so much pain. But I've certainly paid for it."

"Have you now? Looks like you've done pretty well for yourself." Erik looked her over with a critical eye.

"You've no idea what I've been through Erik, so don't stand there and judge me like a Sunday preacher. You're no saint, and you've no right to hold me to account."

Marta nodded. "No he doesn't, but the good Lord does. And you've done all that he asks of you, Elaine."

"Elaine! Is that what you call yourself? Heavens Eleanor. I just don't understand." Erik shook his head.

"Well if you'd give me a chance, I'd like to try and explain." Elaine sat exhausted by the emotional reunion and the following debate over right and wrong.

Over the next hour, she explained everything to her brother, who after initially holding so much resentment towards her, finally softened when he heard of Gerrard's treatment of his younger sister. Although she sat before him as a grown woman with a child of her own, she couldn't help but feel humiliated by her past. To her brother, she must have appeared as naïve as the day she left.

Elaine patted a tissue to her nose. "Gerrard was everything to me, I worshiped him. He took care of me and made me feel like I was valuable. So valuable, that he never let me out from under his spell. And since I was so dependent on him for everything, he knew I wouldn't dare rebel against his wishes. It wasn't till I realised that he might have stolen my child and given her to his mistress that I began to uncover his deception."

"Well, he won't get away with it, Eleanor. I told him once I'd break more than his face if I ever saw him again, and now I hope I will." Erik clenched his right fist and punched it into his left hand. His eyes were laced with hate. There was no doubt Erik's words came with actionable consequences, and for a moment she regretted telling him the truth.

Elaine sat up straight and touched his arm.

"Don't do anything you'll regret, Erik. He's not worth it. And don't forget - he's the only person who can tell me where my daughter is."

"Well, what do you propose then?" He sighed heavily.

"I'm not sure. I was thinking I would go to Paris and confront him. Then I'd ask him where Joanna is. I don't see any other option."

Erik placed his fist on the table.

"Well I do. Leave it to me. I'll get your answer without you being deceived by him again. He's managed to elude you so far, I wouldn't put it past him to do it again. You don't want to waste a good lead on emotional outbursts. I'll go."

"Erik. You can't. I won't let you." Marta shook her head fiercely.

"She's right, Erik, you're just as emotionally involved as I am. You wouldn't be able to stop yourself if he goaded you into a fight. He's much older now - but so are you. I don't want anything bad happening to you - not by his hand."

"Fine. What about your son, Joseph. Could he go?"

"No, he's busy with his studies and I don't want to bother him. Joseph doesn't know anything about Gerrard's mistress and I'd rather keep it that way. I'd hate for him to learn his father's been cheating on me. Joseph has no clue that his sister might still be alive. Besides, I think Gerrard would just talk him out of the idea, and probably call me a liar or crazy. I couldn't bear it if Joseph thought I'd gone crazy. You must never tell him who you really are, Erik. I don't want him to know that you're my brother. I could never explain my past to him. Do you understand?"

"Aye, alright."

Elaine was at a stalemate. Who could find Gerrard and hold him accountable for his actions?

"I'll go," Marta's quiet voice uttered.

4th April 2016

Jess

Yawning her way out of bed, Jess reluctantly prepared for school. She wished like anything they were back at Joe's cottage, snuggled beneath toasty down duvets. Ella was already up, humming cheerfully as she went about the room gathering items to be stuffed in her school bag. Jess slowly made her way to the bathroom and noticed Brody and Steve were dressed and ready. Jack wandered around looking for his missing shoe and whined about it in a most annoying tone, setting Jess's nerves on edge.

What time is it? Did I sleep through the alarm clock again?

Quickly climbing the loft stairs she looked at Ella with eyes that begged to be put back in their sockets. "Why didn't you wake me?" She screeched. "You didn't seem to mind waking me up every other morning since we've arrived." Sarcasm steamed from her temples and tongue. She rushed about manically tossing books in and out of her bag, all whilst dressing; popping her arms and head through her jumper. When she finally made it to the kitchen the others were finishing up. Dropping two pieces of bread in the toaster she prayed they would pop before they had to leave - she was starving.

Yesterday Mum had received a call while they were still at Joe's, asking if she would like to take up the duty manager's position at the hospital. Thrilled and not at all concerned by the effects of her decision, Mum had accepted on the spot. Jess knew she should be happy for her, but she wasn't.

Normally, in these types of situations, she'd be able to fake her happiness. But, for whatever reason, she seemed incapable of playing the part. It had been nice having Mum around at the start and end of each day, and the home cooked meals and ready-made lunches were a bonus. Mum's return to shift-work again would ruin Jess's idea of their new start in Scotland. Sadly, reality and the cost of living hit her harder than expected this morning and a familiar sense of monotony returned.

Jess stared into the heat of the toaster and Ella plucked an apple from the fruit bowl beside her.

"We've got that forensic lab technician coming to speak in science class today. That should be interesting,"

"I guess." The toast popped. Jess dipped a knife in the butter and smeared it on thick. "Mum what time will you be home today?" She hoped it wouldn't be too late.

"I'll be there to pick you all up from school, Jess. I'm not spending the whole day at the hospital. It's only site training this week - so I can get to know the staff and facilities. I'll be there to pick you up every day this week except Thursday. Jerry has lined up some more properties for me to view, so you'll have to catch the bus home that day as I won't be home till around six, Alright?" Jess nodded and topped her toast with a spread. Mum wisely pre-empted any protest from Ella.

"Don't worry, Ella, all the properties are between here and the hospital. We won't be too far away from you all." Mum rested an arm on Jess's shoulder. "I don't want you and Brody to have to move schools again. Not if I can help it, but it might mean you'll have to bus to school more regularly, that's all. Right, time to go, everyone!" Mum called to the boys in the snug.

Jess had heard Mum speaking, but hadn't taken any of it in. She wasn't just distracted, she was lost in another world entirely. The evidence of which, was spread all over her toast. Jam. She hated Jam. How had she not noticed? With a rumble in her tummy and disgust on her face she slammed the sorry excuse for a breakfast in her mouth and tore off a bite. Ella grimaced at Jess's foul response to her food and giggled.

"Come on, sour-puss. Or we'll be late!"

School was surprisingly enjoyable considering the depressed mood Jess started out with. By lunchtime, she'd almost forgotten all her woes.

Standing in the outfield waiting for a softball to come her way, Jess day-dreamed about Aunt Gabby's hope chest and the people in the picture.

Spits of rain ended the game, sending them running for shelter. Much to Ella's delight class was released early to get changed.

"We've got to unlock it, Ella," Jess said on the way to their lockers. "I saw something and I know it's important."

Fear swam in Ella's eyes. "I don't think I can do it, Jess. It's not that I don't want to know what's in Ma's chest, but if Pa ever found out that I'd been snooping, he'd... well, I'd be so ashamed. Couldn't we ask his permission first?"

Jess opened her locker and dumped the books she wouldn't need for homework inside - Ella did the same.

"Well, I don't see how we could, Ella. If we ask him, he'll not only want to know why we want to open the hope chest but also how we plan to unlock it. He's obviously not opened it himself before - with the key missing and all, so he'll be awfully keen to know how we came to have it, he'll think you stole it."

Jess didn't like to lead her cousin down an unnecessary path of guilt, but Ella was so gullible sometimes that it was hard to resist.

"Oh no, you're right," Ella's voice quivered. She closed her locker. "So I'm doomed either way. I don't wanna get in trouble, Jess."

"I get it, Ella. But if we're ever gonna find out what happened, we've got to unlock that chest."

"Well what did you have in mind?"

The last bell of the day rang and students began filling the school halls. Jess searched the sea of faces for Brody then eyed the revolving exit.

"Come on. I'm in no mood to walk home this afternoon, Mum will be waiting. We'll think of something, Ella, don't worry."

19th June 1995

Elaine

Elaine sat speechless as the information of a car accident came across the line.

Gerrard was dead. How could that be?

An official from the Aberdeen Police department gave her the details of where she needed to go to identify the body in Paris.

With little time to waste she prepared herself for the journey packing just one small piece of hand luggage. She didn't want to stay, not if she didn't need to. She decided not to call Joseph. Not until she had seen for herself if the words the detective had spoken were true. She wouldn't tell anyone - not until she returned.

20th June 1995

Joe

Joe had finished his exams and was in the process of packing a bag to return home. He wasn't staying long. He'd found himself an internship for the summer in Oxford, starting the following week. He was excited about his chance to work at W. Langdon & Co. The company had an excellent reputation as one of the best business consultancy firms in the greater London area. His opportunity to gain executive experience before taking a junior role at the shipping company would help establish realistic standards, not just those of his father's. He had to prove his worth and if nothing else, show Pa he could stand on his own two feet.

Besides that, it also meant he'd be able to spend the summer with Flo while she continued her studies. She'd opted to complete her courses in three years, rather than four. How or why, Joseph would never understand. Enduring his business economics classes had proved challenging enough without adding years of centuries past into the equation. He had Flo to thank for that. He would have died of boredom in Professor Scott's class if she hadn't made it sound so interesting. He was gonna miss studying with her - Flo made everything seem more interesting. Once, she had explained the collapse of the Roman economy using their dinner ingredients and a giant platter. The result was a delicious example and he wished he could have had all his lessons with her.

The phone rang from the kitchen.

Stuffing the last of his dirty washing in his bag, Joe bounded towards the vibrating bells, expecting to hear Flo's voice on the other end. They'd planned to meet up for lunch after her morning class and Joe was keen to surprise her with a special picnic before he flew north.

"Hello?"

"Joseph - is that you?" a quiet sniff made its way through the receiver.

"Aye, Ma it's me. You're awfully quiet, is everything alright?"

"No. It's your Pa, Joseph. He's dead."

"What? What do you mean he's dead? He's in Denmark, isn't he? That's what ye told me."

"Well, He's...gone..." Joe heard the tremors in his mother's voice and knew it was true.

"I'm coming, Ma, I'm on the next flight out this afternoon. Let me just get some loose ends tied up and I'll see if I can catch an earlier flight. Okay?"

"Alright Joseph, we'll talk more soon. I love you," came her sad soft voice at the other end.

"I love ye too, Ma."

The next four hours seemed a blur. He wasn't sure what to make of any of it. Flo had been understanding, and thankfully, a calm voice of reason. But now, as he sat on the plane, an hour earlier than planned, he started to think it all through. This could change his whole life. For better or worse? He could not tell.

If it really were true, would he have to return to Aberdeen to work for the company immediately? Would the board even accept him as the new chairman? He certainly didn't have the necessary experience they'd be looking for. And what about his summer with Flo, and his internship?

He'd phoned the firm informing them of his family predicament - giving his assurances he'd merely be delayed. But who was he trying to fool - them, or simply himself?

He closed his eyes; overwhelmed by the incessant questions colliding in his mind.

He arrived just before 5:00pm and his mother stood waiting for him at the arrival gate in the airport. Other than her slightly puffy eyes Joe never would have picked she was in mourning. In fact she seemed lighter than usual and her shoulders weren't so rigid when she hugged him. Pa was no saint. Joe knew it couldn't have been easy for her these last few years he'd been away.

"Let's get an early supper, shall we?" Ma said, void of any emotion that might reveal her state of mind.

"Okay, Ma. Whatever you like." He shrugged his bag over his shoulder and Ma hooked her arm through his. She rested her head against his shoulder for a moment.

"It's so good to have you home, Joseph. I've missed you."

He wasn't certain how, but in that moment a burden of responsibility shifted on his shoulders like he'd just pulled an Olympic barbell above his head. Shaking and balancing he knew he had better re-centre himself or the whole thing might crush him. Maybe it would anyway.

Sitting in an almost empty restaurant, Ma explained the facts as she had been informed herself. Pa had been killed in a car accident in Paris, just on the outskirts of the city. Speed had been a factor, but his car had crossed the centre-line and he was crushed by an oncoming truck.

Ma paused, "There's something else, Joseph, but I'm not sure you'll want to hear it. I'm not even sure I should tell you. But given the circumstances, I also don't want anyone else to tell you."

He knew something bad was coming, Ma had kept things from him his whole life when it came to Pa's erratic behaviour. Whatever it was, at least his father couldn't hurt them anymore.

He was wrong.

"Joseph, your father was with someone else when he died - A woman."

Ma looked at him with pain creasing her eyes and forehead. He knew what she was going to say but he still wanted to hear it.

"Her name was Charlotte and she was his mistress... I...I'm so sorry, Joseph. I know it's not what you want to hear. It had been going on for a while. I don't think Gerrard knew that I knew about it, but that doesn't matter now." Ma grasped hold of both his hands on the table. "Joseph, please don't let this ruin the happy memories you do have of him. I know he was hard on you sometimes, but he was only doing what he thought was best. You won't remember him, but Grandpa Naudman was the same. Gerrard became more like his father as time went by and I'd hate for you to be consumed by that same bitterness and deep seated anger. Gerrard made some bad choices and wasn't very nice at times, but there were good times. He read you stories every night and gave you opportunities not many other young boys had. Please don't forget that. I won't ever regret marrying your father - he gave me you. You are the best thing that ever happened to me and I don't want you to lose sight of who you are. You are kind, you are forgiving, you are generous and you are loved. You are **not** your father."

Joe struggled to take it all in and file every thought and emotion that came up. For the rest of the night old memories of his father's temper and strange behaviours surfaced. He tried hard to remember them in detail. But in doing so, he merely buried them in his sub-conscious to fester. For the rest of the night he was entwined in a mind-game which questioned everything he knew or could remember about his father. By the time morning arrived, his eyes had sunk deeper in their sockets and were circled by rings of grey. His shoulders seized and ached with jabs of pain. He'd had drunken nights that took less of a toll, and his head felt the size of a concrete block. His heart was wounded and emotional scars etched themselves more permanently on his forehead. Anger brewed in his chest and he feared it would consume him. Ma's face of pity didn't help. He was angry, and he had a right to be, no matter what Ma said.

"I hate him!" was all he could say at breakfast. He withdrew back to his bedroom to stew in self-pity.

Joe could feel his temper growing and couldn't seem to stop it. He was caught in a rip; becoming more like his father as he let each wave take him further out into a sea of fury. He wanted to fight it; to resist. But underneath, he felt justified and succumbed to it with ease. His father's legacy was too strong and pride would take him without a fight to the darkest parts of himself. Joe knew he couldn't stay like this - He had to close his mind. As long as Ma didn't pry - he could keep it locked away.

Joe returned to the kitchen with his anger buried and his mind ready to focus on more practical issues.

"Right, what can I do to help?" He asked.

Ma looked surprised and then smiled sympathetically.

"You're going to be fine, Joseph, you'll see. Give it time. I don't expect you to be ready just yet. But when you are. You know you can talk to me - anytime, okay?" Ma patted him on the shoulder.

His act hadn't fooled her - she knew him too well.

"Aye, Ma, I will, just not now. I don't want to think anymore. I just want to do something."

Ma took a piece of paper from the buffet draw. "Here's the list of what needs to be done. I could use your help with the arrangements for Gerrard's body. Lord knows who else we might need to call. I still haven't called the shipping offices yet. I'm sure there's a ton of legal stuff that'll need sorting out - but I wouldn't know where to begin."

"Don't fret, Ma. I'll do all of that. You stick to the funeral arrangements and I'll sort out the business stuff, alright?"

"Thank you, Joseph. Where would I be without you?" Ma kissed him on the head like she always did before leaving the house.

"Where are you going?" He asked.

"I've got an appointment with the funeral director at ten and then I'm headed to the florist after that. Oh that reminds me. Max was coming over this morning to see you. I haven't told anyone else about Gerrard yet. You can tell him, but please be discreet about... you know."

"Aye, I will, Ma. He may be dead but we wouldn't want to tarnish his good reputation now would we." He was being sarcastic but it held his true sentiments. "For the sake of the company, I'll keep Pa's secrets. But one way or another I'll make sure he pays for what he's done to you." Bitterness licked his last words.

This is gonna be harder than I thought.

Ma left and Joe started making calls. The list was long and required him to be official in tone and language - there was little room for personal emotion. The newspapers, The Scottish, French and Danish Embassies. The police department, and finally, Shona at the Aberdeen company office - who was extremely apologetic and seemed the most upset by the news.

At the end of it all, he called Flo. The only person he trusted completely enough to express his shattered state of hopelessness to. Unloading his darkest thoughts of anger towards his father, she listened patiently and was a beacon of hope to his present darkness.

"I never want to look at his face again," Joe said through gritted teeth, his pain, still fresh, seething beneath the surface. "The secrets of Pa's life and body will go to the grave and I will not mourn for a man who treated my mother so badly."

"You will, Joe...one day. You're hurting - you're allowed to you know. As time passes, you'll see." Flo soothed with compassion.

"He deserved to die in that crash. The only reason I have to care, is for Ma. She's the one he's hurt the most, not me. He's scum and I'll not give him the satisfaction of ruining my life because of his stupid mistakes."

"Joe. I'm coming - to the funeral I mean. I've only got one class on Friday and I'm sure I can skip it. I can stay for the weekend too if you like."

From that moment he knew he could never live without her. She understood his anger and didn't make him feel badly for expressing it. She was the remedy to his heart and the tonic he needed to keep his spirit in check. He could never hurt Flo the way Pa had hurt Ma. He'd never allow it.

There was a knock at the door.

"I gotta go, Flo. Max is here. Let me know what time your flight arrives and I'll come pick you up, okay? I love you. Bye."

He hung up quickly. He'd never said the words before and they'd slipped out unintentionally. It was true, he did love her, but he wasn't sure how she'd respond. The resulting high left Joe a little giddy when he opened the front door.

"Well you look happy. What's up?" asked Max.

Joe suddenly felt guilty. He was meant to be in the depths of despair or at least appear so. But Ma wasn't around and he was tired of all the tension in the air.

"I was just on the phone with Flo. She's coming up this weekend."

"I see. That's soon." Max grinned. "She must be keen."

Joe wasn't sure how to tell Max about his father's death.

"Well, At least one of us is happy. I haven't heard anything from Gabby all week. I'm worried I've scared her off with my proposal. I thought girls liked that kind of thing. She said it had nothing to do with the ring, but I'm nervous she won't say yes. What do you reckon, should I be worried?"

"Hmm?" Joe hadn't really heard what Max said. He'd opened one of the buffet draws to see if his mother had been keeping anything else from him. Sadly she had.

Shuffling through papers he picked up a letter. It was a final notice for a bill due six months ago. Why hadn't she paid it? It suddenly dawned on him that his mother's troubles were far from over with his father now deceased. She was obviously struggling financially and he had to find out to what extent her debts had grown.

"How could he do this to her?" Joe muttered under his breath and stormed towards his father's home office.

"Wait, Joe, what is it?" asked Max.

"Ma's in trouble. Can ye drop me in the city, Max? Ma's got the car and I need to go to my father's offices and find out what's been happening."

"Sure Joe, I'll take you. Is everything alright? You don't look yourself. I'm sure your Ma will be fine."

"You don't know that, Max. You don't know me father. He's…He's dead! And that's not the worst of it. He's done some terrible things, and I'm worried Ma's way in over her head."

"Alright. I'm sure you're right. But your Pa - is he really dead?" Max asked.

"Aye, in a car crash in Paris."

"So why's your Ma in trouble? She didn't kill him, did she?"

Joe didn't have time for one of Max's jokes, and why wasn't he taking him seriously?

Heat rose to his cheeks. "Look are ye gonna take me or do I have to tell Gabby about… Maxine?" Joe batted his eyelids like a girl for a reaction.

"No. No. Don't you dare say a word. I'm Sorry. I didn't mean it. I was just joking. I'll drop you in the city. Whatever's happened, Joe, I'm sure you can fix it."

Joe hoped Max was right for the sake of his mother and the company.

CHAPTER TWENTY-SEVEN

7th April 2016

Ella

J ESS AND ELLA stood in front of her mother's hope chest. The dark stained timber was worn and well beaten from being moved around a lot. The ornate carved top depicted a sailing ship with its masts full and the sea swelling about its hull. Its origins were similar to that of a Chinese camphor chest, but the design of the ship on this chest was clearly European. The sides were equally embellished with people in a scene of pilgrimage and a black wrought iron disk on the front held the opening for a key.

Aunty Vera wouldn't be home till 6:00pm and the boys were still at the sheds with Pa. Jack had been left in their care, but Ella managed to convince him to stay in the snug watching TV.

Jess pulled out the ring of keys and passed them to Ella. It dawned on her then that they never did get the chance to touch the last key. It sat tightly on the ring beside the black hope chest key and seemed completely out of place.

Now is not the time Ella - focus.

Inserting the small black key into the hole, she turned the lock. The slide clunked and disengaged. Ella lifted the lid casting light on its contents for the first time in years.

"That's it there." Jess pointed to the picture frame she'd described from the vision. Ella held her breath and picked it up from the blanket it sat on. Turning it over, she let out a slow quiet squeal.

"Jess! It's, it's… isn't that the same man we saw in the suit by the green car?" She asked.

"It's Gerrard. But I don't understand. Why is there a picture of Gerrard in your mum's chest?"

"Look, it's not Elaine in the photo with him. It's Charlotte! C.S – Charlotte Sinclaire. It's the same woman, see." Ella took the photo of Charlotte with the kiss mark on the back and held it up next to the framed photo. Then she held up the picture they'd found at the castle of Eleanor and Gerrard standing beside the sports car. "It's him. Charlotte was his mistress."

Jess pointed to the framed photo, "But why did your mum kiss this picture before her wedding? Shouldn't this be in with the others in our box? Why did she hide it here?" Jess looked confused.

"I don't think it's got anything to do with our box, Jess, look." Ella held up another photo. A family of three stood in their swimsuits at the beach, Charlotte smiled, arm in arm next to Gabby who was almost as tall as her mother. Gerrard stood behind them with his arms around Charlotte's shoulders, all looked exceedingly happy. Ella guessed her mother was about eighteen or nineteen.

There were tons of pictures, all capturing a happy memory of her mother's past. None of which Ella had ever seen before. "Why did she never show us these?"

"Who knows? This is weird, Ella. I wasn't expecting to find this. Wait. If Gerrard gave baby Joanna to Charlotte, then why did she call her Elle and not Gabby?"

"My mother's full name was Gabriella Louise Sinclaire. I'm named after her, but Pa liked to call me Ella."

Dots began to connect and her head thumped as hard as her heart.

Jess's expression changed to one of disbelief. "But if Joanna became Elle, and Elle was really Gabby, then your mother is Elaine's daughter!"

"Shhh, we've got to get out of here." Ella was keenly aware she was still standing in her father's room violating his privacy. "I don't want to get caught. Come on."

Ella slammed the lid shut on the chest.

"Wait. Let's at least keep a picture, so we can sort this out." Jess towered over her and the only way to get her cousin to move, was to comply.

Ella lifted the lid, grabbed the beach-side family photo, and thrust it into Jess's hands. Ella locked the chest and made for the door.

Just then, Jack walked up the stairs.

"What's going on, Ella?"

"Oh nothing, I just fell over that's all."

"You're such a klutz." He laughed. Jack made his way back downstairs and Ella followed. On the way she silently gestured Jess to go and hide the picture in the loft. A few minutes later Jess joined them in the kitchen. Ella was finishing a sandwich for Jack, who was licking peanut butter off a spoon.

"There you go. That should keep you happy for a while." She handed Jack the sandwich and grabbed two cookies from the jar on the bench for her and Jess.

Jess raised her eyes to the roof, beckoning Ella to return upstairs.

"Ah, we're just gonna be upstairs, Jack. You wanna go watch some more TV?" Jack nodded and left the kitchen.

"Come on. Let's head to the loft. I'm confused and a little freaked out," Jess whispered.

"Not more than I am." Ella cocked an eyebrow and shook her head.

Safe within the confines of the loft, they sat on Jess's bed and studied the picture.

"So," Jess held out her fist with a thumb poking out as if ready to make a list. "Eleanor was Elaine, she married Gerrard, and she had two babies, Joe and Joanna. Joanna was given to Charlotte, Gerrard's mistress, who named her Elle, who then went by the name Gabby? Well if that's right, then it means that Aunt Gabby - your mother - was Joe's sister."

"But that would mean that Pa and Ma were cousins. Is that even allowed?" Ella twisted a fingernail between her front teeth. "Jess, I'm worried. Maybe that's why Ma never said anything? Ooh - I don't know. She must have known when she saw the photos in Elaine's diary. Why didn't she say anything to Pa about it then?"

"Who knows maybe she did tell him and he already knows."

"No, I don't think he does, Jess, he didn't know Joe was his cousin, or that Elaine was his aunt. I don't want Pa to find out. I'm beginning to understand why Joe said we should just leave the past in the past."

"We'll figure it out, Ella. Maybe we should ask Mrs Jenkins or Lady Ferlie. They might know what to do?"

"Maybe, but they'd have to promise not to tell anyone - **Ever**."

Paris – 19th June 1995

Gabby

The sun, a little past the height of noon, was beginning its descent towards the horizon once more. Cars screamed along the highway above as Gabby stood crying beneath the overpass pillar. She couldn't bring herself to go inside the stark brick building with its arched wood and glass doors. She was trying to understand how any of it could have happened. She was all alone and she felt it deep within her core where an ache gripped her with intense grief.

The front doors squeaked when a woman exited the building wearing a pinstriped navy shirt rolled to the elbow and matching trousers. A white scarf and sunglasses covered her eyes and head, matching the handbag she held tucked under her arm. She looked very smart and elegant, just like a department store mannequin. Holding a brown paper bag to her side, she paused to take in the sky above and then let out a heavy breath.

Gabby looked at her curiously. There was something odd about this woman, but she couldn't say what. Although she wore the face of grief, no tears stained her cheeks as they did Gabby's.

The woman walked towards her and Gabby wondered if it were intentional. Wiping the tears from her eyes she tried to compose herself for public appearance sake.

"Are you alright dear?" asked the woman, her voice had a Scottish accent and was filled with concern. Gabby felt at ease. It made her think of her father. The woman stopped ten metres or so from her, far enough not to encroach on Gabby's space.

"I'm okay. I'm just, just trying to work up the courage to go inside." Another tear escaped her eye and she wiped it away instantly.

"Oh, I'm sorry for your loss. This morgue is a ghastly place for anyone to visit that doesn't actually work here. I've just been to see my husband. He *doesn't* work here." She paused to see if she understood, "But I'm not upset about it anymore. He was a terrible husband. He cheated on me, ran off with some other woman and now he's dead. I can honestly say, I'm not sorry for him one bit. He got what he deserved if you ask me. At least my son and I can get on with our lives without him causing us any more trouble."

Why the woman felt the need to share any of it with Gabby she could not fathom, everyone dealt with grief in their own way she guessed, but sensing anger in the woman's voice she was glad she didn't feel like that about her own loss. Her parents were the reason she could smile at life, well, her mother anyway.

"You'll be alright dear. You're young and life goes on. Whether or not *we* decide to go on with life is a choice we all must make when we lose someone." And with that the woman left her to deal with her grief again, alone outside the Institut médico-légal in Paris.

Paris – 19th June 1995
Elaine

Elaine sat in the empty hotel room with her thoughts and a brown paper bag. Gerrard's personal effects, although of interest to her, were no compensation for the emptiness she felt. She was more annoyed than angry about having to remain overnight in the city. She'd signed all the documents and provided all the paperwork they had requested for

Gerrard's body to travel back to Scotland. But now she had to wait for it to all be approved and the airline to grant passage, which could take up to forty-eight hours.

She had once dreamed of a romantic trip to Paris. Picturing herself and Gerrard staying in a luxurious hotel suite drinking champagne. Never in a million years could she have pictured the scene she sat in now.

Tipping the contents from the brown paper bag onto the bed, each item sat as an object she could only despise. A wristwatch with a black leather strap still ticked, oblivious to the fact it had lost its owner. The inscription engraved on the reverse were her own words, Together Forever - *how naïve*.

His wallet was new and still shiny, not the one she last saw him holding in Aberdeen.

Opening it, a photo of a little girl in a purple dress smiled back at her. She snapped the wallet closed, refusing to see the truth and let her tears fall. She was angry, yes, but not for the loss of Gerrard. Her only link to finding Joanna now lay as silent as the grave he would rest in and the same was true for his mistress.

Picking up a key from among the personal effects, she turned it around. Not like any other key she had seen before, she examined it carefully. The triangular turn grip was sheathed in thick white plastic and the metal shaft was hollow with laser-cut rectangular holes. She had no clue what it might unlock. But rather than toss it back inside the brown paper bag with the other items, she remembered the buffet drawer key she had zipped in her handbag pocket. Retrieving it, she added the strange key to the piece of ribbon and promptly tucked it out of sight.

24th June 1995

Joe

Back in Aberdeen, the mourners gathered around the hole in the ground with the casket resting above it. A few work colleagues from the Aberdeen offices and members of the board made an appearance; more out of courtesy and compassion than grief, Joe presumed.

Pa's mother; Joe's grandmother, Margaret Naudman, stood beside Ma. Bravely waiting at the head of the coffin, watching the cables turn and lower the box into the ground. Both women were dressed head to toe in black; both now having the commonality of being widows.

Flo clung to Joe's hand - his life line of added strength should he ever need to draw on it. Max's parents, Marta and Erik stood behind himself and Flo. He wasn't exactly sure why they were attending the funeral. As far as he was aware, they'd never even met his father.

Max was nowhere to be seen. Perhaps his friend had sent his parent's in his place.

Tears slipped down Ma's cheeks and fell to her hands which held a single white rose. Tossing it in the hole she turned to leave immediately. Joe and Flo followed her example and the mourners disbanded as quickly and quietly as they had all gathered.

"Where's Max?" Joe asked Marta, waiting with her husband by the cars at the cemetery.

"He's gone to Oxford to look for Gabby. He hasn't heard anything from her in over a week and he's worried sick. She was meant to arrive last week, but she never came."

Max's mother wouldn't look him in the eye, hardly anyone did lately; their sympathy or pity preventing them. But Marta seemed more nervous than anyone else. She smoothed her hands over her jacket and lifted her chin. "I'm not much good at funerals. My brother died young and I don't like cemeteries.

Flo touched Marta's arm. "I'm sure Gabby's fine, Mrs Lawson. I'll give her a call and see if I can get a reply if you like."

Max's father looked at his wife incredulously and crossed his arms firmly across his chest. What it all meant Joe couldn't tell, but something wasn't right. Maybe they'd been arguing, it didn't seem unreasonable to think so.

"Oh, would you, Florence? Oh thank you dear, that would be most reassuring," said Marta.

Pa had been buried almost a week when Max finally returned. He'd called and asked Joe to pick him up from the airport and drop him home and Joe had been more than happy to oblige.

Seeing Max's dishevelled state when he exited the terminal, Joe suddenly realised how negligent he'd been of his friend's troubles. He'd been so consumed by his own anger that he'd been deaf to Max's plea for help. Hastily ushering him towards the car, Joe offered an apology. "Sorry I wasn't here for you sooner, Max."

"What do you mean? You're right on time."

"No I mean, there for you - to help find Gabby."

"It's okay Joe. I understand. You've had a lot to deal with. I'm glad you're here now though. I've been looking forward to this day for a long time but you'll forgive me if I'm not as happy as I'd like to be - nor yourself, given the circumstances."

Max's comments were strange and somewhat cryptic.

What on earth is he on about -Happy about what?

As far as he knew Gabby was still missing and the sorrow in Max's eyes was obvious. So what reason could he have to be happy? Joe couldn't explain it and made the only assumption he could.

"Aye, I've been looking forward to seeing you too, Max, and where you live." Having never been to Max's house before, Joe was curious to see where the directions would take them.

"Take this next right," Max paused. "Joe, I am happy to see you, but there's something I need to tell you."

"Aye, well, did you find out anything more - about Gabby I mean?" Joe was hopeful the news would be good for a change. It seemed like he'd not heard something positive in a long time. Speeding in the direction of Alford, Max sighed multiple times. He was wrestling with himself over something and clearly wanted to get it off his chest. Max broke down.

"What is it laddie, has something happened?" Joe asked.

"She wasn't there. I looked everywhere, Joe. Her flat, The Library, the Cafeteria, the gardens, that cafe on Broad Street. Nothing. I even tried the police station and the hospital. Nothing. It's like she's vanished." Max's eyes glassed with tears about to fall.

Joe remained calm and tried to speak steadily, "Well, what about her folks in Paris, have you called them?"

"Of course. I've tried that every day, there's no answer. I'm running out of options and my head thinks the worst." Max paused. "Take a right up here at the round-about and the first road on the left after the next one. Then follow the signs to Alford."

"Okay, got it. Max, someone must know where she is."

"I've booked a flight to Paris for tomorrow afternoon. It's the only thing I can think of left to try. I've got to find her, Joe."

"Alright. Well, I'm coming with you. We found her in Italy together, I'm sure we can find her in Paris. What's her address?"

"I, I… I don't know. She never told me. Does Flo know?" Max's eyes begged him for any sort of answer.

"I'll call Flo and ask her to look for the address at their flat. She still has a key. She might be able to find some clues amongst Gabby's things. Flo has classes till two, so she should be home soon. Don't worry, Max, we'll find her."

"What about you?" Max asked.

"What about me?"

"Well, what about your Pa?"

"We buried him last Saturday."

"Oh, I'm sorry I wasn't here for you, Joe. Are you alright?"

"Yeah, I'm fine. I have bigger things to worry about."

"Yeah, like what?"

"Och, it's nothing, Max. I'll figure it all out, eventually." Joe surveyed the road as he approached an intersection.

"You sure? I could use a distraction. Take a right up here. What's the problem - You and Flo alright?"

"Aye, we're fine. She's the best bit of my whole existence right now."

"Aye, well I hope you've told her so. Don't wait till it's too late, Joe."

Max's cautionary comment gave Joe reason to doubt whether he had made his intentions clear to Flo. A fact he would ensure was unquestionably clear when he returned to Oxford. If, in fact, he ever was able to return.

"It's the company, and Ma. She's in trouble, Max, and I have to sort out the mess my father has left behind."

"I guess you'll be busy with lawyers and accountants for a while then?"

"Aye, and Ma has a lot of explaining to do too. There wasn't a lot in the fridge when I got home from Oxford. I think she's been struggling for a while from what I can tell. My account's been fine. Pa has covered all my expenses at university, and my flat in Oxford is paid up till the end of next year. I just don't understand. Why would he do this to her?"

"Sounds like you've trouble enough on your hands. Best you stay here than go travelling with me."

"No Max, it can wait. Gabby might be in trouble and need our help." The suggestion disturbed Max and he sat quietly till they arrived in Alford.

"So this is where you're from?" Joe pulled off the road where Max indicated and parked outside the Alford Bistro. He looked about the small village with general interest.

"Well sort of," Max said. "I live another ten minutes or so just out of town, in Tullynessle. But Ma won't mind coming to fetch me."

"Well, tell me where and I'll take you. I don't mind." Joe turned the engine over and looked to Max for directions.

"Uh, well, about that. It's what I wanted to talk to you about." Max paused and looked at him squarely. "Joe, you know me, I'm not one to tell lies, but there's something I haven't told you about me."

"Aye, well, what is it?" These days it seemed everyone he loved had dark secrets they didn't want him knowing. He never would have placed Max among them. He only hoped Flo wasn't hiding something from him as well. His trust had taken too many knocks lately and a blow from her would devastate him.

"Well, my name is not Max Lawson. It's Max Lockheart."

"You're joking with me, aye," Joe chuckled to himself. "Surely ye'r joking. Why on earth would you lie about your surname? I suppose it tis a wee bit girly. Lockheart." He laughed and shoved Max's shoulder.

"I'm not joking, Joe. It's the truth. I wanted to tell you sooner, but there's some strange reason about the Naudmans and the Lockhearts not getting along. To be honest, I don't really know me'self. It doesn't matter all that much to me, you're my best friend and I want you to be my best man at my wedding. That is, if we can find Gabby of course - and she says yes. But now that your Pa's gone, I thought you should know the truth. I know you're sick of all the secrets and I didn't want to keep this from you any longer."

Joe looked at Max stunned by his confession. He wasn't sure what to make of any of it, but he knew one thing. Max was a good friend and he would never want to hurt Joe on purpose.

"I don't know what's happened in the past, Max, but let's leave it there and never let it ruin our friendship. I'd be honoured to be your best man." He grinned at Max so hard he felt muscles in his cheeks which hadn't been used in ages.

"Now, where do you live?"

The two of them drove to the farm and along the way, Max pointed out various places he'd injured himself.

"It's a wonder ye'r still breathing Max." Joe chuckled.

Max pointed to a metal letterbox. "Just here's fine, Joe." Max got out, and poked a head back inside the car. "Thanks for the lift. I'll see you tomorrow - it's the two o'clock flight."

"Okay, bye, Mr Lockheart." Joe chuckled and waved.

Making his way back to the port offices, his first order of business was to call Flo. Without any success, he left her an urgent message to check the flat and call if she found anything that might aid their search for Gabby in Paris.

Channelling his frustration into work, he turned his efforts to finishing the task he'd started earlier that morning. Joe had spent most of his days, since arriving home, wading through files; trying to familiarise himself with how the company was being run.

Tapping on the computer keys he brought up a spreadsheet of the company assets. Scanning the list he noticed a property with a downtown address. The location did not correlate with the port offices and it peaked his curiosity.

I wonder what that's used for - storage maybe?

Sitting at his father's desk he made a search for the property's records.

Nothing. *That's strange, it should be here.*

He'd have to follow up with the accountant about it when he returned.

Picking up the phone, he asked Shona to schedule a meeting with the head of accounting for Thursday the following week.

"Will that be all, Mr Naudman?"

"Ah, please don't call me that, Joe is fine. I'm going to be out of the office for a couple of days. Heading to Paris to help a friend. Would you please see if you can get me on the 2 o'clock flight tomorrow? Oh, and book me a hotel too. You can forward any correspondence to me there. I hope to be back on Wednesday."

"Why of course, Mr… Joe. We're so glad to have you here and I hope you'll be able to stay on. I'll have the bookings arranged for you."

He could get used to this. Having a secretary made office life seem effortless. It also helped that Shona had worked for his father, which made it easier to learn how he used to run things.

Collecting his jacket from the back of the worn leather chair he decided he couldn't wait till next Thursday to see the accountant. Instead, he detoured off his usual route home to check out the address. What was it, an industrial building, a commercial property, Pa's ghost office?

Driving down Union Street he slowed as the number drew closer. It was right in the heart of the city and the busy crossing foot traffic aided his slow pace, enabling him to scan the building. Hugging the steering wheel he looked as far up the building face as he could.

Its edifice was akin to the detailing of Dutch renaissance in style and at the top sat two decorative steeply pitched gable roofs. Four round bay windows held two Juliet balconies above them with the top two windows enjoying a view of the city no doubt. One of the top sash windows was open slightly. *Someone must be there.*

A sharp horn blasted from his rear and he startled from his search of the building. *Guess I'll have to wait till Friday to find out.* He frowned and pulled away. Just as he did, he spotted something. A familiar set of curls walked along ahead of him on the opposite side of the street.

"That's Gabby, isn't it?" He tried to speed up so he could glance back at the woman's face, but before he got the chance a truck passed, blocking his vision momentarily, and she was gone.

Where did she go?

Maybe it wasn't her. Had he dreamed it? He couldn't be certain of anything and he wouldn't raise Max's hopes without proof.

Joseph spent the next two hours wandering up and down Union Street trying in vain to find the woman he'd seen. Finally, he gave up and returned home.

CHAPTER TWENTY-EIGHT

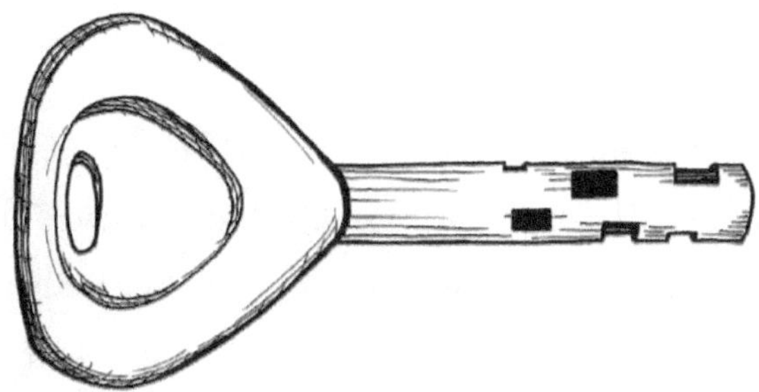

8th April 2016

Ella

ELLA TRIPPED ON the rubber mat in front of the school's main entrance when a gust of wind threw her into the glass doors.

"You alright?" Jess asked.

"Aye, I'm okay." She rubbed her arm.

"That was close - you could've broken it."

"What - me - or the door?" Ella asked sheepishly.

Jess giggled. "Come on, let's find Mrs Jenkins before the bell rings."

Inside the library, Mrs Jenkins sat typing frantically on her computer with such fierce concentration that she never heard the girls enter, let alone call her name.

"Mrs Jenkins? Mrs Jenkins - Anyone home?" sang Jess.

"Oh, Hello, girls. Sorry I was just... never mind, how can I help?"

"What were you doing?" asked Ella, more curious to know her answer than raise the topic they were here to discuss.

"Uh, I'm writing a story," She said.

"Really, what's it about?" Ella rose on her tip toes and leaned over the counter to peer at her screen.

"Oh, you know. Just a story about romance and betrayal - that sort of thing." Mrs Jenkins touched the tips of her fingers to her glasses and re-settled them on her nose.

"Really, cool. What's it called?" Ella asked.

Jess tapped on the counter.

"I'm not sure. I can't decide between *Chelsea's Choice*, and, *A Change of Heart*." Mrs Jenkins blushed and stared, waiting for their suggestions.

"They both sound good to me, will you publish it?" asked Ella, trying to forget her own dilemma.

Jess's frustration boiled. "Uh, Ella, we've got more important things to do than ask Mrs Jenkins what she's writing about. Sorry. No disrespect, Mrs Jenkins, but we really must ask you something very important."

"Well, yes, what is it? Have you uncovered some new information?" She gave the girls her full attention.

"Yes, we think so," said Jess. "Yesterday we uncovered some slightly disturbing new information about our family. Well, Ella's mum to be exact. You see, we found a photo of her parents in her Hope Chest and it seems..."

Ella's body tensed and she did all she could not to plug her ears with her fingers.

She butted in, "...it seems that my mother was Gerrard's daughter - and I'm freaking out!" Ella nibbled at her finger nails. It wasn't a habit she was prone to, but five had vanished overnight.

"I see. So what's the matter?" Mrs Jenkins asked matter-of-factly.

"Mrs Jenkins. I'm ninety-nine percent sure that Ma was Gerrard's and Elaine's daughter, and that makes her Joe's twin sister. And... since Elaine was my grandfather's sister that would make my mother and my father cousins. Is that even allowed? Can you marry your cousin? I don't think it's right!" Ella's voice peaked and a cool sweat dampened her face.

Jess touched Ella's arm. "Shhh, calm down, Ella. You're the one who didn't want anyone else to know about this."

Just then, Lady Ferlie entered the library. Jess had called and asked her to meet them there in the morning. Not only did they want to return her books and photo albums, but also the key to her writing desk at the castle. Jess also thought Lady Ferlie might be able to assist them now they had uncovered the truth about their family.

"Hello, girls, everything alright?" She asked with a smile. Her rich perfume lingered heavily and seemed to fill the whole library in a matter of minutes.

"Not really, Lady Ferlie. Ella's really upset about what we've uncovered and we're not too sure what to do about it."

When she saw how upset Ella was, Lady Ferlie's interest became more like that of a concerned mother than a detective.

"Oh lass, what's the matter, how can I help?" She pulled Ella into her arms.

"Oh, Lady Ferlie, my mother and father were cousins. Isn't that wrong? What should we do?" She sobbed. Lady Ferlie looked at Mrs Jenkins who had been trying to say something since Lady Ferlie arrived.

"Girls. It's perfectly fine to marry a cousin. Although it's not recommended in our times, they used to do it often back in the old days; usually to keep the money in the family. But there were occasions where cousins just fell in love with each other. Queen Victoria married Albert, her first cousin, and even Einstein married his cousin."

Ella's angst melted away when she finally grasped the information.

"So it's not against the law?"

"No, nothing like that. It's advised that you don't marry your second cousin, for health and genetic reasons, but other than that it's generally acceptable."

Lady Ferlie rubbed her shoulder. "I'm sure there were cousins who married within the Ferlie family. It was often done to keep the clans strong, or to unite two clans. If a daughter had married into another clan, often the resulting cousins were married to each other. Don't worry girls, it's not as disgraceful as you might think."

"See I told you, Ella, everything's fine." Jess smiled at her.

It was easy for her to say, her parents weren't cousins. Ella found it hard to accept the truth and wondered if Pa would struggle the same way. After all, it was he who had married his cousin without knowing it.

"So how did you find out they were cousins?" asked Lady Ferlie.

"Well, we uncovered all sorts of things when we visited Joe at Rattray, didn't we Ella?"

Ella was getting annoyed by how casual Jess was about it all and just nodded.

"Is that Joseph Naudman?" asked Mrs Jenkins.

"Yes," said Jess. We found a locked box under a bed with notes from his wife and mother. And then we found a shipping crate with a baby coffin in it."

Lady Ferlie looked horrified. Jess smiled.

"Don't worry, it was empty. But that's how we learnt that Joseph's twin sister wasn't dead after all. It's weird, I know. But then, when we read the letters we found in the buffet drawer - that was locked too and one of our keys opened it." Jess gleamed with pride. "We found out from the letters that Gerrard had a mistress in Paris and she was raising a girl, that she called Elle. Gerrard gave baby Joanna to his mistress, her name was Charlotte..."

"Hang on, you've lost me," said Lady Ferlie.

The girls carried on trying to explain it all, and when they finally had it out, Mrs Jenkins decided to make up a family tree flow chart for them.

"I'll have it ready for you at the end of the day." Mrs Jenkins gleamed. She loved that sort of thing. Ella had heard many of her stories in the Library over the years. Stories of family feuds, mysterious deaths, and runaway children. But none of them seemed as unbelievable as her own family history now.

"You know, I remember now why I knew Joseph Naudman's name." Mrs Jenkins chuckled.

"Really, how?" Jess asked.

"Well my father used to run the Aberdeen Scouts group and I remember him telling us a strange story at supper time once, about how one of the boys mother's had wanted her son's name changed on the role. It was Joseph's mother. She wanted his name to be Joseph Newman. I thought it was a funny story because anyone who wanted to change their name would usually only change their first name, not a surname."

"Well, she must have done that to prevent Pa from finding out that he and Joe were cousins."

"I wonder why though?" Mrs Jenkins twirled a pen through her hair.

Ella shrugged. "I dunno, we're still trying to figure that out."

"What about your grandmother? She must know." Mrs Jenkins looked from her to Jess.

"She probably does, but it's unlikely she would actually remember." Jess sounded like Aunty Vera and Ella wasn't fond of their indifference. She did understand though. Grandma hadn't been very pleasant to Jess when they visited. But somehow, Jess's presence had also unlocked Grandma's memories - more so when she talked to her as if she were Aunty Vera. That was puzzling in itself.

"Well, why don't we invite your family to sit down at the castle one afternoon and see if anyone knows what happened?" Lady Ferlie's offer was very generous and Jess seemed quite taken with the idea at first. But then hesitated.

"Oh that's really kind of you, Lady Ferlie and we just might take you up on your kind offer. But I think if we could just find that last piece of the puzzle. Then we'll be able to let everyone know the truth."

Ella's frustration was mounting. She too wanted all the facts, but Jess seemed to care little for the feelings of those whom the revelation effected most. Keeping everything secret seemed to trump anyone else's wishes. What was she afraid of - losing control?

"I understand," said Lady Ferlie. "Well, you've come this far. What about those keys, are there any left that you still haven't found homes for?"

Jess pulled the keys out of her bag and held them in the cloth. Ella remembered holding Jess's hand and touching the small black one in Joe's shed. It felt wonderful to see her mother again - even if it was a bit scary.

"Yes, this funny looking one here." Jess pointed it out.

"It is really odd, isn't it? Is there anything magical about that one?" Lady Ferlie asked.

"Oh, we haven't touched that one. I was going to at Joe's, but we were interrupted and never did."

Jess's realisation glistened in her eyes.

"Why don't you try now, Jess?" Ella said.

"Okay, I'll give it a go."

Everyone looked at the odd white key and Jess placed a finger on its hollow shaft...

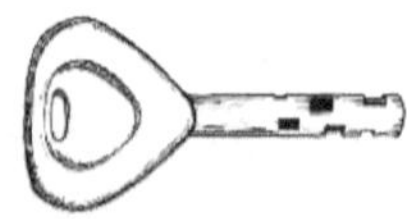

Jess

...Jess found herself seated in the back seat of a car. In the driver's seat she saw Gerrard, he was smiling at Charlotte who sat beside him and looked admiringly into his eyes. Jess glanced out the back window and saw the Eiffel tower in the distance. The couple were driving away from the city towards the countryside. Gerrard's eyes glanced in the rear vision mirror and Jess's pulse raced. Could he see her? She believed he must have because he kept doing it and swerving across the road. The corners of the narrowing road became tighter. Gerrard sped up and looked worried. An engine revving behind them made Jess turn to see what it was. Another car accelerated towards them, then backed off.

Someone was following them.

Gerrard tried to speed up, putting more distance between them and the tailing car. But he couldn't shake them. As they rounded a left-hand corner Gerrard took his eyes off the road to look behind. He drifted across the centre-line and straight into an oncoming farm truck.

Jess floated out of the car and from the side of the road watched the crash unfold before her like it was happening in slow motion.

The car was a wreck. Gerrard's face lay smashed over the steering wheel. Blood dripped down his temples and the crumpled mess of metal consumed the whole left hand side of the car where Charlotte had been sitting.

The tailing car passed the accident and pulled over. A woman got out and ran to check on them, her face was stricken with shock and tears, but she returned to her car and drove away before the man in the truck regained consciousness. Jess saw her face. *It couldn't be, could it?...*

"Jess, are you alright?" Ella asked. "You screamed. What did you see?"

Tear's welled in Jess's eyes and her voice trembled. "I saw Gerrard and Charlotte. They were driving in a car and were being followed. Gerrard couldn't shake it and he lost his focus. They crashed into an oncoming truck. But that's not the worst of it. I saw who was driving the tailing car."

"Well, who was it?" asked Lady Ferlie.

"It was Grandma Marta!"

"Really, are you sure?" asked Ella.

"She looked younger than she does now, but I'm sure it was her. She was really upset about it, but she just left them there in the car." Jess wasn't sure she could believe her own words.

"My goodness. Well what do you make of that?" asked Mrs Jenkins.

"I'm not sure." Jess sought Lady Ferlie's thoughts with a desperate stare.

"Well I think, if Marta ran them off the road, she must have had a pretty good reason for it. Maybe she was trying to get retribution for Elaine?"

Ella frowned.

"I can't imagine my grandmother going to that extreme. She's a good Christian woman of the Alford community, she would never have said an unkind word, let alone run someone off the road. I bet it was a mistake. Maybe she was trying to help Elaine find Joanna."

Jess nodded. "I reckon you're right, Ella. She looked so scared after the crash, she wouldn't have done it on purpose. I'm sure it was an accident." Jess hoped the adults would agree.

"Well, you never know. Some people are very clever at hiding their true identity." Mrs Jenkins gave them a mischievous look. "Maybe Marta hated Gerrard so much for what he did to Elaine that she just snapped. It can happen. They call it 'stress under duress'; an out of character act in the heat of the moment."

Both girls looked at her, horrified by her suggestion.

"Well it's true, it *can* happen. Just saying." Mrs Jenkins shrugged her left shoulder.

Jess didn't much like the librarian's opinion. Could she be trusted to keep this new revelation to herself? If not, then it was possible they'd be the talk of the school before the day was out. Jess had no intention of becoming Alford Academy's latest hot gossip.

"Well, I don't believe it, and you've got no proof, besides my vision, that Grandma killed Gerrard. I suggest you keep your opinions to yourself, Mrs Jenkins. If I hear one rumour that dares mention it - I'll know who to blame. Come on Ella, we've got to talk to Grandma - well - at least try anyway. I don't care about school. I'm going. You coming?" Ella flashed Mrs Jenkins an apologetic look before heading for the door with Jess.

"Girls, wait!" called Mrs Jenkins.

They paused mid-step.

"I didn't mean to upset you. I'm sorry. I won't say another word. I promise. Jess, why don't you try touching that key again? See if you can learn anything more about the accident before you go upsetting your Grandmother."

Ella tugged her arm. "That's a good idea Jess. It's worth a try. Maybe you didn't see everything correctly." Ella looked into her eyes so hard that she had to at least try. It was probably a waste of time, but, for the sake of Grandma Marta, Jess would give it another go. She was prepared this time and would try not to be afraid.

Jess touched the key...

Nothing happened.

She tried again...

"Something's wrong. It's not working."

"What? What do you mean it's not working?" Ella asked. "Here, let me try."

Ella placed her finger on the key and crushed her eyes tight.

"Nothing. Why isn't it working, Jess?" Ella looked at her expectantly. "We made the key work a second time when we touched it together - let's try that."

Jess nodded and they placed their fingers on the key together like they'd done in Joe's shed.

"Nothing's happening, Ella."

"Well, maybe it's run out of magic," said Lady Ferlie.

"Well that's convenient... I mean, inconvenient." Mrs Jenkins corrected herself when Jess scowled at her.

The school bell rang.

"Come on, Ella. Let's go see Grandma. We need answers and we're not going to find any here."

Both of them headed for the door.

"Wait, Girls. I'll take you," said Lady Ferlie. "At least if you're seen leaving with me you shouldn't get into too much trouble."

"Thank you, Lady Ferlie. We'd really appreciate that, wouldn't we, Jess?" Ella tugged her arm.

"Yes, thank you Lady Ferlie." Jess was in no mood to play games with her grandmother today and wanted answers - not crazy talk.

When they arrived at the rest home, Jess prepared herself for what could be an emotional ride - for all of them. Entering Grandma's room Jess noticed how peaceful the soft old lady looked. Her eyes were closed and she worried that she might be dead, not asleep.

Ella walked to her bedside and touched her arm; gently nudging her awake. "Grandma, are you awake?"

The old woman moved her head and her eyes fluttered open.

"Who's that? Freda is that you?"

"No Grandma, it's me, Ella. And Jess is here too. And this," - she gestured towards the doorway - "is Lady Ferlie."

"Oh, I wasn't expecting company. Ella could you hand me my shawl, please. I'd like to sit up."

"Of course, here you go, Grandma."

Ella helped Grandma Marta pull herself to a seated position and then wrapped the cream loose knitted shawl around her shoulders. Jess took a seat in the vacant chair near the end of the bed while Lady Ferlie stood just inside the doorway. Once Grandma was settled Ella knelt on the floor beside her. Cupping Grandma's hands inside her own, she smiled.

Grandma looked at all three of them. "Well, it's so lovely to see you all."

Ella wasted no time getting to the reason for their visit. "Grandma. Have you ever been to Paris?"

Grandma's face turned paler than it already was and her eyes started to well up. "I, I...I can't remember."

"Are you sure, Grandma? Have you never seen the Eiffel Tower? Or taken a drive out of the city?" Ella asked.

Grandma dropped her head into her hand.

"Oh it was terrible, Ella, I didn't mean to, it was an accident." Her voice was shaky and frightened. "It was all my fault. I didn't mean to scare them off the road." Her eyes glassed with ripples of water and looked earnestly at Ella and Jess.

Grandma was eager to unburden herself. "Elaine is so mad at me and won't speak to me. I've ruined her chances of finding her daughter." Grandma sobbed into her shawl, "She won't even come to Max's wedding. I'm so sorry. What should I do? How can I fix it?"

Ella wrapped her arms around Grandma.

"Shhh, it's alright. We know it was an accident. We'll figure it out."

CHAPTER TWENTY-NINE

29th June 1995

Elaine

ELAINE WAITED; STARING out the kitchen window.

Where is he, he is never this late.

Her nerves had been unsettled for months and with Joseph back from Oxford, she suddenly had someone to care for again. Uncertain how to fulfil a mother's duties for an adult son, she'd possibly resorted to treating him like he was still a young lad; fraught with worry when he didn't return home at the specified time.

The lights of the car shone through the window when Joseph pulled in the driveway. Elaine jumped up to take his jacket and bag when he opened the front door.

"Thank heavens you're home. I was so worried." She hugged him tight.

"You were, why?" He asked, oblivious to her distress.

"Well, I don't know. I guess I was worried that something might have happened to you too," She said. She realised then that she might have gotten carried away a bit.

"Nothing's going to happen to me, Ma. I was caught up at the office, that's all. I'm home now."

Elaine sighed. "You're right. I know I'm overreacting. It's just that you reminded me of your father; working late and not coming home. I'm sorry, it's not your fault."

"I'm sorry too, Ma. I never want to be like him." Joseph said; an undertone of hatred still seethed beneath his breath. He had improved since the funeral, but in future, she would resist making comparisons between her son and Gerrard.

"I'll be sure to call you if I'm going to be late next time. Okay?" Joseph smiled and gave her a hug.

"Alright. I'm sure you don't want me bothering the police if you're just working late, do you? Anyway, how was your day?" She asked trying to change his focus.

"Well, it was interesting. Max is back and he still hasn't found Gabby. He's going to Paris tomorrow to search for her, and I've offered to go with him. He was in such a panic this morning. He could sure use some help." Joseph paused and looked her in the eyes. "He also told me his name isn't Max Lawson - it's Max Lockheart. Did you know that, Ma?" The way he said it made her feel like he already knew the answer, but she dare not confirm it.

"Gabby's still missing? Oh, poor lad. I bet he's beside himself with worry." She said, avoiding his question.

Joseph shook his head unimpressed. She was lucky he didn't push her further.

"Yeah, I hope we can find her. I'm not sure what Max would do if..." He cut himself off. Did he do it for her benefit - or his own? "Well you know."

Grief was too familiar to both of them presently and she understood what he meant without him having to say it. All she could do was try to reassure him.

"I sure know what it's like to have someone you love go missing, and I wouldn't wish it on my worst enemy." She was referring to Joanna, but Joseph would presume she meant his father.

30th June 1995

Joe

Next morning, Joe was up later and decided not to go into the office until closer to midday before his flight that afternoon.

"Would you like to have lunch with me in the city, Ma, before I head off with Max?"

"Well, that would be..."

Just then the phone rang and Ma stopped to answer it.

"It's for you, Joseph, it's Max, and he sounds happy." Ma handed him the phone.

"Hello, Max, what's happening? ... Och well, that's wonderful." He smiled at his mother. "Gabby's back," He whispered.

"Ah, lunch?" Joe looked at his mother and she motioned for him to go.

"You go with Max, we'll go some other time," She whispered. He nodded.

"Well how about we meet at Café 52, on the green, in the city." Joseph held up his wrist. "Say about twelve-thirty, is that alright? ... Okay, I'll see you then." Joe hung up the phone.

"Well, it seems Gabby is back so that's a relief. Max sounded very excited. Are ye sure you don't mind about lunch, Ma? You could join us."

"No, you young ones go and enjoy yourselves. I have a lot of cards to write anyhow."

"I promise I'll take you to lunch sometime later this week, how's that sound?"

"I'll hold you to it." Ma stood and kissed his head.

"Well, I suppose I'll head in to the office this morning then. I'll need to cancel my flight and re-arrange a few things before lunch. I'll be home for supper, Ma, and I'll let you know if anything comes up that might delay me."

Joe kissed his mother on her cheek and went to get his things ready.

Thirty minutes later and Joe breezed into the office with a smile on his face.

"You look like the cat who got the cream, something you want to share?" asked Shona.

"No, it's just nice when things all work out, that's all. Can I see you in my office for a moment, Shona?"

"Sure thing, Joe." She said emphasizing her use of his Christian name.

Seated at his desk he flicked on the computer and waited for Shona to enter. As soon as she did he started dictating instructions.

"Shona, I'd like you to cancel my flight to Paris and also the hotel. I won't be going anywhere, it seems my friend has found his girlfriend and so there is no reason for us to go searching for her." He paused while she took notes. "Also, I'd like you to reschedule that appointment with the accountant for Monday if it's possible. Tell him not to panic, I don't need a full report immediately, I just have some questions I want answered. That's all. Thank you," Shona left still jotting down his statements as she exited his office.

"Okay got it." She said, almost completely out the door.

"Oh, one more thing. Sorry."

Shona popped her head back inside the door frame.

"Yes?"

"I'll be out for lunch today from noon till about one-thirty."

"Yes, Mr... Joe." She grinned just remembering in time.

Twelve o'clock arrived sooner than Joe expected, and he wanted to take another look at the building before meeting up with Max and Gabby. Announcing his departure for lunch to Shona, he headed out the door.

The sun was high and although it was summer the draughty streets kept him comfortably cool on his way to Union Street. Busy with traffic, both foot and motorised, he made his way west towards the Music Hall at the far end. Colourful shop fronts lined the street like spectators at a horse race and the grey granite offices and apartments above sat tall like top hats on gentlemen's heads. With a steady pace and a spring in his step he made excellent time, arriving in front of the building in just under ten minutes.

He stood on the opposite side of the street and gazed up the face of the building. He noted the ground and first floor housed the Lakeland kitchenware store. The name had been etched into the store front glass, and the window frames painted in its signature blue. To the left stood a tall door - the entrance to the rooms above. The window sat open still and a pot-planted creeper wound itself across the left side balcony. Joe believed it was likely an apartment and not just an office space.

Clearly, the building could only have served as part of the shipping company's property portfolio and wasn't in direct use by the company itself. But why were its financial records missing from the computers? It made no sense to Joe and he looked forward to grilling the accountant about it on Monday. Just as he turned to begin his walk back towards the Café he noticed something strange. The tall blue door opened and out popped that familiar set of curls, along with Max. Joe couldn't believe it. Why would Max and Gabby be exiting from his company's building? He watched them amble up the street; hand in hand, gazing at each other and chatting between themselves.

Trying to assemble his thoughts he followed them from the opposite side of the street. What would he say? Should he ask her if she was in town yesterday? He was now almost certain it was her that he'd seen. How long had she been there? Joe felt sickened by the thought of Gabby being there all along, while Max crawled the streets of Oxford searching for her.

Finally, they looked as if they would cross the street. He didn't want to bump into them on the pavement and held back until they took the stairs to the green. When they had reached the bottom, he followed, catching up to them as they arrived at the café.

"Hello, Max. Gabby. Och lass, am I glad to see you. We were all gett'n so worried. What gave you the idea to put us in such a panic? You nearly had him flying off to Paris to find ye." Joe slapped Max on the shoulder.

"It's lovely to see you too, Joe," She said. Apart from the lack of a smile, Gabby's mannerisms would have anyone believe nothing had happened over the past week few weeks.

"Aye, well, like Ma was telling me last night. If you're gonna be late - at least give me a call so I don't bother the police about ye."

They all laughed and followed the waitress to their table. Once she had left with their orders, Joe decided to come clean about stalking them.

"Umm, I have a wee confession to make." He slunk his gaze to the ground - returning it so he could see his friends' reactions. "I was just follow'n you now, and I seen ye exit a building in Union Street. How did ye come to be in there?"

Joe's question didn't fluster Gabby, but Max looked like a Scout busted with contraband. Gabby was quick to deter any ill thinking on his part.

"Max came to pick me up - I have an apartment on the top floors."

"Did he now?" Joe caught Max's eye and teased him with a cheeky grin. "That's really interesting, you see, because I just found out yesterday that my father's shipping company owns that building," He waited for their reactions.

"Oh?" said Gabby. "That's a funny coincidence. I guess it has to be owned by someone I suppose. My mother has rented that apartment since I was about fourteen I guess. We shared it with another couple as a holiday let. I used to stay there for a couple of weeks each summer. I've occasionally used it as a study base and between terms too while I've been at Oxford."

"Aye, well it would have been nice to have known that a couple of days ago, aye Max? Would've saved ye an awful lot of worry." Joe took a swig of his ale and let the two of them sweat over how to respond.

"Of course I checked the apartment, Joe. She wasn't there." Max shot him a stern look; warning him to back off.

"Leave Gabby alone, Joe. It's no concern of yours no more." Max took a sip from his glass of cider and Joe took it as a cue to move on.

Max looked at Gabby and his smile returned. "Joe we wanted to see you today because we have some great news."

"Really? Well I'm sure I can guess what it is."

Max's chest heaved. "Good grief, Joe. Can't you just play along?"

"Fine. Sorry." His apology seemed pathetic - even to himself.

"We're getting married." Max beamed like he'd won a great prize. Gabby held up her ring finger to display the engagement ring, while Max told some story about his grandmother.

"Och, that's wonderful news." Joe smiled as warmly as he could, given their awkward interactions so far.

Wanting to make amends, Joe stood to offer Max a congratulatory handshake. He hugged Gabby and gave her a kiss on the cheek.

"Your Ma must be so pleased, Max."

"Aye, she is. She wouldn't stop crying last night when we told them. Poor Gabby, you handled it really well though, Luv." Max gave her a quick kiss on the lips, which she happily returned.

"Och, you two. Maybe you should head back to the apartment." Joe chuckled. "No, I really am pleased for ye both." He tipped his glass before taking another swig.

The waitress arrived with their food and Joe was saved from being told off again. Munching on their meals, he was certain they hadn't told him what really happened. So, against Max's warning, Joe questioned Gabby further.

"So where've you been this whole time, Gabby? I know you wouldn't have left Max in the lurch like that if you hadn't good reason."

Max kicked him in his shin and wrapped an arm around Gabby's shoulders.

"You don't have to talk about it if you don't want to, Luv." He spoke softly to her side.

"It's alright, everyone will find out eventually," She said.

"Not if you don't want them to, Gabby. It's up to you. It's okay if you don't want to talk about it just now." Max squeezed her shoulder and watched her profile attentively.

Joe grew more inquisitive by the second.

What didn't they want him to know?

"Well, Joe, I didn't reply to Max's calls because - I was in Paris..."

"Yeah, but weren't ye meant to come here first?" Joe interrupted.

"Give her a chance, Joe." Max's voice was almost a growl.

He was very angry - Why?

"I was in Paris because both my parents were killed in a car accident," Gabby said flatly, looking beyond his stare. "I didn't know what to do. The police called me and I just left as quickly as I could. I've apologised to Max. He didn't deserve to worry like that, but I had a lot to deal with and I needed to be alone. You can understand that, can't you, Joe?"

Her question made him uncomfortable. The fact that Gabby was trying to liken her own trauma to his loss seemed absurd. He didn't want to think about his father any more, but people kept bringing him up.

"Well, I guess so. Max has obviously told you that my Pa just recently died too, but I'll not grieve for him. He was a bastard and I'll never forgive him for what he did to Ma - and to me." Joe's anger rose beneath his calm exterior and he fought to keep his cool in the presence of his friends.

"Well, whatever the case. I loved my parents and now I'm all alone. At least you still have your mother, Joe." Gabby's eyes fought back tears.

Max kissed her forehead. "You're not alone anymore, Luv. You have me and my family. We're your family now."

Gabby reached across her chest and grasped Max's hand which still cradled her shoulder. "And I'm so grateful not to have lost you too." The dams broke in Gabby's eyes and Joe felt guilty for pressing her.

Keen to break the emotional tension, Joe decided to change the subject to something more cheerful for everyone. "So...when's the wedding?"

Max frowned microscopically. "Oh, not till the end of summer. Gabby is heading back to Paris at the end of the week to settle her parent's estate and then she's transferring up here to finish her degree at Aberdeen University. We plan to stay in the apartment initially..."

"You could buy your own farm, Max, from the estate money - that is - if Gabby agrees, of course." Joe nodded and tilted his glass of ale at her respectfully.

"Well, as I was saying... We'll stay in the apartment initially till Gabby finishes her studies and then Pa has agreed to sell us the Lockheart farm. He'll still work the land with me of course for a while, but Ma has asked him to step back and let me take charge. He can gradually retire when he likes then."

"But what about your parents, where will they live?" Joe asked.

"Well, Ma is keen to live in Alford, close to her friends and the church. I know they'll miss the farm, but at least they'll still be close by."

"That'll come in handy when you start a family." Joe grinned, biting back a full blown laugh. Max shook his head and Gabby looked a little horrified.

"Well, I think that calls for a toast!" Joe flagged the waitress and asked her to bring them a bottle of champagne.

Popping the cork, he poured them each a glass and raised it above his head.

"To new beginnings - and to burying the past. Cheers!"

CHAPTER THIRTY

10th April 2016

Jess

WITH EVERYONE ASSEMBLED at Castle Ferlie on Sunday afternoon, Lady Ferlie ushered them all into the sunny reception room on the south side. Dark timber beams lined the high ceiling and the pale green walls were adorned with numerous paintings. The ladies took their seats, leaving Max and Joe to sit uncomfortably close on a small pink settee. When everyone had settled, Jess spoke.

"Thank you, Lord and Lady Ferlie for hosting our family this afternoon. You have been most generous and we are truly grateful. Were it not for yours and Mrs Jenkins assistance, Ella and I might never have succeeded in finding the answers we were searching for."

Mrs Jenkins sat in a dark leather chair, most likely Lord Ferlie's given its size and masculine look. She smiled and nodded at the girls, giving them encouragement to continue. Ella acknowledged her and looked around at the others.

"Pa, Joe, Aunty Vera. We would like to explain what we've found out about our family and my hope is that it will bring us closer together and not upset anyone." Ella emphasised her last words with a glint of fear. Jess wasn't sure they'd succeed, but their time was up and they had to come clean regardless of what might happen.

Jack, Brody, and Steve were crammed together on a second small settee. They seemed to care little for anything the girls said. The busy pattern of the carpet, and the framed Ferlie ancestors, were of far greater fascination.

Lady Ferlie, sitting in a velvet wing-backed chair, was enjoying watching the boys' attentions shift about the room and she smiled at the girls every so often to show she was still listening. Her husband, Lord Ferlie, stood assertively between her side and the large reception window. Lord Ferlie looked a little out of place, given his present company, but seemed ready and willing to take the lead at any given moment, should the need arise. Jess wondered how he could assist them at all, given he was relatively clueless to the true purpose of the gathering.

Ella and Jess stood in front of the glossy grand piano. Ella cleared her throat.

"It started years ago when Joe's mother, Elaine, gave Aunty Flo a box. In the box was a set of keys and some clues about Elaine's past. But, because Aunty Flo was unwell, she decided to give the box to my mother before she died. Aunty Flo wanted Ma to continue to try and find out what happened to Joe's sister."

Joe looked at Ella, his full attention focused on what she would say next.

"Joe had a sister?" Steve asked, looking up from the floor in shock. Lady Ferlie looked surprised by his comment, but Jess wasn't. Kids often tune in to listen when adults least expect.

"Aye, he did," said Ella. "Her name was Joanna and they were twins. It was thought that she died soon after she was born. However, from what we've learnt, we now know that she did not die, but grew up to become a lovely woman."

Jess grinned. She knew Ella was talking about her own mother, but few others in the room did.

Ella pursed her lips. "After we spoke with Mrs Jenkins, we found out that Elaine was once called Eleanor Lockheart - before she married Gerrard Naudman. Eleanor was Grandpa Erik's younger sister. This meant that Joe, Pa, and Aunty Vera are cousins, which you already know."

Ella looked at Jess as if to pass the baton.

"So, then we visited Grandma Marta." Jess looked at her mother. "I didn't even know I had a Grandma until Ella introduced us."

Mum glanced at Uncle Max and blushed. She seemed more concerned with his response than Jess's lack of knowledge about Grandma's existence.

Jess frowned. "Anyway, Grandma told us that Elaine visited her and confessed that Gerrard was hitting her. With the link between Elaine and Gerrard now confirmed we decided to see if we could learn anything more about Elaine's past. So, we called Lady Ferlie, and asked if we could visit the castle. We thought since Elaine was Rosalie Ferlie's daughter there might be some pictures of her here. With the help of Lady Ferlie, we found photos of Rosalie, and Joseph Lockheart; our great-grandfather – and the man who built the Lockheart farmhouse."

"Cool. So you're saying my great-grandfather built Uncle Max's farmhouse?" asked Brody.

"Yup, he sure did." Jess was pleased he'd finally taken an interest and ceased poking his fingers into the buttons on the couch. She'd been praying Lady Ferlie wouldn't be bothered by his constant fiddling. Jess picked up the keys and held them casually in her hand.

"So. Rosalie married Joseph and moved from the castle to the farmhouse. They raised their children, Grandpa Erik and Eleanor there. But that's not all we found at the castle. We also used one of these keys to unlock a writing desk upstairs in the *Girls Room*."

Lord Ferlie looked surprised and became more engaged with the story when he realised it might involve the Ferlies just as much as the Lockhearts. Jess handed the keys to Ella and picked up a piece of paper.

"Inside the desk, we found a photo of Eleanor as a teenager and a note to her mother Rosalie." Jess held the paper up for all to see. "In the note, she apologises to her mother for running away to marry Gerrard, but she is certain she will be happy with him."

Ella put the keys on the piano, grabbed the Lockheart Family Album, and resumed their story.

"Once we realised that Eleanor's Ma was Rosalie, we wondered if there might be something of hers at our farmhouse too. So, we searched the loft and found Rosalie's wedding dress and this family photo album. In it there are photos of the farmhouse being built and photos of the all the Lockhearts - including Erik and Eleanor as children. The last photo in the album was of Grandpa Erik and Grandma Marta's wedding."

Mum shifted in her seat.

"In the loft, Jess and I also found a locked jewellery box which belonged to Eleanor. Inside, she kept a lock of her hair and a silver locket. We also believe that she hid her engagement ring in it too." Ella nodded at Jess.

Mum leaned forward and raised her eyebrows. "I'd like to see that album, can I take a look?" Mum's hand extended ready to receive the album.

"Aye," said Ella. "You can all take a look at it later. I'll leave it over here on the table. If you can just be patient with us a little longer, there's more to the story that we must tell you first...now where was I?"

"Joe's." Hinted Jess.

"Ah yes. So, then we asked if we could go visit Joe at the coast to see if we could learn anything more about Elaine.

"In her journal, Elaine wrote a lot about what Gerrard was doing. She suspected he was keeping secrets from her.

"We spoke to Joe"- Ella nodded at him -"and he told us all sorts of interesting information about his Ma and Pa that was quite useful. While we were there, we wanted to see if there was anything on his property that his mother might have left him that was locked. Our search led us to a locked box in the cottage, under the bed I slept in. Inside it were notes from Elaine and Aunt Flo."

Steve looked at Ella when she mentioned Flo's name and he turned his gaze toward Joe. Ella did the same. Joe gave them both a sympathetic look, smiled and nodded for Ella to continue.

"Anyway, Elaine's note led us to a shipping crate in Joe's storage shed. We had the key, so we unlocked it, and inside it – was a white baby size coffin."

A collective intake of air echoed around the room and everyone fell silent.

"Did you open the coffin too?" Uncle Max asked with trepidation.

Jess held the room in anticipation until Mum bugged her with eyes that said 'well?'

"Well, the coffin was locked, but yes, we opened it. And inside…it was empty."

Relief exhaled like a charge of lightning to the ground. Steve and Brody let their heads roll back on the settee to re-gather themselves.

"Well, it wasn't exactly empty," said Ella. Both boys sprang their heads upright immediately.

"What do you mean?" asked Steve. "Was it empty or not, Ella? It's a simple question."

"Aye Steve. There was no body inside the coffin, just another note."

"…and some rocks and a blanket too," said Jess.

"Well then it wasn't empty then, was it?" said Steve.

"No Steve - but that's not the point," said Ella.

"Well what is the point, Ella? You're walking us in circle's here."

"No I'm not. Just quit jabbering at me and I'll tell you." Ella winced her eyes at Steve.

"Now as I was saying - Inside was a note from Elaine, it was to Joe and Joanna. Joe's baby blanket was also inside and was covering a pile of rocks - which lay in the bottom of the coffin. The note said that if Joe could find a matching blanket, that he would know he'd found Joanna."

Jess looked around the room and all, bar Mrs Jenkins, seemed completely absorbed.

"Then you guys got back from the beach," Jess looked at her mother, "and, Mum, you came to the shed and found that buffet with the stuck drawer. Well, it wasn't stuck, it was locked - just like you said, and we had the key."

"I knew it." Mum blurted, "I knew you girls were up to something."

"Well, once we'd convinced you to leave, we unlocked it. Inside, was a pile of blue and white letters addressed to Gerrard. We also found that boarding pass, matchbook, and those French coins in there too," Jess admitted.

"I knew something wasn't right," said Mum. "I just couldn't figure out what it was. I can't believe this whole time you've been keeping this all a secret. Well, we know where you get that from now, don't we?"

"You." Uncle Max said quietly.

"No! Elaine, silly."

"You're right, Aunty Vera, we have been keeping it a secret, but only because we didn't know if we might uncover something that might make people very angry. We didn't want to risk hurting the people we love most, *our family*! But what we have to share, just might do that anyway." Ella cast her eyes to the rug and her shoulders slumped.

"Oh come on, Luv, what could possibly make us angry about the family's past," Mum said. "Nothing can tear us apart. Nothing you say could ever make me think any less of you. You're my family and I'll love you no matter what you have to tell us." Mum's attempt to comfort Ella was a welcome tonic.

"Aye," said Joe, "It won't matter to me what ye've got to say. I love you, Max, the boys, and Vera's too. Nothing you have to say would make me angry. Be sure lass, everything will be fine."

Ella straightened and her mood improved. "Well, we read the letters and we found out that Gerrard…had a mistress." Ella and Jess looked at Joe to gauge his reaction. He was neither stunned nor angry.

Ella's voice jittered, "Gerrard's mistress was called Charlotte and she lived in Paris. She raised a child called Elle - Gerrard's child." She paused again. Joe's eyes froze confused.

"So I have a half-sister - called Elle?" He asked.

"Not exactly," said Ella.

"What do you mean - exactly?" asked Joe.

Ella looked at Jess. Jess knew she wouldn't be able to explain it without bursting into tears. Jess would have to do it.

"Well, the thing is, Joe. You know how we mentioned that the keys were magical?"

"Yeah, but, I wasn't sure I believed ye."

"Neither did I at first," said Lady Ferlie.

Lord Ferlie looked stunned by his wife's admission.

"Magical Keys?! I don't believe it. You've never believed in any of that sort of thing before, Janice. What makes you think their keys are magical?"

"Well. I...I... I just do," said Lady Ferlie, unable to sound convincing. Lord Ferlie paced the floor in front of the window.

"You see, Lord Ferlie," Jess said, "When I touch the keys, I have a vision. Sometimes I see what the key might unlock and other times I see a moment in time when the item was used or important. When we left Joe's, there were only two keys left that we had to find homes for. In order to find out what they might unlock, I decided to touch one - on purpose."

"Did you really, Jess?" asked Brody. "Did you see a ghost?" Brody raised his eyebrows and laughed. Jess struggled to maintain her composure since his guess was entirely accurate.

"Yes, Brody, I touched this black key here." Jess held it up for them all to see. "In my vision, I saw Aunt Gabby in her wedding dress opening a wooden chest. She took out a framed picture and kissed it. Well, naturally we had to find out why. So while everyone was out, except Jack - he was watching TV, we went into Uncle Max's room, and unlocked Aunt Gabby's hope chest."

Jess looked nervously at her uncle having confessed what they'd done. "It was all my idea, of course, Ella tried to talk me out of it, but I just knew it was important, I'm really sorry, Uncle Max." Jess rubbed her sweaty palms together. She prayed her apology was enough to atone for their betrayal.

"Is that what you were up to?" asked Jack.

"I'm so sorry, Pa." Ella crossed her arms about her waist and chewed her bottom lip.

Uncle Max sat motionless and straight-faced. Jess couldn't tell if he was angry or just annoyed. She wanted the confession to end and decided it was best to yank the Band-Aid off, so-to-speak, before anyone could yell at them.

"Yes, Jack, we opened your Ma's hope chest. Inside we found the picture frame I'd seen in my vision and behind the glass was a photo of her parents. There were lots of other photos in the chest, some of which had of all three of them together as a family. Ella said she'd never seen any of the photo's before and that her Ma didn't like to talk about her parents."

"No. They were both killed in a car accident," said Uncle Max; his flat tone hinting annoyance more than anything.

Jess's voice broke in chunks, "We...well... The people in Aunt Gabby's picture frame - were Gerrard and Charlotte."

Jess stopped and waited for their little bombshell to go off.

Looks of surprise, shock, and horror passed across the faces of Joe, Uncle Max, Mum and Lord Ferlie. The boys took a little longer to grasp the enormity of the statement.

Uncle Max finally broke the silence. "So I married Joe's half-sister?"

Tears rolled down Ella's cheeks and Uncle Max tried to grasp what they already knew.

"Well, I'm afraid it's even more complicated than that," Jess said. "You see, the child Charlotte raised - Elle. Her full name was Gabriella Sinclaire, and she was the daughter of Gerrard and Elaine. She was Joanna."

The shock of it hit Uncle Max like an arrow in his chest and he stared into space trying to comprehend it.

Meanwhile, Joe burst into tears. "Gabby was Joanna, my twin sister? But she's gone now. I never even got to meet her." Jess knew it wasn't the truth, but she understood what he meant. He'd never known her as a sister, only as Flo's friend and Uncle Max's wife.

"Hell Janice!" boomed Lord Ferlie. "What sort of mess is this? If I'd known this was to come, I would have offered drinks before we even started."

Lord Ferlie went to pour the men some whisky, hoping it would help ease the tension.

"Max, Joe?" He asked, tipping the bottle in their direction.

"Aye" came Uncle Max's vacant reply. Joe looked up and simply nodded.

"Vera, what about you? Mrs Jenkins?" asked Lord Ferlie. Mum shook her head but Mrs Jenkins said, "Aye."

The boys looked around clueless. Mum sat speechless and confused. Her calm exterior was likely only for show so as not to add to the drama. But Jess knew she'd be going off inside like a fire cracker.

"Now, I'm afraid that's not all." Jess had everyone's attention once more. "We still had one key left. When Ella and I found out from Mrs Jenkins and Lady Ferlie that it's perfectly fine to marry your cousin..."

"Ewww! Who would want to marry their cousin?" said Steve looking oddly at Jess.

"Steve - Ma and Pa are cousins," said Ella.

"REALLY?" Steve's eyes bulged and his face skewed.

Jess grew impatient. "Yes really. Anyway, as I was saying, we decided to touch the last key to see if I'd have a vision of what it might be for. Well, I did, and the results were completely unexpected.

We needed to confirm if what I'd seen was true, so we went back to Grandma Marta to ask her.

3rd July 1995

Joe

Joe sat staring at the accountant, Mr Johnson, across the desk.

"Well, where are they? The files aren't here, and they should be." Joe said with stern authority.

"Um, I'm sorry, Mr Naudman, but I'm not exactly sure. Sometimes there's a glitch in the computer software and records don't always show where they're meant to." The nervous accountant, strangling a pen between his finger and thumb, was dressed far more professionally than his position required. Though his own suit did not exude an experienced CEO, Joe leaned forward and clamped two fists on his desk.

"Well fix it, damn it." He thumped vibrations through the desk. "I want to know by tomorrow afternoon where the files for the Union Street property have vanished to. And so help me, if ye don't have an answer - you'll not have a job here any longer."

"Yes, yes, of course, Mr Naudman, I'll have it for you as soon as possible. I'll just run it past legal - just to be sure it's still an asset we own," He stuttered.

"What do you mean, if it's an asset we still own? It's written right here in the company files." Joe slammed a folder in front of him.

"Well, it is possible the property has been sold, and that's the reason our records no longer show it." His theory on the matter was valid and Joe felt foolish for not considering the possibility himself. He'd only recently completed his financial management classes, so how could he have forgotten something so fundamental? He was angry with himself more than Johnson but he was too proud to let the poor man know it.

"Well, wouldn't **you** know if a property had been sold? Ye'r the god damn accountant for crying out loud."

"Yes, yes, of course, Mr Naudman. I should, but if the transaction was completed somewhere else - not in Aberdeen, then our files can take a couple of weeks to be updated." Johnson flicked a palm in the air to aid his explanation.

"That's ridiculous," Joe growled.

"Well maybe so, but have you tried checking the records in Denmark?"

"No, but I will. And I suggest you start making inquiries ye'self before I send you packing." Joe dismissed the accountant with a stare towards to the door.

"Of course, Mr Naudman, right away, Sir."

Johnson skittered away in a flurry of ungraceful manoeuvres. Joe couldn't help but smile at the terrified look he'd inflicted in the man's eyes. Just as quickly, he made his smirk disappear, worried that he was more like his father and grandfather than he liked to admit.

Turning his attention to his computer he tried to access the Denmark files. But having no success and feeling considerably frustrated, he resigned himself to the fact he might need help.

"Shona, can I see you in my office please?" He called through the phone's intercom. He'd upgraded the phones as soon as he saw how antiquated their systems were. Now he was beginning to think that the same was needed for their computers. Their processors were slow and if they couldn't keep up, how did they expect to compete with the more advance systems of other shipping companies.

A few seconds later Shona entered the room.

"Yes, Joe?"

"Ah, Shona, do you know how to access the Denmark files?"

"Yes of course. Which ones would you like?"

"Uh, well. How about the transactions for the last six months."

"Oh. That could take me a while. I'm sure Mr Johnson will find what it is you're looking for."

"Just do it, Shona." He hated the sound of his own voice - it was too much like Pa's. He'd have to work on it.

"Yes, Joe." Shona left.

Joe slumped in his chair feeling defeated. Even though his demands were being dutifully carried out by the staff, he felt more like a mean nuisance, than actually offering them any help.

He didn't much like the way he felt at the office. His own personality seemed to disappear the moment he sat in his father's chair. Even Max had mentioned the change. But how could he escape it? It was his duty to carry on the legacy his father and grandfather had built. No one had ever asked him what he wanted to do, it was just expected.

Although it had come to him sooner than he'd planned, Joe felt cheated. No longer was he expected to work his way up the company under his father's guidance. Instead, he was thrust into the very position he thought he'd never achieve.

As chairman of the Naudman Shipping Company, Joe found the job financially rewarding, but not hugely satisfying. He wasn't even sure if he was doing it all right. Not only did everyone expect him to step in and fill his father's shoes, they depended on him. For the first time, the full weight and burden of responsibility fell on his shoulders alone. He now understood how consumed his father was by it, and it scared him to see it happening to himself.

Lost in thought he never heard the faint knock on his door.

"Hello? Joseph?" His mother spoke softly from outside. "Joseph?" Ma opened the door and peered in. "Oh, you are in here. How's it going?"

"Och, okay, I guess. Just having a rough day." He admitted reluctantly.

"Well, how about that lunch?"

"Aye. That would be great, Ma. Let me get my jacket."

He stood and pulled it from the back of his chair. His mother went to help him, but Joe already had his arms inside it. She smoothed his shoulders and ran her eyes over him.

"Oh, look how refined and smart you are," Ma patted the lapel of his suit. "I'm so proud of you, Joseph. Everyone says you're managing things far better than they expected. I told them, of course you were, you're..."

"Oh Ma, whatever ye do, don't tell me I'm just like Pa. I hate it and I'm worried I'm becoming more like him the longer I stay here."

"Nonsense, Joseph, you're a good man. You're nothing like your Pa. But you are a Naudman, and that name holds weight around here, and much of the northern ports of Europe too. You're talented and I know you'll succeed." Ma knew when it was best to change the subject. "Well now, when is Flo coming to visit next, or are you heading to Oxford for the weekend?"

"She's too busy; swamped with papers to write. To be honest, it's what I should be doing too if I want to finish my studies by correspondence." Joe exhaled deeply. "Flo will be up in three weeks. Och, I miss her terribly, Ma. I want to go see her, but I also don't want to distract her. I'd never forgive myself if I was the cause of her failure."

"Well, you do what you think is best. Flo loves you - I've seen it. But don't forget, Joseph, a girl still needs a little romance in her life. It can't all be about the books." Ma pointed a finger into his chest. "It was very generous of you to offer her your flat, especially since Gabby will be moving up here. No doubt that will ease the pressure on Flo, at least in the finance department. And what about Gabby, will she be returning to university in Aberdeen?" Ma shook her head not waiting for his answer. "I don't know, girls these days, seems they want the career and the family. Something's got to give. Raising a family is a full-time job. Something Max and Gabby will no doubt figure out soon enough, someone's got to compromise." Ma held onto her old fashioned values with such pride. Didn't she realise it wasn't the 80's anymore?

Knowing he hadn't heard the last of his mother's advice and opinions, he ushered her towards the door. If he had to listen, it was better done with a good meal and a shot of whisky.

Taking her son's cue to leave, she walked a few steps ahead of him, pausing her chatter only when they were within ear shot of the staff.

"I'm heading out for lunch, Shona." Joe said - then whispered, "Wish me luck."

Shona smiled and nodded.

Joe had only just returned from lunch when Shona said he had a call waiting. He quickly fare-welled his mother and resumed his position behind the desk.

"Hello?"

"Mr Joseph Naudman. I am Mr Garrick, the company's solicitor. I hear you've been making inquiries about the Union Street property."

"Aye, that's correct."

"Mr Naudman. Your father sold that property just before he passed away."

"Oh, I see. Well, do you know who he sold it to?"

"Ah, yes, he sold it to the Yohan Foundation in Denmark."

"I see, and who are the trustees or shareholders of this Yohan Foundation?"

"That, I am not too sure. The signature on the sales agreement is of Victor Nielsen, the director."

"Well, thank you, Mr Garrik. You have been a great deal of help. Did my father say why he wanted to sell the property?"

"No, he gave no explanation or reasons. Maybe the company just needed some more cash flow."

"Well, thank you again, Mr Garrik. Goodbye." He hung up the receiver.

Joe called through the intercom, "Shona. I want Johnson back in my office in thirty minutes. Do ye have those transactions?"

"Yes, Joe. Uh, they're just about finished printing."

"Great send them through with Johnson."

Exactly thirty minutes later Mr Johnson walked into Joe's office for the second time that day, with a mountainous armful of files and the transaction print outs from Shona.

"Thank you, Johnson. Take a seat. I want to go through every transaction in the last six months. I want to know exactly how my father was running this company and we're not going home till I'm satisfied I understand."

Joe held up his finger before Johnson could rebut him. The accountant seemed to accept his fate and opened up a file.

"Shona?" Joe called through the intercom. "Would you please call my mother and tell her I'm going to be late home tonight? Johnson and I have some catching up to do. That's all. Thank you."

CHAPTER THIRTY-ONE

24th August 1995

Joe

JOSEPH HAD BEEN chasing his tail for weeks trying to figure out the company finances and operations. The mystery of the Union Street sale still bugged him. He'd tried everything to find out who the Yohan Foundation actually was. He'd run searches for their shareholders and requested a list of its trustees, all of which had resulted in dead ends. Even Victor Nielsen was dead.

The summer had all but come to an end and he longed for the break he so deserved. He hadn't seen Flo in over a month and was desperate for the relief she could bring to his nine to five life. He would decide after this weekend whether he would propose to her or not.

Seeing Max and Gabby so happy with their life mapped out before them, Joe envied their ability to see each other every day. If only his dreams could be so easily achieved. Every day he wished he could escape his life at the company, even if only for a short while, in the arms of the woman he loved.

Flo would arrive at six tonight, in time for the respective stag and hens parties. Although he wouldn't get to see her until tomorrow, just having her in the same city helped clear his mind and ease his tension. The wedding was only two days away and he had neglected to complete his given task; the best man's speech. He was determined to make Max proud, but as yet no words deemed worthy had come to him. Promising himself, and Max, he would have it done by tomorrow, he decided he would finish it while Flo was at the dressmaker's with Gabby tomorrow morning.

25th August 1995

Joe's stress had increased substantially these last few weeks and Max's stag night was just what he needed; time to unwind, blow off some steam, and forget all about the company's troubles. He was paying for it now though with a sore head and a speech to write. It felt like a case of high school déjà vu and seemed a fit punishment for the excess he'd enjoyed at the party last night.

Sitting at the kitchen table with a steaming cup of coffee fuelling his brain cells, he wedged an ice pack between his hand and forehead. The mixture of both, kept him uncomfortably awake so he could finish his task. Crafting his best lines into an ode to friendship with Max, he penned what wit he possessed into a string of entertaining one-liners for the guests at the reception. Although he wasn't entirely happy with his final result, the speech was done and his headache finally eased.

Joe went to clean himself up. He was due to pick Flo up from town at eleven. He'd dreamed of this day since he last saw her at Max and Gabby's engagement party six weeks ago.

With a picnic packed and time to spare he collected a dozen red roses on his way there. His extra effort was commended by all the ladies at the dress shop, and Flo blushed like jam in a sugar dusted donut.

Now nestled close beside him in the car, Flo embraced the flowers and looked out the window towards the horizon. Her silk hair rested squarely on her shoulders. She'd cut it since he last saw her. It looked okay but he preferred it longer. He didn't care. Today he was floating on cloud seventeen sitting right next to his favourite angel. In that moment he definitely knew he wanted to propose. Not only was the weather better than he'd hoped for, but the drive to Fasque Castle was breathtakingly memorable. Surely it would aid his proposal and make it harder to refuse.

Flo hadn't said much and he could tell something was weighing on her mind. He prayed it wasn't bad news. He'd had enough of that kind lately and wasn't at all keen to spoil such a lovely day with negative sentiments.

No. He was determined nothing would ruin this day for them and he'd make sure his plans succeeded. Flo would agree to become his wife, and - if she permitted, they would stay for the night in the master suite at the castle. Joe couldn't wipe the grin off his face. A glimmer of hope peaked out from behind his gloomy cloud of company spreadsheets. Joe would happily place bets Flo would cheer up once he'd made his offer.

Settling into each other after nibbling on the picnic baskets delicacies, Flo looked up at him, "Joe, I've been..."

"Wait, don't say anything," He interrupted, "I, I know it's been difficult these past few weeks. I've missed you terribly. But, I, I just want you to know, that I have given this a lot of thought and...Florence Rogers, I'd like you to be my wife. Will you marry me?"

"Oh, Joe." Pain flooded Flo's face. "I wish you hadn't. I'm flattered of course, and I'd love to say yes. In fact, I know I would have. But I've been offered a job in Rome and I've accepted. It's a three-year contract, Joe. I can't agree to marry you and expect you to wait that long for me. I know you're disappointed, but it's what I've studied for all these years, and I'll finally have the chance to pay my parents back."

Tears swelled in her eyes and Joe wanted desperately to wipe them away. It made him upset to see her so distressed. But at the same time he was also angry that she hadn't even bothered to speak to him about it until now.

"Och, I see." His voice choked; ill-prepared to say anything better.

"Oh please, Joe, say you'll be alright. I know you probably had other plans and I still love you very much. But you and I both know we've been drifting apart over the summer. I thought you might have come to visit me a little more often."

"Well, I didn't want to be a distraction to ye. I thought we could move in together - when ye finished your studies. I was willing to wait and at least try and make things work, ye've barely even called me." Joe steadied his voice; stifling his frustration into his clenched fist.

"I have - you were just never home. Your mother said you were working late. I started to think that you'd found someone else."

"No Flo, I've been working and waiting like a damn fool, for **YOU.**" His temper gave way.

"Please don't be upset with me, Joe. I don't want to ruin Max and Gabby's wedding."

"No we wouldn't want that, would we." Joe scowled and lay back on his elbow. He stared at Flo and she bent forward to kiss him.

"Don't." He placed his hand to her lips. "I'll be fine, but please don't make it any harder."

Tears dripped from her eyes. "I'm so sorry, Joe. Couldn't we work this out? Please don't hate me. I love you."

"Ye've a funny way of showing it." Joe fussed with a thread in the picnic blanket and wouldn't look at her.

She got up and wiped her face. "I think I'll take a walk. Would you like to come with me?" She offered her hand.

Joe was no longer in the mood to share a romantic stroll through the gardens. Not when any chance of romance had fled the property - along with his self-respect.

"No thanks. I'll wait here. Let me know when you're ready to leave." His icy words stung his heart, and would probably sting hers just as much. Her face was a sculpture of agony. He'd never forget that look. Never. Flo's betrayal wounded him more deeply than his own father's had. He would never risk loving someone so foolishly again. Not if this could happen.

How did I not see this coming? I'm a damn fool - that's why.

Nothing during the next forty-eight hours came close to lightening his mood - not the celebration of Max and Gabby's wedding, nor the bottle of whisky he'd consumed. His smiles were fake, and his cheers were forced. The burden, resting heavily on his shoulders, seemed to double. His anger condensed into an armour of hate and his jaw locked; setting his features like a mask of stone. Closing himself behind another door of protection, Joe lost hope of ever leaving the prison inside his head. And fearing he might lose himself entirely - He nailed the door shut.

26th August 1995
Elaine

Elaine stood at the rear of the church. Memories of the confession she'd made the last time she entered the parish flooded her mind. Thoughts of Joanna seemed to consume her every day and she struggled to release the anger she felt towards Marta. She knew Marta hadn't intended to run Gerrard and Charlotte off the road, but losing all chance she had of finding her daughter sat like a pebble in the base of her shoe.

Erik spotted her hiding behind a large arrangement of pink and white peonies with lavender-coloured hydrangeas. Hastening his step he made his way over to talk to her.

"Come sit with us, Eleanor, you're family."

"No Erik, I'm only here to wish Max and Gabby well and then I'm leaving." Her cold tone could not be masked, even for the sake of a wedding.

Erik attempted to smile and nod at the other guests arriving inside the church as he dealt with her under his breath.

"Marta is truly sorry about Gerrard, I hope you understand that. If she could take back that day she would. I'm grateful to you, for not mentioning anything about it to the police, or the boys. I'd hate for Joe and Max to be at odds with each other, they've become such good friends. Don't you think they ought to know they're related though, Eleanor?"

"Don't call me that, and No, I don't. If Joseph found out he was related to Max and that his best friend's mother was responsible for the death of his own father, they might end up hating each other and resenting us. They don't need to be mixed up in our mistakes."

"I suppose you're right. At least stay for the ceremony, I won't say a word to Marta about it."

"Alright. Now get going with you." Elaine shooed him away so he wouldn't draw any further attention to her.

The bride looked beautiful; dressed in a simple soft white chiffon dress with a ring of daisies around her dark curls. Max, in his Lockheart family kilt, was all smiles from ear to ear when he saw her.

Elaine admired them, as did the other guests. Awash with emotions, something about the bride seemed familiar - though she couldn't pick why.

Tears collected in her eyes and she recalled her own wedding to Gerrard. It boasted none of the happy celebrations of this wedding, nor the company of loved ones to share it with. She felt a terrible ache for the lost opportunities in her life. She wanted to run, to escape the truth of her own failures. The only solace to her crumbling world was Joseph and the hope of new beginnings - which Max and Gabby exemplified.

Outside the church, a shower of rice rained over the newly-weds. Friends an family congratulated the charming couple, and Elaine waited to do the same. While Marta was distracted she ascended the stairs and held out her arms to Max. Gabby was talking to Flo, but Elaine didn't mind. It was Max she wanted to speak to.

She kissed him on the cheek.

"Congratulations, Max. I'm sure you two will be very happy together. Best of luck."

Elaine turned and walked away. She heard Gabby ask,

"Who was that?"

Max replied, "That's Joe's mother. She's..."

Elaine could no longer hear Max's reply when the crowds cheered the couple on for another kiss. Glancing back she caught sight of Max pulling Gabby into his arms before dipping her for a kiss.

Moments later, the happy couple rushed past in a flurry of cheers and streamers, heading for the wedding car.

Joe followed behind and Elaine grabbed his arm, detaining him briefly.

"I'm heading off home now," She said.

"Are you sure you won't come to the reception, Ma? Max and Gabby won't mind."

"No. I'm tired. I just want to be alone for a while. Good luck with your speech. I'm sure you'll do a marvellous job, Joseph."

She released her grip on his arm, looked into his eyes and ran her fingers down his cheek.

What would Joanna look like on her wedding day?

"Okay, Ma. I'll see you later then."

"Aye. Have fun." She gave a brief glint of a smile and then left.

Elaine wept as she drove home. She felt hopeless and fatigued from the countless hours she'd spent thinking about Joanna. Walking through the front door she went straight to the buffet drawer and removed her blue journal and the keys. In their place, she threw Charlotte's letters to Gerrard inside and locked it.

What shall I do? If I can't find Joanna, how can anyone?

Taking the keys on the ribbon from her handbag she twisted each of them onto a single large ring. Adding the other keys she had collected over the years she said a prayer over each of them, hoping that one day someone might find her missing daughter.

The odd white key, they'd found on Gerrard's dead body, she held tightly until her fingers ached. With difficulty, she added it to the ring and sat them on the bed. Taking out a little baby's gown with an embroidered pink bow, she wrapped the keys inside, placed them in a box and stowed it under her bed. She vowed never to give up hope that one day she might get to meet her daughter.

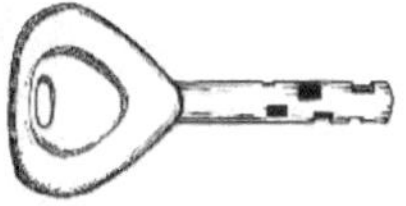

10th April 2016
Jess

Jess held up the white triangle topped hollow cut out key.

"In my final vision when I touched this key, I saw Gerrard and Charlotte driving a car. I also saw the accident that killed both of them. Grandma Marta had been tailing them when they crossed the centre-line and crashed head-on into a truck. She had gone to Paris to confront Gerrard for Elaine about the whereabouts of Joanna. It was an accident and she didn't know what to do, so she fled back home to Scotland. Elaine was so furious with her that she never spoke to Marta again. Her only link to finding Joanna was Gerrard - and he was dead."

Uncle Max and Joe looked at each other. Confusion reigned. Neither spoke; perhaps fearing what the other might say.

"Does anyone know where this key might belong?" asked Jess.

Handing the ring of keys to Uncle Max, she thought he would be the one most likely to know the answer. He shook his head, obviously clueless to its origin. He handed it to Joe, who having already seen it and knew nothing, handed it to the boys. Steve, Jack and Brody, all took a good look at the keys, but each shook their head.

Jess grew impatient, it was unlikely her mother would know either, but she passed them to her to inspect anyway. She took the keys reluctantly. Jess hadn't considered whether anyone else may be affected by the keys. She had accepted that their magic had in fact, 'run out' - as Lady Ferlie suggested. That wasn't to say she and Ella hadn't tried re-instating it. But so far nothing had worked. With no one else affected by the keys, it seemed that the magic really was gone. Mum quickly looked them over and passed them on to Lady Ferlie. She, in turn, passed them to her husband, since she had already seen all the keys before. Lord Ferlie looked at the white key in question and recognition creased his face.

"I know what this is for." His tight lips smiling like a child with a new toy.

Everyone's eyes darted in his direction. "It's a safe deposit box key for the Royal Bank of Scotland in Aberdeen. They no longer offer safe deposit boxes to new customers, so whoever owns that box, must have owned it for a while. The key is of little use though, unless you have the box number," said Lord Ferlie.

Jess shot a stare at Joe.

"Did you bring everything we asked you to, Joe?"

"Aye, I did, it's in me car, why?"

"That slip of paper we gave you with that hundred pound note, it had a number on it. What if that's the deposit box number?" said Jess.

Lord Ferlie swilled the last drop of whisky in his glass. "If it's a five-digit number that'll be it alright. A bank account number is at least ten digits or more, the box numbers are shorter."

Steve looked at Joe - ready to burst.

"Well don't just sit there, Joe - go get it!"

CHAPTER THIRTY-TWO

7th November 2007

Gabby

G ABBY TOOK THE box from Flo reluctantly.

"I don't know why you think I'll have any more luck than you, Flo. I only wish you had more time to work on it yourself."

"Well, you at least know more than Joe and that's a start. I'm sure you'll be able to find the answers. But promise me this; look after Joe for me. He's gonna struggle when I'm gone; running that property on his own. You know he won't ask for help, but he'll need you all the same. I was a fool to wait so long. If only I hadn't taken that job in Rome, Joe and I might have had more time together. Don't waste it, Gabby. Make every moment count." Flo gripped Gabby's hand.

"Well Joe was the fool, Flo, he should never have let you go. But he got awful stubborn after his Pa died and your leaving was the last straw. I barely recognised him that Christmas after you'd gone, and even Max struggled to tolerate his tempers. I know Joe hated his Pa, but that bitterness probably made him more like him than he realised. It was such a relief when you came back. Though it can't have been easy for you."

"No. Joe had a lot of issues to work through, but he did - bless him. He's much more like the man he was when we first met now. Do you remember the first time I told you about him? I fell so hard. It was only your straight talking that kept my head below the clouds.

"If there is a link between the Lockhearts and Joe, I'll be praying you find it. But you take care of yourself Gabby. When that little one comes, you give him a big kiss from his Aunty Flo for me, won't you."

"Of course. But how do you know it's a he?"

"Awe, I have a feeling, that's all." Flo smiled.

Gabby balanced herself upright, her swollen belly protruding under her dress. She stood beside Flo and bent to kiss her friend's deathly pale head. Holding her hand she gave it a squeeze.

"Bye, Flo. I'll miss you." Her eyes washed with sorrow.

"Bye, Gabby. Take heart, I'll be watching you all from above." Flo's thin lips formed a gentle smile.

Gabby left with streams of tears staining her cheeks and a brightly coloured box tucked under her arm. She longed to run from the closing walls of the hospital, but her pregnant state prevented it. Instead, she steadily waddled her way to the main car park where Max would be waiting for her with the two children. Their innocent smiles lightened her heart the moment she saw them.

"You alright, Ma?" asked her sensitive five-year-old, Ella.

"I'll be alright, sweetheart. But Flo won't be with us much longer." Gabby struggled to turn and let her daughter see her tears.

"I'll miss her, Ma."

"Me too, sweetheart, me too."

It was early January 2008 when Gabby first looked at the box. Jack, just seven weeks old, lay settled in his crib and Gabby welcomed the silence.

Jack was born three weeks after Flo died and Gabby worried whether a baby, born in grief, would suffer for it.

Steve, her rambunctious two year old, was finally down for a nap and Ella wasn't due to be picked up from school for another hour. Trying to decide between reviewing the contents of Flo's box, or taking a nap herself, she decided she was long overdue in keeping her promise to her friend.

Flo had worked as hard as she could right up until she passed away, trying to solve the mystery of Joe's missing sister. But would she be able to do any better?

Opening the lid of the box, she looked at the journal and read a few pages. She picked up the keys that lay swathed in the baby's gown. Unwrapping it she studied them once again, with similar conclusions. None of them were familiar to her, except maybe one. She thought she remembered seeing her father once with a key similar to the modern plastic topped one.

She read a few more pages of the journal and came across a photo of a baby. There was something very strange about the photo. It looked an awful lot like one she had of herself as a child. Standing up to go and look in her hope chest, the journal fell from her lap and out slipped another photo. Flo had never shown her these pictures, so how did they get there?

Picking up the picture from the floor she noticed a kiss mark on the back. She flipped it over and there staring back at her was a beautiful picture of her own mother.

She sat bewildered.

What's going on? How did Flo get a photo of my mother?

She'd locked every photo she had of her parents in her hope chest and only ever opened it on the anniversary of their death. Maybe Flo had found them when they moved out of their flat in Oxford? But she herself couldn't remember ever having a photo of her mother with a kiss mark on the reverse.

It puzzled her greatly and with no one to question, she decided the only thing she could do was talk to the author of the journal - Joe's mother.

Flo had warned her that Elaine never wanted to talk about it. But surely she'd be able to explain why a photo of her own mother was in her journal - wouldn't she?

Gabby knew time was short. Joe's mother was very ill and delaying a trip might lose her the opportunity forever.

11th April 2016

Jess

The bank attendant, seemed nervous when all five people entered his office.

Joe, Uncle Max, and Mum stood behind Ella and Jess. They'd managed to convince Joe and their parents to take them with them to unlock the safe deposit box at the bank in Aberdeen.

"Well now, how can I be of assistance today?" asked the tall genteel bank clerk.

"We'd like to open it, Sir." Jess held out the key and slip of paper with the security deposit box number printed on it.

The bank attendant took the items from her and looked at the printed slip. "Alright, one moment, please, while I get authorization to open the vault. We wouldn't normally let this many people in there at once. How about just two of you retrieve the box, and you can open it in my office, hmm?"

Everyone looked to her to answer, so she did.

"Fine. I think Joe and Ella should go." Jess felt as confident as any adult in the room and everyone agreed with her suggestion. Joe and Ella followed the attendant out the door. They returned five minutes later with a steel case box. Its number was engraved on the front and a keyhole sat in its centre on top.

Joe placed it on the attendant's desk. Ella placed the key in the lock and turned it until the slide came free.

Lifting the long lid, all that could be seen was a loosely knitted baby blanket. Ella pulled it out and passed it to Joe. Underneath lay a few envelopes. Opening the first one she read:

"My dear Gabriella." Ella stopped, realising the letter was to her mother.

"I am sorry to have to tell you but you are not the daughter of Charlotte Sinclaire & Victor Nielsen. Your true identity is Joanna Naudman. You are the daughter of Gerrard Naudman and Eleanor Lockheart, also known as - Elaine Naudman. You were born as a twin sister to Joseph Naudman on September 27th, 1974. You were gravely ill at birth and so I took you to Aberdeen to be treated. I stole you from your mother and gave you to my mistress, Charlotte Sinclaire, whom I dearly loved. She was the one who nursed you back to health and raised you as her own. You were the joy of her life. I know what I've done is unforgivable, but one day I hope you will be able to forgive me and find peace with it all. Your loving father,

Victor Nielsen / Gerrard Naudman.

Ella passed the letter to Joe who took it from her and muttered to no one in particular.

"Why that good for nothing piece of... He's still wreaking havoc even though he's dead."

Ella picked up the next envelope. Pulling out three pages she looked them over. The top page was her mother's birth certificate. The child's name written at the top was, Gabriella Rosalie Sinclaire, Father; Gerrard Naudman and Mother; Charlotte Sinclaire.

Underneath the birth certificate was a forged death notice for Joanna Naudman. The cause of death was written: Died at birth, September 27th, 1974.

The final piece of paper was a signed and dated document written by Gerrard stating that Joanna Naudman did not die and had been stolen and renamed, Gabriella Sinclaire. Any and all deeds or titles left to either of them were to become the property of Gabriella Sinclaire.

The final envelope was thick and obviously contained multiple folded pages. Ella handed it to her Pa.

Uncle Max opened the letter and flipped through the pages. "It's the deeds to 145 Union Street," He said, confused.

"Let me see that," Joe grunted. "But I spent months looking for this company's trustees and shareholders. Pa certainly fooled the shipping company here. If he was Victor Nielsen, then he sold that property under very false pretences. He must have made it a blind company. Aye, here" - Joe pointed to the company details - "I'm right. But why didn't Gabby just tell me? I really wish she had."

"Maybe she didn't know, Joe," said Jess.

"So, Ma never got to meet her real mother, nor Elaine her daughter - that's so sad," Ella said - her voice breaking.

Uncle Max wrapped an arm around Ella's shoulder and smiled.

"Aye, but she did meet her mother. Elaine was at our wedding. She congratulated me and wished us well. I thought she was just a friend of the family, but she was more than that, she *was* family. They may not have known each other as mother and daughter but your Ma did not lack a mother, she had Charlotte. Losing both her parents in the car crash devastated her. I think that's the reason she wanted to get married so quickly. But I wouldn't change anything - not for a million dollars. I have you, and I have Joe. Even if Elaine and Gabby never truly knew each other as mother and daughter, it doesn't matter. They're together now and that's what counts," Uncle Max said resolutely.

"Aye, but they did meet," Joe said with a sheepish smile. She made me promise not to say anything to you Max. "Gabby came to see Ma just before she died. Ma asked me to give Gabby her emerald necklace. It all makes sense now."

"Really? She never mentioned it to me," Uncle Max said. "I clearly didn't know my own wife very well at all, did I?"

"You did, Max. Gabby came to visit us at Rattray just before Ma passed. Maybe she knew the truth, maybe she didn't. I guess we'll never know."

9th January 2008
Gabby

Gabby rose early and prepared Ella's lunch for school.

"I thought I might go into the city today, Max." She wrapped an extra sandwich in cling-wrap and popped it in a container for herself. "I'll pop in and visit your mother after I've dropped Ella at school. I thought I'd see if she wouldn't mind looking after Steve for me. I'll take Jack with me."

"You sure you don't want me to drive you?" asked Max. The roads would be icy and a trip to town with a baby could be challenging enough.

"No, I'll be fine. I promise I'll be careful. I really need to get out of the house."

Max walked up behind her and wrapped his arms about her waist, and she smeared another piece of bread with butter.

"Well alright, but do be careful, the roads may be icy. Tell Ma to call me if Steve gets too much for her and I'll pick him up."

"I'm sure she'll be fine."

Gabby knew that if Max knew her true intentions he would never have let her go alone. The drive, although not more than two hours away, could be difficult at this time of year, but delaying her trip even a day might lose her the opportunity to speak with Elaine at all.

The fields lay thick with snow and earlier travellers left impressions of their journey in black trails along the roads. Gabby scanned the road carefully, keeping an eye out for any diversions off the road that might indicate a slippery spot. Grit laden snow slushed about the tyres and Gabby felt relieved when she finally pulled into Marta's driveway.

With as little explanation as possible, Gabby excused herself leaving Steve in Marta's arms. Steve waved his chubby little hands at her from the window as she pulled away. She hoped she was doing the right thing and would live to regret it if she wasn't. The photos and journal sat on the seat next to her as reminders of the mystery she had promised to unfold for Flo. She could only hope that Joe wouldn't berate her for driving in such conditions like she knew Max would, if he ever found out.

Before Joe could question her unexpected arrival, Gabby thrust baby Jack in his arms and poured steaming hot water from the kettle into a bowl. Placing the bottle of milk into the bowl to warm it through, she fired instructions at Joe about how to check when the milk was ready. Wiping the droplets from her wrist she asked, "Could you feed him for me, Joe? I really must talk with your mother - it's important."

Bewildered, Joe could really only give one answer, "Sure."

Joe rocked and cooed at the baby resting in his arms, and Gabby entered the bedroom where Elaine lay. Edging closer she pulled up a chair beside the bed and held her hand.

"Elaine, are you awake?" Gabby asked softly. "Elaine, it's Gabby."

Elaine roused with a warmth in her face that contradicted her state of ill health.

"Oh, Gabby, it's so nice of you to come. Joe will be pleased." Elaine's voice was weak and Gabby leaned closer. "He's been stuck here with only me for company and I've not many words left I'm afraid. I'll be gone soon and my son will be all alone. Will you keep watch over him for me?"

"Yes. I will."

"Thank you, dear. Now, I want you to have my emerald necklace. Joe will give it to you." Elaine closed her eyes and took a few deep breaths.

"That's very kind of you, Elaine. Thank you. The reason I've come today is because Flo gave me your journal and I have some questions." Gabby didn't want to wait for Elaine's approval to ask them so she carried on. "Why are there photos of me as a child and of my mother in your journal?"

Elaine locked eyes with her for a good long moment, and tears swelled on her bottom lashes.

"Elle, is that you?" She asked faintly.

"Nobody's called me that since I was about ten. I went through a phase where I hated that name and my mother said I could change it to Ella or Gabby. My father liked Gabby, so that's what I chose. But Mum would still call me Elle - or even Gabriella sometimes. But how did you know I went by that name?"

"Oh Elle, I've been looking for you for so long, and now that you're here, I can hardly believe it." Elaine said, her face locked in a battle of excitement and agony. She coughed, weaker than ever.

"What do you mean, Elaine? I don't understand?"

"You, my dear, are **MY** daughter. When you and Joseph were born, you were very ill...near death. Your father, Gerrard, stole you from me and said you were dead. He gave you to his mistress, Charlotte, and sent you far away so I could never find you. Oh Joanna, look at you."

"I don't understand. My father's name was Victor, and who is Joanna?"

"You are. You are Joanna. You were born Joanna Rosalie Naudman. Your father changed your name and probably his own too, to prevent you from ever knowing the truth." Elaine chuckled softly and then coughed. "Gerrard, sometimes like to call himself Victor when we lived in Denmark - He thought it was a great joke since we'd changed my name when we were married. My name was Elea..."

Elaine seemed to run out of breath just as she was about to tell her something important. But regretfully the dying woman was so tired, and a peaceful calm fell over her.

"Elaine, Elaine!" Gabby yelled. Puddles of tears slipped down her cheeks.

Joe burst into the room and Elaine's eyes fluttered open once more.

"Och, Joanna. Tell Marta I forgive her," She said on a breath.

Elaine slipped into a deep sleep. One which neither Gabby nor Joe would wake her from. But the smile on her face told them she had at last found peace.

Gabby sat at the kitchen table sipping on the hot cup of tea Joe had made for her. "Your Ma was very confused. She called me Joanna. I think maybe she thought I was."

"Aye well, she's been looking for Joanna for so long and I'm sure ye brought some peace to her. Joanna is dead. She died a long time ago. She's buried in a field on our auld land."

Gabby wasn't sure what to say. She knew there was more to it than that, but she wasn't sure if she wanted to pry any further. Joe might hate her if he found out that her mother was his father's mistress and that he had left him and Elaine for her and Charlotte. Not to mention he'd kept a second family hidden from them all these years. And then there was Max and the children to consider too.

Gabby was content, and she didn't want to cause any trouble between Max and his closest friend.

So she didn't.

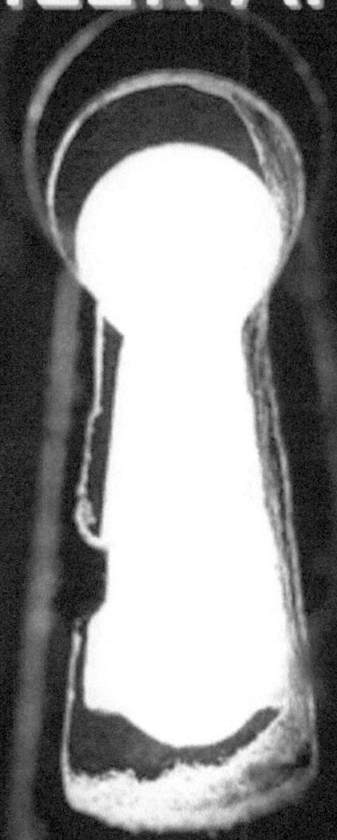

CAUTION!
SPOILER AHEAD
Proceed only after finishing the book

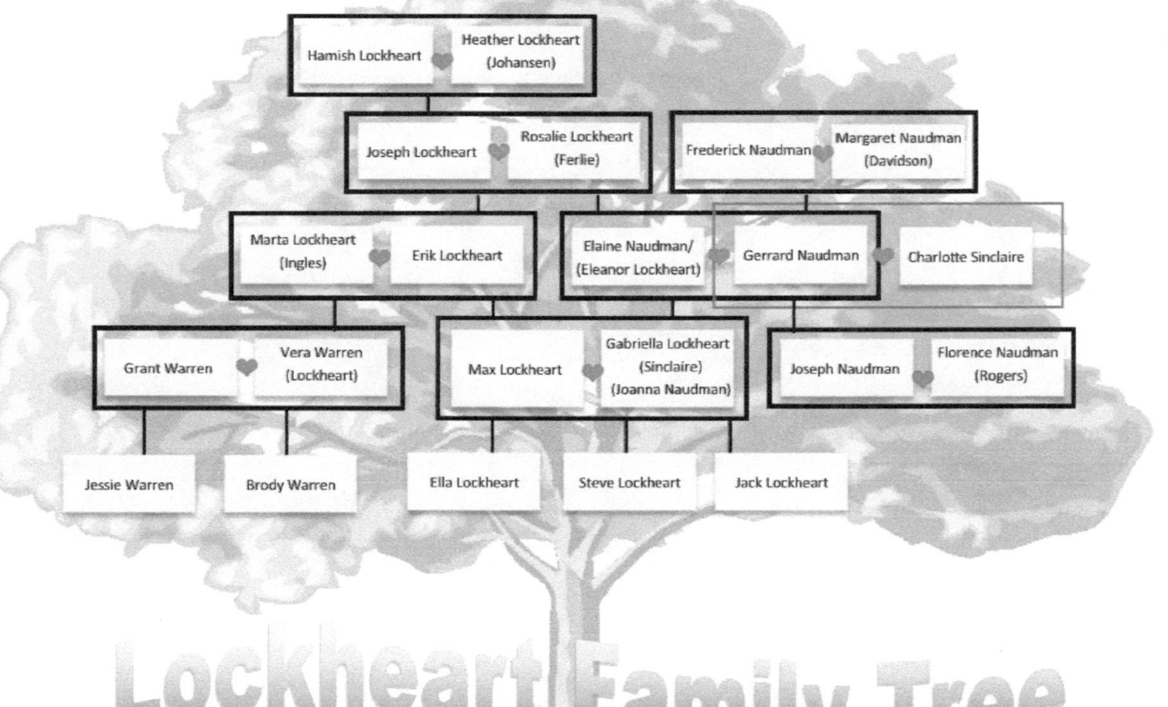

Hamish Lockheart
Heather Lockheart (Johansen)
Joseph Lockheart
Rosalie Lockheart (Ferlie)
Frederick Naudman
Margaret Naudman (Davidson)
Marta Lockheart (Ingles)
Erik Lockheart
Elaine Naudman/ (Eleanor Lockheart)
Gerrard Naudman
Charlotte Sinclaire
Grant Warren
Vera Warren (Lockheart)
Max Lockheart
Gabriella Lockheart (Sinclaire) (Joanna Naudman)
Joseph Naudman
Florence Naudman (Rogers)
Jessie Warren
Brody Warren
Ella Lockheart
Steve Lockheart
Jack Lockheart
Lockheart Family Tree

Note from the Author

My sincerest thanks for reading my book. It is because of readers like you that make getting up in the morning so rewarding. I hope you liked the first book in my Lockheart Mysteries Series, and I trust you'll be eager to read the next one too.

It has been a roller-coaster journey writing and revising my first novel. What began as a home-schooling exercise to encourage my daughter with her writing, became a three month long daily word-count challenge. Sitting in our kitchen-living room, during the winter months of 2016, we spent many days trying to 'beat' each other – announcing our word count at the end of each session (She gets that competitiveness from me) It's true that words come more quickly and easily when you have less grammar & punctuation rules to restrict you – Ah the beauty of childhood. After a session, we would read aloud sections of our work and do a little editing of basic punctuation & spelling. To my surprise my daughter's writing was actually quite good with amazing descriptions and pacing. I put that down to her love of reading the Warrior Cats series.

This book began as a bit of fun for me, but quickly became an obsession. Writing it has made me seek the help and experience of a wonderful group of writers. The Romance Writers New Zealand - Central Coast to Coast chapter (RWNZ – C2C), have been an amazing source of advice and support, and I am most sincerely grateful to all of them. A huge thanks also to my family for their love and support and to Catherine Hudson who has been a wonderful source of guidance and motivation.

A final shout-out also goes to my wonderful Beta-readers who have helped me shape the final book you have just read.

With a new appreciation for what writers go through when they begin a new book or series, I was thrilled to discover that two more stories from within *Locked & Found* are waiting to be written. Both Marta's and Vera's tales will soon follow (and who knows who else might show up and demand to have their story told too!) The best way you can show your support to any author is by posting your honest review on your chosen online bookseller, or on Good Reads. I trust you'll consider writing a few lines about your experience reading *Locked & Found* at www.goodreads.com.

It is my truest wish that you enjoy this Tale from the Tea Cup and that it lingers with you in some way.

Until next time,

Meredith

About the Author

Meredith Reece is addicted to tea and spends much of her time crafting her tales over countless cups of the stuff.

Meredith has authored high stakes Young and New Adult Family mystery sagas that'll make you wonder if any such secrets lurk in your own family tree.

While sifting through her grandmother's photographs, for use on a heritage quilt, Meredith became fascinated by the countless generations who had come before her and lived seemingly ordinary lives just like her own. But searching deeper, she found their stories were filled with loves, losses and life's little triumphs. It is these home truths that have become an integral part of her writing and form the life lessons that are woven throughout her tales.

Meredith's debut novel, *Locked & Found*, is the first of three in the *Lockheart Mysteries* series. The assortment of adventures, both sweet and savoury, are best enjoyed alongside your favourite beverage - whether it's tea or not ;)

Writing is one of Meredith's latest feathers in her cap. In the past she has been a fashion designer, self-taught cake decorator, Clinical Massage Therapist, craft business entrepreneur, and travel blogger.

She has climbed Mt Taranaki. Walked the Milford, Hump Ridge, and Grand Canyon tracks (with much moaning & sweat I might add). One day, she would like to walk the PCT (from Mexico to Canada).

She is mother to one amazingly talented daughter, and wife to a husband who patiently reads everything she writes (Bless him). They live in New Zealand with their cat, Willow, and are often travelling in their campervan, 'Boots,' during the summer.

To find out more about this author's
upcoming releases and free giveaways,

Sign up for her newsletter & join the community.

Or, come chat with me on Facebook at:
Meredith Reece - Author

You can also visit the loft on my website @

www.meredithreece.com

You can find me on Pinterest @meredithreecewrites
or on Instagram @meredith.reece.writes
Meredith hasn't bothered to sign up for Twitter yet -
but give it time and she'll get around to it eventually

– if she believes she is 'Twitty' enough to do so.

Titles to look for next:

LOCKHEART MYSTERIES SERIES
Locked & Found
Locked in Lies
Locked in Time